SHADOWS OF CARDUEL

First Calliope Press paperback edition published 2024

Manufactured in the United States of America.

SHADOWS OF CARDUEL
ISBN 979-8-218-37266-8

SHADOWS OF CARDUEL

by

David R. Witanowski

CALLIOPE PRESS

THE REYNARD CYCLE

I love you little maid,
Said the sunbeam to the shade
As all day long she shrank away before him
But at twilight, ere he died
She was weeping at his side
And he felt her tresses softly trailing over him

- John B. Tabb

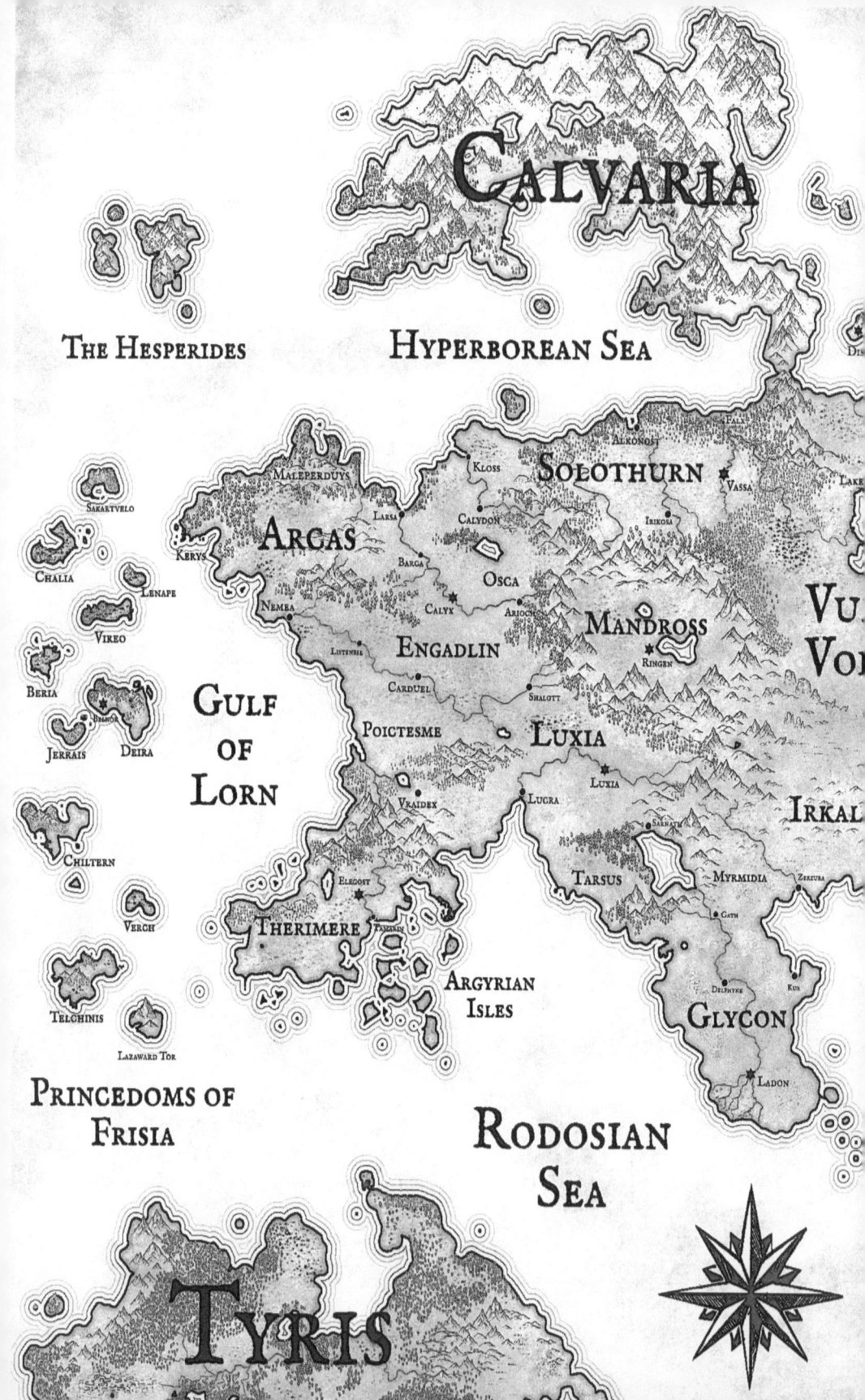

SHADOWS OF CARDUEL

I

The wind was sweet. It smelled of oleander and rosemallow and the sea. Sugarbirds flitted amidst the blooms that stretched beneath the villa, untroubled by the breeze. And there, far below in the rocky cove that served as the island's eastmost bay, white ships sailed, their masts unfurled.

Who sailed them? Roland wondered as he leaned against the parapet. *Fishermen most like, returning with the morning catch. Crabbers maybe. The crab here is always fresh. Or perhaps a merchant, holds laden with tobacco.*

Roland took a deep breath, released it.

I envy them, he mused. *And why should I not?*

Such men do not have the cares of a king.

The door to the villa swung open behind him, hinges whining.

"The air is sweet here," Roland said, not bothering to turn.

"Beria's was sweeter," a voice answered, and let out a heavy sigh.

Roland waited for Pinoteau to join him on the terrace. His cousin was robust, crude, and five summers his senior. He was also the heir to Engadlin and Roland's closest friend.

He was dressed for the voyage, and already sweating beneath his sea cloak. The Frisian sun had long since baked the flush from his cheeks.

"I was speaking of the air," Roland said, "Not the women."

"Of course, Your Majesty." Pinoteau smiled broadly.

"I am not King yet, cousin," Roland chided, though he could not help but grin. "Are you ready to sail?"

"We are," Pinoteau said. "Bloody captains are eager to launch while the weather holds. And yet-"

Roland let the man think, fixing his gaze on the ships again.

How small they look from here. How safe.

"Why should we wait?" Pinoteau burst at last. "We have more than enough men. We could land in Cadwallon five days hence with a good headwind. By the time the usurper's dogs knew it-"

"Cousin-"

"And with all of Lorn and Engadlin at our backs?" Pinoteau stormed on, his voice sending the sugarbirds to flight. "Why, Carduel would be ours by Wulf's Night! You could wed her proper then, eh? Serve her the usurper's head on a pike before you bed her!"

"Peace, cousin," Roland urged, aware of how silent it had grown. "You frighten the birds."

"Peace?!" Pinoteau scoffed. "There'll be none while the Tyrant still draws breath!"

"Caution, then," Roland amended, and moved towards the shade of the beach apple tree growing alongside the terrace.

"Caution?" Pinoteau repeated. "We have been *cautious* for far too long."

"Caution is what has kept us alive," Roland said as he brushed one of the tree's branches aside with a gloved hand.

"Your mother's words."

"Perhaps," Roland said. "But true nonetheless."

Roland's mother, Rosalind, was not cut from the same cloth as his grandsires, Firapel and Escaldos. They had fallen at the battle of Dandilin alongside his father. They all had fought bravely, the stories said, and against hopeless odds. And now they were dead.

Nor could she equal his grandmother, the Lady Felice, sister to King Nobel. Some tales had it that she had refused surrender and burned with the fortress during the sack of Nemea. Others whispered that she had been cast into the White River by the usurper's men, in mockery of Vasilisa the Beautiful. He did not know which version of the story he preferred. The former perhaps. The thought of her spirit drifting beneath the waves had kept him from sleeping many a night. But either way, she was long since dead.

His mother, though, was not dead. Nor was she a coward. A coward might have married a wealthy princeling from Vireo or Jerrais and left her name behind. But no. Wherever they had traveled, she was Rosalind, the Baroness of Landuc and mother of the rightful heir to Lorn.

And that was not all. She had been crafty too, in her politics. Roland had once thought that it was shame that had prompted the princes of Frisia to grant his mother their hospitality. Now he realized it was greed that motivated them. For he was promised to be wed to the Princess Larissa, and it was on that promise that they had been fed and kept and ferried from island to island whenever the agents of the usurper drew too close.

When Roland becomes king, his mother would whisper, *When Roland sits the throne, how richly his friends shall be rewarded.*

Yes, greed. And fear too, he guessed. He could not blame them. Solothurn had sworn vassalage to Arcasia, the new Grand Prince little more than a puppet. Half of Calvaria called the usurper friend. Glycon trembled. Even Therimere, long ally to the isles, had turned its back on them. The mountains that stood between Elegost and Pocitesme were high, but not that high.

Frisia stood alone. And now their only hope lay in him.

Even now, the Prince of Lenape sheltered them in a villa far from the port. The Princess of Beria had lent them her ships and the Prince of Verch, sailors. From Lazaward Tor, Telchinis, and Chiltern had come fighting men and from Deira the gold to pay them. Sakartvelo and Chalia had opened their granaries, for an army must surely eat.

And Larissa? Larissa was on Vireo, a guest of the lord of Pikria, waiting.

Waiting for him to send for her. Or so his mother said.

What a mystery she was to him, her thoughts in especial. The first time he had taken her hands in his, he could not help but wince at the white scar running up her left wrist. She had noticed, he could tell, but had said nothing. Her pet chimera had spat and hissed at him, and her Calvarian 'brother' had all the charm of a block of ice. As for the rest of her retinue, he did not know who scared him worse: The She-Wolf, or the Telchine and her *thing* of metal.

It could not be helped. The usurper could not stop them from landing. He had his sea-reavers and his Southern fleet, but their numbers could not match that of the princes. But landing an army would not win them a war. Not alone.

Larissa. The Queen of Arcasia. She was the key.

The sugarbirds were singing again.

"We need allies, cousin," Roland said. "*Arcasian* ones. And for that I must be wed."

"But where would you look for them?" Pinoteau snorted. "Lothier? Astolat? They quake in their boots, while Osca licks the Tyrant's shit and calls it sweet."

"You know I mean the South."

"Feh!" Pinoteau spat. "The Old Goat would sooner pluck her own whiskers than see a Northerner on the throne."

"Especially when she learns that we call her the 'old goat.'"

Pinoteau laughed then, the rancor in his voice draining.

"Wulf, boy," Pinoteau swore, wiping at the sweat on his brow. "It is not even midsummer. Are you truly in such a rush to bed her?"

Roland hoped that the shade would hide his blush.

"Not that I blame you," Pinoteau went on. "Though she's a fair bit wild, cousin. You're certain you don't want her broken in?"

"I am certain," Roland answered.

"Hm," Pinoteau mused. "I suppose I could make do with that Telchine of hers."

"What would your wife have to say about that I wonder?"

"Something I suppose." Pinoteau scratched at his neck. "If she were here."

"You dog."

"Says the young leopard yowling in heat," Pinoteau laughed and flicked at his coat, where the great cat of Lorn prowled amongst the wool.

"A ceremony will do," Roland said, blushing harder. "When Crowning comes-"

"I jest, cousin, I jest! I'll fetch your bride for you. Her, and that pair of ghosts she calls family. Marry her if you must, Crowning be cursed."

Pinoteau plucked an apple from the tree and turned it in his hand.

"Who knows?" Pinoteau said. "You may even start a fashion. Is that not the way of Kings?"

"We will see," Roland said. "If we can retake Cadwallon-"

"If?" Pinoteau tossed the beach apple into the brush. "*When,* cousin, *when.*"

Something cawed in the forest below. Not a sugarbird.

Roland pursed his lips. His mouth had gone dry.

"We should go inside," he said. "We've said too much."

"You do not like the look of the birds?" Pinoteau chuckled.

"No," Roland answered. "It's not that. Only, they say-"

Larissa says.

"They say the usurper's gaze has grown very long."

"It must be long indeed to see us all the way from Carduel," Pinoteau said. "You worry too much."

"As any king should," Roland said, and clapped a hand to his cousin's shoulder. "Come. Let us share a glass of rum at least before we part, to toast to your voyage."

"At last," Pinoteau laughed. "You speak sense."

They slipped into the cool of the villa. The wind picked up then, a strong trade wind that shook all the hillside. The door to the terrace swung shut behind them.

The sugarbirds took flight at the sound.

So did the quails scratching amongst the brush.

And one other.

* * * * * *

The city lay beneath the sea.

Its towers had turned to breakwaters, their ancient stones now thick with seagrass. Along its dim avenues great wrecks lay, large as whales. Fish swam through the halls where lords and ladies once laughed and danced, long ago.

In the depths, its bells were silent.

Of Kerys that was, only its fortress remained. And there Reynard held council.

He sat atop the highbacked chair that Baron Gradlon had given up to him. The Lord of Kerys quivered now under the cool gaze of the Graycloaks, a dozen of whom stood watch near every door. Their captain, Ulfdregil, stood but a sword's breadth away from his master, like a pale shadow.

It was cold in the hall. Cold and dim. All but one of the high windows had been curtained and there was nothing in the hearth but ash.

Reynard shifted in the chair and raised his good hand.

Two of the Graycloaks slipped from their posts and swung wide the doors.

Boots scraped against flagstone as the Lords Julien and Devoye were admitted. The stench of the low tide came with them. The Baroness Rukenaw's lip curled at the sight of them, as though she had bit into something particularly sour.

The one was as light as the other dark, the Oscan all silk and polished steel that looked as though it might crumple under a lance point. Devoye favored Mandrossian plate, nearly as black as his wooly locks.

They bent their knees and knelt.

"My Lord Protector," Lord Julien said, cradling his owl helm beneath his right arm. "We await your command."

Waves swelled against stone. The Baroness took a swallow of wine from her glass. Gradlon coughed into his fist as gently as he could.

Reynard turned towards the lean figure that stood near the foot of the dais.

Tiecelin nodded.

The Warden of the Muraille wore the rough wool and leathers of a huntsman. Behind him, a far stranger figure lurked: A shrike in the shape of a woman with piercing green eyes. Necklaces and baubles strung on filaments of silver were her only modesties. That and the cloak she made of her wings.

"My lord requires an escort," the Luxian said, addressing the men kneeling before Reynard's feet. "The remainder shall serve here as a diversionary force."

Devoye cleared his throat. "Does the Lord Protector have a preference?"

"Osca or Tarsus," Tiecelin answered. "He cares not which."

The Count of Osca and the Baron of Ylourgne spared a fleeting glance at each other.

"My lord," Julien said, rising quicker than the older man. "Let the honor be mine!"

The words echoed long after they had been spoken.

"You do not object, Lord Devoye?" the Baroness asked mockingly. "Or is your armor too heavy for you?"

"I do not object," Devoye answered, carefully. "Though I maintain my reservations."

"Reservations," Tiecelin repeated. It did not sound like a question.

"Surely," Devoye said, "If my lord *knows* the pretender is on Lenape-"

Julien could hardly contain himself.

"Do you question the Lord Protector's judgement, Devoye?" the younger man asked.

"No," Devoye answered, darkly. "But should Roland slip now from our net- Should he *run-*"

"He will not run," Reynard said then, and the room went silent. Julien re-bent the knee.

"How can you be so certain?" Devoye asked. "My lord."

"Roland is still a young man," Reynard answered, rising from his seat. "Not twenty summers old. Tell me, Devoye, were you never young?"

Devoye bowed his head, very low, as Reynard strode down the steps.

"He is in want of a woman," Reynard said. "And this one is very rare. Yes?"

"Yes," Devoye said. "Lord Protector."

"Roland will tarry on Lenape," Reynard said. "Cradling hopes we soon shall dash."

There was a bird-like whistle and cry as a winged shape swooped through the hall's only open window. Baron Gradlon shrank at the sight of it and made a quick study of the stones beneath his feet.

"Lyra returns, father," the shrike-woman said. Her voice was raspy, almost deep.

The Luxian outstretched his arm and the other shrike lit atop it. She was far smaller than her cousin, no bigger than a falcon. With the beaked hood she wore over her face, she could easily be mistaken for a bird. Her eyes were more human than most, but far too large.

Tiecelin slipped the hood from the shrike's head and offered her a morsel from the pouch on his belt. She took it, twittering, then sidled up his arm so that she might whisper in his ear.

"Two ships as expected, my lord." Tiecelin said at last. "And they have already sailed."

"Rukenaw," Reynard said, turning to the Baroness. "You will launch at once. Land on the far side of the island and encircle the city. Let no one escape."

The Baroness drained her glass and tossed it into the hearth. Baron Gradlon winced as the last of his best crystal shattered against the firedog. Then she retrieved her morningstar from the mantle and made for the door.

"And Rukenaw," Reynard said.

She turned on her heel, a questioning expression on her face.

"Do not fail me again."

"Fail you, my lord?" she asked, all innocence.

"Were it not for your captains, we might have caught the princess in Solothurn. Or have you forgotten?"

"Hartnet was," the Baroness searched for the right word. "*Impatient*, my lord."

"Her impatience cost me Tybalt."

The Baroness smirked.

"I weep for him still," she said.

"I am certain that you do."

She did not wait to be dismissed, but left, her cloak wafting behind her.

Reynard turned his gaze towards the men still on their knees.

"Lord Julien," he said. "You will remain here and make a show of the number of our horse. Send too for the reserves we left in Cadwallon. They will serve for distraction should there be any eyes watching the coast road."

"As you wish," Julien breathed. "Lord Protector."

"Devoye," Reynard went on, "Pick your men carefully. We may lose a ship in the crossing and every sword will count."

"You honor me," Devoye said, bowing his head once more, "Lord Protector."

The shrike called Lyra spoke something low and chirped noisily. For a moment it sounded as though a flock of birds were in the room, like the ones that suckled plants for nectar in the Frisian isles.

"My lord," Tiecelin said softly. "There is more."

"Leave us," Reynard said to the men who crouched near his feet. "Now."

"My lord," they said, rising quickly. Baron Gradlon slipped after them, relieved to have been overlooked. The Graycloaks shut fast the doors behind them.

Reynard climbed the stairs and moved to the thing that lay beside the chair, a tall shape concealed beneath a cloth. He took hold of the cloth and pulled, revealing a black sheet of glass. A dark mirror, so thick that it stood on its own.

It was empty at first, save for his reflection. The forked crack made it seem as though three Reynards stared back at him: Gray-haired, solemn, their ruined eye hidden beneath its black patch.

Slowly, he passed his hand over its face and stared into its depths. Visions played there. Dim shadows from the past.

"Tisiphone," he said at last.

The shrike-woman lifted her head at the sound of her name.

"Fly now to Carduel," Reynard went on. "Tell Galehaut to make ready for our guests."

"And where shall I find you, my lord," Tisiphone asked, her taloned 'fingers' flexing as she loosened her wings, "When I am done?"

"Nemea," Reynard answered, turning from the mirror. "I will see to it that you are expected. Now go."

"My lord," she said, her wings spreading wide.

"Daughter."

Her spine stiffened at the sound of Tiecelin's flat voice. Her wings drooped.

"A gift first," the Luxian said, drawing something from beneath his coat. A necklace of fine silver, no thicker than a thread. "Something pretty."

She folded her wings tight about her.

"Come here," he said.

She drew near to him. He leaned closer and gathered up her hair the way she could not. His fingers moved deftly as he slipped the necklace over her head and guided it into place across her breast.

He bent her head upwards then and pressed his lips to her mouth.

"Does it please you?" he said as they parted.

"Yes, father," she replied.

"I am glad."

He pulled away from her. She turned, spread her wings, and was gone.

Reynard had already turned back to the mirror.

Tiecelin moved to his side, the little shrike still perched on his arm. She tilted her head and stared into the mirror, where the shadows of two figures stretched across the sunbaked tiles of a villa by the sea. The men who cast them were hard to make out, for they stood beneath a wide-branched tree. But they were there.

"You do not like the look of the birds?" a coarse voice spilled from Lyra's lips.

She sang like a sugarbird for a moment. Then she spoke like a young man, afraid.

"No. It's not that. Only- They say- They say the usurper's gaze has grown very long."

"It must be long indeed to see us all the way from Carduel."

Reynard passed his hand over the mirror, and it was dark.

"Longer than you think, my friend," Reynard said. "Longer than you think."

* * * * * *

Pinoteau flipped over the stock. For the third time, The Eclipse stared back at him.

"Shit," he swore.

He gathered up the cards and poured himself another dram. The game was Patience, for none of the men could be spared to play and the captain was fast asleep.

He could not sleep.

His cabin was in the forecastle of the *Celaeno*, just beyond the galley. It was a cramped, creaking place that stank of garlic. He might have paced were it not for the ship's great wooden sprit. It practically carved the room in two.

But at least there was privacy. The rowers sleeping in heaps in the hold could hardly say the same. He imagined the Queen of Arcasia would not be forced to quarter in a place so wanting.

Oh, to be ashore. The coast of Vireo could not be more than a short swim away. Earlier, he had even seen the lights of some little village, low in the hills. Corsi, he thought. There were fine girls in Corsi. They danced as well as priestesses, even on their feet.

Too dangerous, of course. He didn't need to be told *that*, not that it stopped the captain from doing so anyway. To slip past the usurper's reavers they were taking the long way round the island, where there were few ports and many a cove to shelter in. Tomorrow they would round the salt cays off the western spur and come to Pikria with the wind at their backs.

For now, they must row. At least, the men would, and gods how they grumbled. Pinoteau could not blame them. The *Celaeno* and *Nymph* were no war galleys, but freighters whose holds had all the sweet tang of tobacco. There would be soldiers in them upon their return. Soldiers and fresh supplies for the crossing.

He drank and grimaced at the bite of the rum. It was white, and it was Argyrian.

No character at all.

What he wanted was palm wine. Yes, palm wine, and in a proper gourd. And why not the best, as long as he was dreaming? A calabash full of bell-palm grown in the tiered gardens of Trimount. That would help him sleep.

He shuffled the cards as the ship groaned about him.

Trimount. Now there was a city. Bravos fighting every noonday on the street of scars, summer festivals amongst the red bricks of the old fortress. And courtesans, of course. Were there ever such women to be found anywhere else?

What was that one's name? The one who said she had a taste for giants? Heh. She made one feel like a giant, at least.

Those had been simpler times, free from care. Was he not the son of Lampreel of Engadlin? Was he not wed to Opal of Lazaward Tor, the prince's eldest daughter? And was he not bosom friend to Roland, true heir to the Arcasian throne? Why should any door be closed to him? One day he would sit on the right side of a king.

Though there was no rush. No harm in sampling a cup or two while the usurper skulked in Carduel. And so, he and Roland had made the streets of Trimount their own, and no one could say they were not men.

Until Larissa came.

A ploy, Pinoteau had thought at first. A ruse. Another false Larissa. Different leopard, same spots.

He still remembered the sight of Lettice's head. The usurper had dipped it in lacquer so that it would keep long enough to be shown to the court before it was set atop one of the spikes of Traitor's-Gate. It had hardly looked real to him then, but his father had assured him that it was.

There, son, his father had told him, *there lies the fate of all traitors.* And yet his father too had been gulled by the second false Larissa. She had been some chevalier's whelp from Cordeliers. Or was it Vyonnes? He could not remember. Had he not sailed to Frisia, he might have joined his father at the fork of the Isoile. They say the river ran red that day. He could not argue. He was not there.

He had Opal to thank for that at least.

Nine summers, now. Has it been so long?

And now, a fourth Larissa. It beggared belief, or that was what he had said. But no. You only had to meet her to know that she was true.

And even if she were false, why would the usurper hunt her so?

He dealt out the tableau and played.

Star to Lance, that was quick. A pair of serpents joined a third. Beneath the serpents The Maiden dallied.

Now if only he had a Huntsman . . .

He shuffled through the stock. The three of seeds. The seven of skulls. The nine of skulls. The Lioness. The High Priest. The eight of serpents. The ten of stars. The Watcher.

No help.

Wood scraped against wood as he rose from his seat and strapped on his sword.

He needed fresh air. And at least on deck he could watch the stars as he dreamed of palm wine and Corsi girls.

The galley was dark as Domdaniel, but he managed to pluck a pear from one of the barrels as he sidled past the hollowed stone that served as the hearth. It had gone quite cold.

It cannot be that late. Can it?

He pushed through the door to the deck.

He'd expected to hear crickets singing on the shore, but there were none, just the lap of waves against the hull. Nor were there any stars to be seen. All the bay was shrouded in fog. Were it not for the ship's lanterns, he doubted he would be able to see at all.

He took a bite out of the pear.

There were twice as many guards than usual posted on deck. The captain's doing no doubt. He approached one of them, a Berian marine by his armor. The man was gripping the gunwale so tightly that one might think there was a storm on.

"When did this roll in?" Pinoteau asked, peering down the length of the ship. He could barely make out the shape of the aft.

"It come up sudden," the man answered gruffly. "From the west."

The man clucked his tongue, as though tasting the air.

"Don't like it, m'lord," he went on. "Don't seem natural."

"Come now," Pinoteau chuckled. "The usurper's no sorcerer."

"M'lord," the man nodded, but he did not sound convinced.

"We should be glad of fog anyway," Pinoteau said. "Keeps us hidden."

The Berian said nothing and kept staring out into the fog.

Pinoteau finished the pear as he made his way along starboard, trying to pick out the outline of the *Nymph* amidst the mist. The men stationed near the mizzen barely straightened as he approached.

"Where is the captain?" he asked, irritated.

"Went to fetch you," one of them answered.

"To fetch-" Pinoteau sucked at his gums. "Hydra's Teeth, what for?"

A distant scream carried over the bay. Or *was* it distant? The fog played tricks with the ear. Steel clashed against steel. Another scream.

Pinoteau drew, his heart racing. The men near him readied their crossbows.

"Ahoy, the *Nymph*!" Pinoteau barked. "Ahoy, curse you!"

No one answered.

Then, suddenly:

"Eyes, portside!" the *Celeano's* lookout called out. "All eyes, to port! To po- araahaghaah!"

The man's scream was soon joined by a ragged, cawing shriek, like that of a hunting bird. Pinoteau's head snapped upwards, his gaze bent on the crow's nest.

There were *shapes* hovering and swooping above the sails. Winged shapes.

Some of the men on deck let loose their bolts. Others merely stood, too stunned to act. Then the lookout sailed from the nest. His body hit the deck with a brutal *crack*.

"All hands!!!" the captain's voice roared through the fog. "*All hands, on deck! Prepare to repel boarders!*"

Pinoteau still could not see the man. But he could see the black shape emerging from the fog. A ship. But not the *Nymph*.

Something massive swung out from the fog and struck the side of the *Celeano* like a weighted club. Wood splintered as part of the gunwale cracked under the weight. The force of it rocked both vessels, and Pinoteau grabbed onto the mizzen to keep his feet.

When he had steadied, he could see what had struck them. It was a boarding ramp. There were already men pouring across it. Tall men with pale faces and gleaming steel in their hands. They carved through the first men to meet them as easily they would children armed with sticks.

"Calvarians!" someone managed to shout before he too was cut down.

No, Pinoteau realized. *The Graycloaks! Which means-*

There was no time to think. One of the Northerners was already on him. It was all he could do to put the mizzen between himself and the man's sword.

The timber splintered from the impact.

Pinoteau put his own sword up, painfully aware that he wore nothing thicker than shirt and breeches.

"Come on!" he snarled. "Is that the best you can do?!"

The Graycloak took up his blade in both hands and waded in, swinging.

It was all Pinoteau could do to deflect, giving ground. The man was so quick, yet his cuts had so much weight behind them that they nearly ripped Pinoteau's sword from his grip.

Ground! Pinoteau's mind raced as he backpedaled. *I need more ground!*

There was none. He hit the gunwale and tried to spin away.

He was too slow.

A sharp twinge of pain ran up his left arm, and then blood began to flow from the slash he'd taken. He ignored it and managed to parry the Graycloak's reverse. The force of it knocked him backwards.

Then the Graycloak kicked him, hard in the gut.

He fell, a coiled rope knocking the breath from him as he hit the deck. He tried to raise his sword, but there was no strength left in his arm.

Metal rang across the deck. Chimera screeched. Men cursed and screamed and died.

And yet, somehow, he was still alive.

Pinoteau shook his head, gasping. The Graycloak was gone, and where he had stood two of the watchmen lay. He had been speaking to them just moments ago. Now one was trying to crawl towards the aftcastle, blood pulsing from his neck. The other lay on his back, dead, his crossbow still cradled against his chest.

They fell trying to defend me, he realized, ashamed.

The fight was still raging about the bow. He supposed the captain was there, making a last stand of sorts. It was pointless. The usurper's reavers had joined the Graycloaks: The wretched dregs of Lothier from Maleperduys to Thelema given cutlass or axe and a share of plunder to make the killing easy.

Pinoteau was bracing himself to stand, to fight afresh, when he saw the figure striding across the gangplank.

The usurper.

His mail was enameled steel, the visor of his helm a mask of his own face. His artificial eyes wept tears of steel.

Pinoteau turned towards the dead man lying not ten paces away.

His crossbow was still loaded.

Pinoteau began to creep forward.

"Cast the dead overboard." The usurper ordered over the din. His voice was chillingly calm.

"And the wounded?" one of the reavers asked.

"There can be no survivors."

The reavers did not hesitate to obey. The cries wafting from the deck began to be silenced, one by one.

Pinoteau scrambled the rest of the distance and, taking hold of the dead man's hand, gently tugged it away from the trigger. When he had the thing in his own grip, he stood, and aimed at the figure surveying the carnage with cold detachment.

Die, you son of a bitch he swore silently, and squeezed the trigger.

Something struck him hard in the chest. His own shot went wild, streaking over the usurper's shoulder. He stared at the arrow protruding from his breast.

It had red fletching.

Something whistled and then another arrow caught him in the thigh. He tried to cry out as he sank against the gunwale, but naught but a wheeze came out. The arrow had pierced his lung.

Sword, he thought. *Where's my sword. Dropped it- Must have.*

He saw it. Not far. He could reach it. Could at least take one of the reavers with him.

He crawled.

There was a loud splash. Then another. They were already throwing the bodies overboard.

He crawled, favoring his left side. If he pulled the arrow free it would surely kill him.

His sword lay just beside the rope, not even bloodied.

I can change that-

He reached for it, fingers stretching.

A booted foot stamped down on his hand.

"That will not help you, Master Pinoteau."

The usurper stood over him. Pinoteau groaned.

"Bas-," Pinoteau managed. It was hard to form words. "Bastard!"

"Hrm," the usurper hummed, his thumb loosening his sword from its scabbard. The ship's lanterns played against the ruby set into its hilt.

"No-" Pinoteau wheezed. "Mercy."

"As you wish," the usurper said.

The ruby flashed in the lamplight.

II

Arsinoe came in fast, her bare feet kicking up sand as her stave drove Lara back into the tide.

"Give up?" Arsinoe asked.

"What do you think?" Lara shot back.

Arsinoe shrugged and sent the end of her stave sailing towards Lara's face.

Lara smashed it aside and took another step into the surf. Seawater soaked her breeches, icy cold despite the heat.

"If you fall over," Arsinoe said, planting her own feet more firmly, "I'm going to call this in my favor."

Lara ignored the tug of the sea and lowered her stance, the tip of her wooden blade sinking beneath the foam.

Arsinoe jabbed at her as she took another step into the surf. A lazy strike. Just a test. Lara did not flinch.

Arsinoe winced as the saltwater surged about her toes.

"Cold?" Lara asked.

Arsinoe did not answer, but drove forward, her stave flying before her. Lara did not hesitate. She swung as she lunged past the Telchine's strike, and for a moment wooden sword and sea spray were as one.

Arsinoe leaned away from the blow, but only just. The saltwater hit her right in the eyes. Lara could not help but revel for a moment and reversed her grip for the follow up.

Then Arsinoe spun about, her feet barely touching the sand as her stave whirled. Lara tried to sprint, but the rush of the surf slowed her step.

Arsinoe's stave caught her right between the shoulder blades. She fell face first into the sand.

"That was a dirty trick," Arsinoe panted. "Where'd you learn it?"

"From your sister," Lara said, spitting some of the sand from her mouth.

"Aren't we a sore loser." The beetle on Arsinoe's cheek flexed its wings.

"Sore, at least."

Arsinoe offered her hand. Lara took it.

She got to her feet, blinking. There was sand in her eyes too.

"Thirsty?" Lara asked.

"Very," Arsinoe answered.

They made their way up from the shore, Lara sparing a moment to wave towards the riders watching them from the dunes.

I'm fine, the gesture said. *No need to come to my rescue.*

Captain Scyron nodded back. His men shifted in their saddles, relaxed.

There were only five of them today. She remembered when it had been a hundred. The princes' faith in her had grown since the usurper's raid on Verch.

They knew she could handle herself in a fight. A dozen or so dead men had taught them that.

But they still gave Dramsind a wide berth.

The hollow man had hunkered down amongst the sea grass, looking more like a boulder than anything else. Bannertail was snoozing in the shade of the giant, belly up like a dog upon a dry patch of sand.

The fox-squirrel's ears twitched as they approached. Dramsind was still, but Lara could tell he was staring at them, watchful. She had grown used to it by now.

"Go back to sleep," Lara murmured to the fox-squirrel.

The chimera's tail thumped against the sand. He yawned, stretched, and then was still.

Their horses were foraging amongst the scrub grass beneath the palms. Maiden and Jumper got along well enough, but the mare was hogging the tastiest wildflowers for herself.

Just like her mistress.

"Hello there," she said, giving Jumper's withers a good scratch.

The horse turned, snorted, and went back to nosing at the grass.

Lara lifted a skin from Jumper's saddle and drank. The water was lukewarm, but still good on the tongue. It was easy to get thirsty here. You could almost taste the salt hanging in the air.

She passed the skin to Arsinoe.

The Telchine buried the head of her stave in the sand and took a good long swallow. Her real spear was strapped to Maiden's saddle, safe in its sheath. Its blade was broad as the knives the farmers of Trimount used to cut sugarcane. The Prince of Lazaward Tor had made a gift of it to her. *How long ago now? Two summers? Three?*

Lara had lost count. It always seemed to be summer in Frisia.

"You would have had me, you know," Arsinoe said, returning the skin. "But you hesitated."

"I wasn't sure if it would work," Lara admitted.

"Pity," Arsinoe said. "I'll be expecting it next time."

"We'll see," Lara said, and retrieved a pair of leaf packets from her saddlebag.

"What's that you got there?" Arsinoe asked.

"Guess," Lara said, and gently tossed the Telchine one of the packets.

Arsinoe unwrapped the packet and smiled at the sight of the fried conch within.

"How did you know?" Arsinoe asked.

Lara rolled her eyes. "How did I know you were *hungry?*"

"Piss off," Arsinoe said, and stripped off her gloves to eat. Her hands were as green as her feet now. The patina had spread to her forearms. It climbed higher every year.

They sat in the sand and ate.

Waves swelled against the sand. Palm leaves whispered in the wind.

Across the bay stood Pikria. It had been a Telchine city once, though most of that lay buried. The Aquilians had built terraces and bulwarks atop the old foundations of the citadel, and around it a place of sun-bleached stones and tile clung.

A wall, crumbling but still solid, defended its approaches from the forested hills, and a pair of towers the bay. Between them, lying somewhere beneath the waves, a great chain lurked. At the sight of an enemy, it could be raised between the towers, and then not even the strongest ship could pass.

Their makeshift sparring ground lay more than halfway between the city and the eastern tower. They had done so inside the city at first, but too many people tended to gather and watch. Even in the prince's manse, the servants would flock towards whatever court they had chosen.

It was better outside the city. Better still near the sea. The drag of the waves against one's legs and the uneven sand made for a challenging sparring ground. After a month, it made fighting on solid ground seem almost easy.

Even Moder had approved.

Of course, no wall or chain could keep Reynard's eyes from watching them. The princes had taken measures, of course. Shrikes, or any bird larger than a gull for that matter, were shot from the skies without a second thought by anyone with a bow.

A shrike was worth gold. A bird? Well, you could always cook it.

Of course, not all of them were shrikes. The Prince of Jerrais had hanged his own steward for taking the usurper's coin. That had been a close thing. There had been a boat waiting to spirit her away, doors to the manse left unlocked.

She had become quite a light sleeper.

Then there was the mirror. She was certain that he had it. After all, was he not still alive? Perhaps he watched her even now, chewing.

Something soft brushed against Lara's leg.

She turned. Sure enough, Bannertail was staring at her with his honey-colored eyes. There was more silver in his fur than ever, especially about his muzzle.

"Greedy old man," she said, and tossed the last of her conch to him. "Greedy."

"Hmph," Arsinoe grunted, licking a few errant crumbs from her fingers.

"Another match?" Lara said, stretching. "It's still early."

Arsinoe flexed her right hand, watched it flake. The sea breeze carried them away.

"Not that I mind," Arsinoe said, "But I thought we were going riding today."

"A figure of speech."

"Sure," Arsinoe sighed and pulled on her gloves.

"What is it?" Lara asked.

"What is what?"

"*Arsinoe-*"

"Alright, alright," Arsinoe gave in. "It's just, if you're really going marry that boy who fancies himself a king- I mean, if you're *really* going to do it- Then isn't it a different, ah, *breed* of experience you should be seeking out?"

"Oh," Lara said. "That."

"That," Arsinoe said.

"And how do you propose that I do . . . That?" Lara asked.

"How else?" Arsinoe said. "We passed a hut or two on the way here, didn't we? We could find you a fisherman."

"Ugh."

"One of those fruit boys, then," Arsinoe amended. "A coconut trimmer. They're a bit like racing dogs, you know? No fat."

"Who am I?" Lara asked. "Pinsard?"

Arsinoe snickered.

"She is skinny, isn't she?" the Telchine said. "Volk, but I guess that shouldn't surprise me."

Doricha was her name, a merchant's daughter. Pinsard had met her on the street that led to the dyer's market. Or, rather, that was where she had snared him. She had been walking ahead of them and had slipped- or seemed to slip- on an uneven stone. Her sandal had come off, but she had kept on walking without it.

Of course, Pinsard had picked it up. Of course, he had caught up with her.

"Just like Princess Rhodopis," Lara mimicked, daintily pressing a hand to her chest. "Oh, how gallant!"

"I would have checked the bottom of the sandal first," Arsinoe sniffed.

Lara bit her lip to keep from laughing. Some of the prostitutes in Pikria wore sandals with words etched into them, so that their footprints read *follow me* in the dust.

"She's nice at least," Lara said. "Moder likes her."

"Now there are words to set hearts ablaze."

Arsinoe rose. Lara rolled her shoulders. Her back muscles ached.

"Do you," Lara ventured. "Do you think that they-"

"You have seen them together?" Arsinoe asked. "Haven't you?"

Lara nodded. They kept so close they were practically the same person.

"Little minx," Arsinoe said. "Doesn't she know he already has a wife?"

"Pfft," Lara snorted. "Still, I would have thought he'd have fallen for one of those washerwomen."

"Which ones?"

"You know," Lara said. "The ones by the river. Always wet, always . . . *Bending*."

"Sounds like it's not Pinsard who's interested," Arsinoe said.

Lara flashed the fingers.

The Telchine ignored her and pulled her stave free from the sand.

"What about you?" Lara asked.

Arsinoe cocked an eyebrow. "Me?"

"Surely," Lara went on. "There must be someone who's caught your eye."

Arsinoe's beetle squirmed.

"Getting *that* close takes a certain amount of trust," Arsinoe said, giving her stave a whirl. "I don't really do trust, girl."

"No," Lara said. "Suppose you don't. Must be lonely."

"Are *you* lonely?" Arsinoe asked, bluntly.

Lara checked the grip on her practice sword.

"Sometimes," she said at last. "But I've never been . . . Close. To anyone."

"Well, come on then," Arsinoe said, planting her feet. "Try and get close to me."

They fought.

* * * * * * *

The Firebird was high by the time they were done. The men on the hill had dismounted and were taking their own meal beneath the palms.

"We should head back soon," Lara said, rubbing at her calf. "I'm tired of losing."

Arsinoe leaned on her stave. Sweat made her golden skin shimmer.

"You don't have to marry him, you know," Arsinoe said, wiping her brow.

"I *don't?*" Lara asked.

Arsinoe wet her lips.

"We could just run off," she said. "Be free."

"I won't be free until Reynard is dead," Lara said. "You know that."

They walked back up the beach. Lara found her boots in the grass. Arsinoe slipped her practice stave alongside her spear.

Maiden whickered at the interruption.

"Do you want to marry him?" the Telchine asked.

There was no bitterness in her words.

"How could I?" Lara answered, flatly. "I know so little of him."

"Then why are you?" Arsinoe asked.

"I need his ships," Lara said. "His men. That's all."

"And here I thought I was the cynical one," Arsinoe sighed.

Lara pulled on her boots and began to coax Jumper out from the brush.

Another horse's whinny carried across the dunes. A man's voice called out, one of the guards, but the tide drowned out his words.

Lara turned. Scyron was pointing towards something in the bay.

She peered, shielding her eyes from the sun. There was nothing to see, just whitecaps rolling in from the sea.

Curse me if that old man's eyes are sharper than mine.

Then she saw them: White, triangular shapes on the water beneath the western watchtower. *Sails.*

There were ships in the bay.

Had the day finally come?

No time for the bridle. No matter. She could ride well enough with rope and halter.

Lara slipped her makeshift sword into her belt and pulled herself up by a stirrup. The brush shook as Bannertail sprang from it, catching her by the leg.

Still spry, Lara laughed as the fox-squirrel scrambled up her back. She was glad her leather jack was too thick for his tiny claws to pierce.

"What is it?" Arsinoe asked.

"The ships are coming!" Lara answered, pointing now herself.

Arsinoe did not bother to look. "*The* ships?"

"I don't know!" Lara cried. "But I know where we can get a better look!"

"Is that what you want?" Arsinoe laughed as she leapt onto Maiden's back. "Or are you looking for an escape route?"

"Come on!" Lara laughed, spurring Jumper on. "I'll race you!"

"Dramsind!" Arsinoe said. *"Fiki!"*

"Wopa," the giant answered, his bulk rumbling up from the sand. The prince's men cried out as their horses spooked at the sight.

"Your Highness!" Lara could hear Scyron crying out with alarm. "Your Highness!"

They rode, the prince's men cursing as they made to follow.

This too is practice, she told herself as they cleared the first of the canebrakes. *Best put them through their paces!*

They crested an embankment and then they were on the trail that led to the eastern watch. They picked up speed, Jumper and Maiden kicking up clouds of red dust as they raced.

Dramsind kept pace behind them. She could hear his limbs slamming into the dust like the beat of a drum.

The trail hugged the shoreline. It was little more than red earth stamped flat, carved by the thousands of mules that had trod from Pikria and back. On their left the wild palms climbed, their roots threatening to trip up the horse of a careless rider.

She was not careless.

Whenever she tilted her head she could see them, the ships growing more distinct as the noonday sun was reflected upon their sails.

He is my cousin, she told herself. *The only blood I have.*

What then is this dread?

Their first meeting had been a cautious affair, after a week of being kept at arm's length by the Prince of the Tor. She had taken no slight at that. After all, she might have been an assassin, a fetch, or some other pretender wearing her name.

Curiosity had won out, though. And there was no denying the resemblance between them. He had her curling locks, the same set jaw.

She might have called him handsome.

Too dangerous, of course, for the two of them to be together for longer than was necessary. And so, they had met no more than thrice since the crew of the *Kite* had brought her to Trimount. And then, always under watchful eyes.

He *was* polite. It helped mask his nervousness, though not as much as she guessed he would have liked . . . And at times she preferred her other cousin, boorish though he was.

At least you knew what he wanted.

Gradually, the trail began to curve, rising slightly as it skirted a low hill. The trail grew serpentine here, Lara knew, winding this way and that as it followed the contours of the island.

She let Jumper set the pace.

They rounded the first curve, losing sight of the prince's men behind them. Loose rocks flew from the trail as Dramsind made the turn less gracefully, skidding into the canebrakes.

Arsinoe let out a wild *whoop*. Lara hoped there were no tern nests in the reeds.

Bannertail's long ear tickled her neck. He was riding on her shoulder, his face thrust into the wind.

He must feel like he's flying.

They came around another curve, and then Jumper came skidding to a halt. Maiden rode off trail, Arsinoe cursing as she took a branch or two to the face. Dramsind merely *stopped*. His momentum dug a sizable furrow into the dirt.

The trail ahead was clogged with goats. Bells jangled and kids bleated after their mothers. A shepherdess was wading amidst them. She turned to stare at them, eyes widening.

"*Pigaine piso!*" she cried out in the old tongue. "*Tromazeis to zoa!*"

A sandy colored mutt came bounding out from the flock and began to bark at them. The fox-squirrel squalled back, his tail whipping against the back of Lara's neck.

"They'll have landed by the time we're clear of this mess," Arsinoe called out, doing her best to shake a twig free from her hair. "Should we turn back?"

The hoofbeats on the trail behind them were growing louder.

"No!" Lara shouted, turning Jumper away from the trail. "I know a shortcut!"

She gave Jumper's flanks a squeeze. He mounted the embankment and was off.

"Volk," Arsinoe cursed again. "Wait for me!"

Fronds and branches whipped against Lara's legs as she rode, but the palms were not as thick here. Beyond them a forest of giant cane grew, rows and rows of it, and lanes between wide enough to ride in.

Old plantation. Cutters and goats kept the weeds from overtaking it.

Another trail cut through the cane. She took it, urging Jumper to speed as it leveled out. Behind her she could hear stalks snapping as Dramsind changed course.

Something broke above the cane ahead of them. A steepled roof, plaster peeling to expose red brick beneath. At its apex a brass Firebird was set, wings outstretched.

The temple was right where she thought it would be.

Let's just hope the back gate is open!

It was. As they burst from the cane, they flew over a patch of wildflowers and then shot through the gated arch that led to the Temple's work yard. Chickens scattered and pigs squealed. A bearded priest stumbled backwards as he dove from their way, spilling the pail of slops he carried all over the front of his fiery robes. Acolytes atop the steps of the inner shrine whooped and hollered at the sight, their mirth turning to terror as Dramsind barreled after his companions.

The horses' hooves kicked up gravel as they came around the yard and onto the path normally walked by the petitioners. A plump priest bearing a ceremonial lantern was kneeling beneath one of the Firebird statues flanking the walkway, but at the sight of them he scrambled back to his feet and ran. When he realized he could not outpace them he dove into the saplings growing by the wayside.

"Sorry!" Lara called out to him as they passed, catching a whiff of the burning pine incense the man had been lighting.

A string of curses wafted from the brush, and then they were through the main gate and on the country lane that led to the cliffs along the watchtower.

They went slower as the lane began to climb the heights. The lane was wide, but a fall would be long and fatal.

"Do you think the old man's still after us?" Arsinoe asked.

"No doubt," Lara shot back, "Though he just might stop to make an offering!"

The path grew steeper still, so that the horses strained to crest the final ridge, but then the watchtower loomed above: A brutal-looking turret of piled stone with a wooden scaffold at its peak. The only way in was through a pair of banded doors, and those were a quarter of the way up its base. To reach them you had a to climb a ladder.

"Who goes?" a voice called from the top of the tower as they dismounted.

"Larissa of Arcasia!" Arsinoe hollered back. "Open up!"

There was some commotion from above.

"Dramsind," Lara said, *"Tipet!"*

"Wopa," Dramsind answered, and his head began to swivel as he looked no doubt for a good place to settle.

Bannertail clung to her as she climbed the ladder's rungs, the two of them reaching a shelf-like balcony just as the doors to the tower swung inwards. The watchman, a graybeard with a shaved head, offered her his hand. She took it, trying to ignore the stink of his breath.

The interior of the tower was dark, ill lit, and smelled of sweat, oil, and burnt tar. Still, it was cheery compared to the chainworks of its bowels. Lara had seen them once. Its gears and wheels and hooks made it look like a torture chamber for giants.

"Your Highness," he said, ignoring Arsinoe as she hefted herself into the room. "We did not expect-"

"No time," Lara said, and made for the ladder that led up to the watch. She could practically feel the man's eyes boring into her as she climbed.

It was fresher up above. There was sweetgrass piled in the signal cauldron and, if the other watchman stank, the sea wind masked it well.

"Highness," the man said, bowing his head. "There are ships-"

"I saw them from Sugar Bay," Lara said. "Are they my cousin's?"

"They fly his flag, Highness," the man nodded. "Look."

He stepped aside as she made for the edge of the scaffold and peered down into the bay. Sure enough, there were two galleys coasting through the channel. A half dozen smaller ships trailed behind them.

She could not make out their emblems.

Bannertail leapt from her shoulder and paced along the railing.

"There are more ships than I expected," Lara said.

"Prince of Lenape must have sent an escort," the man said.

"Perhaps," she mused. "Hand me that glass."

The watchman flinched but gave up his spyglass.

"Thank you," she said, squinting through its scope.

Yes, those were the ships that had brought them out of Beria. Or, at least, they had the same figureheads: A shrike and an antlered faun, both predictably underdressed. The spotted leopard of Lorn and the red flower of Engadlin flew on both ship's sterns, while the others bore the flag of one of the sea princes, something with shells and knots.

"Those are his ships, alright," Lara said. "But-"

"But what?" Arsinoe asked. Lara had not heard her haul herself up from below.

"There's damage," Lara said. "All along their hulls. It's almost like they were-"

Boarded.

The ships, all of them, were well past the chain.

"Light the beacon!" Lara shouted, straightening.

"What's that?" the bald man started.

"Light the bloody beacon!" Lara repeated. "We're under attack!"

Arsinoe already had the tower's firebrand in her hand. She tossed it into the cauldron. The rushes caught, and with them the packets the priests of the nearby temple had prepared.

Red smoke billowed from the pyre, and for a moment that was all that Lara could see. Then the sea wind caught hold of it, and it blew from the tower top like a river of blood against the sky.

"Your Highness!" the graybeard shouted, choking a bit on the smoke. "Watcher take me, if this is one of your jests-"

He was quiet then.

There was something *boiling* out of the larger of the two galleys. It almost looked like smoke to her, black and wild, but then it broke apart.

Shrikes. Dozens and dozens of them were pouring into the heights of the bay. She had never seen so many in one place, all at once.

Even from here she could hear them shrieking.

"Gods," the younger watchman breathed. He was backing away from the railing as the flock continued to swell.

Bannertail was trembling. Lara scooped him up.

The gods won't help us, boy. Not now.

III

Is it him? Hirsent mused, her eyes drawn back to the red ribbon streaking from the eastern watch.

Lara. Good girl.

The screams of the prince's daughters brought her back to the matter at hand. One of them had toppled the wicker table, spilling kettle, plate, and the midday meal across the veranda. Their ribboned shoes were trampling pineapple and whitefish into paste.

A pity. The tea was good today.

"Get them inside!" Prince Mydas barked at his wife. "And have the windows shuttered!"

The daughters of Vireo, young and old, fled to the false security of the manse. The house guards were jabbering to each other, their posts abandoned as they scrambled for a better vantage point.

Sloppy. No discipline.

"Moder?" Pinsard breathed, his piercing eyes still locked on the ships below.

"He will be expecting us to panic," Hirsent said, "Yes?"

"Yes," Pinsard said, and took a deep breath. "But we will not."

"Good," Hirsent said. "Keep breathing."

There were bells ringing in the city below. Hirsent turned to regard the prince.

He was staring at the advance of the shrikes, his mouth gaping like one of the embroidered fish on his silken robes. He was shaking too. The shard of the Southerner's supposedly unbreakable sword jingled against the rest of his finery, hung from a golden chain. She had seen similar shards over the years, each to an island. The metal was unlike any she had ever seen, forge-bright for all its age.

Some of the princes kept theirs under glass. He wore his like a bauble.

Fitting.

Her gaze finally seemed to rouse him.

"Lityerses," he said, addressing the young man who stood by his side. "Take half of the guard and get to the harbor before they land! If they do-"

"We'll throw them back into the sea, my lord!" the young man shouted, his cloak billowing as he leapt from the veranda.

Mydas' son-of-passion is fiercer than his father, my love. You would have liked him.

White plumes blossomed from one of the smaller vessels as it came about. Then she could hear the *pop pop pop* of distant artillery. A high whine rose above the cries of the shrikes, and then one of the ships laying at harbor buckled against its pier. Smoke rose from it, and with it the bright lick of flames.

"What was that?!" Mydas gasped.

"Calvarian fire," Hirsent said, as a second ship opened onto the port.

The roof of a warehouse crumpled, split, burst into flames.

"The harbor-" one of the guardsmen said, stunned.

"The whole fleet will catch," Mydas said.

Let us hope not.

The shrikes were over the harbor now, banking between the plumes rising from the fires below. The prince was barking out more orders: More men to the harbor! Form fire brigades! Launch the ships!

Panic. Panic.

She turned. Pinsard was still, his breathing even.

Good.

"How many ships do you count?" Hirsent asked.

"Eight ships," he answered.

"Swords?"

"No more than a thousand." He had already done the calculations. "The shrikes were in the bigger galley."

"And what is that telling you?" Hirsent asked.

"We outnumber them," Pinsard said. "Unless-"

"My lord!" a voice cried out from one of the towers. "My lord, the north bridge is breached!"

The prince began to move, his silk swishing as he left the polished wood of the veranda for the thickness of the parapets that guarded the approach to the manse. The guards hastened to follow, mail jingling.

Hirsent shot Pinsard a knowing look. He almost smiled.

They were not halfway past the wall walks when she caught sight of the troops emerging from the wooded hills that ringed Pikria. From the heights they resembled great curling centipedes, glistening in the sun.

They already held the bridge that forded the river. And the banners they flew were all too familiar: A mailed fist on a field of blood.

"The Baroness," Pinsard said.

"Rukenaw," Hirsent nodded.

The hundreds she could see were quickly becoming thousands. Horse and cart were following close behind the van. More artillery.

Outnumbered. Surrounded.

Reynard is here.

"Send-" Mydas croaked. "Send our birds! There are men west of here that could-"

"They will not be reaching us in time," Hirsent said. "Besides, nothing on wings will be escaping from here."

The prince turned to answer when the first of the shrikes dove at them, wild-haired and screeching like a demon.

Pinsard drew his sword neatly and would have cut the thing in two, but it swerved at the last moment, its momentum carrying it well beyond the parapet.

It cackled as it started to come about.

Then a second shrike shot past the wall walks. Another circled the manse's highest tower, cawing, almost lazily. The archers on the wall walks, what few there were, let loose with their arrows.

Their shot shattered against the stones or, worse, went sailing into the city.

"Be saving arrows for Reynard's soldiers!" Hirsent shouted, taking hold of Mydas by the front of his robes and yanking him close. "Shrikes are to distract! Now, seal gates! Defend city!"

He gasped and sputtered. The house guards did not move an inch to defend him. She was not surprised. They feared her more than any Vanir raider.

She was the She-Wolf, after all. The White Lady.

"Yes," the man finally managed. "Yes, of course! Sergeant-"

"My lord!" one of the house guards said, ducking as one of the shrikes came in low.

"Take the rest of the guard and by all the gods, hold the gates!"

The guardsman moved at once, roaring out orders as he hastened to comply.

Hirsent released the man. He wheezed, his fingers fumbling for the shard hanging round his neck, as though it might protect him.

"My armor!" he bellowed, making for a nearby archway.

Hirsent wondered if he would emerge before the battle was done. Not that it mattered.

"City is doomed," she said, turning to Pinsard. "Get to the *Kite*. Is best way off island now."

"But Lara-" Pinsard blurted. "She and Arsinoe are still outside!"

"Do not be worrying about them," Hirsent said. "They are handling themselves, yes?"

A shrike risked another dive at them. This time Pinsard's sword sheared a handful of feathers from its tail.

"Yes," he panted, keeping his eyes on the shrikes.

"And your *lufestre*?" Hirsent prodded.

Pinsard's cheeks flushed, his sword wavered.

"Her family's manse isn't far from the Spell," he said, using the name for the little bay where the fishermen moored their craft. "I can get there, but only if I go now!"

"Then run," Hirsent said.

"What about you?" he said, sheathing his sword.

"I will come," she said. "And if I do not-"

She took him by the shoulders and kissed his brow.

"Do not wait for me," she said, and released him.

He bowed his head, *yes*, and then broke into a sprint.

Hirsent rested her hand on her pommel and spared a last look at the ships advancing on the harbor. The galleys were launching longboats. The steel aboard glittered like the sunlight off the waves.

Not much time.

* * * * * *

Lara could already smell the harbor burning. They rode into the wind, and on it came a bonfire of ships' timbers wreathed in flame. She could taste the sharp bite of black powder in her mouth as well.

"Shrikes!" one of the escorts cried out as a pair of the things swooped out of the palms. One was white-bellied, the other rich as a plum.

The lighter of the two came about for another look.

Lara leaned ever so slightly and nocked an arrow from the quiver on Jumper's saddle. Smoothly she drew, trusting in the horse's momentum. She took aim.

The shrike saw her and began beating its wings to gain some height.

She loosed.

The thing cawed, flexed its wings, and plummeted, almost rolling as it fell.

She was reaching for a second arrow when the plum too crumpled in midflight. If it had seen them, it would not tell the tale.

She turned and saw Scyron gripping one of the lacquered bows the Frisians favored.

"Good shot, old man!" Arsinoe shouted at him, speeding past.

"Old man-" Scyron made a series of noises that made Lara grin.

Then the ships in the bay fired another salvo. Shot squealed through the air, louder even than the bells crying from the city.

Jumper spooked and bolted for the palms. Lara tried to slow him, but between the bow in one hand and the lack of a bridle it was hard going. Gradually she managed a turn, Jumper slowing to a trot as they crested a low rise thick with white-tailed grass.

There were soldiers no more than half a league away, hustling beside the shallow river that ran east of Pikria. They were too far for her to pick out their banners, but she knew they weren't Frisians.

Jumper snorted as his head bobbed in the grass. Lara massaged his withers, ignoring the prick of Bannertail's claws as he scrabbled across her neck.

"Hoo," she soothed. "Hoo, boy. You're safe. You're safe."

But for how long?

The others were circling back to join her. The escort's horses were frightened as well, their riders fighting to control them, all save Arsinoe.

She and Maiden cantered up the rise as smoothly as though this were any other noonday ride.

Lara was not surprised. Maiden had been Tybalt's horse, after all. She was probably used to far worse.

"You alright?" Arsinoe asked.

"I'm fine," Lara replied, straightening.

One of the escorts lost his seat as Dramsind barreled up the far end of the rise.

"Get back on your horse!" Scyron snapped at the man, struggling to control his own.

Flames bloomed from the city. Another salvo roared across the dunes, far closer than before.

This time, Jumper reared. Lara managed to keep her seat, but only just.

"We're going to have to run," Lara said, letting Jumper circle a bit.

"Well, I figured that," Arsinoe sniffed.

"I mean, *run*," Lara said. "Maiden can't carry all of us."

"She can carry you and me."

Arsinoe shot Scyron a wry smile. He glowered back.

"I know," Lara said, "But we're going to need all the help we can get if they're already inside the walls."

"Inside?" Arsinoe blanched. "Inside the *city*? The one that's on fire?"

"Where did you think we were going?"

"I thought we were trying to escape!"

"We are," Lara said, and brought Jumper to a halt.

"Lara," Arsinoe seethed, practically leaning out of her saddle. "Reynard's blundered for once! You're *supposed* to be in there, remember?"

"And you know we can't leave them behind," Lara shot back. "Would you abandon your husband?"

The beetle danced as Arsinoe moved her jaw.

"I never should have taken that knife," she said.

Lara dismounted and unstrapped her sword from Jumper's saddle.

A gift from Roland, it had been forged in Damas, the city of steel. A bravo of Princess Zara's court called it 'Three-Merits.' Lara had wondered at the name until she learned it was what Frisian wives called their cooking knives.

She had been certain to leave the bravo three reminders of that insult during their duel, but the name had stuck all the same. To soothe her perhaps, Pinsard had named his own sword 'Sparrowgrass,' whose shoots were quick to cook.

Another bravo had laughed at that, and in Pinsard's face to boot.

'As quick as sparrowgrass' had taken on a new meaning since then.

She strapped on her sword and said a silent farewell to Jumper. She doubted she would see him again.

Bannertail leapt from her back and slipped into the whitetails.

"Have one of these men lead the horses somewhere safe!" Lara ordered, uncertain of where that might be. "The rest of you, follow me!"

"Your Highness," Scyron said, dismounting.

The man chosen to be left behind looked distinctly relieved as he took hold of Jumper's reins.

"Somewhere safe," Lara said again.

"Yes," the man said, "Your Highness."

Lara mouthed a silent prayer and began to sprint through the whitetails.

Scyron and his men followed, fanning out. Dramsind brought up their rear. Lara could hear the hive beginning to swarm within him.

Arsinoe brought Maiden alongside them, riding at the single-foot.

"I'm not leaving her," she said before Lara could comment.

"They'll shoot her for certain," Lara said between breaths. "And you!"

"We'll see," Arsinoe said, clicking her tongue as they picked up their pace.

They broke from the whitetails. No more cover.

Ahead of them were the tobacco fields that kept Prince Mydas in silks and damask. Reynard's soldiers were trampling the unripe leaves underfoot as they brought horse-drawn siege engines to bear on the walls. Some of them were already firing, discharging shot at the towers seemingly at random. The edge of the forest was so thick with powder that it looked like morning mist.

"Lara!" Arsinoe called out to her. "Don't know if you've noticed, but there's an army in our way!"

"I see them!" Lara shouted back.

"They have cannons, Lara!"

"I see them!" she panted. "And they're facing the wrong way!"

They were amongst the tobacco now. The soil was still damp from the morning's work. Maiden's hooves were kicking up clods and leaf alike.

Any moment now, they would be spotted.

More soldiers than she could easily count were storming Lark's Head by force. The little village by the bay was already ablaze, but it was impossible to tell who had set it alight.

There were just as many incendiaries flying from Pikria's walls as towards them.

"Riders!" Arsinoe cried out.

Lara saw them. A dozen of them at least, tearing from the tree line beyond the fields. Some sort of rearguard, no doubt.

"Can you slow them down?" Lara shouted.

"We'll bloody their nose!" Arsinoe called back, freeing her spear from its sheath. *"Dramsind! Motaju tifeke!"*

The swarm inside the giant shivered into a bright rage as they both veered towards the riders.

Lara almost felt sorry for them.

She made for the low bridge fording the river. There were no river girls here today. The enemy had taken it. Arbalests took cover behind wooden shields as engineers busied themselves about the artillery. She could make out the emblems on their tunics now, swallow-tailed birds on a sky-blue field.

Would that I were in white. They might take me for Moder and run.

They had been seen. An arbalest took to horse, no doubt to summon reinforcements. Scyron let loose an arrow at the woman, but his shot sailed into the river.

"Fire!" a woman's voice roared out.

The cannon jumped. The blast made Lara's ears ring. Smoke made a haze of enemy and bridge alike.

Ah well. Let them learn to fear me instead!

Lara drew as she burst from the tobacco and leapt into the haze. Swords scraped from their scabbards. She could not tell whose.

Good. They won't know how few we are.

A dark shape loomed out of the smoke. One of the arbalests. Lara drew her knife and drove it into her throat before she could call out.

The woman took the knife with her as she fell.

Another soldier emerged from the haze, her bow held out before her. Lara slashed at her forearm, knocking the thing from her grip. The arbalest back peddled, ignoring her wound as she drew sword from sheath.

She could see the cannon now, more soldiers, and the river beyond it.

The smoke was clearing.

Lara swung as she made for the woman, hoping for an easy kill.

The woman parried the blow and riposted without hesitation. Lara leaned away from the cut, but only just.

Not one of the arbalests, it seemed. *This one has some skill.*

The wind picked up as Lara waded forward. There was no time to be cautious.

Her opponent gave ground, her eyes widening as she realized who she was fighting. Lara pressed her, making a bludgeon of her blade before sweeping the woman's legs out from under her with a well-placed kick.

"No, wait-" the woman cried out.

A single thrust silenced her.

Steel rang against steel behind her. A man cried out.

One of the escorts.

Then one of them came at her with sword and shield, the swallow on its front seeming to leap as she bulled forward. Lara dodged about her and took a swing at the back of her head.

Three-Merits glanced off the back of the woman's helm. The woman stumbled forward and tried to bring her shield back to bear, but then Lara had slashed open her sword arm, just above the elbow.

They still hold back she mused as the woman dropped her weapon and turned, this time to run.

She had only taken a step or two before Lara cut her down.

A shadow on the road.

Someone behind me!

She did not hesitate, and slashed as she spun. Her sword met bone.

A woman fell against one of the barrels the enemy had stacked by the roadside, gasping as blood spilled from the cut. It was one of the engineers. A Northerner.

She was as fair as Moder.

Lara drove her sword through the fox above her breast.

The engineers were running now, most of them upriver. Scyron was putting one of the arbalests out of their misery. One of the escorts had taken a bad cut to the brow. Another lay dying, his lifeblood darkening the golden carp of Mydas.

More shadows on the ground. Shrikes overhead.

No point in shooting at them now, she supposed.

Arsinoe.

She scanned the fields. She could see horses wandering without their riders, but no giant. Perhaps she had led them off. Perhaps she was calming Dramsind. He would kill Scyron and his men in a heartbeat when his blood was up . . . So to speak.

Somewhere upriver another cannon went off. Plumes of smoke wafted downriver, as thick as it was acrid. This time she could not help but cough.

When the smoke cleared, she could see Bannertail atop the siege engine, circling nervously.

I know, I know.

"Follow me!" she shouted, scooping up the fox-squirrel as she mounted the bridge.

It was not long. Twenty strides, no more, and they would be across it.

"Highness!" one of the escorts shouted, nearly tossing her into the river as he caught hold of her arm and yanked backwards.

Arrow shafts whistled as they thudded into the bridge from the wall above. The man who had pushed her aside had taken one to the thigh. As he tried to rise another sank into his breast.

"It's us, you idiots!" Lara screamed, but she knew her words were lost amidst the reports of the cannons. Bannertail squirmed in her grip, but she held him fast.

She took a step towards the wounded man, but then Scyron was dragging her back.

Another volley sank into the planks.

"Stay back, Highness," Scyron said, tearing at the clasps of his captain's cape. When the thing was free he held it aloft and took a few steps onto the bridge.

"Open the gates!" he bellowed, ignoring the fresh flight of arrows that rained down around him. "Open the gates!"

Artillery screamed overhead. Lara flinched as one of the towers exploded from within.

Scyron gave up yelling and waved his cloak in the air.

Finally, the archers stopped firing.

"Old man has a pair!" Arsinoe's voice rang out. "I'll give him that!"

Lara turned. Arsinoe was still on Maiden. Both were speckled with blood. It did not look like their own.

"They give you any trouble?!" Lara asked, straining to be heard.

"Some!" Arsinoe answered, dismounting. "You?!"

Maiden shook her mane and nosed at the weeds growing along the riverbank. The soldiers had not trampled them all. She did not even flinch as Bannertail leapt from Lara's arms and squeezed himself into one of her saddlebags.

Wulf, Lara mused. *That horse must be stone deaf.*

"Some!" Lara said. "Where's Dramsind?"

"Over there!" Arsinoe pointed. The giant was standing, very still, amongst the tobacco.

"What's wrong with him?!" Lara asked.

"Don't know!" Arsinoe answered. "He just stopped there! Didn't even need to calm him!"

"Dramsind!" Lara shouted at the giant. *"Kelowo bujeti?!"*

Dramsind's head swiveled towards her, but he did not answer. Instead, he took a step backwards, his long arms hanging limp at his sides.

"*Something's* got him spooked!" Arsinoe said. "But if they're lobbing invisible fire at the walls, well then I guess all bets are off!"

"Highness!" Scyron called out. "The gates!"

The gates were opening. And, as they did, Lara could not help but doubt.

Those wooden doors are over a hundred years old. The damp and ivy have rotted them through. All it would take is a single cannon blast to blow them to tinder.

They don't want to break them down. Just keep us in.

"Lara!" Arsinoe said. "I know this spot is lovely and all, what with all the bodies, but we might want to keep moving!"

Arsinoe pointed over Lara's shoulder.

A wedge of a hundred or so horse was pounding towards them from upriver. A banner bearing the mailed fist of the Baroness rode at their head. Soldiers were streaming towards them from the flames of Lark's

Head as well. A chevalier in full plate was leading the charge. If she was a woman, she was the biggest one Lara had ever seen. Her great sword was nearly as tall as herself.

"Dramsind!" Arsinoe said, practically leaping onto Maiden's back. *"Fiki!"*

Dramsind moved, but slowly, his legs sidestepping each other like a crab as he kept his distance from the artillery works.

Lara, on the other hand, ran towards them, sheathing her sword as she searched amongst the barrels of black powder.

"What are you doing?!" Arsinoe shouted at her.

"Flashing them the fingers!" Lara shouted back, lifting one of the corded fuses the engineers had dropped.

It was still smoking.

Lara tossed it into one of the open barrels.

Arsinoe did not wait, but spurred Maiden towards the gate, nearly running Scyron down. Dramsind picked up speed as he reached the far side of the bridge.

Lara ran for the gate. The chevalier was roaring something she could not hear.

She was still on the bridge when the powder blew. She could feel the furnace at her back, could hear timbers splintering.

Then she was through the gate. Its doors closed behind her, shuddering.

* * * * * * *

"Forgive me, m'lady," Bradamante said, dropping to her knee as Rukenaw rode up. "I take full responsibility. I thought scuttling the ships of that rat's nest of a village took precedence! Had I left a company behind-"

"No need to beg my pardon," Rukenaw said, shifting in her saddle as she scanned the walls of Pikria. "We did as we were bid, if only by happenstance."

"M'lady," Bradamante said, bowing her head.

"Now get up," Rukenaw said, "And see to our flank."

"At once, m'lady!"

Bradamante rose and broke into a sprint, moving fast for all her armor.

Rukenaw looked to the bridge. Bradamante's Flycatchers were already clearing the bodies from the wreck of the cannon.

"So close," she breathed.

She considered the whistle hanging round her neck. One blast would bring one of Tiecelin's flock down on them before long.

No need. She had already sent Briser.

Let 'Father' be blamed.

"Gunnery!" she called out.

One of her staff broke from the line of horse behind her.

"My lady?"

"Bring up another engine," Rukenaw ordered, leveling her mace. "I want that gate gone. Not just the doors, the whole bloody structure."

"M'lady!"

"No one gets out of this city. Not past us."

* * * * * * *

The city was on fire.

Frisia was always hot, of course. Even in winter Pinsard would sweat through his shirt by midday. He was sweating now, and glad of it. The flames spreading up from the port had drawn much of the moisture from the air. Every breath made his chest ache.

He picked up his pace. This place would be a furnace before long.

There were shrikes wheeling above the city, there were soldiers beating at its gates, and no doubt there were reavers already inside its walls, but here, in Oldtown, the streets were almost empty. He had counted on that.

Too close to the fire for the enemy to brave, and too far gone for the city's bucket brigades to bother saving.

But even he was forced to take the long way around Whitesmith's Row, where the tinkers plied their craft.

The flames had already taken it.

Pikria was a city of stone, the better to withstand the storms that traveled the gulf, but that made no difference to the fire. The shops and homes here might not burn to their foundations, but they had become ovens within.

He could picture iron boiling like wax in their crucibles as he raced through one of the alleys that ran beneath the walls of the citadel. Tin running in rivulets through the gutters. Nothing could survive such heat.

He put on more speed.

What if Mulberry Square is already alight?

What if I am too late?

The alley ended. Men, women, and children were racing away from the spreading flames, their arms full of anything that could easily be carried. Others were busy hurling cloth, baubles, and furniture into the street from the windows above. Were they tenants? Looters?

It did not make a difference.

He leapt over the shattered remains of a wardrobe and made his way downhill. A man shouted something at him in the old tongue. It sounded like a plea.

He kept running.

Soon he could see blood on the cobblestones. Then, bodies. They were prince's men most of them, though he spotted at least one with spurs on his boots.

One of the Steel Heels. Their captain had been father's second, long ago. Now he served as the seneschal of Carduel.

Coward. Lackey. Traitor.

A cry rang out from the next block. Steel rasped against steel.

Fighting. Somewhere close.

He took a turn onto the winding lane of the dyer's market, and for a moment he had a clear view of the Spell. The fishing boats and merchants' cogs were untouched by flame, but there were figures swarming over its wharves like rats. He could not see the *Kite*, but it was moored in the far end of the bay, where the wall had begun to fall into the sea.

Then the lane wound back on itself.

He was close now.

He ducked under a low awning, ignored the slap of wet yarn as he shoved straight through one of the smaller stalls, and at last he saw her, a slight girl with a ream of linens gripped to her chest.

Doricha.

She said nothing but ran to him, dropping her burden without a second thought.

He took her in his arms and kissed the top of her head. She shook.

"Are you hurt?" Pinsard panted.

"No," she said, her eyes widening as she stared up at him. "Your face-"

"Just dye," he said. "I ran all the way."

A giggle escaped her. She had to stand on her tiptoes to press her lips to his.

"Madder," she murmured as they parted, "Madder, my love, a talent a pace-"

"Doricha," Pinsard said, "We need to go. Now."

"Now?" she blurted. "Is the fire so close?"

She has no idea what's going on.

No. She must know. The rumble of artillery could be heard clear across the city. But she was panicked. So were her kin, who were loading the cart before their shop with far more than either of their mules could bear. The Irkallan carpet on which they had first taken tea together was laid in front of the house, the best of the silver laid atop it.

"Doricha!" a voice called out. Her mother's. "Where are you girl?"

On instinct the girl began to pull away from him, but he held her fast.

"It is not safe here," he said to her. "The whole city- Doricha, please-"

"Mother!" she cried. "It's Pinsard!"

"Lord Pinsard?" The woman came jogging about the cart, her hair jingling with beads of amber. "Oh, thank the gods! You can help us empty the house before the fire takes it!"

"Leave it!" Pinsard shouted, releasing Doricha. "We need to get to the ship!"

"Ha!" Doricha's mother laughed. "My lord, you cannot expect- These silks alone are worth a dozen ships!"

"And soon they will be ash! Leave them!"

By now all of Doricha's kin, her sisters, her brothers, her cousins, her aunts and uncles and their wives had stopped what they were doing and were gaping at him.

Doricha's father, silent as ever, came to stand beside his wife.

"The city is surrounded!" Pinsard said. "There is no way out of here. Not on foot. Not with a cart to slow you down. Now you have to come with me, all of you!"

Mother's lip stiffened.

"If you will not help-"

Doricha screamed.

There were men coming up the street. A dozen of them, armed. *Steel Heels* Pinsard thought at first, sliding his blade free from its sheath. Then he saw their boarding axes, their long-knives and cutlasses. *Reavers.*

"Stay back," he said, putting himself between Doricha and the men.

"Look who we've caught," one of them blustered to the others. "The pup! Or are you some fool got lost on the way to Domdaniel?"

"'e's pale enough," another agreed, but did not laugh.

Pinsard did not answer but loosened his cape from his shoulders. It could prove a hindrance against so many.

"Where's your mother, pup?" the first reaver asked. "Or better still, your sister?"

They were spreading out as they approached. Hoping to surround him.

He did not wait for them to strike first.

The closest one managed to begin a swing before Pinsard's blade slashed straight through his sword arm. He stepped away from the next one's clumsy slash, deflected the man's riposte, and then let his own blade sink home in the man's chest.

Someone behind him took a swing at his head, missed, and then lost his footing on the cobblestones.

Pinsard spun. The edge of his blade sliced into the tendons of the man's neck.

The reaver slid free from his sword, gasping.

Four came at him then, or was it five? They were as much in each other's way as anything else. He could smell them as he weaved. Sweat, black powder, and the stink of liquor on their breath.

He let them get around him, his blade his only shield. A mistake and he would be dead, but it made them overconfident. Sloppy.

He was not sloppy. And he and Sparrowgrass were very quick.

They died. Their ends were quick. It was almost easy.

He only needed to picture Reynard on the end of his blade.

"Who is next?" Pinsard asked as the last of them fell.

There was as much blood on him now as dye.

One of the reavers tripped over a loose cobblestone as the rest turned to run. Pinsard drove his sword through the man before he could rise.

The others lay where they had fallen: Dead or choking on their own blood.

"Doricha," Pinsard said, turning.

She was standing with her family, her sisters holding her close.

Her eyes were very wide.

She had seen him train. She had heard the stories. The ones that made it seem romantic rather than brutal. She had sighed at them, how brave, how gallant.

But she had never seen him kill.

She's scared of me now. Just like all the others.

"Linen," he said.

Doricha's father tossed him one of the smaller bolts. The beads in mother's hair quivered, but she kept her peace.

Pinsard cut free a swatch and wiped his blade clean. Sheathed it.

"The ship," Pinsard said. "There is room for-"

They stared at him. He could read the look in their eyes.

Stay away from my daughter. Stay away from us.

A salvo went off in the harbor. It sounded very close.

"Goodbye," he said, taking up his cloak as he turned from them.

"Pinsard!" he could hear Doricha crying out. "Pinsard, wait!"

But he could not. There was no more time.

* * * * * *

Maiden tossed her head, her whinnies as loud as the screams rising from the Spell. The sailors cursed and struggled to keep hold of her as she beat at the boarding plank with her hooves. When Lycus reached out to calm her, she snapped at his fingers.

"Keep 'er steady!" Damon barked at the men gripping the end of the plank. "It's the water's got 'er spooked!"

"You'd think she'd be used to it by now," Arsinoe grumbled, shoving Lycus aside to take the reins herself.

Lara shot her a look. "You throw up every time we're at sea."

"I've got a sensitive disposition," Arsinoe said. "Now move, *seni sefil canavar!*"

She managed, somehow, to coax Maiden aboard. The sugar in her palm helped no doubt.

"Get her below deck," Lara said. "And make ready to sail at my command!"

Her orders were obeyed at once, and without question. Hylas might be the captain of the *Kite*, but she was the Queen of Arcasia's vessel.

Sailors raced up the shrouds, seeing to the lines as Dramsind worked the capstan.

Bannertail, for his part, sat upon the gunwale, and squalled.

Hylas was frowning at the battle in the bay, looking as nervous as he'd ever been. One of the enemy galleys was sinking into the shallows. Its sails were on fire and men were leaping from it in swarms. If it had been set ablaze by boarders or one of the ballistas of the citadel Lara could not say. There was enough smoke in the air that even the shrikes were forced to keep their distance.

What little she could see was far from encouraging. The few Frisian ships that had escaped the fire engulfing the harbor were engaged with the brigantines of the enemy, and they were outnumbered two to one. One of the usurper's vessels had anchored just outside the Spell, its cannons ready to fire on anything that dared leave the cove. It had struck the shells and knots and raised its true colors: A fanged eel vert with a naked wretch caught in its jaws.

The Spell, its shallows so full of lashed together ships that they had formed a floating village of sorts, was a mad confusion of people. Some were bargaining with the captains of boats no bigger than a skiff for passage. Others brawled when words would no longer suffice. Many wept, and huddled beneath the shadows of the larger ships, praying to whatever gods would listen for mercy.

"Below there!" Daimonax called from the crow's nest. "Boots on the pier!"

Lara turned, hopeful. But it was only Scyron. He was alone.

"It was like this at Quivira," he panted as he mounted the gangplank. "Only we were the raiders that day. Gods, what a fight that was!"

The man's voice was ragged from the smoke. Lara handed him her waterskin.

"You were at Quivira?" Arsinoe said, popping a sugar cube into her mouth.

"I was," Scyron said, taking a swallow. "I am surprised you know of it."

"My people fought there. For the Hivans, of course."

"They fought well," Scyron said, "As I remember."

"Volk," Arsinoe cursed, sucking on the cube. "Just how old are you?"

"Feh!" Scyron spat. "I might ask you the same ques-"

"You two can trade war stories later!" Lara interjected. "Did you find them?"

"No," Scyron said, returning the skin. "I got as close to Prince Street as I dared, but the fighting was too hot."

"They're making for the citadel then," Lara reasoned. "But how close are they? To us, I mean."

"Bravos and militia are holding them at the fish market. Or at least they're still scrapping over it. Some of the usurper's pirates are ashore too. What they're doing this far from the fighting though-"

"Looking for us, no doubt," Arsinoe said. "That bounty's large as it ever was-"

An explosion ripped across the Spell. Lara ducked beneath the gunwale and braced for impact, half-expecting the hull to shatter beside her. Bannertail leapt onto her shoulders and tried to burrow under her jack.

Then Daimonax sang out from above: "All clear! All clear!"

She rose and could see that the brigantine guarding the bay had opened on a small flotilla of vessels making for East Point. The smoke of its cannons drifted inland as the little ships turned about, their sailors rowing like mad.

"Wulf!" Lara cursed, freeing Bannertail from her shoulders. "Where are they?"

"Here," Pinsard said, striding up the gangplank.

"Blood," she worried.

"None of it mine," Pinsard said.

She embraced him. The fox-squirrel weaved between his feet, chattering.

"There are reavers in the city," Lara said as they parted.

"I know," Pinsard said.

"How many did you kill?" Arsinoe asked.

"Ten," Pinsard said. "I think."

"You think?" Arsinoe smirked.

"I did not stop to count."

"Less of them to worry about at any rate."

"Fewer," Pinsard said, wiping the blood from his blade.

"Siktir git," Arsinoe snapped.

"I know what that means, you-"

The brigantine opened up again, its cannons vomiting smoke and flame. Their shot sent up great plumes of water at the mouth of the Spell.

"Is there any other way out of here?" Pinsard asked, trying to extricate Bannertail from the leg of his breeches.

"Not unless you've learned to fly," Lara said, helping him. "The Baroness' grip on this place is getting tighter by the second."

"How did you get past them?" Pinsard asked.

"Oh, that?" Arsinoe said, feigning a yawn. "Easy. Hardly broke a sweat."

"You exaggerate," Pinsard said. "But I am glad you are safe."

"It's good to see you too, lover boy."

He flinched at that.

"Doricha?" Arsinoe prodded.

"With her family," he said.

"Ah well," Arsinoe sighed.

"Where's Moder?" Lara asked.

"She's-" Pinsard said, his brows knitting. "She is not here?"

"We thought she was with you," Lara said, her mouth gone suddenly dry.

"She said to meet here," Pinsard said. "Told me to find Doricha. I thought she might get here before-"

Lara turned her gaze to the citadel. Flames were licking at its western approaches. Shrikes were thick about it; the enemy was making for it with all their strength.

But somehow its gates still stood.

"She said," Pinsard whispered. "She said not to wait."

He turned and flew back down the gangplank, his long legs pumping as soon as he hit the pier.

"Pinsard!" Lara shouted. "Stop!"

He did not slow.

"Hold the ship!" she shouted, not caring who obeyed. "I'll bring him back alone!"

"Are you sure?" Arsinoe shouted at her as she mounted the gangplank.

"I'm sure!" Lara shot back.

"Lady, I am sworn to protect you!" Scyron cried out after her.

"Then see that I have a ship to come back to!"

Lara ran.

But Pinsard was faster.

IV

The prince's men held the harbor for as long as they could, each man selling his life but dear. The brigades pulled back and let the counting house catch fire, hoping that the flames would make the way to the citadel impassable. Archers rained arrows down upon the enemy, until the cobbles of Prince Street ran red with blood.

But Reynard could not be stopped.

The Steel Heels had brought up a mortar from the harbor, a stubby thing that half resembled a cooking pot mounted on a wheeled harness. Devoye's soldiers cleared the way for them, tossing bodies into the pyres that had once been rich men's homes. When archers emerged to fire upon them, they themselves were shot down. Tiecelin had brought his own marksmen: Handpicked men from Riva and Ormond who were echoes of their master.

Their aim was keen. When no man dared stir atop the walls, the engineers aimed the mortar at the gatehouse of the citadel and let fire. The gates were thicker than they looked. It took three touches of shot to bring them down, the keystone above failing as they gave way.

The Tarsus men were the first through the breach, two score sword and pike bearing the golden ram on their tunics, eager for a fight.

The White Lady was waiting for them. The She-Wolf.

She stood at the far end of the first court, tall and fair and terrible. She had freed her storied blade from its sheath, and there was death in her eyes.

The remains of the house guard stood behind her. There were no more than twenty of them, and they had all been bloodied in the streets . . . Yet even they kept their distance from the woman in white.

The Tarsus men wavered, their pikes quivering as they ground to a halt at the edge of the court's reflecting pool. The fish that swam its waters were as brilliant as citrus.

"Kill her, you cowards!" their captain shouted from the safety of the rear.

She struck.

The first of them hesitated as she mounted the bridge that spanned the pool, tried even to back away. Her first cut sliced through the bridge of his nose.

Her second separated his arm from his shoulder.

Another of the men rushed her, thinking perhaps to skewer her on the tip of his pike. She stepped around his thrust and sent Harrower whistling into his shoulder.

The man next to him turned to run.

She let him go. She needed all her strength.

Others were beginning to panic. They had expected to face men here, not a demon clothed in mortal flesh. Some dropped their pikes and reached for their swords. It made no difference. They were middling swordsmen at best. She slew them where they stood, and ignored what wounds she took.

She hardly seemed human.

When one of the arbalests took aim at her, she threw one of his fellows into the path of the bolt. The man had not hit the cobblestones before she cut down the marksman as well.

"Stand your ground!" the captain was roaring at his men. "She's only one-"

His words died in his throat as the She-Wolf drove her blade straight through his skull. He had barely lifted an arm to defend himself.

The Tarsus men broke.

Those that could fled back through the ruin of the gate, ignoring the flames that had caught amidst its fallen timbers. The house guard fell upon the rest, the prince's men rushing into the fray with new heart. They drove some of the Tarsus men straight into the pool, where they died amidst the fishes.

Hirsent caught her breath, glancing at the blood that now stained her woolen coat. Some of it was hers no doubt, but she felt no pain.

Not yet.

Somewhere beyond the gates the mortar *boomed*. There was an ear-splitting shriek and then the wall of the second court exploded outwards, masonry flying as bits of the walls rained down on living and dead alike.

Hirsent choked on the kicked-up dust but found that she was still standing. Her ears rang, but she could still hear the men crying out about her.

There were shrikes landing on the remnants of the outer curtain. Dark ones with red-breasts and plum ones with violet eyes. Some were no bigger than falcons.

They were all staring at her.

"Back," she said to the men floundering about her. "Back, all of you."

They had no time to obey. A sheet of flame leapt up between the ruin of the gates, so hot that even the shrikes shied from it.

Through the fire, a figure stepped. A shadow wreathed in smoke.

He was gripping a pair of severed heads in his right hand, his fingers finding purchase in their locks. The shattered remnants of a violet ruby had been embedded into his breastplate. The sword that her lover, her husband, the father of her children, had built with the skill of his own hands hung from his belt.

Of the man beneath the mail, there was nothing to be seen. Not even his eyes.

"I have been waiting for you," Hirsent said. "Reynard."

He flicked his wrist.

The severed heads sailed across the court and came rolling to a halt beside her feet. The first had been dipped in lacquer and belonged to Lara's crude cousin, Pinoteau. The other was Lityerses'. It was so fresh that the young man looked as though he might open his eyes and speak.

The house guards gasped and shuddered and hastened towards the gate of the second court, some of them stumbling into the pond in their rush.

Hirsent merely straightened and flicked the blood from the edge of her blade with a shake of her wrist.

"There is trick to it, no?" she asked. "The fire."

"Stand aside, Hirsent," he said, his voice sounding odd to her ears, harsh and metallic. "Stand aside, and I will spare your life."

"No," she said.

He took a step forward, his cloak still smoldering about his shoulders.

"Where is she?" he asked, the fingers of his left-hand quivering.

"Be coming closer," she said. "And I will tell you."

He cast his gaze over the courtyard, the flames playing against his counterfeit face.

"Not here it seems," he said. "I have fallen for that ruse once before. Or have you forgotten?"

"I am not coming here to *trick* you, Reynard."

The shrikes cawed and chattered.

"You've grown reckless, Hirsent," he said, undoing the clasp at his throat. "You would truly risk it all? Just for the *chance* of killing me?"

Her knees bent as she planted her feet.

"Very well," he said, shaking off his cloak. "I accept."

With a press of his false thumb, he loosened Right-Hand from its sheath.

She took a step forward, sweeping aside Lityerses' head with a gentle kick.

One of the shrikes took flight, cawing.

Reynard drew as he lunged: The fishing cast. Hirsent parried it easily, giving ground as he pushed into the strike and drove his left fist towards her breast, the hidden blade springing from its sheath.

She smashed his blade aside, deflected his quick riposte, and then tested him with a flurry of her own strikes.

Their swords sang across the court as he parried every blow.

He is quick as ever. Quicker, even.

She tried to plant her foot for a kick to his legs, hoping to put him on his back for an easy kill, but he was already drifting about her, winding into a slash that would open her neck.

She spun into her parry, putting all her weight behind her sword.

Their swords met, and he buckled. Before he could recover, she brought her sword down on his shoulder.

Steel rang as the blow glanced off his mail. Then she was backing away from his left hand, her heels slipping over the blood-slick stones. She had barely regained her balance when he came at her again, more furiously than ever.

He's not even stunned.

Suddenly she found a wall at her back. He pressed into her, both true hand and false gripping Right-Hand as he swung.

She slid under the strike and landed a blow to his back as he whirled to counter. She doubted he even felt it through the plate.

She gained some ground, panting for show.

Let him think I tire.

He took the bait and thrust at her, using the full reach that Right-Hand afforded him.

She stepped into the blow as she dodged and caught hold of the gorget protecting his throat. He struggled to lean away from her, his grip on Right-Hand loosening as the blade sprang from his left wrist.

Hirsent kicked him then, as hard as she was able.

Something gave in her hand as the straps of the gorget sprang free.

He managed to catch himself as he fell. But only just.

She tossed the gorget aside, ignoring the agony in her fingers, and swung at his head.

He brought sword and blade up to catch her blow and then pushed, steel rasping on steel as he cast her blade aside.

His reversed the cut of his sword, slashing open her thigh.

She drove her sword through his throat.

Reynard dropped Right-Hand as he slid from her blade. He gurgled beneath his mask, tried to speak perhaps, but all he could do was wheeze as his lifeblood spilled from him. When he tried to stem the flow, Hirsent put her boot down on his hand and twisted her heel.

The fingers of his left-hand quivered. Then they were still.

Her own fingers throbbed. Broken, no doubt.

But worth it.

"You," one of the house guards said, as wide-eyed as any boy. "You killed him."

"Yes," Hirsent said.

She slumped against the ruin of the gatehouse, her weariness no longer an act.

"He's dead," the man said. "The usurper is dead!"

"The tyrant's dead!" another of the house guard echoed. "Long live Vireo!"

By the time Hirsent had knelt to examine her leg, the words had become a cheer.

The cut was bad. It would need cleaning, then stitches. Her fingers, a splint. The fourth and fifth digits would not bend on their own.

She laid down her sword and loosened her belt, meaning to make a tourniquet of it.

She stopped.

Tiecelin lives. So does Rukenaw. Reynard may be dead, but the fighting is not yet done.

And yet, it was so quiet.

A shiver ran through her as she turned towards the flaming timbers that stood between her and the plaza outside the citadel.

Where were his men? Surely, he had brought his Graycloaks with him. Tiecelin too.

Then where are they? Why are they holding back?

She was still wondering when the arrow struck her.

It took her in the back, just beneath the shoulder, the shock of it enough to force a cry from her throat. She could hear other missiles whistling down from the heights of the second court, the cries of the house guard as they were struck down.

Tiecelin was standing atop the second gate, nocked and ready. His marksmen had taken up positions along the inner curtain. Men with spurs on their boots and foxes on their breasts were pouring from the second court, their blades putting an end to the suffering of the men groaning on the cobblestones.

The citadel had fallen.

She wrapped her fingers about the hilt of her sword and made to rise.

Tiecelin loosed. A red-fletched arrow caught her in the chest.

She staggered towards the pond, gasping. Her legs shook. She reached out with her broken hand to catch hold of one of the little statues that housed the pipes. This one was shaped like a naga. Water poured from the conch it cradled.

Tiecelin put an arrow through her thigh. Just above the cut.

She fell against the statue. The arrows twisted within her.

She could not help but scream.

One of the smaller shrikes flew across the court and landed atop Tiecelin's outstretched arm. It tilted its head and stared at her with its all too human eyes.

Then its mouth opened, and Reynard's voice spilled out.

"You've grown reckless, Hirsent," it said. "Reckless."

"Hirsent," another of them warbled. Rohart, she thought. Or was it one of his sons?

It did not matter.

"Hirsent, Hirsent, Hirsent!" the others cawed.

It sounded like laughter.

"Enough," a voice rang out, and the shrikes were quiet.

A man wearing an eyepatch stepped from the ranks of the enemy. He was dressed as one of the Steel Heels. His good eye blinked at the smoke in the air.

"Ah," she gasped. "I thought he had some skill."

He smiled at that.

She tightened her grip on her sword.

"Who was he?" she asked.

"Lord Reynard," he answered, the fingers of his false hand flickering.

"And you?"

"No one," he said simply. "A shadow."

"A black one."

"So, you've finally grown some wit," he said, drawing closer. "Or will you call me 'dog' as well, and spoil it?"

"Dog!" she spat, and lunged at him, ignoring the pain as her sword whistled towards his face.

He dodged the blow easily. Then Tiecelin put an arrow through her knee.

She dropped her sword as she toppled.

By now the Tarsus men had braved the fiery wreck of the gate to secure the first court, and with them the Graycloaks. The Calvarians looked on her with indifference, the Southerners with awe.

Here lay the She-Wolf, bested at last.

"Search the citadel," Reynard said, addressing one of the Southerners, a high captain judging by his plate. "The storerooms. Mydas will be in one of them."

"My lord," the man said, already moving.

The Tarsus men followed, pressing past the Steel-Heels.

"Your orders?" Tiecelin asked. He had a fresh arrow nocked.

Reynard raised his hand, *hold*, and knelt beside her.

"Where is she?" he asked.

"Safe," she said.

"Someone once told me that there is no such thing as 'safe.'" He said cooly. "Where is she?"

"Lenape . . . This morning she is going."

"Comb the bay," Reynard said, raising his voice as he straightened. "Her ship is still there. If not, turn the city inside out."

"As you command," Tiecelin said.

The Luxian whistled to his children. The shrikes perched atop the battlements burst into flight. The Steel-Heels were moving too. Their spurred boots thundered past her.

She closed her eyes.

When she opened them, Reynard was still standing over her.

He was wearing her husband's sword.

They were alone.

"Are you in much pain?" he asked.

A laugh shook her frame. Every heave was an agony.

"I could send for my priestess," he said. "She is no *fisicien*, but she has a very steady hand."

"No," Hirsent hissed.

He nodded and was silent.

She tried to turn on her side, but the pain was too much. She forced herself to look at her leg. Her breeches were soaked through with blood.

"You are," she breathed, "You are cheating me."

"I had to," he said. "I never could have beaten you."

"Another lie," she said, trying to rise. "You killed him. You killed-"

"He won, Hirsent," Reynard said. "Isengrim. He won."

"You *dare* say his name?"

"I do," he said.

She closed her eyes again. The earth seemed to lurch beneath her. She was so thirsty.

"What are you waiting for?" she managed.

He took a deep breath and squeezed his left hand into a fist.

The hidden blade sprang from its sheath.

"Did you really think it was me, in that armor?" he asked. "Don't lie."

She nodded.

"I believe you," he said, and readied his blade to strike.

"No!" a voice cried out.

Reynard's blade wavered, then retracted. Hirsent turned her head, and for a moment she thought one of the Graycloaks had turned his colors. Or was it her husband, come back from the dead?

Then she saw him clearly.

"Pinsard," she tried to shout, but she did not have the breath.

* * * * * *

Pinsard flew towards Reynard, his own sword ringing from its sheath as he closed the distance between them.

Reynard leapt backwards.

Pinsard drove on, his cuts quick, but all his sword found was air. Reynard stepped away from them almost casually.

"Coward!" Pinsard snarled, pressing his attack.

Reynard began to use his false hand, casting aside Pinsard's strikes with the flat of his palm.

"You are very good," Reynard said, still weaving.

"You mock me!" Pinsard panted.

"Not at all," Reynard breathed, letting the boy's own momentum carry him past his left shoulder. "You are like your father's sword. Strong yet supple-"

Pinsard spun about neatly, and then exploded towards Reynard, his sword sweeping wide.

Reynard leaned away from the strike, no more than a step.

Then he drove his palm into Pinsard's face. He staggered into the pond, the fish darting away from his boots.

"But your rage unbalances you," Reynard said.

The Graycloaks were rushing back into the court by now, their blades drawn.

Reynard waved them back.

"Draw!" Pinsard snapped, wiping the blood from his nose as he took a step onto the bridge. "Draw, you bastard!"

"As you wish," Reynard said, and mounted the span himself.

The Graycloaks formed a circle about the pool as the boy found his footing.

Reynard took a step forward, his good hand touching the hilt of his blade.

The sword flashed in the sunlight as he drew.

Twice their blades met.

Then Sparrowgrass snapped in two.

Before Pinsard could recover, Reynard flicked his wrist.

Pinsard took a step back. His undershirt was soaked through with sweat, but he could still feel the heat coursing down his chest.

He pressed a hand to his collarbone. He was bleeding.

He had not even felt the cut.

"Just a scratch," Reynard said, leveling his blade. "Now. Do you yield?"

"Never!" Pinsard answered, lowering his stance.

"You've lost your sword, boy."

"I will not need one," Pinsard said. He tossed what was left of Sparrowgrass aside.

Reynard smiled ever so slightly.

"All the same," he said taking hold of Right-Hand by its length.

Then he offered it to Pinsard, hilt first.

Pinsard's eyes widened at the sight of the blade, but he did not move to take it.

"Take it," Reynard said. "It was your father's. But you know that."

Still, Pinsard did not move.

"Hm." Reynard sheathed the blade and crossed his arms. "You are catching on, aren't you? Faster than your mother."

Pinsard could not help but flinch.

"I lay with your mother once, you know," Reynard said. "Naked beneath the stars."

"Liar!" Pinsard barked.

"Do I lie, Hirsent?" Reynard said, turning ever so slightly.

Pinsard turned too, only for a moment.

Something struck him in the gut, hard enough to make him double over. A booted foot drove itself into the back of his right knee. Suddenly, he was in the pool. He flailed against one of the dead men floating amongst Mydas' fish, his feet slipping against the slimy bottom as he tried to rise.

A hand took hold of him and dragged him up by his collar.

Then there was a blade at his neck.

"Don't struggle," Reynard said, applying some pressure to the blade. "Or I'll open your throat."

Pinsard coughed. He had swallowed some of the water. His mouth tasted like an old coin.

"She is somewhere close, yes?" Reynard said, pressing his knee into the small of Pinsard's back. "She wouldn't let her dear brother run off alone, would she? Not Lara."

The blade nicked his throat.

"Call out to her, boy," Reynard said. "Call for help."

"You'll have to," Pinsard choked, "Kill me."

"Perhaps I will," Reynard said. "If I cut you down, boy, will she come running to save you?"

He nicked him again, deeper this time. He could feel the blood as it ran down his neck.

"Does she care for you that much?" Reynard mused. "I wonder, boy. I wonder."

"Reynard," a voice called out.

She had managed to crawl to the edge of the pool. Her voice had grown very weak. One had to strain to hear it.

"Do not," Moder said, laboring for the words. "Do not. I . . . Beg you."

"Moder-" Pinsard said, his voice catching in his throat.

Reynard had gone still beside him.

"I beg," Moder repeated.

Reynard lifted the blade from Pinsard's neck.

"Go to her, boy," he said, giving Pinsard a shove with his boot.

Pinsard began to turn and felt the prick of a blade in the small of his back.

"Go," Reynard urged. "Before I change my mind."

He went. The Graycloaks made way for him.

She looked so small to him now. Her coat and breeches were more red than white.

He knelt by her. He helped to turn her.

"I told you not to wait," she wheezed.

"Moder," Pinsard said. "Moder, why?"

"You know why."

He nodded. His cheeks were burning.

"Is she safe? Is she-"

"She-"

The words caught in his throat. Reynard's reflection was staring at them from the waters of the pool.

"Yes," he said. "She is safe."

She took his hand in hers and squeezed.

"You do your father honor," she said, laboring at the words. "He would be proud."

She tried to wet her lips.

"As proud as I . . ."

He shut his eyes and tried not to weep.

She squeezed his hand again.

"Now," she said. "Stand aside."

"No," he said, his voice catching in his throat.

"Do," she said. "As I say."

He obeyed.

She turned towards Reynard.

"Finish it," she said. "I am . . . Ready."

Reynard slid Right-Hand free from its sheath.

Pinsard lurched forward, his feet carrying him towards the man, but then strong hands had caught hold of him. They dragged him from his Moder.

Reynard placed the tip of the blade over her heart and took a breath.

He exhaled as he drove it home.

A howl escaped Pinsard's lips. There were no words in it. He struggled against the men holding him, his feet skidding against the cobblestones as he fought.

One of the Graycloaks, a woman, punched him in the soft part of his gut. The blow knocked the air from his breast, and he went limp.

Then he could hear it.

Somewhere close an animal was squalling.

Pinsard forced his head back up.

Reynard had tilted his own head back and was scanning the outer curtain. The Graycloaks were doing the same.

A stone clattered against the cobblestones of the court.

"There," Reynard said, pointing towards one of the tiled roofs just outside the wall. "It's her. Don't let her escape."

The Graycloaks began to move.

"Run!" Pinsard called out with all his strength. "Run, Lara, run!"

The woman struck him again, this time under the jaw.

* * * * * * *

Devoye found him standing vigil by the pool. He had dismissed over half his guard.

"Pikria is yours, my lord," Devoye said. "And Vireo with it."

The Baron of Ylourgne knelt and offered him a golden chain. From it dangled a fragment of Thunderclap, the soul-crushing blade.

Reynard took it and turned it in his palm.

"They say it has no equal, my lord," Devoye said. "No stronger steel than-"

"I have heard the stories," Reynard said, slipping the trinket under his jack. "Mydas?"

"Dead, my lord," Devoye said. "We found him in his wine cellar. His heart gave out, I think."

"His household?"

"Taken, my lord."

"Escort the Lady Damodice's daughters to my ship," Reynard said. "Young Anchurus will return to find himself a prince, but he will be less inclined to strike back at us once he learns that we keep his sisters as guests."

"And the treasury, Lord Protector?"

"One third shall be a gift to Tarsus," Reynard said. "See that you find something of the house that will amuse the Lady Belisent."

"My lord," Devoye said, and rose.

Reynard turned his eye on the woman who lay by the side of the pool. The fingers of her right hand were floating just atop its waters. The nipping of the golden fish lent them some semblance of life.

"The She-Wolf," Devoye said.

"Yes," Reynard said.

"Shall I tell the men that you slew her?"

"No," Reynard said. "Say that she cut down more than a dozen men before she fell, amongst them a chevalier and one of the bodyguards of the Lord Protector. But for her wounds she might have fought on, for no man could stand before her . . . No honest man, at least."

"That tale will grow tall in the telling," Devoye frowned. "My lord."

"As it should," Reynard said.

Devoye did not press him further. The Lord Protector's stratagems did not always make sense to him. At least, not at first.

"Her body?"

"See that she is burned apart from the others," Reynard said. "I would have her remains sent to Kloss."

"My lord," Devoye said, and removed himself from the court.

"What would you have of this one?" Ulfdregil asked, nodding towards the boy.

The boy still slept, but he had been tied and gagged all the same. Four of the Graycloaks stood watch over him.

"We will take him to Carduel," Reynard said. *"The perfect bait to catch a Queen."*

V

Lara was numb as she leapt from rooftop to balcony, not daring to look down, not daring to slow. She barely felt the shock of each landing, or the ache in the small of her back.

All she knew was that she could not let them catch her.

She could not let him win.

She leapt and ran the length of a rich man's villa. The tiles made the footing difficult, and more than one of them slipped beneath her feet. She could hear them smashing against the cobblestones below and hoped that at least one of them would stove in the heads of her pursuers.

She could still catch glimpses of them, racing through the streets and alleys beneath her. The Graycloaks they were called, Calvarians that Reynard had bent to his service during the wars. The men could have been Pinsard's uncles. The women-

She thrust the thought aside and leapt.

She was over High Market now. One of the Graycloaks vaulted onto one of the low hanging awnings ringing the square, but the weight of his own mail was enough to send him plummeting into the stall below. She did not look back to see him fall, but took the next leap at a run, catching hold of one of the washing lines that crisscrossed the rooftops as she tumbled onto a terrace. Bannertail was using them as he would a tree limb, keeping pace with her far more easily than the Calvarians beneath.

She was not surprised. He was a fox-squirrel after all.

She had done this before, though nowhere near as quickly. The roof tops near the citadel were the easiest way to slip in and out of the prince's manse undetected, if you had the courage to take the leap.

Had the usurper's men done the same? Or had they come up with grapnels?

She threw herself aside just as a jet-black shrike came swooping down on her, its claws outstretched before it. There was no balustrade to stop her, so she let herself drop onto the roof directly below.

Its tiles gave beneath her weight. She flailed her arms, trying to catch herself, but the fall was too sudden.

Fabric ripped. A shock ran up her legs as they met something soft, but solid. Wood creaked, then snapped. Feathers flew into the air.

She rolled from what remained of the bed, threw open the shutters of the nearest window, slipped from the balcony onto the street below, and ran.

The shrike had begun to call out her name. She could hear bootsteps racing behind her, but she knew the city better than they. She slipped into the narrowest alleys she could, leaping over carts, barrels, and anything else that stood in her way, keeping beneath what cover she could.

The only one who could keep up with her was Bannertail.

She lost them near Soursop Lane . . . But by then she could hear the roar rising from the Spell. It was not over.

She pressed a hand to the cool stucco of the tenements and rested, just long enough to catch her breath. The fox-squirrel took the opportunity to clamber up her leg and find his usual perch.

He had saved her. She knew that now. She had been frozen when he began to howl. She had not even noticed him following her through the streets until they had climbed atop the merchant's villa beside the gate, and then he had been still beside her as she had watched Pinsard cross swords with Reynard . . . Watched him fall.

Watched as Reynard had stood over Moder and drawn his sword.

"Just a bit further," she whispered to the fox-squirrel, and forced herself to keep moving.

The whole of the bay had turned to battleground. Bravos and reavers were fighting amidst the quays, and Lara was hard pressed to tell which was which. Arrows were whizzing into the crowds from the heights of the western approach. A section of the city walls had collapsed onto the wine sinks and bawdy houses of the Spice Way. Dozens upon dozens of people had already leapt into the bay. Some were swimming for safety, others clung to anything afloat. Overhead the shrikes wheeled, screaming amidst the smoke riding the westerly wind.

The *Kite* itself was under attack. A mob of all sorts had flocked about it and were trying to board. Lara thought she could pick out Arsinoe atop the deck, slashing at the men who were scaling the hull with her broad-leafed spear. The crew had kicked free the boarding ramp but the men assaulting it had snagged it with hook and rope.

But it was still afloat.

Lara had no choice but to draw as she waded into the fray. She had barely stepped onto the quays when a couple of men came at her. They weren't even the enemy. Sailors, or bravos, or back-alley thugs, they saw her and saw what most men saw when they looked at her. Either that or the price on her head.

"It's her!" one of them grunted, barreling towards her. "Get 'er!"

She slashed open his chest before he could close. Bannertail threw himself at the face of the other. The man howled as the chimera sunk its teeth into his cheek. Lara did not wait for him to recover and gave a swift kick to the groin.

Bannertail sprang from him as he fell.

She dodged about barrels and coiled rope. She put her sword through the back of a reaver who had pinned a fisherman's daughter against one of the barges tied to the quay. She climbed atop the boards of the shipwreck-cum-tavern at the heart of the Spell and, when she had come down again, was forced to find her way through the maze of alleys near Eastgate, for here the mob was so thick that she might be crushed in the press.

At last, she climbed over an iron gate blocking one of the smaller alleys and made for the *Kite*. There was no hope of muscling through the men crowding the pier, so she sheathed her sword, ran the length of one of the smaller docks, and dove straight into the waters of the bay.

The shock of the water made her gasp. Her boots felt like lead. She rowed with her arms, slower than she would have liked, but was relieved to see that Bannertail was already paddling past her, making for the anchor.

She thought she could hear someone shouting her name above the din.

The rope nearly struck her in the head as it came down. She caught hold of it and held on tight as the men on the other end began to pull.

When she was free of the water, she used what was left of her strength to climb.

"Ruiner be praised!" Arsinoe swore as she came tumbling onto the deck. "We couldn't hold them much longer!"

Lara choked on salt water as she tried to catch her breath.

"Pinsard-" Arsinoe began to say, but Lara shook her head.

Arsinoe blinked. Then she helped Lara to rise.

"Raise anchor!" Lara shouted. "Raise anchor and set sail!"

"My lady-" Hylas began to protest, gesturing towards the brigantine bottling up the bay.

"Just do it!" Lara snapped and moved towards the bow.

The crew moved as one. Skelmis began breaking out the oars. Damon, Mimon, and Lycus cut loose the last of the mooring lines as Scyron fired a few warning shots at the men on the pier. Arsinoe set Dramsind to the task of lifting the anchor, his arms extending as he took hold of its chain and yanked. Bannertail came up with it and shook himself dry on the deck.

Lysagora took the helm as Hylas gave the order to row.

The shrikes saw them first. A dozen of the smaller ones came screeching towards them across the bay.

Scyron and Daimonax took bead with their bows and loosed. The lookout had the better vantage point and managed to wing one of them. The thing tried to bank away, but it was too slow. Scyron's second shot sent it plummeting.

Good! Lara wanted to shout. *Kill every last one of those monsters!*

But the chimera had not come to fight. Merely to pick them out.

Daimonax was lining up his next shot when he suddenly crumpled against the side of the crow's nest, a red-fletched arrow lodged in his neck.

"Row!" Hylas shouted.

Antaeus fell next, the big man letting go of his oar as he clutched at the shaft in his breast. When Scyron bent to see to the man, a third arrow struck the foremast behind him.

The crew did not need to be told to pick up the pace.

Lara could not see the archer, but she knew which direction he was firing from. She moved to Starboard and did her best to weave amongst the rowers, doubling back more than once to keep her pace unpredictable.

Mimon took an arrow to his upper arm. Another buried itself in the gunwale beside Lycus. Then the barrage ceased. Mimon even chuckled at the wound, claiming he had hardly felt it. Arsinoe took his place at the oars and put her back into it.

The wind was just beginning to catch their sails when the brigantine opened fire.

Perhaps they had not seen the shrikes circling above the ship. Perhaps they thought to sink her in the shallows. Perhaps it was intended as a warning shot, and their marksmen had a poor judge of distance.

Whatever the case, the shot struck them straight across the bow.

Lara flung herself to the deck as wood shattered about her. Something seemed to catch hold of her jack and she felt herself being flung backwards.

There was a *clang*. Then she hit the deck, harder this time. Stars danced behind her eyes.

When her head had cleared, she could see that Dramsind was standing over her. When he turned about, she could see the massive dent in his left breast. And the iron ball lodged in the deck beneath his feet.

"Thank you," Lara said, shakily. "Old friend."

"Bama jifi jalawe," the giant said, his fingers groping as they found purchase about the ball. He lifted it easily, wound back his arm, and then sent the missile sailing back towards the brigantine.

It sailed over their bow, but the cannons on the reaver vessel did not fire on them again. Their own lookouts had no doubt spied the metal giant and knew who they might kill with an errant shot.

Instead, the men aboard the brigantine made to come about, the ship's yellowed sails unfurling as they climbed into the shrouds.

"Hard to port!" Hylas sang out. "We'll outrun her, lads!"

The *Kite's* own sails were blossoming in the wind, the crew trading oars for rope as the ship began to turn.

"Volk," Arsinoe swore, grabbing hold of the gunwale as she began to retch. "Not already!"

The brigantine was still raising its sails as the *Kite* glid past its stern. Some of the reavers raced for their aftcastle and sent a round of bolts whistling into their hull. Scyron managed to pick one of them off with his bow, and then they were flying across the bay, the bright water deepening as they cut towards the straights.

"Starboard!" Skelmis called out from one of the tops. "Two more, coming on us fast!"

Lara could not see them at first, there was so much smoke on the far side of the bay. Then a pair of black ships issued from the haze, their courses set to intercept. They were narrower than the brigantine, with three masts apiece. Built for speed.

So, however, was the *Kite*. It had been a smugglers ship for many a year. It still was, really. Only she was the cargo now.

"Stand by to set stun'sl!" Hylas roared.

Lycus and Damon climbed, spider-like, across the rigging and then to the yards.

"Haul taut!" Hylas cried as the studding sails were cast loose. "Rig out! Hoist away!"

The *Kite* caught the wind, and now she truly seemed to fly. The reaver ships were forced to jib into the wind as they made for the straights themselves.

"They'll never catch us now!" Lara exclaimed, leaning off starboard to catch a glimpse of the reavers' prows.

"Don't be so certain," Arsinoe groaned, catching hold of Lara's arm, and wresting her about.

Lara saw it then: The chain.

Reynard's troops had either taken the western watchtower, or the prince's men had seen the signal from the east tower and set the mules to work without thinking, for the western end of the chain was already hanging clear of the waters of the straight, a good part of it as taut as a clothesline aside the escarpment.

And it was still moving.

The length dangling from the eastern watch had risen too, though it was impossible to tell how high it was beneath the waves.

"We could sail under it!" Lara said, racing to the helm. "Between the cliffs and-"

"No!" Hylas said, grown decisive at last. "Masts will catch for certain!"

"Course, Captain?" Lysagora grunted, her callused hands gripping the wheel as she squinted at the rising chain.

Hylas gestured towards the center of the straight. "Steady on!"

"And pray," Lara added.

All eyes were on the chain now, the shrikes and reavers behind them forgotten. It continued to rise, length after length slipping from the waters of the straight as the unseen wheels above them continued to turn. Lara made her way to the bow, and could *see* it, like the tail of some great sea serpent rising from the depths.

"Steady!" Hylas shouted as the bow shot straight towards the chain. "Steady on!"

Lara wrapped her arm around one of the lines.

They struck the chain.

The *Kite* lurched. Lara could hear the metal rasping against the hull, and for a horrible moment the ship threatened to broach. Rope, metal, and men slid across the deck as the booms swung free. The men in the rigging cried out, wood splintered as something heavy gave to the pressure, and then, miraculously, they righted.

The force of the ship evening its keel nearly threw Lara off her feet, but she clung to the rope until her palms were raw.

The crew began to cheer. Behind them the reavers had given up the chase. The chain was too high for them to follow.

They were away.

* * * * * *

They did not stop until the sun had set, dropping anchor as far from shore as they were able. Even then they lit no lamps above deck, for fear of ships patrolling the coast. If the usurper chanced to gaze upon them from within the depths of his magic mirror, he would see nothing but The Watcher playing fitfully against the sea.

And so, it was under starlight that they saw to Daimonax and Antaeus. Both men were stripped bare, scrubbed, and then laid within an aged cask. To both honor and preserve them, the captain had each cask filled with rum, from which each crewman took a sip.

"My eyes as sharp," Lycus said, drinking from the lookout's cask.

"My arms as strong," Skelmis grunted, giving Antaeus' shoulder a soft pat as he drank.

Scyron blamed himself for the big man's death. "I stood too close to him," he said. "The shaft was meant for me."

"No," Hylas demurred. "For they say the Sure-Shot does not miss."

And yet Lara wondered. She did not know the number of Tiecelin's summers, but he had fought in far older wars. Perhaps his aim, or his eyes, were suffering. It was not the sort of suffering she wished on him, but she thanked The Watcher for it all the same.

When they were done, both casks were lowered into the hold, and set aside for landfall, when they could be properly burned.

Makelo saw to Mimon's arm. She had a smattering of herb-lore and could mend a broken limb well enough before the *Kite* had taken aboard the Queen of Arcasia, but Hirsent had taught her a fair bit of Northern wisdom over the years, so it was a simple matter for her to clean and dress the wound. And, like some others of the crew, Mimon was from Tyris. He was not of as pure Telchine stock as Arsinoe perhaps, but Lara had no doubt that he would have nothing but a verdigris scar to remind him of the wound come a month or two.

As Makelo worked on Mimon, the others saw to the ship. The damage to the deck was ugly, but superficial. What worried them was what the chain had done to the hull.

They put Damon on a scaffold, no more than a plank really, and lowered him from the aft. When he came back up, his face was grim.

"As we feared," he said. "Rudder's snapped, Captain."

Hylas took a deep breath. "How bad?"

"She can still come about," Damon said as the men helped him clamber back on deck. "But I wouldn't brave the gulf."

"Will she hold 'til Lenape?"

"Has to," Damon said.

"We're not going to Lenape," Lara said.

She had been quiet since they had escaped. During the day she had busied herself with knots and lines. She had taken no food when offered, and at the funeral she had said some few words before falling into silence. The crew had asked no questions and Arsinoe had kept her distance, fussing instead over the dent in Dramsind's breast before seeing to Maiden in the hold below. Only Bannertail would not let her be, until she picked him up and let him rest upon her shoulder.

"My lady?" Hylas blinked at her. "Deira is many leagues further, and we would be fighting the wind-"

"I am not going to Deira either," Lara said.

"Then," Hylas stammered, "Where, my lady?"

"Make for the coast of Poictesme," Lara said. "And there we shall go our separate ways."

Hylas' eyes widened. The crew began to murmur.

"Poictesme?" Hylas managed. "Surely, you do not mean-"

"I would take the White River to Carduel, Master Hylas," Lara said. "But I doubt we'd make it past the sea gates of Nemea. And so I must make land as close as I am able."

The crew was speechless, and so Scyron spoke for them.

"Carduel?" the old man balked. "Your Highness, have you taken leave of your senses?"

"Not at all," Lara said. "Now, do as I command, Master Hylas. A ship can still sail with a broken rudder. Can it not?"

"It can, my lady," Hylas began to protest. "But-"

"Then plot your course," she said.

She could feel their eyes on her as she went below. She could hear them whispering as she found her way to her cabin. She could still hear them as she bolted shut the door behind her.

She lifted Bannertail from her shoulder and laid him down on the end of her berth. He was so sound asleep that he did not even stir.

She lay down beside him and pulled her blanket close to her chest.

Then, finally, she wept.

* * * * * *

Knocking woke her. She did not remember falling asleep, nor could she tell the hour. Her whole body ached, especially her calves. For a moment she thought it was Pinsard come to wake her.

Then she remembered.

She sat up.

"What do you want?" she asked.

"Open the door," Arsinoe said, simply.

"Why?" Lara said.

"They need to see you," Arsinoe said. "The crew."

"I need time," Lara said, kneading a fist into the small of her back.

"You are a Queen," Arsinoe said. "You do not have time."

"I am not a Queen," Lara grumbled.

"You give orders like one," Arsinoe said, and tried the door handle again. "Now open the door. They're worried."

"I don't care," Lara said.

"*I'm* worried," Arsinoe said.

Lara got to her feet, undid the bolt, and cracked open the door.

Arsinoe did not need to say anything. The look on her face was enough. Then she pushed into the cabin and was holding her. Her hair smelled of fresh cut garlic.

Bannertail slipped between their legs, his tail twitching.

Eventually, Arsinoe closed the door and they sat atop her berth. The fox-squirrel hopped onto Lara's lap. She scratched him behind the ears until he settled.

"Was it hard for you?" Lara asked, when she could form the words.

"What?" Arsinoe said.

"Losing your family," Lara said.

"They lost me." She said, tapping at the beetle on her cheek. "It's different."

"It," Lara said. "I saw it. I saw him do it. But it doesn't feel real."

"It will."

They were silent for a time. The timbers of the *Kite* creaked.

"Pinsard tried to stop him," Lara said.

"Is he alive?" Arsinoe said.

Lara nodded.

"Is that why?" Arsinoe said. "Because you think he will take him there? To Carduel?"

"I know he will," Lara said. "And he knows that I know."

"Then he'll be expecting us."

"He'll be expecting *me*," Lara said.

"I won't abandon Pinsard, Lara," Arsinoe said. "But walking right up to his doorstep? There must be a better way."

"I wish there was," Lara said. "But it's the only way. The only way to end it."

"You think you can kill him?"

"I can try," Lara said.

"Like Pinsard?" Arsinoe asked.

"I am not Pinsard," Lara said.

Or Moder.

Lara gave Bannertail's head another scratch.

"You're right, though," Lara said.

"About what?"

"The crew," Lara said. "They need to hear my plan."

"So," Arsinoe said. "You do have a plan?"

"I do," Lara said.

She scooted Bannertail from her lap and stood. There was still some freshwater in her basin. She washed the tears from her cheeks.

"It's funny," Lara said. "I can almost hear her."

"Yes?"

"There is being no time for tears, *dohtor*," Lara said, deepening her voice. "Now is time to be strong."

"Heh," Arsinoe chuckled. "That's not bad."

Lara wiped at her eyes.

"She was a great warrior, you know," Arsinoe said. "Better than many I've known, truly. The bastard *must* have fought dirty."

Lara merely nodded. She could not bring herself to speak of the arrows she had seen.

"Do you think she was sick?" Arsinoe said then.

"Sick?"

"When one of my people grew beyond their years," Arsinoe said, "When they could no longer fight, they would go 'hunting.' Seeking the Maiden, we called it."

"No," Lara said. "I don't think so."

"Maybe she was just tired of Frisia," Arsinoe said.

"Tired of running at least," Lara said. "That I can understand."

* * * * * *

The Firebird had not fully risen, but the sky was already pink as a peach. Vireo was little more than a hazy shadow along the western horizon. They were in the gulf of Lorn now, with little but the waves for company.

Lara was relieved. They had followed her orders.

She was not normally one to make speeches, but she knew that something must be said. Anything to lend the crew some heart. And so, she moved slowly as she crossed from the hold to the foot of the helm, making certain that she had caught the eyes of every man and woman working the sails before bowing her head neatly to Hylas.

"Captain," she said. "My apologies for my shortness last night. I was not myself."

"My lady," Hylas said. "It is not for you to apologize. When you returned without the Lady Hirsent-"

"She is dead," Lara said, swallowing. "Slain by the usurper."

"The She-Wolf?" The words slipped from Lysagora's lips before she could stop them. "Dead?"

"Yes," Lara said. "And my brother taken."

The crew were silent at that, and hard faced. The Northerners had frightened them over the years to be certain, Vanir and Calvarians were the terror of the seas, but they had frightened their enemies more.

"And yet we sail for Poictesme?" Lysagora again. "With the usurper's ships snapping at our tail?"

"We do," Lara said. "And we must pray that they follow us straight across the gulf."

"Pray he doesn't catch us, rather."

"That too," Lara said. "But the longer he hunts for us, the longer he chases *me*, the more time we buy for Roland."

"Roland?" This was Arsinoe. She was leaning against the mizzen, her arms crossed. "That beardless boy?"

"That *boy* has an army of his own," Lara said. "And his own ships, ready to sail. What do you think will happen when word of Pikria reaches Belnor? Will the princes sit quietly, and wait for the usurper to pick them off one by one?"

The crew shot glances at each other.

"No!" one of the men, Lycus maybe, called down from the rigging.

"No!" Lara repeated, louder. "They will retaliate for certain, and there's not a fleet in the world that can stand before the might of Frisia. Not the Glyconese, not the Calvarians, and not the usurper. He will quit Pikria and race back to the mainland as fast as his ships can carry him. And when he does, mark my words, Roland *will* land."

"Then you mean to join him?" Scyron said, hopefully. The old man had climbed down from the crow's nest, his eyes bleary from keeping watch.

"No," she said. "We sail to Poictesme. And from there I will make my way to Carduel."

"But *why*?" Arsinoe prompted.

"Were I the heir to Lorn," Lara said. "I would first free Kerys and Cadwallon from the usurper's yoke. Then I would march down the coast with the aid of the Frisian fleet and take Nemea. From there one might strike at Listenese, Dandilin, even Carduel itself."

"If they are not destroyed," Scyron said.

"They will be for certain," Lara said. "If the usurper leads the army. But if he were *distracted* . . . If he were to sit in Carduel while other men fight his battles-"

Scyron's eyes widened. "You would use yourself as bait?"

"Bait he will not be able to resist," Lara went on. "I am all that he wants now. I am all he has ever wanted. The rest is just a game to him, a play to prove how clever he is."

"And you think you are cleverer?" Arsinoe asked.

"No," Lara admitted. "But I must do what I can."

The crew was silent. The wind whipped against the sails.

"I will go with you," Lysagora said, ignoring the look Hylas shot her. "You may need an extra blade."

"And I," Damon said, slipping from one of the spars. "Lycus and I both will go."

Lycus nodded, smiling.

"No," Lara said, before anyone else could speak. "No, I thank you, all, truly, but the way I must take will not- *cannot*- be won by force of arms. The fewer of us the better."

She clapped a hand to Damon's shoulder.

"Besides," she said. "You have done more for me these past three years than I could ever have hoped to expect. You have all been loyal friends, and true."

"And well paid," Damon said.

The crew laughed.

"Perhaps," Lara said. "But still true."

Damon's smile faded, but he nodded his head.

"Take me at least, Your Highness," Scyron said then, taking to his knee. "I may be an old man, but my aim is still keen as ever."

"It is not your aim that concerns me," Lara said. "Rather, I would not have you risk yourself merely to satisfy your honor."

"My honor?" Scyron laughed. "Highness, I was sworn by Prince Mydas to protect you. And were he to so order it, I *would* leave your side . . . Alas, I fear my prince is dead. Perhaps one of his sons lives, perhaps not. Until then I am like a man cast from a ship into the waves. Will you not take my hand so as to pull me out?"

Lara smiled at that and offered him her hand. He took it and pressed his lips to her palm and let her help him rise.

Then she turned to address Hylas.

"Once I am away," she said. "Sail to Therimere. Use my coin to repair your ship. Then, if you and the crew so choose, make for Lenape with my blessings. I am certain you will have a place of honor amongst the fleet. If not, well, I hear there are fortunes to made in the Argyrian Isles."

Hylas nodded at that; a touch shamed but relieved.

"Now get me to Poictesme," Lara said. "And let me worry about the rest."

The crew moved with a purpose. They kissed their fingers and pressed them to their brows as she passed. There was fresh admiration in their eyes.

"How was I?" Lara asked when they were out of earshot.

"Queenly," Arsinoe answered, and popped a sugar cube into her mouth.

* * * * * *

Even without the threat of the usurper's ships behind them, the passage across the Gulf would not be easy. The damaged rudder forced the crew of the *Kite* to repeatedly luff and trim and flatten both jib and sail. It was exhausting work, even in the lightest breeze, and more dangerous by night, for Hylas would have no lamps lit once the sun had set.

On their second night out, Nicon nearly fell from the foremast when one of the stays suddenly caught the wind and sent a line whistling into his back. He held firm in spite of the pain until Skelmis helped to free him, but from that point on it was deemed too risky to chance sailing after dark. As the waters of the gulf were too deep to drop anchor, every dusk the captain would order the sails struck and let the current carry them towards the coast.

Lara trusted the man, he knew his charts, but it was still a frightening prospect to drift on the open sea. She had no love for The Destroyer, but as it was in her coils that they now placed themselves, she whispered what few prayers to her she knew.

The crew kept her in their own way, though calling her the 'Sea-Bitch' hardly seemed a term of respect. More often than not they drank and gambled, and shed a drop of blood or two for The Watcher's delight, for had he not wooed her long ago, so that even now she rose and fell at his pleasure?

The Firebird's stars might guide them, but it was hard to ignore the skull-moon's grin.

Every night, Scyron would tell tales to the crew. He had been a sailor long before Hylas had set foot upon a thwart and had been as far east as Leng if his stories were to be believed. When the sea was choppy, he would liken it to the night he had seen the Vanir driven from Sakartvelo. When it was calm, he would tell them of the stillness of the water gardens of Metnal, where the fourteen Hivan youths marked for sacrifice spent their last night before going to the Dreamer.

One evening, when there was hardly any wind and they had struck sails long before sunset, the crew gathered about to hear what he would have to say. Mimon even gave up his rum to help loosen the man's tongue.

"It was like this on the *Asteria*. We were becalmed for a fortnight off the eastern coast of Tyris. No winds, no land. Just a hundred of us, too proud to say we were frightened. Heh."

He stared into his rum.

"You do queer things when you're frightened," he went on. "Some as thought we were too close to Domdaniel. Others swore they saw dragons circling in the clouds. We had a priest of sorts aboard, Askander I think his name was . . . By the tenth day he had turned half-Glyconese, thought the world had come to an end and there were no lands left to sail to. I remember him shouting at us from one of the spars. Gods know how he got up there, man was afraid of heights."

He shook his head and drank.

"Anyway, Captain had to gag him before throwing him into the bilge. Me, I just kept my nose to my work, and thanked the gods for rum."

The crew murmured at that and took a sip from their own cups.

"How did it end?" Lara asked.

"Wind picked up," Scyron said, scratching at his nose.

"What were you doing there?" Skelmis asked. "Off the coast?"

"Never you mind," Scyron said, and drained his cup.

Brevity and reticence did not satisfy the crew. And so, to pass the hour, Lara told them instead of Prince Rience, who so resembled his bootblack that the two traded places from time to time, with none but his mother the wiser. She told them how it was that having switched places, Rience came to know his people firsthand, whilst his double delighted the court with his common sense. And how, long after he had been crowned King, men still called him The Bootblack, and whispered that it was in fact the servant who wore the crown and that the prince had given up his duties to live a quiet life in the country.

She omitted the darker parts of the tale. That Rience had grown to be the worst sort of tyrant, more terrible even than Queen Grisana, having been cut down by his own chevalier and whose outrages could only have been committed by a man of low birth (or so the nobles claimed) was hardly a tidy end to the tale. The bootblack who became a prince was good enough for a lonely night, alone on the sea.

As for Arsinoe, be it working the sails or drinking on deck of a night, she would have none of it. She spent as much time below as she could take, lurking with Dramsind in the deepest part of the hold. The crew would not bother either of them, for there the hollow-man's lead-lined box was stowed. Even Lara did not like to be near the thing, though Arsinoe reassured her that it was perfectly safe.

Provided you were not around when it was opened.

Maiden was as restless as her rider was miserable. The horse wanted exercise, but there was not the room to do much more than walk her about the upper hold, and even that was difficult. Lara did her best, but more often than not the mare's ears were pinned when she greeted her, and she would nip at her fingers.

Arsinoe was almost as prickly.

"Water you can't drink," she complained. "Food you can't keep down."

"Should I stop bringing you the fish I've caught then?" Lara asked.

"No," Arsinoe said.

Lara laughed but could not help but pity her. She retched in the morning and moaned through the afternoons. She had found a root on the Tor that had helped to settle her stomach for a time, but she had chewed it up so quickly that she always had to go without.

Some years back, Antaeus had joked that she had a baby in her belly, but the big man had quieted when Arsinoe threatened to break his nose before having Dramsind throw him overboard. Lara missed the man. He had a laugh as broad as his chest.

Daimonax too. He knew all the sea birds by name and had taught her knots.

And Moder. She missed her very much.

* * * * * *

They were five days out from Vireo and still fighting the wind when Scyron rang the general alarm.

"Wings off our stern!" he sang out, pointing.

Lara was helping Mimon to tack one of the jibs, but only needed to turn to see the dark shapes gliding against the horizon. There were three of them, and they were far larger than any gull.

Makelo was good enough to take her place on the lines. She shimmied down one of the shrouds and made her way to the aftcastle, where Hylas stood with his spyglass.

"Shrikes, my lady," Hylas said.

"I see them," she said. "And they us, no doubt."

He nodded and put away his glass.

"How far behind us are they?" she asked. "The enemy, I mean."

"I do not know how long a shrike can stay aloft," he said. "A day perhaps?"

"And how long before we reach the coast?"

"We could make land by sundown," Hylas replied. "But I doubt it. We have drifted south with the tide."

"Tomorrow then?" she asked.

Hylas considered the matter, then nodded.

Lara watched the shrikes, until one of them veered from the others and turned back into the wind.

Then she went back to the lines.

That night Scyron told no tales, but kept watch up in the nest. The crew slept in shifts as well and kept their blades close by their berths. Arsinoe roused herself and Dramsind from the hold, stretched her muscles, and kept Lara company.

Neither of them could sleep.

"You think it's *him*?" Arsinoe asked, pacing.

"No," Lara said. "Probably his shrike-tamer."

"The Sure-Shot," Damon growled beneath his breath.

"Maybe they were wild," Lycus said hopefully. "The shrikes."

"Maybe they were 'Dancer," Arsinoe snipped, "Turned to a flock to keep us company on the way to Domdaniel."

The next morning the sky was red.

"Storm," Lara said, rubbing at the white scar across her wrist.

"Lovely," Arsinoe said. "I don't suppose we'll land before it hits?"

Lara searched the horizon. She could not see the coast.

She shook her head: *No.*

"Volk," Arsinoe swore. "I miss the wastes."

There could no longer be any doubt that they were pursued. The three shrikes they had seen the day before had become a dozen, their wings spread wide as they soared just out of bowshot.

"Ignore them!" Hylas shouted. "And mind the sails!"

The crew redoubled their efforts and for a while they made good headway. Skelmis sang a Glyconese field call as they worked, and some of the men laughed as the shrikes seemed to abandon the chase, peeling from the flock one by one until there were only two of them left. Even Arsinoe helped with the lines, taking a long bolt of rum before mounting one of the spars 'to help settle her stomach.'

Then the wind changed. The waves turned to chop as dark, towering clouds loomed up from the west. The sails were rippling wildly even when trim.

"At least *they're* giving up!" Damon called out as he and Lara traded places atop one of the spars. "Don't blame 'em either!"

Lara looked. The last of the shrikes were quitting the pursuit, their wings beating desperately against the wind.

Then she saw the sails on the horizon.

"They're not giving up," she said, and raised her voice so that all could hear: "Ship off our stern!"

"Three ships!" Scyron corrected from the nest above her. "Riding the wind!"

"We've still a league on 'em," Hylas shouted, unshouldering his sea cloak to take one of the lines himself. "Keep on trim! Lysagora, you have the wheel!"

"Aye, Captain!" Lysagora answered.

The *Kite* was fast, and the crew worked as though The Watcher himself were chasing them, but the usurper's ships were whole. And so, they gained on them as the sky turned dark and rain began to lash the deck. Lara worked until her arms ached but whenever she turned about, she could see them: *Five* ships now, not three.

She could see the monstrous eel amongst their colors, but the closest had a chimera emblazoned on its mainsail: A wolf (or was it a fox?) with the hindquarters of a fish. With each fresh billow it seemed to paw at the air, eager.

She blinked as the clouds overhead flashed. The rain began to fall in sheets, and then a peal of thunder rolled over the gulf.

Lazy girl who shirks her chores, Lara hummed to herself as she helped Damon luff, *when thunder roars, run indoors . . .*

"Rocks!" Scyron roared then. "Rocks off our port!"

Then the sky lit up and she could see them, a broken line of massive stones like jagged teeth jutting from the waves.

Hylas shouted something, but his words were lost to her in the thunder. Then the line began to slip from her palms as the ship veered to Starboard. She redoubled her grip, wincing from the burn, and held firm.

"Hydra's bloody Teeth!" Damon shouted. "We must've drifted south!"

"That's the coast?" Lara shouted back.

"Beyond the rocks!" Damon answered as he struggled to keep the sail trim. "Yes!"

"Take my line!" Lara shouted down to Nicon, who scurried up to take her place on the spar.

She made for the mizzen, where Hylas, Makelo, and Skelmis were fighting their own battle against the wind. As she did, Bannertail came bolting out of the hold and clung to the dubious safety of her left leg.

"Captain!" she cried out, ignoring the fox-squirrel's claws digging into her calf. "How close can you get to these rocks?!"

"Close?!" he shouted back. "One chance wave and they'll break us to splinters!"

"That's what I want them to think!"

When she told him what she intended, Hylas stared at her, blinking against the rain.

Then he laughed.

"Skelmis!" he bellowed, "Take Nicon and Critias and get the skiff unlashed! When you're done-"

Lightning lanced overhead. The thunderclap that followed shook the bones in Lara's chest. Bannertail abandoned her leg and took shelter atop her shoulder.

"Anything we can spare!" Hylas continued. "Make it jetsam! Go!"

The Telchine sailor did not question but moved. Lara followed, her hands shaking as they cut loose the lines holding the skiff. By the time they were done, Hylas had taken the helm.

"Below," Skelmis grunted when the last line was cut.

He did not wait but made for the forward hatch. The skiff rocked in its cradle as the ship let the wind catch her sails.

Lara followed, catching a glimpse of Lysagora as she leapt onto the lines. Then she was in the hold. The lanterns were swaying with the waves. Maiden was tossing her head in her stall, whinnying as the ship continued to lurch.

"The ramps," Skelmis said, pointing to the seasoned timber. "Critias, with me!"

Nicon helped Lara fasten ramps to the hatch as the two men disappeared into the lower hold. Bannertail found a perch atop one of the hammocks and stared, his tail quivering.

Skelmis and Critias were rolling the first of the empty casks up from below when Arsinoe came storming down the aft hatch. She was soaked from head to toe.

"What in the name of all the demons are we doing?!" she demanded.

"Abandoning ship!" Lara answered.

"Ah, Volk," she swore. "I'll get Dramsind!"

Arsinoe was moving towards the entrance to the lower hold when Maiden gave the door of her stall a kick strong enough to send its latch clanging against the berth. Freed, she bolted loose, throwing Nicon aside as she mounted the ramp and erupted out of the hold.

Lara raced after her, the rain slapping against her face as she cried out for the horse to stop.

It was too late. With a single leap Maiden soared over the gunwale and plummeted into the sea.

Poor girl, she thought, and then she saw how close they were to one of the rocks. The tide had them, and for a horrible moment they lurched towards its mossy crops, so close that Lara could make out the cracks running through the stones.

Then the *Kite* shot forward, the hull scraping against something beneath the waves. There was an awful crack when what was left of the rudder gave perhaps, or was it one of the spars breaking as the wind sent the booms swinging from starboard to port?

"Man overboard!" Lara could hear someone shouting, but it was the sight behind them that kept her arrested. The reaver ship with the chimera on its mast was braving the rocks as well, emboldened perhaps by their success. Lara could see the dark figures hanging from its own shrouds, and the panic in their eyes as a wave struck them clear across the bow.

The force of it drove them straight into the rock, the ship buckling as its port side split wide open. She could hear the men aboard screaming as the tide carried them away from the hazard, only to slam them into it again. This time the ship came apart, its stern spilling men into the sea as it rolled into the rush. The chimera on its mast crumpled as the waves rushed up to meet it.

A hand caught her by the arm. It was Scyron.

"Highness!" he shouted. "The shore!"

She could see it too. The waves were breaking against its shoals, and as the lightning played overhead she could see hills rising beyond. They seemed to tilt as the ship was tossed on the waves.

"I need my pack!" she shouted and ran back into the hold, but Arsinoe met her halfway up the ramp, her pack already in her grip. She shoved it into Lara's chest, along with her sword belt.

The pack squirmed under Lara's grip as Bannertail tried to squeeze from its flaps.

"Thank you-"

"Later!" Arsinoe snapped, caught the spear Skelmis tossed up to her, and then pushed her way onto the deck. Dramsind came lumbering after her, dragging the lead chest behind him. He was cradling one of the spare spars under his free arm, as easily as one might a bedroll.

"Prepare to come about!" Hylas shouted from the helm. Lara could see the crew moving from line to line, but then she was helping Scyron to roll one of the casks brought up from the hold towards port.

The ship lurched again, timbers straining. Lightning lit up the sky, and Lara thought she could hear shrikes screaming in the wind.

"Now!" Hylas shouted. "Now! Run, curse you, and go over!"

They threw what they could over the gunwales as the ship began to turn against the wind. Empty casks, bits of lumber, frayed coils of rope, it all went into the sea. Dramsind let loose the spar into the main, and then leapt in after it, the chest held close to his dented breast. Then Skelmis helped guide the freed skiff over as well. Lara suspected they would have thrown loose the figurehead if it were not so firmly attached to the prow.

The waves were carrying flotsam and jetsam both towards the shore. The skiff smashed against one of the rockier shoals before the waves took it.

"Volk!" Arsinoe swore and leapt in herself.

Lara spared one look at the rocks behind them, but she could see no other ships willing to brave the passage.

"Highness!" Scyron urged.

Lara turned back to the shore. She could just make out the shape of Arsinoe's head being carried above a swell, but she was already growing distant. The *Kite* had already caught the wind.

She mounted the gunwale, held her breath, and leapt.

VI

There was wreckage on the beach. Broken casks, ropes, and shredded sails, half-buried by the tide.

And bodies.

Tiecelin strode past them. Most were the crew of the *Seal*. His men were laying them out on the sand in neat rows, face-up.

Three were not like the rest.

One had been mauled by the rocks. His face was a shredded mess, but his skin had the sheen of Tyris.

The other two were pale and bloodless. Naked, their flesh had puckered.

"I shot these men," Tiecelin said, noting the wounds at neck and breast.

"And this one?" his lieutenant asked gesturing to the ruin of the man's face.

"A casualty," Tiecelin said.

"Perhaps the rest washed further ashore," his lieutenant offered. "Tides might have carried them."

Tiecelin shook his head. The wreckage stretched across the beach was too sparse.

"They escaped," he said.

His lieutenant straightened.

"Shall we pursue, my lord?"

Tiecelin held up a palm, *no.*

The man held his tongue.

He tilted his head to the skies above them. His children were there, circling. He watched them, their forms dark against the clouds.

Then one of them stooped to meet him.

His lieutenant stood away as she landed atop the broken hull of the *Seal.*

"Yes?" Tiecelin prompted.

Griffe could not speak. Her father had been Voleur, one of Rossignol's brood. Her mother had been wild. But she understood commands. And her eyes were better than any of his flock. Amber they were, and her pupils black as jet.

She tilted her head southwards, then caught his eyes in hers.

He nodded, and she took flight.

"My horse," Tiecelin said.

His horse was brought.

Griffe made a lazy circle overhead, then turned south.

He followed.

He rode for the better part of a league. He saw no prints in the sand.

The tide took them.

They reached a place where a river met the sea. It was not wide, nor very deep, hardly more than a stream that cut through a stretch of salt marsh.

Griffe flew inland and then lit on a tree far upriver.

He skirted the marsh. When he lost sight of her beneath the trees, she would cry out to him. Her cries were long and lonely.

He whistled back to let her know he was close.

He found her atop a dead elm. She quieted at the sight of him and turned her gaze to the ground near the reeds.

He dismounted and made his way across the forest floor.

The soil here was sandy. Ferns and moss struggled for purchase amongst the marsh grasses.

He stopped at the foot of the tree.

Tracks. Not very fresh.

He crouched.

They were deep.

The ground had been soft.

Dew clung to the blades of grass that lay within them.

They walked by night.

Tiecelin pressed his boot into the soil and compared its shape to the others.

Small. A girl's foot.

Beside them an animal had walked. Something clawed, like a weasel.

Her chimera.

"Good girl," he said, nodding to Griffe.

Her head bobbed back and forth. Then she flew towards a clearing beside the riverbank.

He followed.

Other boot prints joined the first.

One had a quick stride. The other, a wider stance and a rolling gait. *The Telchine. And one of the sailors.*

The prints were mixed. They had stopped to argue their course, perhaps.

Then they had taken it.

He examined the shadows of the trees.

North by northeast, he decided.

"Fetch the others," he said to Griffe.

She took the air with a savage cry.

Slowly, he began to follow their trail.

Then he stopped.

No sign of the giant.

He crouched again and traced his finger about one of the deeper prints.

He frowned.

Hooves.

They had a horse.

* * * * * *

"Gods be good," Arsinoe said as she slipped from Maiden's back. "But this girl has more lives than a cat."

"More than her previous owner at least," Lara sniffed, slumping beneath one of the larger trees. Bannertail scooted up its trunk and found a roost of his own.

"How did she know it was safe to jump?" Arsinoe mused as the horse nosed through the ferns.

"Been in a wreck before, I'll warrant," Scyron said, finding his own seat atop a fallen log. "Shame we don't have more like 'er."

Lara nodded. The sight of Maiden cantering up the beach had her thinking that she had drowned or been smashed against the rocks . . . But she reasoned that if she had been dragged down to Domdaniel then there would not be sand in her mouth, or the Firebird beating down on her.

She had kept a grip on her pack at least. Arsinoe was less fortunate. All she had managed to save besides the clothes on her back was her spear. Scyron still had his bow, but no quiver.

Dramsind still had the box.

They might have found some provisions in the wreckage on the beach, but there was no time to scavenge, not out in the open.

"Couldn't we have just died?" Arsinoe had said, squeezing the sea from her locks as they had made their way down the beach.

Lara had mollified her with a strip of salt-pork, but she knew it wouldn't last.

They had followed the river up to its source, a shallow spring framed by moss covered rocks. Lara had feared coming upon a town as they had pushed upriver, but this was lonely country it seemed. Once they had cleared the marsh there had been nothing but leagues of dense, dark woods. It was not on any of the maps she had seen, but its boughs were thick enough to give them cover.

And that was enough for now.

Dramsind had kept to the river, dragging the chest behind him. He did not need to breathe, and if he feared rust, he did not show it. For a long time Lara could not make him out amongst the reeds, but as the river narrowed his head emerged from the rush.

She wondered what the fish made of him.

Now he stood in the midst of the spring, statue-like, his burden a darker shape amidst the rocks.

"We have to leave the box," Lara said.

Arsinoe's mouth curled into a frown, but she nodded.

"No time to bury it," Lara added.

"Dramsind," Arsinoe said. *"Jasupa lujusi."*

Dramsind released the chest. It did not have far to sink.

"How do you say-" Lara began, but Arsinoe waved for silence.

"Dramsind," she said. *"Josipi lujusi."*

"Wopa," The giant said, wading towards the nearest bank, palms and fingers flattening until they resembled shovels.

"Bopup Mipesi," Arsinoe amended.

"Wopa," Dramsind's voice crackled, his digits separating.

He almost sounded disappointed.

Then he took hold of one of the stones that littered the banks, yanked it loose, and laid it atop the box. He repeated the process, until Arsinoe's prize lay buried beneath stones too large for men to move unaided.

"*Babulu,*" Arsinoe said, and Dramsind went still. His head swiveled until he seemed to find a spot to his liking, and then he too laid to rest amidst the grass.

"Does *this* remind you of anything, old man?" Arsinoe shot at Scyron.

"As it so happens," Scyron answered, "I knew a Lornishman once, name of Allardyce, served on a whaler-"

"Nevermind," Arsinoe said, her beetle twitching. "What if they find it, Lara?"

Lara shrugged. "Getting it out from under those stones will slow them down at least."

"Do you know what river this is, at least?" Arsinoe asked.

"It's not the Roigne," Scyron said. "I can tell you that much."

"I'm not asking-"

"Let's catch a bit of rest," Lara said. "And, if at all possible, try not to bicker."

"And after that?" Arsinoe asked.

"We keep going," Lara said. "Until then, please, rest. And let me worry about what really matters."

"Food," Arsinoe grumbled.

"And a warm pair of socks," Scyron added.

* * * * * *

They broke camp long before daybreak. It was difficult to rest, knowing that the usurper's best tracker was somewhere behind them. Lara had no illusions about him being fooled by the jetsam on the beach, or by the way they had taken.

Tybalt had managed to track them through Vulp Vora with the aid of shrikes. She doubted the shrike-tamer would prove less able.

Lara had packed enough cured meat and tack to feed herself for a fortnight. Split three ways, and rationed, it might last them as long as it took the demons to conquer the world entire. Which is to say: Seven days.

Of water, they had as much as they could carry in their skins. Arsinoe knew many a desert trick for catching water from the air and plant dew, but such things took time and time they did not have. They took advantage of every rainfall to slake their thirst, and let Maiden drink from what streams they crossed, but they kept moving.

The forest grew tamer the further they went. The brush had been cleared and many of the smaller trees had been coppiced. Scyron cut a few shoots free so as to fashion crude arrows, though he lacked the fletching to finish the job. Then, on the third morning since the storm, they came to a place where a wide swath of the woods had been felled. For firewood perhaps or ship's timbers, for the trees here were very tall.

"There must be a town nearby," Lara said, staring at the range of peaks far beyond the woods. "Are those the Taunenfels, do you think?"

"I don't know, Highness," Scyron said. "Could be."

Lara decided that they were, which would mean that they had drifted east as they had traveled.

"North," she said, retreating to the cover of the trees. "Carduel is north."

"Lara!" Arsinoe hissed, pointing across the clearing.

There was a shape atop one of the taller trees.

Lara held her breath as the thing sidled across the branch it had perched upon, wishing for a bow. Then it spread its wings and flew.

"An eagle," Scyron breathed. "Only an eagle."

"You're certain?" Lara said.

Scyron nodded, but they kept a watch on the trees all the same.

Arsinoe began serving as their scout, riding Maiden for short stretches before reporting back. Lara might have gone herself, but the horse's saddle and tack had been left on the *Kite*. She could ride bareback, but not at speed.

One afternoon Arsinoe was a long time returning. They had made a temporary camp within a ring of briar patches so tangled that they had deterred even the woodcutters from their work. Dramsind had torn a path for them easily enough and, once Arsinoe had taken food and sleep, she had mounted Maiden and gone off.

Lara was so tired that she had fallen asleep to the sound of the mare's hooves pounding against the loam. When Scyron woke her, she was surprised to find that the Firebird was in the west.

"How long?" she asked.

"Too long," the old man answered.

Lara was still resolving whether to go out in search of her when the Telchine came racing from between the trees, panting. Lara touched the hilt of her sword, but then she saw the smile on Arsinoe's face.

"What is it?" Lara asked. "Where were you?"

"Lara," she said when she had caught some breath. "You have to see this!"

"Where's Maiden?" Lara asked.

"Come on!" Arsinoe urged. *"Dramsind, fiki!"*

"Wopa," Dramsind boomed as he rose. Bannertail had been chewing the head off a bird he had caught atop the giant's shoulder, but he leapt free as they cleared the briars.

Arsinoe moved with a purpose through the trees. Lara and Scyron followed, the old man cursing with every branch that tripped his feet.

The woods thinned as they went, until the lanes between the trees were so broad that one could have driven a coach between the trunks. The forest floor was littered with shellbark husks. The trees were green with new growth. Even as they ran, she could see boot prints in the soil.

This is an orchard, she realized.

When they reached the tree line, Arsinoe stopped short of its edge and waved them forward.

Lara joined Arsinoe and looked.

Maiden was grazing in the long meadow that lay beyond the boughs, her tail flicking at insects flittering amongst the grass. Beyond her there was farmland. Great earthy stretches of tilled fields and pasture, broken by acres of golden wheat. There were meadows closed in by woodland and fenced-in crofts that dotted the hills.

"Well?" Scyron huffed as he came to a halt beside them. "What is it?"

"What is it?!" Arsinoe gasped. "I've never seen anything like this! Is that all grain?"

"Course it's grain," Scyron said. "This is Engadlin, or close enough."

"Engadlin," Arsinoe repeated. "Is all of it this . . . *Fertile?*"

"It should be," Scyron answered, leaning against one of the shellbark trees. "There's enough blood in its soil for seven generations of rich harvests. Wulf, more even!"

"Blood," Lara said. "War, you mean?"

Scyron nodded.

"When I was a younger man," he said, "There were tales from this place that would make even Vulp Vora seem tame."

"From here?" Arsinoe said, shaking her head.

"I have been to Vulp Vora," Lara said. "And I find that difficult to believe."

"Begging your pardon, Highness," Scyron said. "But you are too young to remember the wars your fathers fought. In the isles we called them the hundred summers of blood and were glad of the waters that lay between us and the dark land."

"The dark land is hardly dark," Arsinoe said.

"Not to look at," Lara agreed.

"I do not know what lands these are," Scyron went on. "But they could easily be The Moulins, where Black Petros sent six thousand Arcasians to meet The Watcher. Even more fell at the Sicoris they say."

Scyron bent to pluck a nut from the orchard floor.

"Here the dragon host made the rivers run red," he went on. "Here a hundred thousand died for love of Vasilisa. Here the armies of Elissa were ground into so much meal."

"I see now your meaning, Master Scyron," Lara said.

Scyron nodded, sadly, and cracked the nut in his palm.

Arsinoe shrugged.

"Still," she said. "At least it's *worth* fighting for."

Lara shot her a look. Scyron chewed on the nut.

"I mean," Arsinoe went on. "There's been more blood spilled on the sands of Irkalla than there is rain, and nothing grows there. But this . . . This is paradise!"

"Arsinoe," Lara said, "Have you been gawping at this view the whole time you've been gone?"

"Of course not!" Arsinoe said, growing arch. "There's a town not a league away where three roads meet, and an old farmstead up on that hill."

She pointed to a clustered wood atop one of the rises. Sure enough, Lara could make out the outline of a structure jutting from the trees.

"So," Arsinoe went on, "There's food enough to feed an army, and so many tracks on the lanes to lose the shrike-tamer."

"Provided we aren't seen," Lara said.

"It's open country," Arsinoe admitted. "But just wait until you see how high the barley grows. Tall as Maiden, I swear!"

Arsinoe held her palm above her head and Lara could not help but smile. Her friend was rarely so moved.

"Let's wait until nightfall at least," Lara relented, "Then we'll see how high."

* * * * * * *

When it was dark, they broke from the wood and pressed towards the far hill, mindful of the fires dotting its peak. Arsinoe had not been exaggerating, either. The grain was so tall that once they were amongst it, they had to rely on the stars for guidance.

"How big is this farmstead?" Lara asked as they followed one of the lanes skirting the fields. "Did you see many people?"

"Place looked half a ruin to me," Arsinoe said. "Though I didn't get too close."

"Dogs?" Scyron asked. "Were there dogs?"

"Didn't see any," Arsinoe answered. "Doesn't mean they weren't there."

"Let's try and keep downwind," Lara said. "Just in case."

When they reached the edge of the barley fields, the beaten path they had been following widened considerably before plunging into a shallow ditch. And, beyond the ditch, there was a *road*. Not a rutted track or footpath, but a length of paved stones.

There were no weeds growing between its cracks. There were no cracks.

Under the light of the skull-moon, it looked new.

"Never seen something like this outside of Hiva." Scyron said. "Have you?"

"I was on the high road once," Lara said. "In Solothurn. But it was falling apart. Nothing like this."

"I thought it was odd," Arsinoe said as she led Maiden over the ditch. "But anything wider than a game trail looks big to an Irkallan."

"Armies travel faster on roads," Lara said, testing one of the stones with her boot. She had no doubts about who had ordered its construction.

They pressed on, tracing the edge of a fallow field as they left the roadway behind them. Lara winced at the sight of Dramsind's feet sinking into the soil. If they wanted to lose their pursuers, this was hardly the way.

The hill was further away than it had looked from the orchard, and the climb to reach it hard. It was well past midnight when they came to the edge of the woods crowning its peak, and very dark.

They took some rest beneath the trees. Insects sang in the heat. Lara tugged at her underclothes and wondered that she could not smell her own sweat.

"It's just beyond these trees," Arsinoe said, swatting at an insect. "Yards are penned in, but it's nothing you can't jump."

"Your Highness," Scyron said. "Is it really worth the risk?"

"It is if we want to eat," Lara said.

He demurred.

"Don't suppose they'd take kindly to strangers knocking at their gate at this hour," Lara said. "Begging for scraps."

"Begging your pardon, sir," Arsinoe said, "But we are naught but penniless mercenaries, who made a bad turn near Sarnath. Our hollow-man is very hungry. Could you find it in your heart to spare a chicken?"

Lara smiled and turned her gaze towards Scyron.

"Please," she ventured. "My father and I lost our horse-"

"Too many questions," Arsinoe said, shaking her head. "Besides, I'd sooner believe he was my grandfather than your father."

"What if you were my wife?" Scyron said.

"Don't flatter yourself, old man."

Lara sighed.

"I will go," she said. "Alone."

Scyron huffed at that but kept his peace.

She drew Three-Merits and passed the blade to Arsinoe.

"Cut my hair," she said, taking a firm grip of her locks.

"Why?" Arsinoe asked.

"So that if they see me in the dark," Lara answered. "They may take me for a boy."

"Fair enough," Arsinoe said.

Scyron grimaced as Arsinoe sawed through Lara's curls.

When she was done, she gave Lara a once over.

"What?" Lara asked.

"You still look too clean."

Lara agreed and began to cast about the forest floor.

"Some mud maybe," she said, turning a dead log over and wincing at the things that crawled out from under it. "Or do you think that will-"

A wet clod of dirt caught her square in the face. It caught her so by surprise that she lost her footing and sat down amidst the muck.

She wiped the mud from her eyes and saw Arsinoe cleaning her glove against her skirts.

"I'd say you should roll around in the dirt a bit," Arsinoe said. "But you seem to be doing just fine on your own."

"Piss off," Lara said, finding her feet.

"Here," Arsinoe said, and offered Three-Merits.

"My knife will serve me better," Lara said, patting the blade. *Though I hope I won't need it.*

"Where's Bannertail?" she asked, looking about the clearing.

"Hunting mice I think," Arsinoe said.

"Well," Lara said. "When he comes back, see that he doesn't follow me."

"Easier said than done."

"Just try," Lara said, giving her shoulder a pat.

Arsinoe's beetle flexed its wings as she chewed on her lip.

"What if Highness is caught?" Scyron asked.

"If I'm not back by daybreak," Lara said, "Come find me."

Scyron grunted with approval and put a tree behind his back.

Lara slipped between two of the slimmer beeches and began the final climb.

"Bring back some eggs!" Arsinoe called softly after her. "Or better yet, a chicken!"

Lara took a breath and pressed on.

She was glad of The Watcher as she went. Without him she might have trod on a dozen dead branches or walked face first into one of the smaller saplings. She was fortunate too that the underbrush was thin. That was no great mystery either, for she imagined that the inhabitants of the steading regularly combed this place for tinder.

What did surprise her when she had scaled the final hill crest, was how much larger the farmstead was now that she could see it properly. The whole of the hilltop had been cleared about it, forming a pasture hemmed in by logs. There were at least two outbuildings she could see besides the main house, which looked to be a long, two-story hall set alongside a crumbling tower. It was hard to make out in the moonlight, but it looked to be more ivy than stone.

She could not see any lights, but a plume of smoke was rising from somewhere beyond the main house.

Someone is keeping the hearth fires going.

She stepped from the trees and crossed to the nearest edge of the fence. It was higher than it looked from afar, and the tops of the logs had been carved into crude spikes, but easy enough for her to climb over.

She landed in what she took to be an animal pen, but rather than finding herself in a filthy pigsty or sheepfold, she found the ground was hard packed and she could see hoofprints in the dirt. The outbuilding she had taken for a barn was clearly a stable and, judging from the number of paddocks she could see, she ventured that this farm bred horses.

How nice, she thought. *But it won't fill our bellies.*

She could hear the horses nickering as she made a circuit about the stable, clearing three fences in turn and cursing inwardly as the next building she came across turned out to be a half open smithy.

Farriers too, she mused, glancing at the tongs, hammers, and horseshoes hanging from its posts. *I bet they have tack and saddles, but how would I carry it all?*

A third outbuilding lay across the yard. A barn, almost as tall as the tower.

And, beside it, a hen house.

She considered stealing back over the fence so as to come at it from the rear of the barn, but the fence was far higher here and to do so would mean passing before the gatehouse of the stead. She did not know if there was a sentry posted atop it, but she did not mean to find out.

She flitted across the yard silently and made for the coop.

It was large, but the size of the barn dwarfed it. It was out of the moonlight, too, so she took her time sizing it up. The one Danica had kept on the farm was partially open, so all one had to do to harvest its eggs was check the rows one by one. This one had multiple hatches for the hens, and a door on its narrowest side.

Carefully, she tried the door, and was surprised to find that not only was it latched shut, but that a padlock was guarding its latch.

The hatches were small, but she figured she could squeeze through if she held her breath.

She nudged one of them with her boot, but the hatch would not give.

She tested another with similar results. Hens clucked as she skirted to the other side of the coop, but the hatches here were shut firm as well.

She was squeezing between the coop and the barn when she saw that some animal had clawed a hole beneath the coop. It was wider than it was deep.

She looked about. No one had seen her. It wasn't too late to slip back over the fence.

Inside the coop one of the hens clucked.

This is ridiculous, she thought as she scooped up a fistful of dirt and began to widen the hole. When she was done she got down on her belly, and squeezed into the gap.

She had worried that her face might be pecked or scratched by an irate hen, or that she would be spitting chickenshit from her lips.

What she had not expected were the bells.

They were attached to a snare, too small of course to catch her own neck, but as she shoved forward, she set them to ringing.

The hens began to squawk. She tried to back out of the hole, but with her shoulders caught she could only push further into the coop.

She set her boots against the side of the barn and pushed forward a hands-length. The bells jingled again. She tried to move her arms, but they were still pinned to her sides.

"We caught 'im!" a man's voice was crying out above the hens.

Wulf! She tried to scurry forward but could find no purchase for her heels.

A key rattled in the padlock. It sprang. Then the door flew open, and she found herself looking down the barrel of a crossbow.

The man wielding it, or boy rather, he could not have been much older than she, froze at the sight of her.

"Don't shoot!" she begged, blowing feathers from her mouth.

"Father!" the boy shouted over his shoulder. "Come and look what we caught!"

The boy took a step aside, but kept the crossbow steady as a gnarled hand thrust a lantern into the coop. Its bearer, a weather-beaten man with a scraggly beard squinted hard at her.

"Hrmph," the man grunted, and then he spat into the rushes.

"What is it, Pelier?" a voice called out.

"A thief, m'lord," the old man answered.

Lara squirmed against the floor of the coop, but it was no use.

A third figure came lurching up behind the others. He too was old to her eyes, pepper-haired and his brow lined with care. He had a cane too in his grip, though perhaps that was just to beat trespassers with.

He stared at her for a long moment.

"Lower your bow, Mattieu," he said at last.

"Father?" the boy hesitated.

"I won't ask again."

The boy lowered his crossbow.

"Help me pull her out," the man with the cane said, bending his head as he stepped into the coop.

The other man scowled but did as he was bid. Lara did not fight them but could not help but wince with pain as they dragged her free. It felt as though her whole back was full of splinters.

"It's a girl!" the boy said, once she was on her feet.

"I can see that," his father said, his grip on her arm still firm.

So much for that ruse.

"What's this then?" the man called Pelier growled, snatching the knife from her belt.

She considered catching his hand or driving her heel into the other man's foot and twisting free before breaking into a run, but something stopped her.

"A knife," she said.

"Don't get smart, girl," Pelier said, squinting at the blade. "Where'd you get it?"

"My mother gave it to me," she said.

"A liar too, m'lord."

"Maybe," the other man said. "Girl, if I let go of your arm, will you run?"

She shook her head.

He released her.

"Let's step outside," he said.

The man called Pelier hesitated in the doorway before moving aside. The boy gave her a nudge with the butt of his crossbow.

She stepped out into the yard.

It took the other man a moment to step from the coop. He limped as he closed to get a better look at her.

"You alone?" he asked.

Lara nodded.

"I believe you," he said.

He doesn't. But . . . He's not angry either.

"Are you hungry?" he asked.

She nodded again. This wasn't a lie.

"You must be," he said. "If you're stupid enough to break into a chevalier's coop."

She blinked at that. He did not look like any of the noblemen she had met in Frisia. His tunic looked roughspun. His only finery was the silver ring on his left hand.

"Well," he went on, "If you're hungry then of course we must feed you."

The man called Pelier let out a deep sigh.

The chevalier motioned towards the hall with his cane.

"Come on then," he said, and began to make his way across the yard. "Mattieu?"

"Yes, father?" the boy said, eager.

"Reset the snare. It would be just our luck to lose another chicken tonight while we see to our guest."

"Yes, father," the boy said, sulkily.

The chevalier pushed through the door to the hall and disappeared into its gloom. Lara followed, aware of the servant breathing down her neck, her own knife at her back.

The interior of the hall smelled of woodsmoke, stale beer, and the savory scent of cooked meat. A dark gallery overlooked its solitary table, and a candelabra hung from one of the beams above, unlit.

"Sit," the chevalier said, tapping one of the chairs near the head of the table.

The chevalier moved to the hearth, bent down and lit a taper with one of the brighter embers. Then he lit a few of the candles atop the hearth. The older ones had puddled right into the wood, the wax running like icicles from the mantle. Above them a shield was hung.

On its face a horse stood atop a field of lilies, a single forehoof lifted.

"Sit," the chevalier said again. "Come, I won't hurt you."

"What about him?" she asked nodding towards the rustic.

"He's just worried about me," the chevalier said. "Aren't you, Pelier?"

The older man grunted.

"Pelier," the chevalier went on. "Go now and fetch mistress . . ."

The chevalier looked at her, his eyebrow raised expectantly.

"Mia," Lara said, pulling a name from the air.

"Go fetch Mistress Mia something to eat."

Lara could hear the servant's teeth grinding behind his jaw, but he moved towards the rear of the hall all the same.

"And Pelier?" the chevalier added. "Leave the knife."

The older man laid her knife on the far side of the table and then they were alone.

"How long have you been sleeping rough?" he asked.

"Not long," she answered.

"Where are you from?"

"Therimere," she said.

Now his eyes widened.

"You're far from home, then."

"Not home," she said. "I worked a ship. A trader."

"What happened to it?"

"Storm," she said.

He studied the knife.

"That where you got this?" he asked. "You didn't steal it?"

"No," she said.

"That's good," he said, and slid the knife towards her.

She took it up from the table and sheathed it.

He smiled, pulled out the chair across from her and sat down heavily.

"That shield up there," she said, "Are you really a chevalier?"

"I am," he nodded. "But I wasn't born one. Had to earn it. And I did, by the gods. Yes, I did."

"You fought in the war?" she asked.

"*Wars,*" he corrected.

"For the-"

She wet her lips.

"For Lord Reynard?"

"For the Lord Protector," he said. "Yes."

Pelier returned to the hall then, bearing a tray laden with some sort of pottage. He set it down in front her with just enough restraint not to set its contents spilling over the edges of the bowl.

Lara's mouth watered. She could smell bacon simmering.

"Eat," the chevalier said. "It's no chicken, but it's hot."

She tucked into the bowl. She could not tell if there were peas or beans in the broth, but she was so hungry it hardly mattered. There was a hunk of barley too.

"It's very good," she said between bites. "Thank you."

When she was done Pelier took a seat beside the hearth and glowered at her.

"Are you thirsty?" the chevalier asked. "I've some ale here, still cool from the cellar."

"Please," she said.

He rose, wincing as he crossed to the sideboard. He poured her a cup and set it down beside her.

"Did you hurt your leg in the wars?" she asked as he found his seat again.

He shook his head, chuckling.

"I was running for my horse," he said. "When I stepped into a tree root. Priestess told me it would heal if I could rest it."

"What happened?" she asked.

"Couldn't rest it."

He chuckled again, only a touch bitter.

"Fought at Larsa, Kloss, Dandilin," he went on. "All with a limp. I was surprised they didn't put a cane on my crest."

"Horse is nice," she said.

"Yes," he said. "And lilies. Cursed if I know what they stand for."

"Was it worth it?" she asked.

The chevalier shot a look at his servant.

"Now I *know* you're not from here!" he laughed. "Who do you think I was, girl? Some nobleman's son, born in a silk shirt?"

"No," she said. "I mean-"

"My father was a fuller," the chevalier said. "You know what a fuller does?"

"No," she admitted.

"They stomp on wool that's been soaked in piss," he said. "To soften it."

"Oh," she said.

"And that was before the Calvos burned down our village," he went on. "You think *I* never stole a chicken?"

Ah. So that's it.

"'Was it worth it?'" He stretched out his hands. "Lands, a title, and a pension. You tell me girl."

Lara shrugged and took a sip of ale. It was so smooth it was almost sweet.

Before she knew it, she had downed it all.

The chevalier laughed.

"Father," a sleepy voice called out from the balcony above. "Who is that?"

Lara looked up to see a young girl staring at her from the balcony above, clearly still half asleep. She was wearing a nightshirt and her long dark hair was half in her face.

"A guest," the chevalier said. "Go back to bed."

She nodded absently and retreated from the balustrade.

"You too, Mattieu," the chevalier said.

Lara could hear the boy mouth something low as he emerged from his hiding place beneath one of the windows.

"What was that?"

"Nothing, father," the boy said.

The chevalier waited for the boy to steal up the stairs before saying, "It was worth it."

He fumbled at his belt and pulled loose a pouch. Pelier got to his feet and pulled a pipe down from the mantle.

"My eldest puts on airs, of course," the chevalier said, taking the pipe with a nod and starting to fill it. "Land will be his one day. Could stay here, raise horses. But no. He wants to be a chevalier."

Pelier offered him a fresh taper. He lit his pipe.

"Do you have family?" he asked, once he had gotten it going.

"A brother," she said. "He lives in Carduel."

"Is that where you're headed?" he asked. "So far from the sea?"

"Heard there's work there."

"Suppose there is," he said, and took another drag. "More ale?"

"Please."

He motioned to Pelier. The old man filled her cup, then poured one for himself.

"The Fairlimb," he said. "Do you know who that is?"

She nodded.

"Fairlimb's always on the lookout for girls need a home away from home." He tapped the bowl of his pipe against the table. "You remind me a bit of her, to tell the truth. She were younger than you, but braver than many a man I've met. Braver than me, at least."

He took a swallow from his cup.

"At any rate, you've got the arms for that sort of work. And it's good pay, provided you don't mind getting your hands dirty."

Lara raised her hands. There were practically black from filth.

"No," he chuckled. "Suppose you don't mind at that."

She shrugged.

"I'm half a mind to take you there myself," he said. "I've some old friends in Carduel, and I do miss the road."

"You've done enough already," she said.

"Pelier would agree with you," he said. "And besides, I've duties here that can't be put off."

She breathed a quiet sigh of relief.

"But," he said, "I can write a few words if you like, put my mark to them. Should get you past the traitor's gate, at least."

Lara did her best to hesitate.

"M'lord," she said. "I couldn't-"

"Nonsense," the chevalier said, struggling to his feet. "Now where's my ink?"

"Here, m'lord," Pelier said, beating the chevalier to the cupboard. He produced ink, quill, and a scrap of parchment and then moved one of the candles close so his master could see what he was about.

The chevalier bent his head low, his hand forming each letter shakily.

"Girl like you shouldn't be sleeping wild in these parts," the chevalier said as he worked. "Nor creeping about after dark. They hang thieves these days."

"Hanged 'em in the old days too," Pelier muttered.

"Mm," the chevalier murmured in agreement, struggling to make a neat 'ene.'

"Whole country used to crawl with 'em," Pelier said. "Father had a fruit tree, when I were young. Gooseberries. Best thing I ever tasted. Brigands come and picked it clean, then cut down the tree for spite."

The old man scratched at his beard.

"Count's men were worse," he said. "Killed our dogs and ate them. Took our women. Burned whatever they couldn't steal."

"What Count?" she asked.

"Don't matter," the old man said, cradling his drink. "Lord Reynard's put an end to 'em. No more lords now come to steal the bread from off our tables, no more brigands to rip our wives and daughters from their beds. No more thieves. High born or low."

He raised his cup.

"Gods bless him," he said. "Gods bless him and all of his."

"Bless him," the chevalier said, raising his own cup.

"Bless him," Lara managed.

The men drank, but Lara spat what she had taken into her mouth back into her cup.

The chevalier went back to his scribbling. When he was done, he folded up the parchment, sealed it with candlewax, and pressed his ring into the join.

"Now then," the chevalier said. "That's that."

He rose and pushed the parchment towards her. She got to her feet, wiped her hand against her breeches and then stuffed the letter into her jack.

"Thank you," she said. "For your kindness."

"It won't be light for hours," he said. "And there's a loft in the barn."

"I can't."

"It gets dark in the woods."

"Not afraid of the dark."

"Thought not," he said. "But still. We can't let you leave empty-handed. It's a long road to Carduel, and I reckon whoever's waiting for you out there is hungry too."

She made a show of looking caught out. Then she nodded.

"Cheese and rye," the chevalier said to Pelier. "And some apples."

The old man sighed but did as he was bid. He returned from the larder with a rough spun sack that he shoved into her hard enough to bruise.

"More'n you deserve," he muttered.

"Well," the chevalier said. "Come on then."

She let him escort her out the door. The old man followed, watchful.

"I remember what it's like to be desperate, Mia," the chevalier said as they crossed the yard. "But don't let me catch you in my coop again. Nor stealing from anyone else under my protection. You understand?"

"You won't," she said. "I promise."

"Good," he said. "You want a place to sleep, or a crust of bread, you just up and *ask* for it. These are good, honest folk. You'll see. The dark days are over."

She nodded.

"Oh," he said as Pelier threw wide the front gate. "And keep a sharp eye if you're going to be sleeping in the wood. Something's been at my chickens. Traps don't seem to work, so I figure it's chimera."

He smiled at her.

"But then I don't expect those frighten you, either?"

"No," she said.

* * * * * * *

"Took you long enough," Arsinoe said. "I was starting to think I'd have to come after you. Where have you been?"

"I got caught," Lara said, laying down the sack.

Scyron ceased his whittling.

"And?" Arsinoe said, eyeing the bundle.

"The farm belonged to a chevalier," she said. "One of the usurper's veterans."

"Volk," Arsinoe cursed. "How did you get away?"

"He let me go," Lara said, "Thought I was a runaway, or something. I didn't bother correcting him."

Arsinoe was already rummaging through the sack.

"And they," she said, discovering a hunk of rye, "*He* fed you?"

"That's not all," she said, pulling the letter from her jack. "He gave me the key to the city."

"What's that, Highness?" Scyron said.

"A letter of introduction," she said. "A simple one. Man could barely write, probably figured I couldn't read."

She offered him the letter, but he begged off.

"Where's Bannertail?" she asked, thinking of the snare.

"Sleeping," Arsinoe said, gesturing towards Dramsind. "With a bellyful of mice."

The fox-squirrel was curled up on Dramsind's shoulder. The giant was silent, his long arms splayed out across the grass.

Lara found a tree of her own to lay beside.

They couldn't stay here, of course. The chevalier might change his mind. The Sureshot's minions might pay this place a call. The old servant might be out looking for her now, a crossbow in his gnarled fingers.

But she needed to sit.

"Lara," Arsinoe beamed, continuing to rummage. "There's so much here. It's- It's a miracle!"

"I know," Lara said.

"Then what's wrong?"

"They love him," she said.

VII

The haunted city lay along the river that the Telchines had called the Leucothea, the White Goddess. Its glimmering waters cut straight across the plain, and alongside it the kings of old Aquilia had made their seat, a place of marble and granite. Here there had been temples to Lioness and Firebird, and wide avenues bathed with sunlight. Here people had tarried amidst silk pavilions and corniced fountains shaded by moly trees.

Carduel had once been beautiful, it was said. Then a hundred armies had sacked it. The dragon host had burned it. Plague, quake, and flood had turned what was left to ruin. Its walls breached, its bridges all but broken, what remained cowered in the shadow of the fortress that lurked atop the promontory overlooking the river. That was a dark place and cheerless. The morning mist hung heavy about its towers, whose windows had the seeming of eyes, searching.

"It was bad enough in the stories," Lara said. "I never thought to look on it."

"And we're not even close," was all Arsinoe had to say.

The path they walked had been longer than Lara could have guessed. It was Rosemonth when they had fled from Pikria. Now it was near to Reaping and the nights were as sweltering as the days.

They had Maiden of course, but one horse was as good as none for speed. Nor could they risk walking the road, no matter how tempting the prospect. Lara and Scyron might have been able to pass as weary travelers, but Arsinoe had been exotic even in Frisia, Maiden was too fine a horse, and Dramsind was Dramsind.

So, they had walked, clinging to wastes and woodland whenever they were able. They had sent Scyron to beg for food at the farmsteads that happened to cross their path, and he occasionally returned with a bit of bread and cheese for his efforts. But not all the folk of Engadlin were as free-handed as the chevalier had promised. More often than not he had been run off by dogs or men with staves. Sometimes both.

There were no steads south of the river. Nor was there pasture. The plain had grown wild from neglect, and amid the creeping briars and scrub-brush lay the bones of the beasts that had seen the downfall of Carduel.

Dragons. Here they had met their end. Winter had done for them where force of arms had failed, and for once Lara whispered thanks to The Watcher with an easy heart.

Many lay in pieces, rib and thigh and wing scattered with the weeds. Others endured where they had fallen, their jaws so wide that you could step between them. Birds had nested in the sockets of their eyes. Their fangs lay in the dirt, more than Lara could count.

As they walked, Lara could trace the lines of rubble where great manses had stood, their stones blackened by fire. In places the shells of structures still loomed, overgrown by ivy, and beside them lay toppled pillars and timeworn statues.

Had Parisa walked the ground she trod upon, she wondered. Had Elissa and Tantilis? Were these the halls where King Leander feasted, turned now to rubble?

"Imagine the heat," Scyron said, patting a crumpled shelf of mortar. The humbler of its stones had run to gloss. "Gods, what monsters."

"Dragons don't breathe fire," Lara said.

"They do in all the stories," Scyron said. "Though, begging your pardon, Highness, I was speaking of the men who brought them here . . . And the ones who came after."

Lara nodded at that, letting her gaze wander towards the citadel that lay on the far side of the river.

It was close on to midday when they came within sight of the crossing. Peering from out of the brush Lara could see that a single bridge served to connect the banks of the White River. Like the road that had led them here, it appeared to have been built anew, and its pale arches were so tall that even a sea-faring caravel might pass beneath with ease.

Its approach, however, was guarded by a rounded barbican that was as strong as any castle Lara had ever seen. The Traitor's Gate it was named, and through it they must pass if they wished to gain entrance to the city. For there were no docks to be seen on the far side of the river, save at the base of the citadel, where a single ship lay moored.

A lean, dark sloop. She did not doubt that it was Reynard's flagship, even though she could not make out the colors of its pennons.

A trio of war galleys lay at anchor about the docks upriver of the Traitor's Gate, and a military camp had sprouted along the nearby embankment. If they were guarding the river, they were hardly necessary, for any fleet hoping to menace Astolat would have to pass beneath the engines no doubt in place along the walls. It would take a bold captain, or a very foolish one, to brave that passage.

Downriver, ships of a more mercantile bent had clustered. Cogs, fishing cutters, and barges jostled for berths as the midday neared. A market town of sorts seemed to have grown out of the ruins there, ancient stones serving as foundations for wattle and daub.

There was life yet in the haunted city it seemed. And laughter too if her ears did not deceive her.

"I don't like this," Lara said, scanning the heavens. "We haven't seen a shrike for a fortnight."

"That's not good?" Arsinoe said, picking a burr from her locks.

"If I were *him*," Lara said, gesturing to the citadel, "I would want us to feel safe. Overconfident. Right up to the point where the noose closed tight around our necks."

"So," Arsinoe said. "What are we going to do instead?"

"First," Lara said. "We'll need to play spy. That might be the usurper's boat moored beneath that rock, but that doesn't mean he isn't elsewhere, and Pinsard with him. I've some thoughts on how to wrinkle it out of an officer, assuming we can find one. If we can find out where they keep their prisoners, even better."

"And then?" Arsinoe asked.

"We free Pinsard."

The beetle on Arsinoe's cheek flexed its wings.

"How?" Arsinoe asked.

"I'm still working it out," Lara said. "But either way, we're going to need to get through that gate."

Lara unshouldered her pack, shooing Bannertail aside as she dug the letter out from under her cooking kit. The fox-squirrel retreated in the brush, sniffing as he went.

"You really think waving a scrap of paper under their noses will work?" Arsinoe scoffed.

"If there's one thing Reynard seems to have a hard time predicting," Lara said, "It's human decency. That chevalier, one of his own no less, took pity on me. His kindness was no act."

"So you say," Arsinoe sniffed.

"You weren't there," Lara said. "And if we're going to walk in the front door, I say we do it in good faith."

"So, what?" Arsinoe said. "We're joining the army?"

"We are," Lara nodded. "At least, we need to seem like we are. It'll be a whole lot easier to steal past the usurper's guards if they think we're one of them."

Arsinoe threw up her hands in surrender.

"Highness," Scyron hemmed. "Perhaps I should make a trial of the bridge first?"

"No," Lara said. "I need you to stay on this side of the river with Maiden. Bannertail too if he'll behave."

The old man shifted from foot to foot, an objection clearly forming on his lips.

"We'll need supplies," she went on, passing him the better part of her coin in a separate purse, "Loose talk, and most of all *a boat*. A small one will do. Hire it if you're able. If not-"

"Highness," Scyron said. "Might we not do these things together?"

"We cannot be seen together," Lara said. "Not for this to work. And besides, you're hardly the sort of woman the Baroness is looking to recruit."

"Suppose I *was* hoping to keep my beard," he conceded. "Been a while since I wore a skirt."

Arsinoe crossed her arms. "You don't seriously expect us to believe-"

"In Leng," Scyron said. "They only let women into the high plateau."

Scyron scratched at his beard.

"Monks made eyes at me all evening."

Arsinoe rubbed at the bridge of her nose.

"You get a whiff of trouble," Lara said, "*Any* trouble, you make further downstream then double back. Either way, keep a sharp eye on the river. If *we* get into trouble, we'll probably need to swim for it."

"As you wish, Highness," Scyron said. "But how will you find me?"

"Dramsind has your scent by now," Lara said. "Maiden's too. Shouldn't be too hard."

Scyron looked a touch unsettled by that, but he nodded.

"Dramsind?" Arsinoe huffed. "You want to bring Dramsind?"

"What about it?" Lara said.

"If we're going to leave anyone it should be him," Arsinoe said. "Least we could say the old man here polishes our boots."

"Hrmph," Scyron grunted.

"Do you see Dramsind feeding Maiden?" Lara asked. "Hiring a boat? Besides, we're going to need him if we get recognized."

"Lara," Arsinoe said, "He's a *hollow man*. We might as well wear signs with our names around our necks."

"You're a Telchine," Lara said. "Who's to say he's not a giant?"

"Is that any better?" Arsinoe shot back. "I bet half the usurper's men think he's a giant."

"Do you remember Trimount?" Lara said. "Or those bounty hunters on Verch? There'll be all sorts here too, I'll bet. Wulf, more even, now that he knows I'm on the run."

"Usurper's famous for his open hand with mercenaries," Scyron mused. "Be willing to wager she's right."

"There's an awful lot of holes in this *plan* of yours, Lara," Arsinoe said. "But let's say you are right, and we do walk right in with no questions asked. Then what?"

Lara gestured towards the fortress.

"Those walls look mighty high to climb," Arsinoe said. "Or are we going to knock at the gates and ask to be let in?"

"I'm thinking we go *under* them," Lara said. "You know what 'under' means, don't you?"

Arsinoe rolled her eyes. "Like the old days, you mean?"

"Even castles have drains," Lara nodded. "And in all the old stories Carduel's dungeons run dark and deep. I bet they stretch straight down the river. Why else would the usurper dock his fancy boat there?"

"You don't know for certain though, do you?" Arsinoe said, pointedly. "I mean, how do we know the Baroness' soldiers aren't camped outside the city? How do we know Pinsard is even here at all?"

"We don't," Lara said. "I never said this would be easy, Arsinoe."

"No," Arsinoe said. "I suppose not."

The Telchine began to undo her belt.

"What are you doing?" Lara asked.

"Lending you some of my skirts," Arsinoe answered. "The least we can do is go in disguise."

* * * * * *

They took the roadway up to the foot of the Traitor's Gate, Lara and Arsinoe walking side by side with Dramsind plodding behind them. They had traded enough articles of clothing to look suitably mercenary. Arsinoe's gloves were bulky, but they hid the white scar running up her wrist. Lara's breezier silks, ragged now, served to veil the beetle on the Telchine's cheek. Mud, dust, and sweat would do the rest.

Or so Lara hoped.

The gate was larger than it had looked from the weed-choked ruins, its turrets and merlons enclosed by hoardings, and manned by some two dozen soldiers. And those were the ones she could see. And yet its doors lay open, its portcullis was raised, and all manner of men, women, and even children were passing freely beneath its arches.

"Market day," Lara said, glancing down the road behind them. Scyron was nowhere to be seen, but if he had cut across the road and was coming at the docks from somewhere downriver or was simply lingering half a league behind them, she could not say.

Better that I don't know.

A line of carts had stalled in the shadow of the gate by the time they came to the crossroad at its feet. A panoply of booths had been erected along the roadway here, and many a ruin had been converted to shops by the more industrious (or unscrupulous) merchants. There were cheese vendors, men selling felt and leather, bins stuffed with charcoal, barrels of tallow, vintners hawking vintages from Osca and Astolat, gowned men fanning themselves beside silks and spices, wicker from Therimere, carpets from Irkalla and, from Hiva, peppers and coffee.

Arsinoe nearly collided into a stall laden with lamps at the sight of the beans on display before Lara yanked her back into step.

"Later," Lara whispered.

The goods on display were far from the only exotics. There were Telchine pillow boys lounging from the windows of wine sinks, and black-robed Mandrossian scholars arguing over steaming cuts of pike. Within a stable yard a smoky-eyed Priestess danced to the delight of muleskinners, much to the disapproval of a prim pair of Calvarians in Southern dress taking tea across the way. And much to Lara's relief, there were giants. A whole dozen of them, half-stripped to the waist and gleaming with sweat, were taking a meal in the shade of one of the larger ruins. Danica had often told her that giants ate men, liking especially the taste of little girls who misbehaved, but she had spent enough time in Frisia to know that they were generally herbivorous. This was not to say they did not have appetites to match their size. These ones, laborers she guessed, were tucking into great bowls of lentils and grilled onions.

Still, Arcasians young and old far outnumbered the foreigners, and more than a few heads turned as they came to a halt behind the carts, though it was difficult to tell if it was due to the sight of two armed women or the hulking figure following in their wake. From the hungry look she could catch in the men's eyes, she guessed it might be a mixture of both.

"Come have a drink, ladies!" a woman cried at them from the upper story of one of the new built taverns. "We've Perigon here! Very pale! The best!"

Lara ignored her. In Frisia she had learned that telling a merchant you did not have coin to spend could be viewed as an invitation to haggle.

Instead, she craned her neck back, and saw that what she had taken for grim bits of decoration atop the gate were in fact skulls, set on spikes. Some still had wisps of hair attached to their leathery scalps.

"Anyone you know?" Arsinoe quipped.

Lara shook her head. If the usurper had brought any heads back from Vireo, he clearly did not think them worth displaying.

One of the carts rumbled through the gates. Lara took stock of the men who were making a survey of the next one's cargo. Their mail was plain, but well-kept, and their coats were mostly gray save for the tawny badge of the usurper sewn upon their breasts. Their captain wore spurs on his boots, but all of them had two eyes, two hands, and were taller than the usurper by a head.

"Let me do the talking," Lara whispered.

"You certain?" Arsinoe said, drumming her fingers against the length of her spear. "I've been a mercenary far longer than you."

"True," Lara said. "But you lack a certain . . . Charm."

"So do most mercenaries," Arsinoe said. "You want us to seem *sincere*, don't you?"

"Fine," Lara said. "Just try not to bite their heads off."

"No promises," Arsinoe said.

The officer waved the last of the carts through the gates and then turned his gaze towards the two of them. He had a week's worth of stubble on his chin.

"What's your business?" he asked as they approached.

"Looking for work," Arsinoe answered.

"Bet you are," the man said, his gaze wandering down both their legs. "Sell-swords?"

Arsinoe nodded.

"What company?"

"Let me guess," one of the other sentries said. "Lady Killers."

"That's right," Lara said, trying to sound curt.

"Heard they were up north," the captain said, "Fighting for the rebel Calvos."

"Gets cold up there," Arsinoe said. "And the Glyconese pay is lousy. Figured we'd head here."

"Hrm," the captain hummed. "This one's a bit young, ain't she?" He gestured towards Lara lazily.

"Calling me old?" Arsinoe asked, switching her grip on her spear.

The captain grinned, his laugh lines deepening.

"Not at all," he said.

"What about 'im?" The other sentry nodded towards the giant. "He a lady too?"

"Dramsind can't speak," Lara said.

"Biwu," Dramsind said, thinly.

The men exchanged glances.

"What was that then?" the captain asked.

"Can't speak Aquilian she means," Arsinoe said, casually. "He's Irkallan. Religious sort. Hardly eats, hardly sleeps. Fact is, I've never even seen him take his armor off."

"Never?" The captain's second looked skeptical.

"Like I said," Arsinoe sniffed. "He's religious."

"If you say so," the captain shook his head. "Now then, you got marks? Papers?"

"We have this," Lara said, and produced the chevalier's letter.

The captain took it from her and blinked at its seal.

"Right then," he said, growing sober as he passed the letter back. "On your way."

"What?" Arsinoe asked. "Not going to search us?"

Lara tried not to choke on her own spit.

"No m'lady," he chuckled. "You'll find the Fairlimb's barracks close to the citadel. Look for ladies in armor if you get turned around."

"Thanks," Arsinoe said.

"And steer clear of Victory Square," the captain called after them. "That's Steel Heel territory."

"Less you like getting chewed up," the other sentry chuckled.

They both flashed the fingers. The men laughed.

"Charming enough for you?" Arsinoe whispered as they crossed beneath murder holes and raised bars.

"Still don't like it," Lara said, glancing back. "Too easy."

"Perhaps he's gotten sloppy," Arsinoe said.

"He's many things," Lara said. "Sloppy isn't one of them."

"Do you want to turn back?" Arsinoe asked, an honest question.

Lara's answer caught in her throat.

Beyond the final gate was the bridge. Its guard rails were of iron and bronze, its stanchions tall shafts of pale limestone. And from each shaft a corpse was hung. Some dangled by their wrists. Others were on their knees, posed like gruesome statuary. Some had bloated, their hands and feet black with rot. Others were beginning to peel. Flies, crows, or shrikes had long since done for their eyes.

There were placards set before them, on which some hand had written in bold neat script. *Rape* many of them read, and *Murder*. Most had been stripped down to their small clothes, but there was one wearing silks and scarlet damask over his fetid flesh. His plinth was marked *Thief*.

"Saves us the trouble of learning the letter of the law," Arsinoe shrugged.

"This is no justice," Lara murmured, and walked on.

It was not long before they caught up to the carts. The oxen were clearly used to the stench of death hanging in the air, but that did not make them any faster, especially as the bridge climbed higher.

"Look," Arsinoe said suddenly, and pointed above the walls of the city.

Sure enough, there was a shrike- it was too large to be anything but- gliding towards the fortress. It had just begun to circle about when another of the things took flight from one of the outmost towers.

"Happy now?" Arsinoe asked.

"That must be their roost," Lara said, watching as the second shrike soared overhead. "Still, I'd think there would be more of them."

"Locals are probably used to them," Arsinoe said. "We should probably stop staring."

"Yes," Lara agreed.

The carts rolled on, and they lost sight of the fortress as the walls of the city reared overhead. They stretched clear across the breadth of the riverbank, crumbling and moss-grown but still very strong. The sentinels at the gate gave them a curious glance or two and then went back to the business of eating lunch.

They stepped through the cool shadows of the gatehouse.

What lay beyond was a city of marble and ivy. Shattered columns lined the throughfare, their hollows thick with creepers. Piles of masonry lay in heaps, and from them trees had sprung. Some looked old enough to have shaded lords who had long since gone to the Firebird. A wide stretch of beaten soil, a market once, had turned to weeds. Amidst them a statue loomed, headless.

And yet there were scaffolds about the ruins, and laborers napping through the heat. Right beside the gate some barracks or garrison had been erected, its archways and domed roof aping the older, Aquilian style. It seemed a crude imitation to her eyes.

"Make way!" a voice cried out from the walls above, and at once the drovers urged their teams to comply. "Clear the road, sharply now!"

The carts had barely moved aside when some two score soldiers came marching by at a light sprint. They were kicking up so much dust that Lara would be hard pressed to guess whose colors they wore, though the spurs on their boots left her no doubt as to their allegiance.

She and her companions stepped into the shade of one of the trees growing beside the gate, Arsinoe making a show of urging Dramsind to hurry. It hardly mattered. The Steel Heels hustled past, sparing no more than a glance or two. Then they were through the gate, and on their way to the far side of the river.

"So many soldiers," Lara said, coughing from the dust.

"And most of them mercenaries," Arsinoe said, tugging at her borrowed gloves. "No wonder they didn't ask more questions."

Lara nodded and made her way towards the fountain set against the curtain wall. Its spouts were shaped like drakes, spewing thin rivulets into a moss-slick basin.

She slipped off Arsinoe's gloves and ran her hands under the water.

"What is it?" Arsinoe asked.

"It's just," Lara said, "This place. I thought it would be different."

"How so?"

"*Darker*, I suppose," she said. "After all the stories I'd heard . . . Well, I always imagined this place was full of ghosts, not people."

"Wait 'til dusk," a high voice said, giving Lara a start. "You'll see ghosts then, m'lady."

Lara turned and found herself staring into the eyes of a young boy, no more than ten summers old. His feet were bare and his breeches little more than rags. The Firebird had turned him dark as a nut.

He held out an open palm.

"Bit fer a veteran?" he said, smiling very wide.

"Aren't you a little young?" Lara asked.

"Naw," he amended. "Fought at Dandilin, I did."

"That was before you were born," Lara said. "And I've no bits to spare. Will you settle for bread?"

"Yes, m'lady," he beamed. "Thankee."

Arsinoe pursed her lips as Lara gave the boy the last of their loaves. The boy saw her staring and held out his other hand.

"Bit for a-"

"Get," Arsinoe said, showing him the back of her hand.

He took off, fast as a rabbit, and vanished down a narrow alley.

"Lara," Arsinoe said. "Tell me you were lying, and you *do* have some bits left to your name."

"I do," Lara said, patting her jack. "More than a few. And we're going to need them."

"What for?" Arsinoe sighed. "Bribes?"

"Drinks," Lara said.

* * * * * *

Bitelas leaned against the rail overlooking the practice yard and stifled a grin. Clorinde was putting the recruits through their paces again, and harder than ever.

There were a score of them, skinny street waifs and lanky rustics armed with staves instead of spears. Less than half of them knew their right foot from their left, so that Clorinde had slipped stalks of straw into their boots.

"Leading by the straw-foot!" Clorinde would bark at them, and still one of them would manage to foul it up.

She could hardly remember if she had done any better when she was green. She doubted it. They had found her hiding in a brick kiln. Back then she had been glad of a crust of bread and a dry place to sleep. Drill would have seemed a luxury compared to the streets of Larsa.

"Hurry it up, sergeant!" she called down to Clorinde. "I have a thirst!"

"Keep your breeches on!" Clorinde barked back.

One of the recruits had the misfortune to laugh.

"Do you find something amusing?" Clorinde snapped, advancing on the girl like a shark with the scent of blood. "Do you?"

"No, m'lady," the girl managed, wilting.

"M'lady?" Clorinde repeated. "Do I look like a lady to you?"

She had shoved her face so close to the recruit's that their noses practically touched. Clorinde's was made of brass and was held in place by a leather harness.

The recruit managed to murmur something low. 'No,' presumably.

"Right!" Clorinde said brusquely and shoved past the girl. "Now, once more, stepping by the bloody *straw*-foot! At the forward . . . March!"

The recruits lurched forward and made a poor circuit of the yard.

Bitelas shook her head, then straightened as she caught sight of the captain coming up the wall walk. She was off duty, but the captain was still the captain.

Her real name was Jenavette, but the troops called her Hatchet. You could tell her girls by the axes tattooed on their skin. Bitelas wore two

- 119 -

of them on her neck, crossed, with her company's number in the crook above.

"Captain," Bitelas said, bowing her head.

The Hatchet nodded at her, *at ease*, and took her own place along the rail.

The recruits marched. The recruits set their staves. The recruits formed and reformed. Bitelas yawned.

The Firebird lowered. The shadows about the yard began to deepen.

"Sergeant," the Hatchet said, her voice carrying over the yard. "A word."

Clorinde nodded neatly and turned the girls over to her second before mounting the stairs.

The Hatchet shot Bitelas a glance. She made herself scarce.

She found Moflete and Salomei smoking beside the cookhouse. This was normally something of a luxury, but the spoils of Pikria had filled their packs with more than silver. Bitelas had traded her own share for fresh small clothes and a pair of decent boots, but she was a more practical sort than most.

"Evening," Moflete said, and offered her a few drags from her pipe.

Bitelas took them slowly. The Frisian leaves had a dark bite.

"Where are we going tonight?" Moflete asked.

"Tyris," Bitelas said. "Where do you think?"

"Oh, not The Poppy again!"

"You like it there," Bitelas asked of Salomei. "Don't you?"

Salomei shrugged and blew a ring of smoke from her lips.

"See?" Bitelas said.

Moflete twisted up her lips. Bitelas returned her pipe.

Moflete was from Engadlin, the fourth of five daughters from some village Bitelas had never heard of. She was stout and her full cheeks made her look a touch soft, but her forearms were thicker even than Clorinde's. She was quick to smile, and quick to forgive.

Salomei was as quiet as Moflete was loud, and so fair that most of the company assumed she was from Carabas, though no one knew for certain. No one pressed her, either. Few of the Baroness' bloody girls had lived happy lives before swearing their oaths to serve.

"Getting dark," Salomei said, tapping her pipe against the heel of her boot.

Bitelas agreed and was just about to check on the yard when Clorinde came trudging around the close end of the barracks.

"What did she want?" Bitelas asked.

"My opinion," Clorinde answered, giving the others a nod.

"What you tell her?"

"New girls are soft," Clorinde said. "No grit."

"You always say that."

"This time it's true. Would have eaten this lot alive back in the Anthill."

"Here we go," Moflete snickered.

"Be food for shot at least," Clorinde said. "Now come on. Let's get skulled."

They left the barracks by way of the bathhouse gate. Two of the recruits were scouring the copper tubs within, and at the sight of an officer they bent to their work with renewed vigor.

The day had been long, and the streets of Carduel were already deserted. Folk did not venture out after dark in the old city, save for criminals, the watch, and thirsty soldiers, and even they preferred to travel in numbers. When the Firebird set the ruins loomed large, and the shadows deepened. The faces carved into the ancient arches looked half alive, and watchful. Salomei had brought a torch to light their way through the alleys, but it seemed a pinprick against the gloom.

The Poppy stood near the foot of the Queen's Steps, that steep climb between plaza and citadel that Bitelas had come to dread. They said the stains on the stair marked the place where Lady Genevieve's daughters had been dashed against the stones, and that no amount of scrubbing could wash them clean. One of the Steel Heels swore he had seen the dead Queen herself, or rather he had seen a *shape*, all in white and silent beside the steps.

Such things were impossible, of course, and easy to dismiss when the Firebird was bright overhead. But Bitelas had seen things herself that were difficult to explain, and she could not help but breathe a sigh of relief as the coarse laughter wafting from the Poppy's stoop broke the silence of the night.

By day The Poppy was flush with custom. The ale was good, the pies usually fresh, and there was dicing and rat-baiting for those who liked to chance their arms. By night it was a touch quieter. Doxies, dissolutes, and soldiers were its chief customers, and tonight seemed no exception. They supped and cackled across the breadth of the common room, a dim but cheery place that half resembled the great hall it must once have been. Tapestries covered the worst of the cracks running through the walls and, above the hearth, where most taverns might have hung arms or the head of some beast, a garland of flowers rested.

There was nothing of war here, save for the patrons.

The Poppy was a place to forget.

"Here, Odette!" Moflete called out as they pushed into the common room. "Four pints, if'n you please!"

"Good even, ladies," the barkeep beamed at them, and set some cups to pour.

"What news?" Bitelas asked, resting her arms against the bar.

"Same as ever," Odette replied. "Another ship come upriver. Tarsus men, but I hear they won't be here long."

"Mhm," Bitelas grunted. This was the third evening in a row they had been given leave, and rest and recreation were usually a sign that they would be back on the march. She had no doubt that their own time in Carduel would be short.

"Forget the men," Clorinde said, grabbing the first full cup. "What else?"

Odette smiled coyly.

"Now that you ask," she said, "There were this lot came in this afternoon. Very strange."

"Go on," Clorinde said.

"Well, one of 'em were a giant, for a start," Odette said. "All in mail, from head to foot. Quiet too. Drank one pint and passed right out."

"One pint?" Moflete tittered, taking one for herself.

"I'd have rolled him," Odette nodded. "But I'd need a winch to lift him, and more than you lot to help. Just lucky he were out back when he tumbled."

"Seen my share of giants," Clorinde said, drumming her fingers against the bar. "And drunks."

"And drunk giants," Moflete giggled.

"I'll bet," Odette said. "But really, it's the two that came with 'im that gave me a start."

"What about 'em?" Bitelas asked, curious now herself.

"Take a look for yourself," Odette said, directing their attention to the snug.

There sat two of the oddest sell-swords that Bitelas had ever seen, if they were sell-swords and not players from some wandering troupe. Their gear looked Arcasian enough, quality even, but their turquoise skirts and sashes made them look half-Glyconese. The older of the two was veiled and golden-skinned, her jet-black hair practically gleaming in the lamplight. Her companion was wilder, ragged-haired, and filthy . . . And yet there was something striking about her.

It was her face, Bitelas decided. If she were an actor, she might have played Ino or Vasilisa. Though she would have to wash first.

Others had certainly taken interest. A brace of men, tradesmen by their dress, were looming about the foot of the snug. She couldn't hear their words, but she could imagine them well enough.

"Who are they?" Moflete asked, wiping ale from her lips.

"Dunno," Odette said. "But that one on the right? She's a *real* Telchine. Wanted roast chicken for her supper. A whole chicken. And she ate it too."

Clorinde drained her cup and made straight for the snug.

Bitelas paid Odette, grabbed her own cup, and followed.

"These idiots bothering you?" Clorinde asked as she came up behind the men.

"Yes," the Telchine said. "Though it's nothing we can't handle."

"Piss off," Clorinde snarled at the men.

Both of them became suddenly interested in the game of hazard being played on the far side of the room.

"Thanks," the Telchine said when they had gone. "You lot come here often?"

"Too often," Moflete said, but shut her mouth when Clorinde glared at her.

"Well, there's room for more," the Telchine said. "Isn't there, Mia?"

The girl nodded.

"Why don't you sit with us?" the Telchine said, patting the cushion next to her own. "We've a whole jug to share and we don't bite."

"Shame," Clorinde said, taking a seat.

Bitelas shot Moflete a knowing look. Salomei squeezed past them and took the biggest of the cushions for her own.

"Sell-swords?" Bitelas asked, leaning against the curtained arch.

The girl nodded.

"Where are you from?" Moflete asked. "Glycon, I bet."

"Irkalla," the Telchine corrected.

"Therimere," the girl murmured.

Bitelas nodded. What was left of the girl's hair had a southern curl.

"Where've you fought?" Clorinde asked.

"You ever heard of Karkadann?" the Telchine answered. "Iram? Simurgh?"

"No," Clorinde admitted.

"Well," the Telchine said, "You're not missing much. Irkallan work is steady, but the pay leaves something to be desired."

"Where's the rest of your company?" Bitelas asked.

"Calvaria, for all I know," the Telchine said. "We parted ways months ago."

"You both stink," Salomei said.

Moflete laughed. Bitelas gave her a sharp nudge to the ribs.

"Ow," Moflete complained.

"No need to apologize," the Telchine said. "Your friend's right. We *do* stink. And we thought about seeing a priestess, but why pay for a bath when the Fairlimb will scrub us for free?"

"How's that now?" Bitelas said. She did not like the Telchine's tone. There was too much mockery in it for her taste.

"We've come to take the bounty," the Telchine said. "Isn't that right, Mia?"

"We've papers," the girl said and drew out from under her jack, reluctantly it seemed, a scrap of parchment sealed in wax.

"Lemme see that," Clorinde said.

The girl handed it over. Clorinde squinted at the seal, and then her eyes widened.

"We should be more careful, girls," she said, holding up the parchment so they could see its stamp. "Could be saluting these two before too long."

"Oh?" the Telchine said. "How's that?"

"That's the Limper's seal," Bitelas explained. "He and the Lady go way back."

"That so?" the Telchine said. "Well, lucky for us then."

"How'd you come by it?" Bitelas asked, growing suspicious. "He gave up his command, what, five summers past? Heard he was living fat on a farm in Cockaigne."

"Heard right," the girl said. "We were coming up from Lucra when we come into some work for him."

"In Cockaigne?" Bitelas scoffed.

"Chimera hunt," the girl said. "Some livestock went missing. Wargs, they thought."

"Were they?" Moflete asked, her mouth agape.

"No," the Telchine snorted. "Just some wild dogs. *Volk*, they had us running through the brush though."

It sounded farfetched, Bitelas thought, but who knew? She had seen far stranger things in her days, and it explained the shabby state of their clothes at least.

"Must have impressed him," Bitelas said. "That or the Limper's getting soft in his old age."

"Wouldn't know," the girl said. "He turned us loose once the hunt was done."

"And now you want to serve the Baroness?"

"Heard it pays," the Telchine said. "And we're quick with our hands."

"How quick?" Clorinde asked.

"Quick as you like," the Telchine said, and poured a fresh cup.

Clorinde *smiled*.

Bitelas shook her head and chuckled. She could not remember the last time she has seen her crack so much as a grin.

This time it was Moflete who jabbed her in the ribs.

"What did you-" Bitelas said, and then she saw that Clorinde and Salomei had risen to their feet.

She turned herself and went rigid.

"Who's that?" the Telchine asked, pointing towards the somber man taking survey of the common room.

"Lord Marshal," Clorinde answered gruffly. "Put your *bloody* arm down."

The Telchine complied.

The Marshal took a brief survey of the room. His eyes had a way of lingering.

"As you were," he said finally, and took a seat beside the fire. One of Odette's girls was already bringing him a cup of the honey wine he was known to prefer.

Bitelas relaxed.

"You'll want to come to attention," Clorinde chided the Telchine, "Next time one of the captains comes round."

"Look at you blush," the Telchine teased. "He *must* be important."

"Marshal Galehaut's captain of the Steel Heels," Bitelas said. "He's *the* Steel Heel, if you take my meaning."

"Where are his spurs?" the Telchine smirked.

"Don't need 'em," Clorinde said, downing her ale. "He's a hard man."

"Has to be, don't he?" Bitelas nodded. "To keep his lot in line."

"How about another round?" the girl asked.

"Who's buying, girl?" Clorinde asked. "You?"

"That depends," the Telchine drawled. "Are we going to get another lecture about military discipline?"

Clorinde turned on the Telchine, her eyes hard, but the golden-skinned woman did not flinch.

"Naw," Clorinde said, a smile struggling to reform amidst the deep lines of her scowl. "Not tonight."

"Another jug here!" the Telchine called out. Odette obliged her.

"Wulf's fancy," the Telchine said, raising her cup.

"Wulf's fancy," they echoed.

They drank. The girl refilled their cups. The Telchine scooched closer to Clorinde while Salomei took out her pipe. Bitelas took a good swallow of the Poppy's dark ale. Odette brewed it herself, down in the undercroft like the mushroom farmers of Larsa.

"Good to have some girls with seasoning," Clorinde said, staring into the Telchine's eyes. "We're going to need more like you. Soon, I'll bet."

Moflete nodded.

"Any news of the rebel?" the girl asked.

"Oh," Bitelas raised an eyebrow. "It's 'the rebel' already, is it?"

The girl shrugged, sheepish.

"Gave 'em a bloody nose on Vireo," Clorinde said. "Lady will give 'em another- *If* they have the brass to swing back."

"You think they will?" the Telchine asked. "Have the brass?"

"Not if they know what's good for 'em," Clorinde said. "Oscans are a poncy lot, but they can fight. Keep those Frisians pinned long enough for the Lady to shove her mace up their ass."

"Where do you think they'd land?" the Telchine asked.

"Dunno," Moflete said.

"They just tell us where to march," Bitelas said.

"And when," Salomei added.

Bitelas chuckled and polished off her ale. The others did the same. The girl refilled their cups.

On their fourth round, Bitelas caught Moflete staring at the Lord Marshal. She did not blame her. Galehaut was easy on the eyes.

She nudged Moflete. "Keep dreaming, soldier."

Moflete sighed, tipsy. "Chief is finally giving him the night off."

"Chief?" the girl said, perking up. "You mean . . . Reynard?"

"*Lord* Reynard," Clorinde corrected.

"He's here then? In Carduel?"

Moflete nodded.

"What's he like?" the girl asked.

"What's he like?" Bitelas laughed. "Wulf, girl, you think we sit down to tea with him?"

The girl wet her lips. "You must know something."

"He saved my life," Bitelas said. "I know that much."

"Mine too," Salomei said, smoke curling from her nostrils.

The girl nodded, her lips thin.

"He frightens me," Moflete said.

"Really?" the girl asked.

"I mean," Moflete said, gulping from her cup. "He's the Fox, ain't he? Say he can't be killed. Say he can walk through walls. Sees *everything*. The future too, like Mehitabel. Knows what the enemy is going to do before they do it. And, well, him and the Lord Tiecelin, up in that tower with those shrikes . . . Makes my skin crawl just to think of it."

She took another long swallow, clearly aware of the way they were all staring at her.

"Lady scares me too sometimes," she finished. "If I'm being honest."

"Only proper," Clorinde said, rubbing at her bronze nose. "Natural even, a soldier afeared of her captain."

"It's Carduel that scares me," Bitelas admitted.

Even Clorinde drank to that. The Baroness was still in Nemea with the bulk of their forces, shoring up the coast. The Hatchet had been given the honor of accompanying the Lord Protector upriver, along with the Steel Heels and the Old Goat's flock. But the Tarsus men were encamped outside the city, which meant that defending the old fortress fell to the Lord Protector's soldiery.

Galehaut's men had the worst of it, taking two shifts for every three, and the Hatchet did her best to rotate the watches, but sooner or later it was their turn to walk the dark halls of Carduel.

"Dungeons must be frightening," the Telchine said, mockingly.

"Don't go down in the dungeons," Clorinde said.

"Whole place is a dungeon," Bitelas said. "If you ask me."

"You ever *see* anything?" the girl asked. "Anything unnatural, I mean."

"No," Bitelas lied. "No, but . . . I hear things. Scratching behind the walls."

"Rats," Clorinde said, stubborn as ever.

"Rats to your rats," Bitelas said. "I heard it, not you. Was too loud for rats."

"There's places too," Moflete said, "Whole rooms even, where it's cold as death even in high summer."

"Bah," Clorinde spat.

"Feel sorry for those little ones," Moflete said, glum.

"Watch that," Bitelas said, eyeing the strangers.

"Not saying nothing," Moflete said. "Chief's got his reasons. Must have. And they're rich snots. I know that. Still, they're just *children*. Must be scared out of their wits."

"Excuse her," Bitelas said, taking hold of Moflete's arm. "She's had too many."

"Hey," Moflete said, wrenching her arm free. "Leggo."

"We should go," Bitelas said. "We've all got drill in the morning."

"So soon?" the Telchine said. "You only just got here."

"We've drill in the morning," Bitelas repeated, trying to catch Clorinde's eye. "Early."

The Telchine leaned into Clorinde then, very close, and whispered something low.

Clorinde shot them a pleading look.

"I'll take her," Salomei said, getting to her feet.

Bitelas breathed a heavy sigh. Moflete whined a bit, but when Salomei took her shoulder, she did not fight it.

"Sharp watch," Bitelas said.

"You too," Salomei said and led Moflete out of the Poppy and into the night.

The Telchine had already helped Clorinde to her feet and was guiding her towards the stair at the back of the house. The two strangers must have already hired a room.

"What's your name?" Clorinde was asking.

"Cleo," the Telchine said.

"Cleo," Clorinde repeated, and took a playful swipe at her.

They disappeared up the stair.

Bitelas drained her cup and found the girl standing close beside her. She wondered where she fit into all this. Was she really the Telchine's comrade in arms or was she a bedwarmer wearing a blade. She was pretty for a sell-sword, hardly any scars. Still, she was fit as a whip. And she certainly didn't look jealous.

"Better make yourself comfortable," Bitelas said, reaching for the jug only to find it empty. "We could be here awhile."

The girl chewed her lip.

"What?" Bitelas spat.

"I'd like to check on my friend," the girl said. "He's out back. Only-"

"It's dark," Bitelas finished her thought. "And you want company."

"Yes," the girl said. "Yes, please."

"Well," Bitelas said. "Come on."

She followed the girl down a dark corridor, through an open door and into the alley that ran behind the Poppy. It was very cool, and there was naught but a sliver of moonlight to see by.

The girl did not wait for her and slipped into the night. She was remarkably quiet.

"Is he here?" Bitelas asked, not liking the way her voice echoed against the stones.

"Over here," the girl said.

Bitelas stepped from the door and felt herself swallowed by the night. She took a breath and tried not think of the eyeless thing she had glimpsed walking the sunken court.

Not real, silly girl. Trick of the light. Not real. Silly.

She crept forward, and then she could just make her out, a slender shadow deeper than the rest.

And something else. A great shape, larger than a man, slouched against the far wall.

She started. Then she had to stifle a laugh.

The giant. I'd almost forgotten.

"Is he alright?" she asked.

"He's not breathing," the girl said.

Bitelas drew closer. The girl was right. She couldn't hear anything.

"Is he dead?" the girl asked, worried now.

Bitelas bent down to listen.

* * * * * * *

Arsinoe dropped into the alley from the balcony above, having traded her skirts and leathers for the soldier's thick jack and pauldrons. The badge pinned to her breast bore the mailed fist of the Baroness.

"Any trouble?" Lara asked.

"No," Arsinoe said. "She let me tie her up."

"Oh."

"Yours didn't I take it," Arsinoe said, gesturing to the crumpled shape laid amongst the cordwood piled against the back of the tavern.

"No," Lara said, squirming in her own borrowed kit. The gambeson hung looser than she would have liked. It smelled sour too, like curdled milk.

"We don't have very long," Arsinoe said. "Sunrise at the latest."

"Then we'll need to be quick," Lara said, checking her straps. *"Dramsind, fiki."*

The giant stirred, planting one of his hands as he pushed himself up.

Lara was already slipping down the far end of the alley.

"Still say we should go in alone," Arsinoe said, falling in behind her.

"It won't work without him," Lara said, peering into the side street before making the turn into the plaza.

"What if they shoot us on sight?" Arsinoe asked.

"They won't," Lara said.

"Promise?"

"No," Lara said. "Now keep your head up and look occupied. We've got a rebel to catch."

VIII

The fortress loomed, sinister in the night. Like many an Aquilian work, it had been built of limestone blocks, stuccoed so as to seem a single piece, but its rooftops and crenelations were far older. Telchine queens had reigned here long before the day of kings and petty nobles. Its round-topped towers and crumbling battlements were lit from fires below, so that they seemed to glow, ghostly against the velvet sky.

There was fog on the river. It clung heavy about the hull of the Lord Protector's sloop and curled in the lamplight, its tendrils playing against the pilings of the dock.

The sound of oars broke the silence. A shape began to emerge from the murk.

The men guarding the river gate stiffened.

A boat was coming their way.

It was not very large, hardly even a skiff, but there were two figures hunkered amidst its thwarts. One at the oars, the other at the tiller.

"Who goes there?" the captain of the sentries called out. His voice did not carry very far in the fog.

A moment passed. The sentries loosened blade and leveled crossbow.

"Hold your fire!" a high voice called back. A woman's voice.

The captain raised his hand, *hold*.

The rower slowed her stroke. The figure at the tiller rose slightly, so that they could see the badge upon her breast. The men shifted atop the dock. Here were two of The Hatchet's company. Some of them began to loosen their grip on their bows.

But the captain did not lower his hand.

"This isn't your watch," he said. "What's your business?"

"We've a prisoner with us," the girl said. "A rebel."

The captain sucked at his teeth as the boat drew closer. He could see the woman at the tiller. She looked young for an officer.

"What rebel?" he asked.

"Caught him downriver," the woman said, giving the heap between her and the rower a shove with her boot. A low groan floated across the water. "Chief wanted him brought here. Gods know why."

"You got orders?"

The woman drew a script from under her belt and held it up. You could just make out its seal in the torchlight.

"Stand down," the captain grunted, turning to his second. He hardly needed to. The man was already making to throw one of the ropes coiled along the pier.

The boat slid close. The rower struck her oars and turned to catch the rope. Her face looked Luxian to the captain's eyes. Genovan even. Her skin glimmered.

"Get up," the woman at the tiller barked, taking hold of their prisoner by the back of his doublet and dragging him to his feet. He was an old rebel, it seemed, a lean graybeard with a bloodied lip. His hands were tied behind his back.

"Go on," she said, giving him a shove. "Move!"

He nearly tumbled out of the boat, but the captain caught him by the collar and half lifted half dragged him onto the pier. He collapsed at the captain's feet, coughing.

The woman at the tiller stepped out of the boat, nimbly. Her silent companion tossed a pack and a quiver onto the pier and then bent to retrieve a broad-headed glaive. The polearm was almost as long as their skiff.

"Get him on his feet," the woman said.

Like her companion, she wore no helm. She was quite pretty.

The captain caught the other men staring.

"Stop gawping," he grunted. "Get back to your posts."

The sentries obeyed. The woman's second gave the prisoner a shove with the butt of her spear.

"Let's see those orders," the captain said.

The woman nodded and extended her papers.

The captain took them, stepping nearer to one of the lamps so as to better make out the seal.

He held it up in the light. It wasn't a fox, a fist, or even a hatchet.

"Here," he heard his second say. "Your pack. Its moving."

"Wuh-" the captain managed before the blade opened his throat.

There was a splash as the man's second fell into the river. The pair of sentries near the sloop turned, bows nocked, but faltered as a great shape emerged from below the pier, planks splintering as its metal hands dragged its bulk up from below.

Their bolts ricocheted off its breastplate, and then the woman with the spear was on them, her broad-headed weapon slicing through fog and flesh.

The other woman tossed the prisoner something from the skiff: A bow. He caught it neatly, his hands suddenly free.

The men at the gate were still debating whether to stand, run, or call for help when the old man put an arrow through one of their eyes. The other managed a solitary shout before the woman at the tiller closed the distance between them. She cut as she drew.

The figures on the dock held still for a moment, listening.

There was no hue or cry.

Lara peered upward, wondering if they might be seen by some guard walking the parapets above, but she doubted it. Both city and cliff were awash in mist.

"I count eight," Scyron said, planting his boot as he freed arrow from socket.

Lara nodded, wiping her own blade as she examined the dead men's faces. They looked far younger than their captain.

Fresh recruits perhaps, untested until now.

"You think anyone's aboard?" Arsinoe said, nodding towards the sloop.

Lara scanned the deck. Nothing stirred, save the ropes creaking against their rings.

"No," Lara said. "Or I think we would know it by now."

"Still tempted to cut her loose," Arsinoe said, eyeing the moorings.

They had discussed the possibility, but Lara had reasoned that the sight of the usurper's flagship drifting downriver would raise enough eyebrows to have the alarm sounded.

Besides, Lara mused, *the anchor must be sunk deep in the riverbed.*

The gate was set deep into the face of the rock, its doors sealed behind a portcullis. A pair of pale women flanked the entrance, carved from the solid rock. Shrouds clung to their faces, and on their brows garlands had been set with flowers that shone like ivory.

"*Dramsind,*" Arsinoe said, gesturing towards the passage. "*Nelete.*"

"*Wopa,*" Dramsind's voice crackled. He stooped somewhat as his arms extended.

He took hold of the gate and lifted. Chains jangled and metal squealed.

The way lay open. There was no light within the passage beyond.

"I do not like this place," Scyron said, staring at the face of one of the statues. "It reminds me . . ."

Here he trailed off and was silent as the river worried against the dock.

"Yes?" Arsinoe prompted.

"Never mind," he said, and tugged at the clasp of his cloak.

"Well," Arsinoe said, throwing Lara a wink. "We have seen deeper and darker places than this. Haven't we?"

Yet she too lingered on the threshold.

Lara grabbed one of the lamps hanging from the bollards and pushed forward. Bannertail trailed after her heels, his tail limp.

The others followed, weapons ready. Arsinoe whispered the command and Dramsind let down the gate. It rang as it settled against the stone.

The passage was not natural. The stones had been worked, and there were tiles underfoot. They were damp, almost slick, and the air tasted stale to breathe.

"No wheel," Scyron said, glancing about.

"What's that?" Lara said.

"For the gate."

"Must be somewhere above," Arsinoe said, staring at the solid rock over their heads.

"Come on," Lara said, patting her leg.

Bannertail clambered onto her shoulder.

Lara went first with Scyron close beside her, arrow nocked against string. Dramsind slunk behind them, his head bent low. Arsinoe brought up the rear, glancing back every few paces.

Their pace was slow. Lara had expected to find guard chambers, or storerooms brimming with supplies for the usurper's ship, not this lonely tunnel. The lamplight picked out dim shapes amidst the stonework: Stag riders rode in relief after a great cat, its hide pierced by arrows. Nudes strained against each other, in strife or passion. A regal figure held a spool of thread between supple fingers. In her other hand were shears, poised to cut.

Then the passage opened onto the landing of a wide stairwell, its steps cracked and worn. The left-hand stair stretched upwards towards a solid wall of rock. The one on their right plunged into a flooded shaft, so that its third step lay submerged beneath dark water. Mollusks in spiral shells clung about its lip.

There were sconces set along the stair, but no torches.

"Hah," Arsinoe breathed at the sight of the pool beneath. It was little more than a gasp, but it echoed down the passage far behind them.

Bannertail leapt down to sniff at the mollusks.

"How deep do you think?" Scyron said, peering into the water.

"Deep," Arsinoe answered. "But we want to go up, not down."

Lara skirted to the left and climbed the stairs, casting about with her lamp as she went and hoping to find the outline of a door amidst the stonework.

There was none. At least, none that she could see.

"Check the walls," Lara said. "There's probably a door here, hidden."

Scyron kept a firm grip on his notched arrow as he gave the walls about the entrance a few taps with the tip of his boot. Arsinoe did the same with the end of her spear, moving gradually up the stair.

Their taps carried far. Lara raised her lamp and peered upwards, but she could not see the ceiling of the chamber.

"Here," Arsinoe said at last, rapping at a section of wall halfway up the steps. "The stonework is newer."

"How can you tell?" Lara asked.

Arsinoe did not answer but gave the wall another rap. She was right. Her knocks sounded lighter somehow.

Lara joined Arsinoe and peered at the stonework. Still, she could not see any seams.

"Dramsind could break through," Arsinoe suggested.

The giant shifted at the mention of his name, but Lara shook her head.

"We've made enough noise as it is," she said. "And . . . Well, there must be a latch or catch *somewhere*."

Lara began pressing at the stones. Arsinoe took a step back, planting her spear.

A sharp *crack* echoed through the chamber. Lara turned, heart beating, but it was only Bannertail chewing on one of the mollusks.

Scyron was half bent over the lip of the landing, his eyes intent on the water.

"That sconce," Arsinoe muttered. "See if it moves."

Lara turned. Arsinoe was pressed against the wall, pointing towards a mounting just out of her reach. It did not look any different than the rest.

Lara climbed up the steps, took hold of the sconce, and twisted. Sure enough it gave under the slightest pressure, swiveling neatly to the right. Something clicked, and Arsinoe drove her shoulder into the stonework.

Silently, the wall swung open. Arsinoe stepped back and let Lara shine her lamp into the gloom.

It looked like the inside of a wardrobe to her at first, for the walls were lined with cloaks and boots. Then she could see the corridor stretching beyond them, and a second set of stairs.

"What's all this?" Arsinoe said, prodding one of the boots. They were mud-caked and cracked from age, and yet the pair standing next to them were of drake-skin. In Trimount they would have fetched a hefty purse of talents.

"They must be his," Lara said, running her fingers along the hem of the nearest cloak. "Disguises, maybe."

"I wonder if these would fit me," Arsinoe said, setting her foot next to a tall pair of jackboots.

"Later," Lara said, turning back to the others.

Scyron had backed away from the water's edge but was still staring at it, as if entranced. Bannertail was too, and his tail was twitching.

"What is it?" Lara asked.

"I saw," Scyron said. "Or, I thought I saw-"

"What?"

"I don't know," he said. "Something in the water."

"You're imagining things old man," Arsinoe said. *"Dramsind, fiki."*

As the giant took his first steps up the stairway, the water *lapped*. Ripples ran across its face.

Bannertail shot past Dramsind. Scyron reached for an arrow, then thought the better of it and hustled past the giant as well. There was a splash, and for a moment Lara thought she could make out a shape beneath the surface, pale against the dark stones.

She and Arsinoe backed into the corridor. Scyron put himself between them and the secret door. Dramsind bent low, his arms and legs shortening by degrees until he could squeeze through the gap.

Behind him, in the stairwell, something wet slapped against the stones.

Lara fretted at the wall, her fingers hunting amidst the cloaks for a second catch.

"Dramsind," Arsinoe said, her voice shaking. *"Bulumu bowata!"*

The giant struggled to turn about in the narrow corridor. From behind him a rumble poured and burbled from some alien throat.

"Now!" Arsinoe barked, backing further away.

Dramsind shoved forward, snapping cloak hooks from their housings, and bent his left arm backwards, his fingers reversing to catch hold of the edge of the false wall.

With a turn of his wrist, he threw shut the door. The boom ran down the corridor.

Bannertail emerged from one of the boots, and then ducked back low as something heavy smacked against the wall. Whatever lay beyond pawed for a time, and then slid free.

They stood in silence, listening.

"My *imagination*," Scyron muttered, shooting Arsinoe a sour look.

"What was that thing?" Lara asked in a low whisper. "Chimera?"

"Didn't sound like one I'd ever heard," Arsinoe whispered back, giving ground as Lara shoved past the last of the usurper's cloaks. "Can't say I'm thrilled about coming back this way either."

"Let's see where these stairs go," Lara said, but this time she let Arsinoe lead them, her spear point ready to strike as they climbed.

The stair was long and narrow. There were no carvings either, just a long run of smooth cut stone.

"Should have brought another lamp," Scyron said as the stair took a sharp turn. "It's dark as Hiva."

They turned round a bend and then another. Lara had the impression that this stair wound its way round the shaft of the old stairwell below.

At last, they reached a door. Or, at least, the outline of one.

Arsinoe rolled her neck atop her shoulders before shooting Lara a questioning look.

"Quietly," Lara said.

The Telchine nodded, steadied her heels against the last step, and gave the door a push.

A chill breeze rushed into the tight confines of the stairway as the door slid forward on hidden hinges. A large chamber lay beyond, its high ceiling supported by pillars. Urns ringed the walls, the flowers within wilted to dust and stalk.

Directly before them a sort of stone table stood, if table was the right word. It had been fashioned out of pale marble, and to Lara it looked like a block atop of which a statue lay as if in sleep: A maiden in flowing gown with a diadem atop her marble brow.

"What is it?" Lara asked, stepping from the door.

"You have no word for it," Arsinoe said. "Ours is *Taphos*. A place for the dead to rest."

"You mean," Lara said, "There's a body under there?"

"An old one, I imagine."

"Whose?" Lara asked.

"Someone important," Arsinoe said, casting her gaze towards the far side of the chamber. "I think there's an archway over here."

Lara nodded, but she could not help but step closer to the block. Bold letters had been carved across its face, but they were of the old tongue, of which she only knew a few common words.

"I cannot read them," Lara said.

"I can," Scyron said and did so.

HERE IS LAID
ANESIDORA
OF THE LINE OF CLYMENE
THIRD OF HER NAME
QUEEN

"What are these words here?" Lara asked of the lines that ran along the rim of the *taphos*.

"Cursed be those who disturb her rest," Scyron recited, tracing the lines as they wound about a seal of soft lead. "Toothless will they be, tongueless, eyeless-"

"That's enough," Lara said.

Scyron nodded and moved to cover the far arch with his bow.

Lara lingered, shooing Bannertail as he sniffed at the edges of the block. The queen's resting place looked undisturbed, its seal unbroken.

It seemed even the usurper feared a curse.

She turned from the *taphos* and brought her lamp to bear on the passage beyond the arch. It stretched deeper into the dark. Along the walls shelves had been carved, but there was nothing within them save a sort of chalky powder.

Eventually they came to a junction. Each way looked the same to Lara's eyes. Arsinoe took a few steps, sniffing at the air, and then gestured towards the middle way.

"Fresher," she said.

This way met another junction, and another, and then they came upon a short stair guarded by a pair of stone watchdogs. One had lost its head, which lay grimacing before the steps under a film of white mold.

Bannertail burred and squalled at the severed head. Lara picked him up and set him on her shoulder.

They climbed.

The stair bent back on itself and deposited them in a place much like the passages below. Only here the corridors were tighter, and the alcoves along the walls were full of bones. They were stacked atop each other, each niche often stuffed to the brim with brown ribs and femurs.

"So many," Lara said, glancing at the sheer number of skulls that lay within one of the alcoves.

"It looks like they threw lime on them," Arsinoe said, doing her best to keep her distance. "Plague, do you think?"

"The Red Death," Scyron said, nodding. "There was an outbreak in the year of the Lion. There must have been too many to burn."

"And no place else to put them," Lara said.

Dramsind's right arm disturbed one of the piles as he swung past. Bones spilled across the corridor, rattling down the tight hall.

"Volk," Arsinoe swore.

Scyron kissed his thumb and pressed it to his scalp.

The way went on, but now it was harder to tell which way they should take. The first turn they took led them down a dead end, where a stone chest lay broken. They retraced their steps and seemed to be making progress until they came to a place where the floor had failed entirely, the burial place seeming to have tumbled into some deep natural cavern.

"I can't see the other side," Lara said, resisting the urge to kick one of the loose rocks over the edge of the gap. "Can you?"

Arsinoe stepped aside to give Scyron a better look. The old man shook his head.

They turned back, coming almost all the way to the stair before making another turn. Lara had lost all sense of direction by now, and wondered if they were heading deeper into the rock or back towards the river face.

They passed two more side corridors and came to a stretch of the vault free of the hastily interred dead. Then Lara quickened her pace.

She could see a patch of light ahead. It shone like sunlight in the darkness.

"Careful," Arsinoe whispered as they approached. "There could be guards."

They reached an intersection. The light, torchlight she guessed by the way it flickered, was streaming from a wide passage to their right. Beyond it the corridor continued to stretch, into the dark.

Lara pressed herself close to the wall, and carefully peered into the passage. It was not very long, maybe fifty feet before it met a bound iron door flanked by burning torches. There were no sentries to be seen, but the statuary that lined its walls gave her pause.

They had all been fashioned to resemble particularly ferocious chimera. Some were a marriage of cat and serpent, others had multiple heads: Goat, wolf, and bird of prey snarled atop clawed forelegs, their necks reared to strike.

The path between them was paved with stones, each about the size of a foot. It was difficult to tell in the light, but some appeared to be more well-used than others.

"Look at the floor," Lara said, moving aside.

They looked. Scyron grunted deep in the back of his throat.

"What do you think," Arsinoe said. "Poison gas? A pit full of spikes?"

"Or darts from their eyes," Lara said.

"Right," Arsinoe said. "But how does *he* get past?"

"He knows the stones," Lara reasoned. "That, or there's a switch on the other side."

Arsinoe sighed. Bannertail switched from Lara's right shoulder to her left, questing with his nose.

"What if we sent the giant?" Scyron said, peering backwards.

"No," Lara said, brushing at the back of her hair. "What if a block comes flying out of the wall and crushes him? Or the whole passage collapses?"

"Thank you," Arsinoe said.

"Let me get a little closer," Scyron said, beginning to pad towards the first flagstone. "There could be a way to-"

The fox-squirrel leapt from Lara's shoulder.

"Hey, wait!" she blurted, trying to catch hold of him.

She wasn't nearly fast enough. But the chimera did not race down the passage. Rather, he bounded straight past it and shot into the darkness of the corridor beyond.

"Don't move," Lara whispered to the others, and made after the chimera, her eyes scanning the floor ahead for hazards as she padded alongside the wall.

She did not have to go far. The fox-squirrel had come to a stop not thirty feet from the junction and was nosing at some shriveled thing laying amid the dust.

"Shoo," Lara said, bending down to examine it.

It was an apple core, brown and withered.

She picked it up. It couldn't be more than a day old.

Bannertail looked up at her, sullen, and then continued to sniff his way further down the corridor.

"Huh," Lara said, tossing the piece of fruit aside.

"What was that?" Arsinoe called down the corridor.

"Someone's pack lunch," Lara said. "Come on, I think he might be onto something."

They followed Bannertail to another split in the corridor, and then down a long gallery with decorations of a martial bent. The peeling frescos on the walls displayed ranks of clashing pikemen, their captains hurrying into the fray from atop white elk, and from the walls shields and helmets of bronze were hung, their luster long since turned to verdigris.

Arsinoe flexed her free hand at the sight, a sigh upon her lips.

Then the gallery came to an end. The decaying remains of some dead warrior's panoply had been set there, some sort of shrine it seemed, untended since the days of King Leander.

"A blind alley," Scyron said.

"I wonder," Lara said, watching as Bannertail paced about the foot of the wall.

The fox-squirrel stopped to sniff at the far-right corner, and then scratched at the stonework.

Lara approached herself and, as she drew closer, she noticed how large the seams were between the mortar of the far wall and the gallery.

"Hold this," she said, passing her lantern back to Arsinoe. Then she stripped off her right glove and pressed closer to the gap, feeling for air.

Her pressure against the wall was enough to send the whole thing gliding smoothly backwards, practically silent. She gave it another shove and could see the greased track it had been set into.

"Together," Lara said, waving Arsinoe forward.

They pushed, Bannertail dodging about their heels. The gallery stretched another ten feet, and then the whole false wall rolled into a low-ceilinged chamber, pillared like the *taphos* below.

Another half-eaten apple lay beside one of the pillars. This one was fresher.

Lara let Bannertail nibble at it before he lost interest.

"Let's put it back in place," Lara said as Scyron and Dramsind came into the chamber, the giant slowing his step as his head began to swivel. "Might as well try to cover our tracks."

But there was no need. As soon as they let go of the wall it began to slide back into the gallery. Lara wondered if the floor was more slanted than it looked.

"Where now?" Arsinoe said, eyeing the apple herself. "I think we've come round the traps, so we must be getting closer . . . Closer to what, though, I can't say."

"Let's follow this hall for now," Lara said. "And keep your guard up."

Arsinoe handed Lara the lamp and gave her arm a pat. Scyron took point.

They moved between the pillars, Lara wincing at the sound of their footsteps echoing off the ceiling. And yet, it was quieter than she might have expected.

She turned. Dramsind was still standing by the track, his head slowly turning.

"Dramsind," she whispered. *"Fiki."*

He hesitated, but then shook to life. And yet his step was slow. *What's bothering him?* Lara wondered. *He can't be hungry.*

"Highness," Scyron hissed. "Look there."

Lara turned back to see that they had come to another archway. This one was warded by a set of iron bars, held fast by a padlock. Beyond it there appeared to be a large, unlit chamber. It reminded her of the prison she had seen beneath The Dragon's palace.

"That lock looks new," Scyron said as they approached.

Lara examined it herself. There was filigree carved into its face.

"Calvarian," Lara said. "It's bound to be complex."

"This is the right way then," Arsinoe said.

Lara nodded.

"Well," Arsinoe said. "Let's not waste time. *Dramsind, jalaju sawena.*"

She tapped at the lock with the point of her spear and then stepped aside. Lara bent down to catch up Bannertail. But Dramsind did not obey. He had come to a halt some ten paces behind them. His arms had gone limp.

"Dramsind," Arsinoe said, more clearly. *"Fiki."*

Dramsind was still.

"This again," Arsinoe said.

Lara searched the outline of the arch, but she could see nothing unusual about the stonework.

"Is it the lock?" she wondered aloud.

"I don't know," Arsinoe said, her beetle squirming as her brows knit with concern. *"Dramsind, motaju?"*

"Motaju wipoba," his voice issued, crackling softly.

Arsinoe took a step away from the gate, eyeing the dark chamber beyond.

"What is it?" Scyron asked.

"Don't know," Arsinoe said. "But *something's* spooked him."

"Powder?" Lara said. "He wouldn't go near that cannon."

Arsinoe shook her head. "I've seen kegs go off right beside him without him so much as flinching."

"Something about the metal, maybe," Lara said, drawing closer to the bars. She took a breath and patted at them.

No cry went up. No trap was sprung. The bars seemed normal. She gave the lock a tug. It was strong, but seemingly just a lock.

"Hydra's Teeth," she sighed.

"I can try picking it, Highness," Scyron said, laying aside bow and arrow.

Lara nodded, moving aside as he unfastened his cloak so that he might use the pin as a pick. He bent down to work, his gnarled hands steady as he tested the tumblers with his pin.

"Might take a while," he said, frowning at each click and snap.

Lara kept the lamp level.

As Scyron worked, Arsinoe did her best to coax Dramsind forward, using words and commands she had apparently kept to herself over the past three years. Still the hollow man stood, a dim flicker of his inner fire pulsing about his upper joints.

After a while, Bannertail left Lara's shoulders to roost atop the giant's. But he too seemed to sense Dramsind's distress and, when he could not settle, he licked at his helm, whining.

Click went the lock at last. Scyron snapped it open.

His pin was so bent that he tossed both it and the lock onto his puddled cloak.

"Dramsind," Lara called back. *"Fepasa. Bolapo."*

"Buse," he replied, his head slowly swiveling towards the hall behind.

Lara clicked her tongue at the fox-squirrel on his shoulder, but Bannertail refused to abandon him.

"Alright," Lara said, and gave the bars a push.

The gate swung inwards with a faint squeal.

"Let me go first," Arsinoe said, girding her spear as she slipped through the gate.

Lara went next, with Scyron following close behind.

The chamber was very large, its ceiling so tall that the lamplight could not reach it, and for a time all that Lara could make out was the mosaic on the floor. It looked brilliant to her eyes after the gloom of the tunnels, its tiles of azure and scarlet looping in geometric patterns like some great Irkallan carpet.

As they advanced, Lara noticed something else. The air was dry. Almost metallic.

She wet her lips as Arsinoe came to a halt.

"I hear something," she whispered.

Lara listened, but all she could hear was Scyron breathing behind her in the dark.

"What is it?" Lara whispered back.

"I don't know," Arsinoe said, "Something . . . Humming? Like an insect. I can't hear it anymore."

Lara turned back. She had lost sight of the gate.

"Let's head back," she said. "I don't want to get lost."

"It's a bit late for that," a voice called out from the shadows.

There was a sudden blast of noise and heat. The chamber filled with light.

She dropped the lamp as she drew, dazed. Glass shattered as footfalls echoed all about her. A metallic *clang* ran throughout the chamber, loud enough to set her ears to ringing.

Her eyes began to adjust.

The chamber they stood in shone bright, its walls an artificial forest of gold and copper. Its domed ceiling glittered with gems hung like the summer constellations. Metallic blooms and lacquered flowers sprung from vase and urn.

Behind them a second gate, this one of reinforced steel, had fallen into place.

A gallery overlooked the chamber. A score of archers stood arrayed along its length, and behind them lamps blazing with an unnatural brilliance. A second company had poured from archways to their right and left, Steel Heels with sword and pike. Even now they were closing the ring about them.

A stairway stretched towards the gallery. At its head stood Tiecelin, the shrike-tamer, an arrow fitted to his string. The archers were his.

And there, beside him, the usurper stood.

"Take them," Reynard said.

Scyron did not hesitate and let his own arrow fly. It struck the usurper clear in the chest, just below his heart, but it seemed to catch in whatever mail he wore beneath his doublet.

Reynard pulled the missile free and tossed it aside.

The Steel Heels surged forward. Arsinoe met them, her spear a blur as she weaved.

Lara rushed the stair, only to find a red-haired Calvarian standing in her path.

He was quick. She was quicker.

Bows twanged. She heard Scyron let out a cry and spared a look backwards as the Calvarian lurched against the balustrade, his hand pressed to the cut she had given him. The old captain was sitting on the floor, a shaft in his thigh. Tiecelin's had gone straight through the palm of his good hand.

Then Reynard loomed up before her, his longsword drawn.

"Majesty," he said, parrying her first cut.

His riposte sent her staggering backwards.

She was still recovering when he came at her again, very fast. Their blades met, a flurry of steel as she tried to gain more ground.

Her heels caught on something laying on the floor behind her. A body. One of the Steel Heels, she hoped.

Reynard lunged at her then, a smile on his lips as she fell.

She gasped as her head cracked against the tiles.

Then his blade was at her breast.

"Don't move," he said, softly. "My right-hand is very sharp."

"Lara!" Arsinoe cried out. She was turning from her own fight when one of the Steel Heels drove the butt of his pike into the small of her back. She fell, tumbling amongst the half dozen men she had downed before the rest descended upon her, beating at her until she lay still.

"No!" Lara cried, gritting her teeth as the usurper's blade nicked her. *"Dramsind! DRAMSIND, MOTOTO!"*

"I said don't-" Reynard began to snap at her, but she cast his blade aside with her free hand and slashed at his face. Her blade glanced off his false arm, but his eyes widened with surprise as he backed away.

She leapt onto her feet. Her head seemed clear enough.

"Dramsind!" she began to shout again when the gate shuddered.

"Ah," Reynard said, taking another step backwards.

The gate shook again as something heavy struck it with enough force to set its rivets clinging across the floor. The Steel Heels gave ground. The archers above retrained the bows.

Then the gate exploded inwards, along with the better part of the stonework about it. From out of the clouds of dust Dramsind emerged, boiling with unchecked rage. At the sight of Arsinoe, and the foes about her, the swarm within him grew to a fevered pitch.

He plowed forward, throwing two of the Steel Heels aside with a dreadful sweep of his arm. As the men flew from him, he caught one by the arm and smote him against the gilded wall. The man barely had time to scream.

"Now!" a voice rang out from the gallery.

There were grunts of exertion and then something whistled through the air. Dramsind's arm shot up to catch it, but it seemed to dance as it flew, and met his chest with a resounding *clunk* and clung there. It looked like a plate to Lara, or one of the disks the Frisians threw for sport.

More of the things whirled towards the giant. He took a step backwards, but they seemed drawn to him somehow, like lodestone to metal.

It *was* lodestone, Lara realized. He took another two to the chest, one to the back of his hand, and fourth straight against his head.

Dramsind wobbled, burbling as his left hand searched the air for support. The swarm within him crackled madly. His right arm went limp, and then he fell straight towards the wall.

When he hit it, he came apart.

His breast split into three separate pieces. His limbs shattered into joints and sinews. His head rolled free. Something within it flashed briefly, and then went out.

There was nothing else inside of him.

Lara was too stunned to cry out.

"Surrender," Reynard said. "Or shall I kill another of your servants? This pirate, perhaps."

He nodded towards Scyron. The old man was bleeding badly.

Lara dropped her sword.

"I thought so," Reynard said, and waved the Steel Heels forward.

She felt her arms being bound behind her back. One of the Steel Heels had caught hold of Bannertail by his scruff and was stuffing him into a sack.

Reynard took hold of her chin then and turned it towards his tin-flecked gaze.

"Welcome home, Lara," he said. "Welcome home."

IX

The rooms of Lara's confinement were very fine. Thin doors separated them, but none were locked. It had taken her some time to discover them all, and even longer to walk them. And even then, when she retraced her steps, she found that she had missed some.

There was a bedchamber, of course. Its bay windows looked west across court, gate, and city, and from them she could tell that she had been put somewhere too high for comfort. Only the tower of the shrikes climbed higher and most of its occupants had the luxury of wings.

Beyond this chamber there was a sitting room of sorts (*parlor* they had called it in Frisia) and off it a snug place whose walls were lined with books. Through one of the thicker doors there was a wardrobe. She called it that, at least, because it was a place of cabinets overladen with high-waisted gowns, silk bodices and, in neat rows atop marble shelves, a whole host of gloves. Luxian hoods and fine linen coifs there were, and pelts of sable, and necklaces of pearl and silver. One nook was full of nothing but shoes. They looked so delicate that Lara guessed they would fall apart if one actually wore them to market.

Some of the drapery hid doors or archways. One in the parlor led to a balcony creeping with ivy. Another, in the hall between bedchamber and wardrobe, led to a privy. Lara wondered how deep the shaft beneath its seat ran, and where it emptied out.

Last, there was a long hall, a dining chamber by its shape. Table, chairs, and cabinets hid now beneath white sheets, and its candelabras were thick with cobwebs. The walls had been done in fresco, but the figures on them had faded to lines and curves that merely suggested riders within a faded wood. If kings or queens they had been, she could not say.

At the end of this lonely hall there were a set of wide doors. They stood wide open, but standing beside them were two of the Graycloaks. They seemed not to look at Lara as she peered at them from across the hall, but she knew better than to think them lazy.

There were more sentries in the hallway beyond, Steel Heels by their dress. She might have chanced a run for it, but where would she go? She was exhausted, they had taken her blades, and she did not know where her friends were kept.

She did not know if they were even alive.

That, more than anything, had gnawed at her as she had been *escorted* to her chambers by the Steel Heels. She could hardly remember her ascent now, all climbing stairs and torch lit passages, and a cold court open to the night sky. There had been food laid out for her, but she could not eat it. She had thought she could not sleep either, until she had laid down on one of the couches beside the windows and shut her eyes.

She woke to find Bannertail resting against the hollow of her stomach. For a moment she forgot where she was, and gently stroked the fox-squirrel's gray fur. He did not start at her touch, but yawned hugely, his tail twitching.

Then, in the dim light peeking through the windows, she saw the clothing laid out on the bed opposite her. A fresh chemise, bodice, and breeches, much like her own. Her own boots stood beside the door.

They had been polished.

Drugged, she thought, rising with a start. But no, she had not touched food or drink since she had set foot inside these chambers. But how? Only someone quiet could have-

She shuddered. Had he watched her sleep?

Bannertail rose, stretched his back, and settled atop the patch of couch she had warmed for him.

"Prisoners again, old man," she whispered.

She eyed the fruit laid atop the tray beside her bed. The fox-squirrel had been at one of the apples, but that was all.

She plucked one of the pears from the table and sniffed at it.

Her stomach rumbled. She took a bite. When she failed to pass out, she continued, staring at the shrikes taking flight from the tower.

News of my capture, she guessed. She wondered how long it would be before Roland learned she had been taken.

Footsteps in the hall. She cast the pear aside and balled up her fists.

There was a gentle knock at the door.

"Your Highness," a woman's voice called out, softly. "Your bath is nearly ready. May I come in?"

Lara smirked at the pretense but lowered her guard.

"Enter," she said.

The door swung open to admit a slender priestess in a dark gown. She blinked at Lara, curtsied neatly, and then went to draw the curtains.

"You should strip off those filthy clothes, Highness," the woman said. "To think you *slept* in them."

"I've been sleeping in them," Lara said. "For months."

The priestess huffed, shaking her head.

"I'll need a finer comb next time," the woman said. "And a sulfur treatment perhaps. But come now, Highness, strip."

Lara had grown used to the forwardness of priestesses. There were so many on Beria that the men of Jerrais called that island *The Baths*, among other things. Still, though, Lara shied as the woman came to help her disrobe.

"You do not remember me, Highness," the woman said, stepping back. "Do you?"

"No," Lara said.

"I have bathed you before, Highness. Bathed you, combed your hair, and for a season I taught you steps. I was meant to-"

She stopped, her lips drawing thin.

"Madam Precieuse I was called," the woman said. "A long time ago it seems to me now, and yet- I had thought you might remember."

"No," Lara said. "No, I am sorry."

"Well," the priestess said. "Whether you know me or not, I am still a priestess, and I swear that I will do you no harm. And, if you wish, I *will* leave you be. But-"

She leaned closer. Her eyes were green as gemstones.

"Know that I do this for your own comfort, Highness," she said. "Not his."

Lara nodded and let the priestess help slip off her jack. The woman's nose curdled as she tossed it aside, and then went to retrieve a robe from one of the dressers. Lara peeled off shirt, breeches, and hose, and threw on the robe.

"This way," the priestess said, gathering up her new garments and gesturing towards the door.

Lara bent to retrieve her boots and stepped into the hall. It was very dim.

"Leave the door open a crack," Lara said. "For my chimera."

"As you wish," the priestess said, but Bannertail did not follow.

She led Lara down the hall and into the parlor. One of the larger carpets had been removed, and in its place a bronze tub sat, steaming. It looked old, having gone almost entirely to patina.

"My brother," Lara said then. "Is he alive?"

The woman did not speak, but she nodded.

"Where is he?" Lara asked.

"Your bath is getting cold, Highness," the woman said, stiff.

Lara set down her boots, slipped off her robe, stepped into the bath and sat, pulling her legs up to her chest.

"You are shy," the priestess said, observationally.

"I usually bathe myself," Lara answered.

"I understand, Highness," the woman said, handing her a scrub brush. "But I should like to take a proper look at you, once you are clean."

Lara nodded, taking the brush.

She scrubbed, dunking her head beneath the water for good measure. The priestess offered her a bar of soap. It smelled like wildflowers.

"How did you get this?" the priestess asked gesturing towards the scar running about her wrist.

"A slime," Lara said. "I had a bowl of its venom in my hand and-"

She mimed the way she had spilled it.

"Does it bother you?"

"Sometimes," Lara nodded.

"I'll see what I can do," the woman said, continuing to look her over. "You are very bruised."

"The usurper's soldiers aren't very gentle," Lara said.

"But nothing broken," the woman went on, unfazed. "May I inspect your scalp?"

Lara shrugged.

The woman ran her fingers through her hair, parting the curls one by one. She was very thorough.

"No lice, Highness," she concluded. "Though your hair is a mess."

"I cut it."

"I believe you, Highness," the woman said, reaching for a leather kit. "Would you allow me to trim it?"

"I suppose so," Lara said.

"Lie back then," the woman said, "And try to keep still."

Lara complied.

"It has been some time since I've cut a woman's hair. I tend to the children's, of course, but-"

"The children?" Lara asked.

"Yes," the priestess said, growing silent again.

Lara let her gaze wander as the woman worked, eventually settling on the view through the windows. They faced south, and through them she could make out the rays of the Firebird streaming through thin wisps of cloud.

Something caught her eye then, through one of the far panes of glass. There, standing perhaps on the balcony she had discovered, a shape, very still. A woman perhaps, for it was slight, and its hair fell in long dark tresses. Or was it a statue? She had seen none the night before.

The shape moved then, drifting across the balcony before passing out of sight.

"Who's that?" Lara asked, tucking her legs in tight.

"Who is what?" the priestess asked, distracted.

"The woman," Lara said. "Outside the window."

The priestess's scissors went still. Lara could hear her take a deep breath.

"There is no one else up here, Highness," the priestess said, her voice grown stiff. "No one but you and I."

"I saw-"

"And the guards, of course," the priestess added. Then her fingers went back to work, the snip of her scissors filling the silence.

A guard, Lara told herself. *One of the guards.*

When she was done, the priestess presented Lara with a hand mirror. The woman had turned her mop of hair into a neat crop, almost as severe as Moder's had been.

Lara liked it, though she doubted Bannertail would.

The priestess laid down her scissors and helped her to dress. The new clothes fit her perfectly. Loose enough to fight in, yet snug in the right places.

She pulled on her boots, grunting.

"Seawater's very hard on leather."

Reynard was leaning against the room's hearth, his false hand resting atop the mantle. Her eyes flicked towards the door to the outer hall, but it was closed.

It was as if he had stepped straight through one of the walls.

"My bootblack did his best," he went on. "But I can send for new ones if you like."

Lara sprang up and snatched up the priestess' scissors.

"What do you want?!" she asked, tightening her grip on the shears as she backed towards the nearest door.

"Only to speak with you," he said, seeming to smirk at the sight of her makeshift dagger. "Before I die."

Lara laid down the scissors.

"Is she unharmed?" he addressed the priestess.

"In body," the priestess said. "Yes."

"Good," he said. "Leave us."

The woman made no obeisance but gathered up her kit and hurried through the door to the long hall.

He moved to the edge of the tub, peering at the cloudy water within. She moved to keep it between them.

"Arsinoe," Lara said. "Scyron. Are they-"

"Quite alive," he said. "Though the Frisian is proving difficult. My *fisiciens* are trying to save his hand, but he's so stubborn that he keeps trying to escape."

He chuckled.

"Reminds me of a sellsword I used to know," he said. "He was a good man. Deserved better."

"So does Scyron," Lara said.

"Does he?" Reynard asked, arching his eyebrows. "He has killed many of my servants."

"So have I."

"Yes," Reynard said. "But he is not a Queen. Is he?"

He moved about the tub. She backed away.

"Nor is your Telchine," he went on. "But she at least has not harmed any of Tiecelin's children. He may be more inclined to spare her for that."

She found that the wall was at her back.

"I like your hair," he said, reaching out. "It suits you somehow."

"Don't bloody touch me," she said.

"Of course," he said, backing off. "Still, I envy you. Gabrielle has not touched a lock of my own since your brother died."

She found her breath.

"And Pinsard?" she said. "Is he safe?"

"Safe," he said, seeming to consider the word. "In a sense, yes, he is *safe*."

"Where is he?" she asked. "What have you-"

"Walk with me," he said. "And I will show you."

He moved then to the far door and turned back to face her.

"Well?" he said.

He was dressed plainly. Gray coat, tawny jerkin. He wore no mail that she could see.

Nor did he wear the sword that had slain her *moder*.

She looked back, towards the small hall, half expecting Bannertail to come yipping through the cracked door, his tail whipping.

Then she followed.

They passed through the long hall. A pair of Calvarians, both men and all in white, waited there with mop and bucket. They bowed their heads as Reynard strode past them, and then straightened.

Are all his servants Calvarians? she mused.

They walked through the archway, a quartet of Graycloaks falling into step behind them, and entered a hall that made her own chambers look quaint. It tapered somewhat, drawing the eye towards the circular stairwell at its end, and as they walked along it, she saw that it served as a pillared gallery for the far larger chamber that stretched below.

It was a wide, cold room, its drapery worn to tatters. Its windows faced east, and yet the sunlight that streamed through them was dimmed by the stained glasswork set amongst the panes. The figures in the glass wore diadems on their brows and held aloft gemstones done in ruby.

And, sitting atop a raised dais, a pair of great chairs sat, equal in all but size.

She tried not to look at them as they walked along the gallery. It had been cleared of the Steel Heels it seemed. Reynard no doubt considered himself guard enough.

They came to the stairs.

"Across the river," she said, coming to a halt. "There is a horse-"

"I had Tiecelin's men collect Maiden last night," Reynard said, not bothering to turn as he began to descend. "Don't worry."

Lara did not ask how he knew her name.

"It is so very like you," he chuckled as he continued down the steps. "To value a horse as you would your own skin . . ."

She felt the gaze of the Graycloaks boring into her back and followed him down the steps.

"You should have taken her and run," he went on. "To run would have confounded me. For a time, at least."

"Maybe I grew weary of running," she said.

He slowed to turn his good eye towards her.

"*Weary*," he said, turning to catch her gaze. "And now your mind is bent towards putting your blade through my heart. Well, *a* blade at any rate."

"Yes," she said.

"It's only natural," he said. "That was the course Hirsent took. And she was far more patient than you."

"Don't talk about her," Lara said, her cheeks growing hot. "Don't."

"As you wish," he said, and slowed somewhat as the stairs came to an end.

They walked another hall, this one carpeted and lined by doors of banded oak. Its walkway was lit by lamps in the shape of the Firebird. The flames flickering beneath their artificial wings made them seem alive.

There were sentries posted by the stairway at its far end and, beside a pair of open doors, a stick-like figure crouched, his eyes intent on the yarn looped about his fingers. His hair was a white mop, whiter even than his raiment.

"Now," Reynard said. "Here is someone to cheer you."

At the sound of Reynard's voice, the figure looked up from his strings, and rose. His knees buckled, and he stumbled forward, but rolled as he fell, until he had tumbled into a neat bow.

Pierrot smiled at her, the wrinkles about his eyes so deep they might have been etched into his skin.

She could not contain herself. She ran to him and threw her arms about him.

"I thought you-" she tried to say. "I thought-"

She squeezed him tight. It was like hugging a packsack full of bones. He patted her in return, then he made a sound in the back of his throat and patted harder.

She released him. He gasped. She started to laugh as he wheezed, until she realized he was in earnest.

"Oh!" she said, helping to steady him. "Oh, I'm sorry!"

Pierrot coughed into his fist, waving away her hand. He searched for something beneath his chalky jack and produced a crumpled scrap of paper. He frowned at it, sighed, and then sank back against the wall, clearly too weary to stand.

"What have you done to him?" she asked, glaring as she turned.

"Nothing that you have not done yourself," Reynard said. "*I* did not force him to follow me into Vulp Vora."

"We would not have been there at all," Lara snapped back, "If not for *you*."

"Nevertheless," Reynard said. "Master Pierrot is rather frail now. And older than he looks. He is like Carduel that way. And so I too am fond of him. He is a proper fool for this place. Don't you agree?"

"Is that to be his punishment?" Lara asked. "To suffer the brunt of your spite?"

"Spite?" Reynard repeated. "You are the one stirring up old ghosts, not I."

"Ghosts?"

"He was dead to you, was he not?" Reynard asked. "Dead and gone. And yet here he is, still drawing breath."

"Spare me your riddles," Lara said. "Or is this meant to be some sad attempt at philosophy?"

"Sad, yes," Reynard said. "But make no mistake: To linger here is dangerous. Life, death, truth, lies . . . It matters not. Within these walls the difference begins to thin."

"For you perhaps," Lara said. "What is true- What is *right* seems very plain to me."

"Does it now?"

He bent down next to Pierrot, exposing his neck to her.

Graycloaks be cursed, she longed for a knife.

"Tell me, Pierrot," he said. "When I am gone, will your mistress say that all my soldiers have deserved death? Or should I say *her* soldiers? They are sworn to serve their Queen, after all."

Pierrot blinked at Reynard and shrugged.

"Even the lame old soldier who unwittingly sped her to my side," Reynard said, nodding. "I will have to remember to thank him for that. Is he to be spared, do you think? Or will she root him out from his home, and hunt him, when I am dead?"

"Leave him alone," Lara said.

"Who?" Reynard asked, straightening as he turned. "Pierrot? Or do you mean your friend, the chevalier?"

In his good hand he held the parchment with its seal.

"He always did have a soft spot for women. Had he known it was you, well, I wonder if he would have done any different."

Lara was opening her mouth to respond when one of the doors further down the hall flew open. From it sprang a huge white dog, who came skidding to a halt at the sight of them. A boy followed close behind, a moppet in a coat of blue serge who nearly tripped on the carpet as he ran from one side of the hall to the other.

"Hurry!" the boy cried, sparing only a fleeting glance at Lara, Reynard, and the servant of The Watcher slumped against the wall before disappearing through another set of doors. The dog let out a low bark, gave its thick coat a shake, and then sped after him.

Lara found herself at a loss for words. Then a fiery-haired Calvarian came storming into the hall. She was clutching a bundle of wrinkled sheets in one hand. The front of her otherwise crisp uniform was marked with paw prints.

"It is no use to run!" she roared. "Now get-"

She saw them, then, and at once she straightened. Then she bowed, crisply.

"Is the Beast giving you trouble again, Sigyn?" Reynard asked.

"Forgive me, my lord," she said, still red in the face. "But that animal-"

She unfurled the sheets with a whip of her wrists. They were quite soiled.

"Must it be allowed *inside*, my lord?"

"Well," Reynard said, "These are weighty matters. But they are for other shoulders to bear, I think. Have you spoken to the boy's chaperone?"

"I have," the Calvarian answered, "My lord."

"And what does she say?"

"That the Lord Protector's wards were given the freedom of these rooms," said the slight woman who emerged from the archway that both boy and dog had used to make their escape. "And that the punishment for their misuse rests with me. Not you."

"Ah," Reynard said. "Faline. I had hoped we might cross paths."

"I am ever at your disposal," the woman said. "Lord Protector."

"Lara," Reynard said. "This is the Lady Faline, of Lothier."

"Your Highness," Faline said, curtsying. Her dark blue eyes matched her gown. A miniature stag, done in pearls, had been sewn into its bodice.

"Are you one of his prisoners too?" Lara asked, bluntly. "Or do you prefer the word 'guest?'"

"It does sound more polite," Faline said with a delicate cough. "Though I am no prisoner, Highness. I am free to come and go as I please. More or less."

"Indeed," Reynard said, "And with more manses than this to call home. Lady Faline has inherited estates from Larsa to Arioch. And yet she chooses to stay in her little apartment, here, off this very hall. I've tried to make it comfortable, but still- It hardly seems fitting for the wife of a great lord."

"My children are comfort enough," Faline said, quietly.

"Of course," Reynard said. "Shall we pay them a visit, Lara? These ones have never met a Queen before."

"Do I have a choice?" Lara asked.

Reynard *smiled* at that.

"You are dismissed," he said to the Calvarian maid.

She bowed, turned on her heels, and exited by way of the far stairs.

"Lady Faline," he went on, "If you would?"

Faline curtsied and then stood aside, her eyes wary as Reynard stepped past. The Graycloaks did not make to follow him.

Lara shot Pierrot a glance. He tilted his head and spread open his finger. The yarn slipped free and pooled into his lap.

"Fair enough," Lara said.

She passed through the doors, the Lady Faline close behind, walked down a dim hall and found herself standing before a lavish chamber laden with potted plants and cushioned seats. An immense table stood at its center, and across it had been thrown a painted chart of Arcasia. Two young men, boys really, were leaning over it, studying the little armies that marched across its surface. Reynard had joined them at the table and seemed just as engrossed. Archers and pikemen in azure and scarlet swarmed about squadrons of mounted horse. A fleet of soapstone ships sailed atop parchment seas.

In the far corner the boy from the hall lay, lounging atop a wide cushion with a leather-bound tome in his lap. His shaggy-coated dog lay before him, watchful.

The elder boys turned from the table and stared at her.

"Who's she?" the taller of the two asked. "Our new sword-mistress?"

"*Manners*," Faline said. "Your Highness, these are my sons. Luisant, Daguet, this is the Lady Larissa. Our Queen."

The boys looked dumbstruck.

"It's alright," Lara said. "I imagine I don't look like any storybook lady."

"Yes, you do," the boy on the cushion blurted, burying himself back into his book.

"And this little troublemaker," Faline went on. "Is Bastian of Astolat. You've already met Labete, I take it."

She motioned towards the dog.

"Yes," Lara said, "She's a sheepdog, yes?"

"How did you know that?" Bastian asked.

"I used to herd sheep," she answered. "What are you reading?"

"A story," he said. "It's very long."

Labete lifted herself from the floor and came to give Lara's leg a sniff. Lara offered the dog her palm. She snuffled at it, eventually deigning to be pet.

"Sweet girl," Lara said.

"You're lucky," Bastian said. "She doesn't like everyone."

"Nor do I," Lara said.

"May we go back to our game now?" the younger of Faline's sons asked. He was having a difficult time keeping still it seemed.

"Bow to your Queen first," Reynard said.

The boys bowed neatly enough.

"Good," Reynard said. "Now then, I see the rebel makes to land in Poictesme."

"Yes," the one called Luisant said, turning back to the table. "With mercenaries, too. I won't say where."

"Naturally," Reynard said, turning to the boy's brother. "And what will you do?"

"Osca and Astolat will send reinforcements," he said, already reaching for the pieces.

"And leave your flank vulnerable?" One of Reynard's false fingers tapped against the table. "What if the South joins the rebels?"

"Those cowards would never dare," Daguet huffed.

"You may be right," Reynard said. "Though the Old Goat is crafty . . . Or so I've heard."

Both boys snickered at that.

"Good luck," Reynard said, taking Daguet by the shoulders. "I think you may need it."

Faline winced. Luisant reached for the dice cup.

"Funny," Reynard said, turning from the table, "The war between Arcas and Luxia never really ended. It's only the pieces that have changed. Isn't that right, Lady Faline?"

"Yes," she said, her voice tight. "My lord."

"Speaking of which," Reynard said. "Have you had any word from your husband?"

"No more than you, my lord," Faline answered. "Unless the Lord Tiecelin's chimera have brought fresh news from the west?"

"Some," Reynard said. "The rebels have landed. And not in Poictesme. Lord Julien made a valiant effort to deny them."

The fingers of his false hand flickered atop the boy's shoulders.

"He failed," Faline said.

"You do not look surprised, my lady," Reynard said.

"Little serves to surprise me in these dark times, my lord."

"Six hits!" Luisant cried.

"Cheater," Daguet grumbled.

Reynard let go of the boy.

"Is he dead?" Faline asked, breathing easier.

"No," Reynard said.

"How did he-"

"Escape?" Reynard said. "Like many a good commander he knew when it was time to cut and run. But I need not bore you with the details. He can do that well enough himself."

"He is coming here?" she asked, confused.

"I would have all of the great lords present for the Queen's coronation," Reynard said. "Osca is no exception."

"Of course," Faline said, wetting her lips. "My lord."

"Will mother be there?" Bastian asked, letting go of his book. He had clearly been listening as closely as Lara.

"Yes," Reynard said. "I have sent for the Lady Elaine."

The boy's face lit up. "When will she come?"

"The shrikes only flew this morning," Reynard said. "But I do not think she will tarry. We should expect her to arrive by Harvest, assuming the weather holds."

"But that's weeks from now," Bastian said, breathing a heavy sigh.

"Not so long," Reynard said. "And so much left to do."

Reynard had drifted as he spoke, his eye falling now on Lara. The sheepdog bristled at his approach, a deep growl rumbling in its throat.

He took a careful step backwards.

"Good girl," Lara whispered.

"If there is anything I might do," Faline said. "To lighten the Lord Protector's burden-"

"Write to your uncle, the Lord Plateaux," Reynard said, suddenly curt. "A coronation will require wine. And given the guests, only the *finest* will suffice. Let us say five tuns of Oscan sweet, six of Barcan, and why not be generous? Another twenty of Felician."

"Twenty *tuns*," Faline repeated.

Lara did not know how much wine was in a tun. It sounded an ocean.

"The Vintners should be able to manage it," Reynard said. "My spies amongst the factors say they've had years of good harvests. Or are they in error? Perhaps I should send for your uncle? He might bring his household. Would your boys enjoy the company of their baby brother, do you think?"

"No," Faline said, "My lord, that is not necessary. I will write to him at once."

"Excellent," Reynard said. "Lord Pescheour downs a third of Felician every *day*, and he's merely a baron. I shudder to think what the whole court will manage."

He sighed.

"A high price to pay for royal circumstance, perhaps," Reynard sighed. "Ah, well. At least it will be a night to remember. I can promise you that."

"My lord," Faline said.

"Does that please you, Lara?" he asked, turning his eye on her once again.

"If you think that watching you threaten an innocent woman *pleases* me," Lara said, "Then you are either mad or far stupider than I took you for."

"Threaten?" he said, feigning hurt. "*Threaten?* No, no. Just a reminder now and then, of where we all stand. And she is hardly an innocent. Are you Faline?"

The lady of Lothier did not answer.

"She plays her own games," Reynard went on. "And with bigger pieces . . . But it is sweet of you to care for her. She was handmaiden to your mother, you know. I had a thought that she might wish to continue in that role, perhaps as your lady's maid."

"If that is your wish, Lord Protector," Faline said and began to curtsy.

"*My* wishes here are irrelevant," Reynard said, brusque again. "But what say you, Lara? Would you care for the Lady's Faline's company? She is a reasonably good conversationalist, though she often knows more than she lets on."

Lara hesitated. Then she saw the pleading look in the woman's eyes.

"I would be honored," Lara said. "Yet, I have no need for servants."

"Think of me more as a companion, Your Majesty," Faline said.

"Then it is settled," Reynard said. "Good."

He cast his gaze over the chamber again, his attention drawn back to the table. The two boys were still at play. The one rolling dice as the other plucked fallen soldiers from the board. They seemed not to have heard a whisper of the usurper's veiled threats.

Lara almost envied them.

"We must be going," Reynard said, genially. "Be sure to tell me how the rebel fares."

With that he made for the hall.

Faline curtsied. Bastian looked up from his book.

"Highness," he said, very polite.

"Goodbye," Lara said, feeling awkward.

Labete followed Lara across the room, panting. Then Bastian called for her, and she padded back to lay by his side.

Reynard was waiting for her in the little hallway.

"A shortcut I think," he said. "Or we shall be all day introducing you."

He touched one of the stones on the wall, and a small door swung open.

"Hurry now," he said, stepping into the dark passage beyond.

She slipped through. The door was already closing on its own.

It shut silently behind her. She could hear him rustling with something, and then sparks flew in the dark. An oil lamp flared to life.

"Follow me," he said, squeezing down the passage.

"What about your bodyguards?" she asked.

"They're used to it," he shrugged. "Keeps them on their toes."

The passage turned sharply. Lara thought she could hear the boys' voices arguing over the throw of a die. Then they faded.

"Then it is you," Lara said. "Scratching behind the walls."

He glanced over his shoulder, a sardonic look in his eye.

"That would be more comforting," he said. "Wouldn't it?"

They reached a spiral staircase, as narrow as it was laden with cobwebs.

He took it. She followed, if only to keep up with the light.

"I see what you are doing," she said.

"Do you now?"

"Yes," she said. "And it won't work."

"Hm," he hummed. "It seems to be working already. Or will you have poor Faline's boorish sons thrown from the battlements before the day is out?"

"No!" she said. "And even if I wanted such a thing, surely no one would obey."

"Not today, maybe," Reynard said. "But soon."

They descended the stairs in silence for a time, passing several small landings.

"She *hates* you," Lara said.

"Faline?" Reynard said. "That's hardly a revelation. All the great lords do. Just as they know the price of rebellion."

"Doesn't that worry you?"

"Should it?"

"They could turn on you at any moment."

"And yet they choose not to," he said, taking a sharp turn into a larger passage.

"Because you will *kill* their children," she said.

"That's what they tell themselves," Reynard said, taking the steps quickly now. "I think half of them would be far more distressed to lose the power they wield. And the other half are probably relieved to have someone telling them what to do. Of course, they all believe that they could *choose* to betray me when it suits them. That helps too."

He came to a sudden halt and pressed his false hand against the stonework of the wall.

"They have the illusion of choice, you see."

There was a *click*. Daylight flooded into the passage.

"And the illusion is often enough."

He slipped through the crack in the wall. She followed suit.

They were in the fortresses' larder, standing amidst racks of hanging game. Through an adjoining archway the castle kitchen bustled with activity. Maids were kneading batter and scouring pots as the full-figured cook fussed over a deep bowl of mince.

One of the maids, passing by the arch, locked eyes with Lara. She did not cry out, but dropped the tray of crusts she was carrying. For a moment the kitchen went silent.

Reynard stepped from the archway.

All the servants made quick obeisance, curtsying, or bowing their heads low. Then they returned to their work as though nothing had happened. The maid dropped to her hands and knees, salvaging what she could of the dough as the cook threw a few choice words her way.

"Look about you," Reynard said, the servants making way as they crossed through the kitchen. "This one a scullion, that one a lady. It's all an illusion. A lie we all have a hand in weaving."

"Even the scullions?" Lara asked.

"Them most of all," Reynard nodded. "Every morning they remind themselves that they must serve. They may hate their service, but the alternative frightens them far more."

"Freedom, you mean."

"*Freedom*," he snickered. "Yes. Little lies usually suffice to convince them to stay in their place. Duty, deference, the circumstances of their birth. For others, bigger ones are required. Or should I say more *creative?*"

He came to a halt beside one of the chopping blocks, plucked a date from one of the bowls laid nearby, and popped it into his mouth.

"Really, Lara," he said as he chewed. "Convincing people that your ideas are actually their own? It's terribly exhausting. You should thank me for relieving you of the burden of it for so long."

"Gods, don't you ever stop talking?" she snapped. "If I had known you were going to lecture me to death, I could have spared you the trouble years ago!"

"You could end it," he said. "Pick up that knife. It's meant to cut game. My hide isn't half so tough."

He gestured towards the carving knife laid on the counter beside her.

It looked very sharp.

"A trick," she said.

"Is it?" he said. "I know you are fast. You must be. Hirsent taught you herself."

"Don't say her name."

"Put that knife in me then, and I'll stop."

He took a step towards her. She snatched up the knife.

It shook in her hand.

"Well," he said. "What are you waiting for? Isn't that what you've come here to do? To kill me?"

"If I try," she said. "You'll hurt them. My friends. My brother."

"Only if you fail," Reynard said.

She laid the knife back down.

"The illusion of choice, Lara," he said. "You would do well to remember it. When you are Queen."

* * * * * * *

He led her through the scullery and then down into a sunken court. A young oak grew there, its roots at odds with the pale stones. It was light here, almost airy compared to the stillness of the long halls they had walked, but to Lara it felt nearly as joyless.

There was a stairway beyond the far arches. It looked as though it led down to the main gate, but Reynard did not make for it. Rather, he slowed his step and made to admire the tree.

She kept her distance.

"Your own plan isn't half bad, you know," he said, examining one of the younger shoots by hand.

"My plan?"

"To distract me," he said. "I admit, you are rather engrossing. But I don't need to lead my army in the field to crush the rebels. My servants are more than capable of that."

"Like the ones Roland routed?"

"Please," he said. "Osca is hardly the backbone of my army. Good horse, yes. A nice bit of shock when properly applied. But they lack versatility."

He let go of the branch. The whole tree quivered.

"Still, Lord Julien played his part."

"And what part is that?"

"To *lose*," Reynard said. "Now all Lorn is in open revolt. Cadwallon, Goscinny, Landuc . . . Even the Baron of Kerys turned his cloak. A pity. His son was such a likeable little chap. Though not very clever."

He turned to face her. He was not smiling.

"A whiff of weakness, Lara," he said, "And all the parasites crawl from the woodwork, hungry for blood."

"It's a mangy dog that has fleas," Lara said. "That's what Danica used to tell me. Before you killed her."

The fingers of his false hand flickered ever so slightly.

"Your cousin too is likeable," he said. "A modest boy, brave. Who knows? In a different life he might have made a well enough man."

"Not a king, though?"

"There are no good kings," he said. "Or queens, for that matter."

"*None?*" she asked.

"How many terrors have been committed in your name already?" he asked, drawing closer. "How many have you committed yourself?"

"Fewer than you," she said, standing her ground.

"You're young yet," he said. "There's still time to make up the difference."

He smiled at her, his gaze wandering. She felt sick.

"Young Roland is wasting no time on that account," he went on, making to round the tree. "His rebels put some three hundred Oscans to the sword after Kerys fell. Even the ones that surrendered."

"A lie," she said.

"I have seen it," he said, simply.

For once, she believed him.

They left the sunken court by way of the stairs. On their left the tower of the shrikes stretched. Below them lay the gate. There was activity in the courtyard. Figures wearing Reynard's colors were coming and going, thick courier bags slung over their shoulders.

"How *did* you steal the mirror?" she asked, her curiosity winning over her disgust.

"Oh, that?" He chuckled softly. "It was ridiculously difficult. Amusing, though. I honestly thought I might die."

He mimed wiping a tear from the corner of his eye.

"Alas."

"Is that how you caught me?" she asked.

"No," he answered. "The mirror is no real guide. For that I needed old tricks."

They had been spotted. A trio of figures, Steel Heels by their dress, were coming up the stairs to meet them.

"Tiecelin was useful," Reynard continued. "I had him follow you and make report. Not too close, I told him, and not with his children lest they spook you. I bade him capture you if you strayed too far from your course, though that may have proven difficult. Your 'hollow man' was very strong. I imagine he would have made short work of men armed only with bows."

"Are they really his children?" she asked, her gaze drawn towards the creatures roosting amidst the ledges of the crumbling tower. "Those monsters?"

"Some," he murmured. "Yes."

The Steel Heels had closed the distance between them. One of them was Galehaut, their captain. They came to a halt on the landing below them, his men standing at attention as he bowed.

"Your Highness," he said. It took Lara a moment to realize he was addressing her.

"What is it, Galehaut?" Reynard asked.

"Forgive this intrusion, my lord," Galehaut said. "But the Lady Rukenaw is in the city."

"She must have ridden through the night," Reynard said. "I suppose I would be impatient too, after all these years."

"Shall I-"

"We have an appointment to keep in the Blue Prince's chamber," Reynard said. "Tell the Lady Rukenaw that she may join us, when she arrives."

Something passed over the man's face. *Fear?* His eyes flicked towards Lara.

Then he bowed.

"My lord," he said, turning. "Your Highness."

"Oh," Reynard said. "Galehaut, before I forget, have you seen to the matter of the bounty?"

"Yes, my lord," he said. "I took the liberty of making arrangements for the widows. And the last of the informers is waiting on your pleasure, just as you requested."

"I'll see him now, I think," Reynard said. "In the court."

"At once, my lord."

Captain and aides strode down the steps at the quickstep. Reynard followed, his pace leisurely.

"Informer?" Lara asked. "So, it wasn't him then?"

"Galehaut?" Reynard snorted. "Wulf, no. He's not exactly the type to slink through the shadows. Why? Don't tell me you remember him from when you were a girl."

"I saw him last night," she said. "In a tavern."

"Last *night*?" The way he lingered on the word made her uneasy. "Tell me, just how long do you think you've been here?"

"How long-" she stammered. "But- It's only been-"

"It's been three days, Lara," Reynard said.

He's lying. Her head swam. *Or did he drug me? Like moder-*

"Yesterday you said you could not sleep and asked for your chimera. I could not see the harm of it, so I had Sigyn bring him to you. Don't you remember?"

"You lie-" she began to snap when her heel caught on the lip of a loose step.

She lost her feet. Her arms flailed, but there was nothing to catch hold of.

Lara's Stair, they'll call it.

He caught her. The fingers of his false hand dug into her arm as he yanked her backwards. She could feel his breath on her neck.

"Let go of me!" she cried, wrenching from his grip.

She took hold of the balustrade, her heart racing.

"You're welcome," he said, continuing down the steps.

It can't be, she told herself as she forced herself to follow. *It can't be three days. It can't- I would know. I would remember-*

"Here you are," Reynard said. His bodyguards were waiting for them at the bottom of the steps. "I was wondering when you would catch up."

They moved aside to let them past, their expressions wooden. She guessed they were used to his disappearing act by now.

"Ah," Reynard said, slowing as they approached the gate. "Here's my chief informer. Would you like to meet him, Lara?"

Another of the Steel Heels stepped from one of the ivy-shrouded archways beside the gate. He was practically dragging a little figure behind him, a young boy. He was a street urchin from the looks of him, ragged haired, shoeless, and brown as a nut.

"I'd like my coin back," Lara said to him.

"Spent it, m'lady," he grinned, the seam of his filthy shirt straining to hold as he struggled. "Leggo of me, ya dumb twist!"

The Steel Heel threw him at Reynard's feet.

"Where's my cut?" he spat as he picked himself up.

"Here," Reynard said, producing a trio of crowns from the purse on his belt.

"That all?"

"It's more than your fair share. After all, you did not capture this lady all by yourself. Did you?"

Reynard held out the coins. The boy snatched at them, seeming to trip on one of the flagstones as he lurched forward. They nearly collided, but then Reynard stepped aside with a sweep his boot.

The boy hit the flagstones harder this time.

"Nice try," Reynard said. "Still, you've done me service."

He tossed down the coins. The boy had to scurry to gather them up.

"Those coins will be a heavy burden," Reynard said. "Especially on the streets. If you wish, I might find a place for you. A hot meal and a warm cot to-"

"Piss on your cot!" the boy swore, and ran, making for the gate.

A half dozen Steel Heels made to block his path.

"Let him go!" Reynard called out. "See he doesn't trip on the way down."

The soldiers made way. The boy shot through the doors. He was gone.

"Was that meant to shake me?" Lara asked.

"No," Reynard said. "Just good timing. Let's see that he makes it, yes?"

They walked through the gate themselves, the soldiers stiffening into salutes as they passed. The boy was already halfway down the steps, his thin legs pumping. Below them the city sprawled, its rooftops floating in the mist creeping off the river.

"He's in for some hard decisions," Reynard said. "His own kind would skin him for that gold. A shop keep might beat it from him. What to do then? Hide it? Bury it?"

"You almost sound like you envy him."

"I do," Reynard nodded, seemingly pleased. "That boy and I aren't that different. Not really. And I'm not just speaking about how close he came to cutting my purse."

He chuckled.

"How could I not envy him?" he went on. "He has far more *freedom* than I do."

"The freedom to starve, you mean."

"That too," Reynard said. "But we all take our chances."

The boy vanished into the mist.

"He won't make it," Lara said. "Will he?"

"Is that such a tragedy?" Reynard asked. "Guild masters and nobles I can cut down in droves. Have done. The guildsmen quake when I send for them. But boys like him? I'll never be rid of them."

"He's not some- Some *lesson*- Or some scholarly *jest* for you to sneer at!"

"You have a kind heart, Lara," Reynard said. "Just like your mother. But I disagree. There is a lesson here. And it's one you still haven't learned."

"And that is?"

"You cannot save everyone."

"And you can't save *anyone*!" she said. "Not even yourself."

He turned to face her, his lips parted.

For once, he had nothing to say.

"Take me to my brother," she said. "I'm tired of listening to your lies. Tired of stories. Tired of *you*."

He shut his mouth and walked along the edge of the steps. His eye was drawn towards the mountains north of the city. Amongst the blueish peaks she could make out the gray summit of the mountain her forebears named Mulciber. It was idle now, but she had read the histories. Secret fire lay deep beneath its roots.

"Tell me," Reynard said, still half in his reverie. "Did that aunt of yours ever tell you of the stone cutter and the mountain?"

"I told you I was tired."

"It's not very long," Reynard said. "Or have you heard it already?"

"No," Lara withered. "And if it's a Watcher's tale then I already know it won't have a happy ending."

"Will it now?" Reynard said, falling silent.

"Oh, Wulf," Lara cursed. "Go on then."

He bowed his head to her, *thank you.*

She spat at his feet. He ignored the gesture.

"There once was a stone cutter," Reynard said. "He lived in those hills below the mountain, and he was very good at his craft."

He came alongside the gate and ran his true hand along the stonework.

"His chisel found the perfect marks. His hammer struck just so. He was an artist. Only no one knew. They merely saw stones. It took a carver for them to see anything more. And so, while he did not starve, he knew very little luxury."

He brushed his hand clean.

"Then, one day, he was on his way back from market when he came upon a stranger, waiting for him near the crossroads."

"The Wanderer," Lara said.

"Perhaps it was," Reynard said. "And perhaps it wasn't. The stone cutter did not know. But when the stranger saw his work, he said, 'Look here, what work! What mastery! Surely, you must be a rich man, to have such skill.'"

"'No,' said the stone cutter. 'I am no rich man.' And his voice was bitter."

"'Would you like to be?' the stranger asked."

"The stone cutter laughed at that. 'Would I like to be rich? Would I like to have a fine house, and servants to do my cleaning and cooking? What sort of question is that?'"

"'An honest one,' the stranger replied."

"'Yes!' the stone cutter said. 'And if you have the coin to make me one, let's see it! No? Then be on your way and let me go mine!'"

"The stonecutter urged his old mule onward but, when he turned back to look, he could still see the stranger watching him from the side of the road, a smile on his lips . . . And when he came to his home, what should he find?"

"A fine house," Lara said, "With servants."

"Yes," Reynard said. "And fine linen sheets, and cabinets full of spice, and a cellar full of wine."

"But he wasn't happy," Lara said.

"He was at first," Reynard said. "It's hard to be unhappy with such luxuries, whatever their source. And, of course, he did not need to cut stone anymore. No more laboring under the hot sun, his back bent. Instead, he filled his days with idle pleasures . . . Until, coming to the crossroads atop his best steed, he found himself being ushered aside by the heralds of some great lord, a prince perhaps of the royal line, coming down the high road with all his retinue. And as the great lord's palanquin passed, how the stone cutter envied the man's silks and jewels. His horse, the best of his stable, looked very plain to him then, his raiment very drab."

"'Oh, if only I were a prince,'" Lara said.

"'Would you like to be?'" Reynard said, softly. "The stone cutter had not seen the stranger standing by the side of the road."

"And after he said, 'yes,' and found he was a prince?" Lara asked, impatient.

"There was a drought," Reynard answered. "He had armies at his beck and call, mountains of treasure, a dozen palaces, but what could they do against the Firebird's glory? His crops withered, his people starved, and he sweltered through the nights."

"But he didn't care about the people," Lara said. "Did he?"

"He thought he did," Reynard said. "So, when the stranger asked him if he should like to trade places with the Firebird, he told himself it was because he could ease the people's suffering-"

"But it was really because he was a small, selfish man," Lara said. "Who did not like to be bested. He didn't care about anyone but himself."

"He cared about who he could hurt," Reynard said. "His fiery rays burnt the fields of those great lords who had slighted him, and with them the plots of the poor. Only the storm defied him now, for only they could capture his rays, and bring succor to the lands he had scorched."

"And when he was the storm?"

"Rivers overflowed," Reynard said. "Dams burst. Town and village drowned alike. Only the great stones of the mountain remained unmoved."

Lara sighed.

"Once he was the mountain," Reynard said. "He could feel no sting of rain, no blazing heat. He stood high, higher than any worldly prince, and strong beyond imagining. Until, one day, he felt something. It was like a sharp-toothed cat, gnawing at his toes."

Reynard rapped his false hand against the stones. *Tap, tap, tap.*

"He trembled," Reynard said. "And cried out for the stranger to make him a man again. But the stranger was gone."

He flattened his false palm against the stone.

"There was only the stone cutter, chiseling away at his feet."

"Am I meant to weep for you?" she said, her rage mounting with every word she spoke. "You, who killed my moder, my friends, my family?!"

"No," he said. "I am not so naive as to appeal to your sympathies. Rather, I merely ask you to put an end to my suffering. You owe me that much I should think."

"You? I owe *you* nothing!"

"Nothing?" Reynard said, his good eye flashing. "Nothing! Really now. Have I not paved the way for you, Lara? Have I not set loose terrors? I have razed cities, slaughtered thousands, piled up the dead in your name, and you say I've done nothing?"

"If only that were true," Lara said. "And I want nothing from you. Nothing!"

"Oh, but *they* do," Reynard said. "Those people you care so much about, they all need a villain. You want change? Real change? That takes a monster. I've done my part."

He stretched wide his hands.

"And now all you have to do, is kill him."

"Kill *you*, you mean."

"Me?" He put his true hand to his chest. "I am nothing. A pebble, casting a dark shadow. The shadow has far more life than I do. You should know that by now."

She wanted to spit in his face. "I suppose I do."

"Yes," he said. "Yours stretches just as far as mine. Further even. It must be a heavy thing to have hanging over you."

Something strange passed across his face. It almost looked like pity.

"Here, on the steps," he said then, taking a look about. "The light is good. You could steal my sword and put it through me before I could stop you. Or would a contest be more believable? I could have your sword brought, your Three-Merits. Then we could fight our way down to the square. That should draw a good crowd. Or would you rather push me down the steps before the end? I might break my neck. And if not, well, you could finish it with the same sword that killed your *moder*."

Her face felt flush. His sword was so close. She could take it. He was fast, she had seen it. And yet-

"This is your chance, Lara," he said. "You won't get another."

"And what if I refuse?" she said. "What then? Will you put my head on a pike?"

"It's not impossible," he mused. "I could always find another false Larissa to groom. A few deaths here and there and no one would be the wiser."

"But you won't," she said.

"No, Lara," he said. "I won't."

He drew close to her once again, his smile fading.

"But if you will not see me dead . . . If you *refuse*, well then, I have another proposal for you."

He looked deep into her eyes.

"Never," she said. "*Never!*"

"Come then," he said. "Let us see your brother."

X

Reynard snapped his fingers. His bodyguards stepped from the pall beneath the gate, their blue eyes fixed. But that was not all. From somewhere within the fortress a horn blew, deep and terrible.

"Bring her," he said, sweeping past them.

"I can bring myself," she said as they bore down on her.

Still, one of them gave her back a shove.

As they stepped into the courtyard, Steel Heels streamed from door and archway, emerging from the barracks lurking beneath the stones. They hurried along stair and walkway, doubling the watch on the walls. A dozen others swarmed past her to throw shut the gates.

Carduel had seemed a lonely place to her. Now its grim strength had been exposed.

Reynard did not slow but made for a short flight of steps clinging to the foot of the tower of the shrikes. They wound about the tower, sagging and split, and then there was a doorway.

It swung open as Reynard approached. Lara could not say how.

"Move," one of the Graycloaks growled into her ear.

She moved.

The interior of the tower was cool, almost damp, like a cellar on a hot summer day. A recessed pool filled most of its vestibule, as bare as it was dry. The chambers beyond were just as stark. Depressions in the stonework suggested ornaments, but any finery had long since been stripped from this place.

"This way," Reynard said, making for a stairwell set against one of the walls. Lara glanced upwards. It seemed to stretch all the way to the top of the tower, which must have been open to the sky, for she could see pale light glimmering far above.

She climbed. Stepping over stones that had been stained white with the filth of the shrikes. She could hear them too, their quorks and chitters echoing in the darkness.

Two flights they climbed, and then they came to a narrow landing. There, set deep into the wall, was an iron-banded door. A pair of sentries were guarding it. Their eyes, half-hidden beneath their helms, glinted in the torchlight.

"Open up," Reynard grunted.

One of the sentries dug an iron key from under his jack and drove it into the lock. A heavy tumbler *clunked,* and the door groaned wide.

The chamber beyond was not so much bare as abandoned. The dusty remains of a table lay at its center, thrown on its side like some wounded animal. Cobwebs hung in shrouds from empty sconces. The fresco on the far wall was peeling, and yet she could still make out the figure who seemed to be taking pleasure of the gardens painted there: A shapely youth in blue, princely in bearing. In his arms he cradled a long-necked lute. His head was bent upwards, as if in song. Other figures were huddled near his feet, but their faces were harder to make out.

Some looked as though they had been scorched with flame.

The walls of the chamber were lined with doors, more than seemed possible. Lara counted five along one wall alone, until she realized that many of them were illusory, paintings against the stonework that fooled the eye. Some of these opened onto fantastic vistas of golden jungle, sea swept shores, or fields of flaming pitch streaked with lightning.

Not all the doors were false, and no two were alike. Here was one with a golden latch, real gold too from the look of it, not filigree. Another was of strips of twisted dogwood. Its knots looked like faces to Lara, bestial and staring.

One door, however, was very plain. It stood beside the hearth and looked rather small compared to the others. It might have been a cupboard.

Reynard reached out and gave the door a gentle push. It swung open.

"After you," Reynard said, gesturing to the dark space beyond.

Lara straightened her back, doing her best to look nonchalant as she crossed the dusty chamber. But when she came to the threshold she halted.

She could smell tobacco, sweet as vanilla. Someone was smoking inside. And beneath that she could smell flop sweat, leather, and the greasy scent of oil. But there was something else wafting from the doorway, something far older, something that had seeped into the very stones of Carduel.

Something horrible happened here. And something horrible was going to happen. Was happening. Now.

She could feel Reynard's gaze on her. Judging her. She steeled herself and pressed forward.

The chamber was pitch black. There were no windows, and only a pair of lamps for light. Tiecelin stood beneath one of them, leaning against the wall almost casually as he drew smoke from a clay pipe. One of his smaller children was perched on his shoulder, its amber eyes fierce as they turned to regard her.

Beyond him lurked a pale, winged figure that Lara might have mistaken for a statue, had their paths not crossed before. The beads and pendants hung round Tisiphone's neck tinkled as she stifled a cough beneath the fold of her wing.

Her 'father' turned at the sound. The shrike-girl quieted.

A heavier chain rattled in the silence, and then Lara could see them. Seven alcoves had been carved into the chamber's curved walls, above each of which a grotesque face leered. Manacles dangled from their mouths.

Five of the alcoves stood empty. The other two were occupied.

In one Pinsard hung, stripped to the waist and bootless. His flesh was a patchwork of bruises and tiny cuts, but he still looked hale.

"Oh," Lara gasped. Her exhalation reverberated against the curved walls and then she was by his side. "Oh, what have they done?"

Pinsard's head lifted. As their eyes met, he managed a smile.

"Lara," he said, his voice hoarse.

They've not broken him. Not yet.

Arsinoe rattled her chains. She looked far worse off than Pinsard, but she was far more alert. Her gag was so thick that it was all she could do to grunt.

"That one talks too much," Tiecelin commented, pointing his pipestem towards Arsinoe. His affect was so flat it was hard to tell if he spoke in anger or not.

"Where's Scyron?" Lara asked.

"Elsewhere," Reynard said. "This place isn't for the likes of him."

"This place?" Lara repeated, looking about the chamber.

"The Blue Prince had seven wives," Reynard answered. "But no faithful ones."

Lara shivered. She did not know the tale, but she could guess it well enough.

"So, Lara," Reynard said. "A test of faith."

He snapped his fingers. One of his bodyguards shut the door to the outer chamber.

The shadows deepened.

"Tell me," Reynard said. "Who do you love the more? Your brother, or your paramour?"

Lara blinked. "She's not my-"

"Your brother, then," Reynard said, cutting her off. "Tiecelin?"

Tiecelin tapped out his pipe against the heel of his boot, and then reached into the folds of his hunter's jack. The shrike on his shoulder baiting its wings.

He drew out a leather roll. It looked like a tool kit.

"I promised Tiecelin some justice for the lives of his children," Reynard said. "Under different circumstances, I would have let him feed you to them. But that won't do, will it?"

There was a little table set beside one of the empty alcoves. Tiecelin laid the kit down upon it and, undoing the clasp, unrolled it.

It was full of knives. The kind you would use to skin an animal.

"So," Reynard went on. "How is it with royal whelps? You cannot strike them, of course. What tutor is the equal of the prince he means to teach? But you may beat a dog before a lion, as the saying goes. Or should I say a wolf?"

Tiecelin selected a knife. A short-handled thing with a hooked blade.

"Stop," Lara said. "What do you want?"

"You know what I want," Reynard said. "And you said, 'never.'"

He made a gesture. Tiecelin approached.

"No!" Lara said, and she made to put herself between them. "Don't!"

"Hold her," Reynard said.

The Graycloaks fell on her. She drove her elbow into the taller one's gut as he grabbed for her arm. He groaned, but then the other caught her by the collar.

She tried to twist away, tried even to throw him, laces snapping as she twisted in his grip, but he was no sea-reaver.

The other took hold of her then. Together, they held her fast.

Arsinoe was trying to shout something through her gag. Tiecelin had taken Pinsard by the hair. The shrike on his shoulder cawed, and then he looked to Reynard for orders.

"Is it still 'never' then?" Reynard said. "Or shall I let Tiecelin have one of his eyes?"

"How could I-" Lara said, still struggling. "You killed them! You killed-"

"Your father killed your mother's father," Reynard said, "And yet she managed to share his bed."

"I'm not my mother!"

"No," Reynard said. "She was not a selfish little brat. Still, I stole something from her. Something I would give back. All you have to do, is say *yes.*"

She shook. "I'd sooner die."

"Now you sound like your father," he said. "Very well."

He lifted his fingers into the air. Tiecelin dragged on Pinsard's pale locks. He groaned, too weak to fight, as the lean man brought the blade up to the level of his eyes.

"Go on," Pinsard rasped. "Go on, you coward."

"No," Lara cried. "Stop! I'll do it!"

Reynard raised his hand. Tiecelin paused.

"Do what?" Reynard asked.

"I'll do it," she breathed. "I'll kill you."

"Oh," Reynard said, dryly. "It's far too late for that."

"But you-" she stammered. "You-"

"I asked you politely," he said, his words tinged with anger. "I practically begged for it. I gave you your chance and you *refused* me. And more than once. You have been walking behind me this whole time. You could have kicked me down the stairs or drowned me in the tub. You didn't even try with the scissors. Why?"

"I-"

"Let her go," Reynard snapped.

The Graycloaks released her at once.

She rubbed at her arms. He was between her and the table with its knives.

"Even now," he said, advancing on her. "You *hesitate*. So, what is it then? Still biding your time? Waiting for the right time to strike? *What?*"

She went for his knee, a quick kick to put him off his footing. He slid away from the strike, dodged the blows she sent whistling towards his face, and then threw a punch of his own.

It was fast, but not fast enough.

She caught him by the wrist and twisted, driving another kick towards his thigh. He took it this time, gritting his teeth as she put more pressure on his arm.

No, she realized. He was smiling.

She tried to release him, gain some ground. It was too late.

He threw her.

She slammed into the wall, and then struck the floor. She gasped for air and began to claw her way to her feet. Her sides felt like they were on fire. Still, she crawled.

He put his boot on her shoulder and shoved.

She collapsed against the cold stones, wheezing.

"Too little, too late," he said. "Now choose."

She panted against the stones, tears streaking down her cheeks.

Heels clicked and scraped. One of the Graycloaks dragged her from the floor. She yelped as knives seemed to run all along her ribs.

She lifted her head, and looked into his good eye. He stared back at her, waiting.

"*Choose*," he said.

She opened her mouth to speak, but no words came out.

"Do it," Reynard said.

Tiecelin pinned Pinsard's head to the back of the alcove. Arsinoe quivered, but she did not turn away.

The shrike-tamer chose an eye. The knife gleamed in the lamplight.

Don't look! Don't look!

But she had to.

Tiecelin cut.

Pinsard did not scream. He was too proud for that. Nor did he thrash. But he made noises from between his teeth.

By the time Tiecelin was done, they had turned to whimpers.

The Luxian loosened his grip. Pinsard's head lolled forward. He offered what was left of her brother's eye to the shrike perched atop his shoulder.

It took it in its jaws, flitted onto the little table, and then swallowed it, greedily, like a child who has never tasted sweets.

Lara could feel the bile in the back her throat. She could taste the tears on her lips. But that was all. She felt empty. Emptier than the hole where Pinsard's eye had been. His other had closed tight as his chest heaved.

"Lara," Reynard said, looming close. "Are you listening?"

She nodded, numb.

"Do not think that I enjoy this," he said. "I do not. And it need not go further. Just say the words, and I will spare him."

"Don't," Pinsard barked, sucking air through his teeth. "Don't *listen* to him!"

Reynard flicked his wrist, and the second Graycloak drove his fist into Pinsard's belly. He did not cry out but slumped against his chains, retching on his own blood as he tried to catch his breath.

A sound escaped Lara's throat.

Reynard's head snapped back around.

"Do you have something to say?" he asked.

She met his gaze.

"No," she said.

"Small," he said, "And selfish."

"Shall I continue, my lord?" Tiecelin asked as he wiped his blade clean.

Reynard nodded.

"No," a husky voice murmured. It was little more than a whisper, but in the cramped chamber it practically boomed.

"What was that?" Tiecelin said as he turned towards Tisiphone. Reproach lurked round the edges of his flat words.

"I said," the shrike-girl said, a touch louder now, "No."

She took a step towards Reynard, her talons scraping for purchase against the floor as she did her best to bow. Lara saw something amongst the cruel angles of shrike-girl's face: Pity, it seemed to her. Or was it more? She could not say.

"His eyes are pretty, my lord," she said. "Please, let him keep one."

"Hrm," Reynard murmured. He sounded surprised.

The shrike on the table let out an angry caw. Tiecelin stepped close.

"Daughter likes her pretty things," he said. "Doesn't she?"

"Yes, father," Tisiphone replied, her baubles jingling as she tucked her wings tight against her chest.

"Then be silent."

Tisiphone nodded and shrunk back into the shadows.

"Hold him," Tiecelin said to the Graycloak, gesturing towards Pinsard with his knife.

The Calvarian obeyed. Pinsard struggled, twisting his head away from the Luxian as he approached.

Tiecelin raised his blade once more . . . And then lowered it, turning his own head.

Lara could hear it then. Footsteps. Quick and hard, and drawing close.

The door to the chamber swung open, and for a moment Lara allowed herself the fancy that it was Scyron who came sweeping into the room, having broken free from the dungeons of Carduel with a host of prisoners at his back, or Roland even, come to rescue her with steel and fire.

The moment was brief.

It was the Baroness.

"You started without me," she huffed, unclasping her cloak. Both it and her boots were caked with mud. She did not carry her famed morningstar on her hip, but a riding crop.

"You are late," Reynard answered.

"I rode as fast as I could," she said, tossing her cloak aside. "Fresh horses are in short supply. And that's not all. Rebels will take Nemea if we don't-"

"Later," Reynard said. "We have a guest."

She noticed Lara then and simply said, "Ah."

"I believe something more formal might be in order," Reynard said.

"Your Majesty," she said, sighing as she bowed. "I caught you once before, you know. You and your so-called brother. It was a long time ago now, of course, but if I'd known then the *trouble* you both would cause I would never have let you go."

"This one is still trouble," Tiecelin said.

"It speaks!" Rukenaw sneered. "Well, what else have I missed?"

"We have taken one of the boy's eyes."

"His eyes?" Rukenaw said. "Not the balls I would have chosen, but I suppose they will have to do."

She crossed the chamber, unlooping the crop from her belt. Tiecelin and the Graycloak stepped aside as she put the end of it beneath Pinsard's chin, leaning close as she pressed.

Pinsard lunged forward, his bloodied teeth flashing as he snapped at her.

The chains brought him up short.

"Pity," she said, inspecting the ruin of his right eye as he glared at her. "I would have liked to have seen it."

"You've had your turn with him," Reynard said.

"Yes," she said. "Nothing he didn't secretly enjoy, of course."

"Bitch!" Pinsard wheezed.

The crop whistled. Pinsard's head snapped to one side before going limp.

"Leave him alone!" Lara said. "He hasn't done anything!"

"Hasn't he?" the Baroness said. "His father turned his cloak. His mother ran like a coward and killed my second. And him? He's killed dozens. He would kill me and the Lord Protector in a heartbeat. And you call him innocent."

"He was defending himself," Lara said.

"He was defending *you*," Reynard said. "Tiecelin?"

"My lord," the Luxian said, nodding towards the Graycloak.

The Calvarian steadied Pinsard.

"One last look, boy," Rukenaw said, toying with her crop. "Choose carefully."

He turned first to Arsinoe, but she was on his blind side. Then his eye met Lara's.

He set his jaw.

Tiecelin went to work. Pinsard's chains shook. The shrike-girl turned away.

"An eye for an eye," the Baroness said when he was done.

Tiecelin offered it to her.

"You can feed it to her if you like," Rukenaw said, casting a mocking glance towards Tisiphone. "It would make a nice change from rats."

"I do not eat rats," Tisiphone said, soft but hard.

"What next?" the Baroness asked Lara. "His ears? He can live without those. Or should we carve a piece from your so-called bodyguard?"

The Baroness moved to the next alcove. Arsinoe did not shrink.

"We haven't been introduced yet," the Baroness commented, running her crop across the Telchine's cheek. "Not properly. That's alright. There's plenty of time to make up for-"

"Enough," Lara said.

"Oh?" the Baroness said, her eyebrows arching. "Oh. Really?"

"*Rukenaw*," Reynard said. The smirk on the Baroness' lips vanished.

Boots rasped against stone. He bent down beside her.

"What was that?" he asked, softly.

"Enough!" Lara cried, though she could not meet his gaze. "For pity's sake, enough."

"Pity," Reynard said. "Pity rarely moves me. I need to hear you say it."

"Let them live," Lara managed. "Prisoners, yes. But not- Not tortured. Please. Let me see them, and-"

"And?"

"And I will marry you."

Her voice had become a whisper.

"Kiss me then," Reynard said. "And seal your promise."

He took her by the hand and lifted her to her feet.

She leaned forward and pressed her lips to his cheek.

"I believe you," he said.

XI

That night, there was celebration. Steel Heels and Bloody Girls made merry in the courts below the citadel. There was wine, and song, and dancing. Word spread quickly, and by dusk both shores of the river were lit by lanterns, ghostly in the fog.

Lara was returned to her chambers. She did not take food or drink but lay in the middle of her wide bed and listened for scraping behind the walls until she fell asleep.

The next morning she found no guards at her door. Not even the Gray Cloaks. She had the freedom of the castle, and servants rather than sentries to keep her company. Pierrot she found sleeping on a cushion beside her door, Madam Precieuse bathed her and salved her wounds, and the Lady Faline broke fast with her, flinching whenever Bannertail leapt onto the table to snatch one the berries from Lara's plate.

Lara said little, but she listened. Faline told her of how Reynard had honored the bounty on Lara's head with lands and pensions. That very morning a small company of his veterans had departed for Carabas, flush with gold and petty titles, while a handful made to return to Mandross, or Lucra, rich enough to buy some chance at contentment.

And yet most of them had stayed. The rebel had come again and who would face them if not the Steel Heels? Who would train the fresh-faced youths come to fill the ranks? The Baroness and her doxies? *Go, Reynard had told them, you have done enough*, and by such snares he held them fast.

Lara knew such wiles herself.

"And the rebel?" Lara asked. "Is there any word?"

"None that I can speak," Faline told her, and Lara retired back to her bedchamber. From its windows she could gaze upon the place where Arsinoe and Pinsard were being held, high in the tower of the shrikes. There the parapet formed a narrow walkway about the base of its crumbling spire, where they would have leave to walk.

If and when they recovered.

The only figure Lara spied that day was one of the larger shrikes. It had perched like a gargoyle atop one of the crenelations, its head turned towards one of the windows. A sentry perhaps, or a spy, listening. Lara watched it for a long time, wondering, until something seemed to startle it, and it took flight.

Only then did she realize it was Tisiphone.

Days and nights passed without much change. She woke, took food, and watched from her window as soldiers came and went below. At night she waited, dreading.

One day she noticed that it was not only soldiers that came marching up the Queen's Steps, but porters and guild-hands bent low with heavy burdens. The fortress swelled with carpenters and plasterers, hammering and scraping as the flagstones were scrubbed. Strings of lanterns went up, some delicate as evening flowers, others weighty firebirds of hammered brass. They hung from tower to tower, even from the citadel to the spire of the shrikes. Leap from one of the windows and she might catch hold of their mooring lines. Strong arms and a firm grip would carry her the rest of the way.

Not that she needed to. She had not been forbidden. No bar had been set. If she wanted to call on them, all she need do was walk.

She could not face them. She was too ashamed.

Harvest came, and with it the Lady Elaine of Astolat. It was permitted that Bastian be allowed to greet her along the bank of the White River, and with him Faline and Lara went, under heavy guard. A pier was built to receive her upriver of the citadel, so that she might enter the city by way of one the northern gates, and there they received her. The boat that bore her was a slender thing, canopied with banners bearing the device of the blue maiden. Bastian ran to meet her as she was lifted onto the thwart, but Labete beat him to her. For a moment Lara thought the dog might knock the slender woman into the rush, but then the woman laughed and bent to accept an errant lick or two.

They were old friends it seemed.

With Elaine came a fragile shell of a man whom Lara took to be her father. He quivered as the servants lifted him from the boat, and only kept his feet by means of a stout cane and the support of a squire. Then Faline introduced them as the Count and Lady Cherax, and she wondered at their contrast. He could not seem to form full words. Nor could he stop shaking, and Lara could not help but notice the way his gaze flitted this way and that, like an animal frightened by a storm.

"The Lord Protector begs your pardon for not greeting you in person," Faline said to them. "There is much to occupy him these days."

"We can imagine," Elaine said, softly, her eyes falling on Lara for a moment.

"Come," Galehaut said. "We have readied horse for you."

"My lord husband cannot ride," Elaine said. "And so, neither will I."

"Then we shall all walk," Galehaut replied, and made motion for his men to dismount.

"You are too courteous," Elaine said, and so they spent the better part of that afternoon keeping pace with Count Cherax. Lara soon gleaned that they had not come alone, for half a day behind them rode some five hundred men-at-arms from Astolat to bolster the Lord Protector's army.

"Astolat is faithful," the Lady Elaine said, loud enough for Galehaut's ears.

From Lothier only some chevalier came, and fewer soldiery, but they were escort to a truly immense caravan of wine. Winches and sledge were employed to cart them into the citadel, a labor of many days, for the casks bearing the bleeding hart of the Vintner's Guild upon their heads were larger than any Lara had ever seen. A tun of Felician was opened to mark to occasion, and that evening Lara sampled a flight of it with Pierrot, having no stomach to sup in the company of the Lord Protector.

"It's good," she said, gasping. She had never tasted wine so strong.

Pierrot grinned at that and held up a finger.

"What?" she asked, as he went to the sideboard, and took up one of the lamps. He found a spare wick, lit it, and when he touched it to the top of his glass the Felician *caught*.

Flame danced in his goblet, and then he downed it, fire and all.

He offered her the lit wick.

"No thank you," she said.

He shrugged and poured himself another.

Redmonth. What remained of the might of Osca came limping back from the front, bloodied and bent. Even their lord, Julien, bore the marks of war, his filigreed mail riven even to his collar. Reynard and the

Baroness received them at the city's westmost gate, as a courtesy perhaps, for Lara did not doubt that any scrap of news he might bring was already known to them. She herself would have stayed behind, but for Faline.

"Husband," Faline said as he stepped from his horse.

"My lady," he said, pressing past to speak with the Lord Protector.

Lara too he snubbed, until Reynard introduced her.

"Your Majesty," he said, bending low. "Forgive me. The dust of the road must have blinded me."

Lara winced, and the Baroness did her best to suppress a snicker.

"There will be time for such pleasantries later," Reynard said. "What news of the rebel?"

"They were massing at Nemea when I rode, Lord Protector," Julien answered. "My rearguard I left to defend the approach to Pardus, but they are far too few to withstand a direct assault."

"To delay them will be enough," Reynard said.

"Should I send the Hatchet to shore up their ranks?" the Baroness said. "If their rear is as chewed up as their van, a strong wind might serve to tip them over."

"They are my *best* men," Lord Julien said with some restraint.

"Do it," Reynard said, addressing the Baroness. "Let Bradamante's Flycatchers have a turn at garrison duty. At least until I am wed."

"The girls will be thrilled," the Baroness said.

That night Faline joined Lara for a drink, saying that she wished to gift her husband some time alone with his sons. Lara wondered if he liked playing with toy soldiers as much as they did.

Faline had two glasses of Felician. Lara had three but still she could not sleep.

Reynard had not spared her a second glance.

The leaves were changing and the nights grown chill when a great party came up from the South. All the court were assembled to greet them as they passed through the Traitor's Gate, a great column trailing behind them.

Pepin of Perigon, the young Count of Tarsus, rode at their head, the ram on his banner shimmering with cloth-of-gold. With him came Terrien of Genova, his heir, Tastevin, and the Dowager Countess Clarissant of Poictesme, riding sidesaddle atop a chestnut palfrey. Coridon, Lord of Luxia, arrived in a wheelhouse. *To match his legs*, the Baroness quipped, but behind him tramped near to a thousand horse, bow, and pike whose standards bore blackbirds on field of burgundy.

Other emblems flew amongst the rearguard: The beast of Vyones, the drake of Nym, and the grim colossus of Ylourgne. The Northern lords peered down their noses at them as they passed, keeping their peace as the crowds about the gate let up cheer after raucous cheer.

"Southern dogs," Luisant spat, and might have gone on had Faline not dug her nails into his arm. When he protested, she dug harder and turned her eyes towards the girls clustered about the hindmost battlement.

Lara followed her gaze. The eldest of them wore burgundy. The youngest held onto a toddler in gold, tears streaming from her eyes as she watched the procession below.

There was a feast in one of the halls beneath the citadel. Lara declined the invitation. As she sat by her window, she caught sight of Arsinoe walking along the battlements.

She watched her until the Firebird grew dim beneath the clouds.

No lords came from Lorn. They had joined the rebels, and on the pinnacles of the Traitor's Gate new heads had been placed. Lord Gradlon's son perched there, and a chevalier from Cadwallon, and between them two young squires from Goscinny.

* * * * * * *

One morning, when the world beyond her windowpanes was still gray and hazy, Pierrot roused her from her sleep. She woke at once, reaching for the blade she kept by her bedside, but the old man shook his head and bade her follow.

One of the Baroness' captains was waiting in the parlor, the fierce one as tall as Moder, Bradamante. She had brought an armed escort with her.

With them was Scyron.

"Majesty," he said, kneeling at the sight of her.

"Get up," she said, rushing forward so that she might help him to his feet.

He did not need it. He looked well, hale even, his new scars blending well enough with the old. His garb looked tidy, if plain: A thick gray doublet, new boots, and riding cloak.

It was only in his eyes that she could see pain.

"I-" she said, gathering her thoughts. "I thought you might be-"

"Oh no, Majesty," he said. "Not old Scyron. Not yet."

Bradamante cleared her throat, her mail rasping as she shifted from one foot to the other.

"Yes," Scyron said, resentfully. "You- You look well, Your Majesty."

For once, he could not meet her gaze.

"Is that why they brought you here?" she asked. "As a witness?"

"I am to be sent to the front," he said, his voice low. "And brought before Prince Roland-"

"The *pretender*," Bradamante corrected.

"I am to tell him that you are alive and well," Scyron went on, "And that- That-"

"That I am to be wed," Lara said.

"Yes," Scyron said. "Majesty."

He shook and, reaching out, took her by the hand.

"I failed you, Majesty," he said. "Forgive me, I failed you."

"No," she said, "You have not."

She turned then to Bradamante.

"Will he be released," she asked. "When his task is done?"

"If he does as The Lord Protector bids him," Bradamante answered.

"Then go," she said. "With my blessing."

He knelt again and pressed his rough lips to her knuckles.

Before he could rise Bannertail was upon him. The fox-squirrel leapt onto his shoulder and nuzzled into his beard.

"I had not thought to see this tree-rat again," he laughed. "Arsinoe was convinced the usurper had drowned him in a bucket!"

A dark look passed over Bradamante's face, but she kept her peace.

"Arsinoe," Lara said. "You- You have seen her?"

"Yes Majesty," Scyron said, growing a touch more sober. "Every morning since-"

He paused and let Bannertail down from his shoulder, blinking at the sight of Pierrot.

"The, ah, Lord Protector has given me leave to join them in the yards beneath the Prince's tower," Scyron said. "We have even been allowed some exercise."

"Why was I not told of this?" Lara demanded of the woman standing in the doorway.

"We assumed you knew, Majesty," Bradamante answered.

I did not ask, Lara realized with a fresh wash of shame.

"Are they there now?" Lara asked.

"Yes," Bradamante said, her jaw tightening. "Majesty."

"Then take me to them," she said.

A moment passed as the tall woman considered. Bannertail leapt onto the windowsill, his tail twitching.

"As you command," she said at last, and motioned for her escort to remove Scyron.

"Shall I bear Lord Roland a message, Majesty?" the old pirate called out as they took him away.

"Tell him he is in my thoughts," Lara answered.

"I will, Majesty," he said. "I will!"

When he was gone, she threw on a cloak against the chill, and let Bradamante lead her down to the lower courts.

* * * * * * *

They were in a court beside the main gate, a bend of stairs shielding them somewhat from the gaze of the great keep above. Reynard's soldiers clearly used the place as a training yard, with wooden pells and straw dummies serving as archery butts. Coarse sand from the riverbanks had been cast across the cobblestones in a rough ring and there, stripped to the waist at its center and surrounded by a half-dozen foes, was Pinsard.

He wore a white strip of cloth over his eyes.

His opponents were Steel Heels wielding wooden swords, off duty no doubt, for the sentries of the hour were all servants of the Baroness. The men laughed and taunted as they took turns aiming blows at his back. Pinsard took each strike with gritted teeth, swinging back with his own length of wood, but always too late. The men danced around his strikes, chuckling before giving him a fresh smack for his trouble.

Arsinoe sat beneath one the walls, her legs drawn close as she chewed on a bit of bread. When she saw Lara coming across the yard, she stopped, but did not rise all at once. She looked older to Lara's eyes. The Firebird was already baking the yard, and the light off the stones made her hair catch silver in the shade.

"Here," Bradamante said, standing aside as they approached.

Lara slowed. A few of the Steel Heels, seeing her, stood aside, staring.

Bannertail leapt from her shoulders then, and ran to Pinsard, making to dance between his legs, but as he drew close one of the Steel Heels let out a cry and made to stomp on him, taking him perhaps for one of the rats that scuttered behind the walls.

Before his boot could land, Pinsard's arm lashed out. His wooden sword walloped the man so hard across the face that he lost his feet.

One of the others wound up his sword arm to retaliate, but then he too saw Lara, and his aim wavered. The other helped the wounded man to his feet and made way.

The yard was quiet then, save for the sound of Bannertail, yipping as he pressed against Pinsard's boots.

"So," Pinsard said, lowering his practice sword.

Lara's eyes met Arsinoe's as she lingered at the edge of the yard. She saw nothing in them save worry.

"Pinsard," Lara said at last. "Pinsard, I'm- I'm sorry."

Pinsard was silent.

Her heels scraped against the sand as she approached. He stepped away from her, his lips growing thinner.

"Pinsard," she said. "Please, speak to me."

"I have nothing to say," he said.

He turned from her and raised his wooden sword into the guard of the hawk.

"Come on," he growled. "What are you waiting for?"

The Steel Heels hesitated.

"Fight me!"

One of them took a few steps onto the sand. Pinsard turned to face him, his stance changing as the man began to circle.

Lara gathered Bannertail into her arms and backed away. The chimera panted in the heat.

The Steel Heel lunged, aiming a blow at Pinsard's head. Lara forced herself not to cry out, but then her brother was moving, kicking up sand as he planted his foot and cast aside the blade he could not see with a single beat of his practice sword.

The Steel Heel back peddled away from Pinsard's riposte, but only just. Pinsard drove on, until one of the man's spurs caught against cobblestones. He went down, and before he could rise Pinsard touched his breast with the tip of his blade.

"Yield," the Steel Heel grunted.

Pinsard lifted his sword, panting. The others chuckled as their brother-in-arms staggered back to his feet.

"That was," Lara said. "That was incredible."

"No," Pinsard said over his shoulder. "It was adequate. But while you were dancing and drinking with murderers, I have been busy, learning again how to see."

"Dancing?" Lara said, her cheeks growing hot. "Is that what you think I've been doing?"

"I do not know what you expect me to think," Pinsard said. "But if you have merely come here to apologize then very well. I accept it. Now, leave me alone. I have so much more to learn."

He raised his sword then and waited for the Steel Heels to come at him.

Lara forced herself to breathe, and bit back words she might regret.

A gloved hand clapped her shoulder.

"He's been like that," Arsinoe said.

"I don't-" Lara said, growing quiet. "I don't blame him."

"He's wrong though."

"Oh?"

"It's not your fault."

"Isn't it?" Lara said, swallowing the lump in her throat.

Arsinoe shook her head, *no*. She did look older. The silver in her locks was real.

"Your hair," Lara said.

"I know," Arsinoe sighed, putting a hand to her locks. "And more to come before the end."

"How is the food?"

Arsinoe smiled faintly. Her beetle quivered.

"Not bad," she said. "Though I'd kill for some pepper."

They walked the edges of the court, weaving through the pells. The Baroness' soldiers shadowed them but at a distance.

"The guards talk," Arsinoe said. "You're to be married soon, aren't you?"

"Yes," Lara said. "On Summer's End. Wulf's Night, they call it here."

"So?" Arsinoe said, expectant. "What's our plan?"

"Plan?" Lara said.

"You must have one by now," Arsinoe said. "It's been long enough."

"Arsinoe," Lara said. "There is no plan. I- I can't risk it. You know that, don't you? You saw. You saw what he did."

"But don't you see?" Arsinoe said. "It will be easier now. He thinks he's broken you."

Lara slowed to a halt.

"He has broken me," she said, quiet. "It's over."

"Don't say that," Arsinoe said.

"Why?" Lara said. "It's true, isn't it?"

"Because," Arsinoe said, her voice beginning to quaver. "Because if you say that again, Lara- If you say that and mean it, then-"

Arsinoe stared into her eyes, and for the first time that Lara could remember she could see tears beginning to well beneath them.

"Then you are no longer my friend," Arsinoe said. "And I don't think I could stand that, Lara. I really don't."

"Neither could I," Lara said.

"Good," Arsinoe said, and they embraced, not caring how the guards stared.

"You think he'll keep his word?" Arsinoe whispered into her ear. "Keep us safe?"

Lara shook her head.

"Then do what you must."

"But how?"

"Think of something," Arsinoe said. "Anything. Outwit *him* for once. Even- Even if it means the end of us."

Lara shivered in the heat. Then she nodded.

"Promise me," Arsinoe said.

"I promise," Lara answered.

She sealed her words with a kiss. They parted.

"I may not see you again," Lara said.

"I know," Arsinoe said.

Bradamante was already bearing down on them, her nostrils flaring.

"I'll try to send you word," Lara said, taking hold of Arsinoe's hand. "I'll-"

"That's enough!" Bradamante barked. They did not touch Lara, of course, but two of the guards took hold of Arsinoe and hauled her backwards.

"Leave her be!" Lara said, raising her voice. "I've seen enough."

The women looked to their captain. She nodded, still glaring, and they loosened their grip.

"Fahiseler," Lara heard Arsinoe mutter as she ripped free.

She suppressed a smile and led her 'escort' back towards the stairs. Pinsard was still sparring on the sand, his hair of mop of sweat.

"Stop," she said. And the Steel Heels stopped.

She pressed through their circle and stood before him.

"What?" he panted at her.

"Go on and be angry," Lara replied. "I still love you. You're my brother."

She turned, but as she did Pinsard's hand caught her by the arm.

"Don't," he said. "Don't let it be for nothing."

"I won't," she promised.

* * * * * * *

She hardly slept that night, save for in the gray hours before dawn. Bannertail followed her as she went from chamber to chamber and pondered the walls. The first time she stepped over Pierrot, slumbering beside her doorpost, he cracked open his eyes and smiled his odd smile. The second time he murmured something and rolled over in his sleep. The third time he got up, joints cracking as he slunk off to the parlor.

In the morning she found him, curled up on one of the couches. She knew where to begin by then.

"Fetch me his steward," she said, waking him. "Sigyn."

Pierrot blinked, intrigued, and slipped off.

Sigyn came, followed by two of her Calvarian footmen bearing breakfast and fresh linens. They looked so alike Lara assumed they were brothers, if not twins.

"The lady called for me?" Sigyn said as her underlings silently went to work stripping down her bed.

"Yes," Lara said, getting up from her seat beside the windows. "I was wondering if any of the craftsmen might be spared."

"Craftsmen?" Sigyn said.

"The ones I hear banging about all through the day," Lara said. "Those craftsmen."

She pointed downwards and, as if to punctuate her words, the sound of some heavy load being shifted clattered up from the floorboards beneath their feet. Artisans and laborers had been trickling up and down the stairs since the arrival of Lady Elaine, seeing to the task of preparing the feast hall for the day of the wedding, but now that the day was nearly at hand the trickle had become a flood of activity.

"And what is the lady wanting with such as them?" Sigyn asked, suspicious.

"I want them," Lara said, moving with purpose towards the vaulted section of wall directly beside her vanity, "To get rid of these."

With an easy shift of her hand against one of the otherwise unremarkable stones, she swung open the hidden door, revealing the tight corridor beyond.

Sigyn's lips puckered as she sucked on her teeth.

"I would have these walls be nothing more than walls," Lara repeated. "All of them. Do you understand?"

"I will take the matter before the Lord Protector."

"Do that," Lara said. "Until then, have some nails sent up from the yard. If I am to sleep here, I would have them spiked shut."

Sigyn's eyes widened, but she bowed her polite bow and excused herself.

She returned less than an hour later. Lara was still nibbling on one of the sweet rolls Pierrot had filched from the kitchens.

"I see no nails," Lara said.

"The Lord Protector bids me ask how many of the doors the lady would have sealed?"

"All of them," Lara said, feigning annoyance.

"He would have her name them."

Lara took a deep breath, letting Bannertail snatch the last bit of her breakfast as she rose.

"Very well," Lara said. "I would have them close the door in my bedchamber, the one in the parlor beside the fireplace, the one in the hall just outside the wardrobe, the one behind the font on the east balcony, and the one in the empty chamber off the long hall. Can you remember all that or shall I repeat it?"

Sigyn shook her head, her brows flashing as she retreated.

It took her far longer to return this time. Precieuse had already done combing out her hair and Bannertail was yawning, ready for the first of many naps beneath the windowsills. She was already a quarter of the way through the surviving memoirs of Lady Blandamour when Sigyn threw wide the doors to the long hall, red in the cheeks and short of breath.

"Well?" Lara asked, shutting the volume and laying it on a pillow.

"He bids me tell the lady that doing all she asks will take some time," Sigyn said. "But, seeing as she no doubt wishes to be undisturbed on her wedding night, he will have the masons seal up the passage leading to her bedchamber. He asks, will that suffice?"

"If it is done properly," Lara said. "Yes."

Sigyn huffed, and called out in her own tongue, too fast for even Lara to understand.

In answer a half dozen men, all but two of them Calvarians wearing chalk white uniforms, filed into the room and began moving the furniture near the door so that they might roll up the carpets.

Bannertail woke with a start and began to squall at them.

"They require room," Sigyn said. "My lady."

Lara took the hint. She gathered up Bannertail, scooped up her book, and left her chambers, smiling to herself as Pierrot followed close behind.

That day, and several days after she spent curled up in one of the snug alcoves of the great room with its painted game table, half-pretending to read as Luisant and Daguet ignored her. The rebels had been crushed it seemed, and now it was Glycon who threatened the realm in miniature, swarming up from the south with their dragon host. Bastian had been given the dubious honor of commanding the Southern armies, which Luisant soundly annihilated in game after game.

She might have felt pity for the boy, but he seemed glad enough to have been included at all. As for Faline's sons, *well* she reasoned, *they might dislike the bookish boy, but he was still a Northerner like them.*

One morning, as the masons were beginning their business, she found herself privy to a different group of boys huddled around a game table, no less petty. This one had been set up before the thrones of the great hall, across which a map of vellum had been spread. Blocks of wooden soldiers stood on it, arrayed atop painted towns and rivers, and over these the nobles loomed, the Northerners on one side, the Southerners on the other, like children arguing over how best to cut up a cake.

She could hear their shouting from the parlor, and by the time she came onto the gallery overlooking the hall she might as well have been standing in the chamber with them. Wishing to observe unseen, she crept up to the edge of the nearest balustrades and settled against the stones.

Bannertail peered from her shoulder as well, warm against her neck.

"Listeneise may hold," a gray bull of a man was saying. *Devoye*, she thought, *he was at Pikria.* "If its stores are good. But they need not take it to march on the capital."

"Or on the granaries in Poictesme," young Count Pepin said, gesturing towards the province. "Might we not spare a force to defend our flank there? With their pirates to ferry them-"

"And split our forces?" a Northern lord sputtered. "We are already stretched too thin!"

"Mind your tongue, sir," Devoye rumbled. "You speak to my master the Count."

"Lord Bourvil speaks sense," said Count Julien. "And with every town that falls more traitors flock to the pretender's banner. If Listeneise falls-" Julien turned to the head of the table, where Reynard stood, watchful and flanked by his own captains. "I beg of you, my Lord Protector, we cannot afford any more delays. Surely, now is the time to strike!"

Devoye jabbed his mailed finger across the table. "Had you held them at Nemea-"

"With what men, Southron?" Julien shot back hotly. "You were not there. You did not see what we withstood. No man could have held against them!"

"No man, perhaps," the Baroness quipped.

Reynard held up his hand, and the chamber grew silent.

"The pretender's victories are but false hope, Count Julien," he said. "A lure we dangle before him. And he is not as strong as you think."

"But the reports," Count Pepin said. "Your own spies, Lord Protector-"

"Lord Tiecelin's shrikes see much," Reynard said, acknowledging the man who hovered beside him. "But even they have their limits. With old tricks the pretender's thousands are made tens of thousands, especially when seen from the heights."

Julien shifted. "So, their numbers-"

"Exaggerated," Reynard went on. "And yet they are still enough to daunt us. Here, Lady Faline, tell these great lords of the enemy's true strength."

Lara's breath caught in her throat as her companion came forward, out from under the shadows of the balcony beneath her feet. The lords in the mail raised their eyebrows at her approach, the Southern barons muttering as they made way.

"All of Lorn the pretender has mustered," Faline said. "But even when joined with his Frisian allies his host numbers no more than six thousand foot. Of horse only some five hundred are fit for battle, the rest no more than scouts and skirmishers."

"And how do you know this?" Count Pepin asked, before adding, "My lady."

"I have many ears within the camp of the enemy," Faline said, quiet. "They tell me much."

Another murmur ran through the ranks of the Southerners.

"And what assurances do we have that these catspaws of yours speak true?" the aged Count Terrien wheezed, resting a hand on the table for support. "Indeed, what false report might the Lady of Lothier give to lessen their number, and thus draw us in?"

"You dare question my wife's honor?" Julien snapped, loosening his blade from its sheath.

Terrien's heir, Tastevin, loosed his own blade as the Southerners began to rattle, but Faline moved quickly to her husband's side and, laying her hand on his sword, lowered it gently.

"Please husband," she said. "Save your blade for the pretender. These Southrons clearly know little of courtesy and, as for my honor, it needs no defending. The Lord Protector knows the measure of my loyalty, does he not?"

Reynard regarded her and nodded. Again, the chamber grew silent.

"But what of their ships, my lord?" Pepin asked, his tone grown cautious. "Surely, we have not the strength here to hold them back."

"I do not wish to hold them back," Reynard said flatly. "We never could have bested the princes' fleet on open water. But now, now that they have bottled themselves at the mouth of the White River, they have lost their main advantage. Fire ships, with wind at their backs will break their armada into so much kindling."

He moved from his place at the head of the table so that he might stand before the wooden ships clustered about the gulf of Lorn.

"Already my reavers sail with fresh ships from Genova," he went on. "In three days' time they will reach the heart of the gulf. Then Frisia will burn."

He reached out with his false hand and swept the ships onto their sides. They clattered.

"And then," Devoye said, "My lord?"

"With their route to the sea cut off, and their allies scattered, they will have no choice but to attack, in the hopes that they might cut off my head before we catch them with their backs to the river. Lady Faline has spun tales amongst them that our numbers are few, and that we squabble amongst ourselves, an army divided."

The men in the room shifted, as Reynard plucked one of the pieces from the map. A white owl.

"But you will deny them, Lord Julien." he said. "I give you the command."

Pepin's jaw dropped, and his barons and chevalier began to clamor. More than a few of the Oscan lords crowed back, and cries of *never*, and *dishonor* echoed off the chamber walls. Even the Baroness Rukenaw looked aghast.

Lara wondered at her face as Reynard returned to the head of the table. *She's as surprised as the others.*

The sharp rap of wood against stone cut through their cries. Three times it sounded, and the Southern men quieted, turning towards a diminutive figure who had been leaning on a cane under one of the far alcoves, where the Count Coridon also sat in his wheeled chair. It was a woman, high-cheeked and prim, her dusky gown almost black in the gloom.

Lara took a step back from the balustrade. The lady was staring at her. Or was it a trick of the light?

Bannertail shifted across her shoulders, his long tail whipping against her locks.

"Thank you, Lady Belisent," Reynard said, looking about the chamber. "I take it then, that there are no more objections?"

The Southerners kept their peace.

"Excellent," Reynard said. "Lord Julien, do you accept?"

"I do, my Lord Protector," Julien breathed. "We will crush the rebels here, my lord!"

Julien drew a dagger from his belt and plunged it into the map, marking a place between Carduel and Listeneise.

"I pray you be gentle with the map, my lord," Reynard said glibly. "We may have need of it later, to mark your victory."

The men about the table, North and South, laughed. Julien retrieved his blade.

"Baron Devoye," Reynard went on, "You and what chevalier you deem fit will serve to guard our person, as well as that of the Queen. Some companies of my own I will keep in reserve as well, but I would know the quality of the South firsthand. What say you, gentlemen? Shall we take some fresh air?"

The men barked their assent, eager no doubt to be gone from that somber place.

"Come then," Reynard said.

The Graycloaks moved from their places along the walls and formed a circle about him, The Baroness and Tiecelin following close behind with their own retinues. Lara could not help but notice the absence of Tisiphone, and wondered if she was about on some errand.

The others followed, with Julien and Faline leading the barons of Astolat and Osca. Count Pepin and his vassals trailed behind, passing beneath the gallery until the last of them had disappeared from her view.

Lara waited until the last of them had gone and made for the stair, half thinking to follow, but as she came creeping down the stairs she realized that she had forgotten about the Count of Luxia and his chair.

A pair of servants were struggling to keep it steady as they laid its wheels down, step by step. Behind them the Lady Belisent stood, frowning at the stairs as another woman struggled to take her arm.

"Leave me be," Belisent said, rattling her cane. "I am not a cripple."

"Mother, please," the woman said, "If you would just let me-"

"Hush," Belisent said. "We are not alone."

Belisent turned to face Lara then, her skin crinkling about her eyes as she peered into the shadows of the stairwell. The other woman turned too, her eyes widening as she let out a shocked cry.

"Oh!" the woman gasped, and curtsied, her knuckles whitening as she took hold of her silken skirts. "Your Majesty, forgive me! I must confess, I took you for a ghost."

"I am the one who should apologize," Lara said. "I did not mean to come on you unawares, Lady-"

"Soredamor," the woman said, curtsying again, more crisply this time. "Of Sarnath, wife to Lord Coridon of Luxia."

Lara blinked. She was a beautiful woman, and vivacious. It was hard to picture her the wife of the weary-looking man being carried down the stairs beneath them. She thought of Lady Elaine and wondered how many other ladies of the court were wed to old men, or maimed ones, bed ridden.

"And this is my mother," Soredamor said, stepping aside so that Lara might have a better look at the little woman still peering at her. "The Dowager Countess, Belisent, of Tarsus."

"I am," Lara said, unnerved by the woman's gaze, "Honored, my lady."

"*Honored*," Lady Belisent repeated, her tongue dripping with derision. "The Old Goat, they call me, girl. Tell me, do I look like a goat to you?"

Belisent was short, and very lean with a long neck. The skin about her eyes and the bridge of her nose had a greenish cast to it, almost jaundiced. There were no whiskers on her chin, but-

"No," Lara said.

"Another liar," Belisent said. "A pretty one. But a liar, nonetheless."

She planted her cane on the first step and began to make her way down, moving quicker than the men with the chair.

"Keep up little liar," she said over her shoulder. "I would speak with you."

She continued to descend, her cane clicking and clacking against every step.

Soredamor shot Lara an apologetic look. She merely smiled and made to follow, Bannertail's claws digging into her shoulder for purchase as she took to the steps.

"Oh, do hurry up," Belisent said, whapping one of Lord Coridon's bearers on the back with her cane as she overtook them. "It will be supper by the time we reach the bottom."

The man had a thick back it seemed. Or he was used to the blows. Either way, Coridon's chair hardly tilted.

"Your husband," Lara said. "Is he- Dumb?"

Soredamor laughed at that. "No, Your Majesty. Not dumb, but very guarded. You might say that he hears much and says little."

"You describe half of the fools I've met," Belisent's voice carried up from below.

"I may be a fool, my lady," Lord Cordion said then, his voice little more than a croak. "But I am still a knowledgeable one."

"Feh!" Belisent's cane clicked on.

They too overtook the bearers, and as they passed Lara saw that Coridon was not as old as she had taken him from the balcony. His legs were shriveled, yes, and his eyes were weary, but the rest of him looked fit enough.

"Do not tarry on my account, cousin," he said to her, "I will be some time on the stairs, and the Lady Belisent does not like to be kept waiting."

Cousin, she thought. *Yes, by my mother's aunt. No wonder he is cautious.*

Lara nodded and quickened her step, Soredamor's skirts swishing as she hurried after her.

They caught up with the Dowager Countess two floors down. She seemed to know the fortress better even than Lara and led them down a corridor guarded by her own soldiery. The Tarsus men straightened at the sight of her but could not help but stare at Lara as she passed. She wondered if any of them had been at Pikria.

They reached an ornate doorway. Belisent struck it with her cane.

"Open up," she grunted, and sure enough it opened. A valet in cloth-of-gold got out of her way as she pressed into the chamber beyond.

Its walls were hung with instruments, mostly strings. Chairs lined it, and overstuffed cushions, and exotic urns from parts unknown. Tall bay windows provided a view of the woods below the escarpment, and the light that streamed through them gleamed against gold and polish.

Belisent moved towards a claw-footed table that stood upon a rug made from the hide of a Tyrian jungle cat and took up the bell that had been set upon it.

She rang. Another door opened, and more servants swarmed into the chamber, moving chairs, bearing dishes laden with cheese and fruit, and decanters of amber liquor. It took them but a few moments to rearrange the room for the midday meal.

"Bring them in," Belisent said to the valet.

The man nodded and motioned to one of his lackeys. Another door swept open, and through it came three young ladies of the court, followed by a maid servant leading a toddler. The eldest of them Lara did not recognize, though she so resembled Soredamor, with her curling hair and gold-green eyes that she might have been her sister. The other two she remembered from the battlements. They each took turns kissing Belisent on the cheek, the maid lifting the fussing child, before taking their places beside the table.

The servants pulled three of the chairs from the table.

"Sit," Belisent said to Lara, settling herself. "Or stand. It matters not to me."

"Forgive her, Majesty," Soredamor said. "Her manners are very Southern. It must seem crude to one such as you."

"No," Lara said, finding her own seat. "Not at all. And after all the lies I've heard over the years, I can't help but find it refreshing."

"Ha," Belisent clucked as her glass was filled. "I should think so. I too am surrounded by liars, but none that compare with the company you keep."

"Lord Reynard, you mean," Lara said.

"Who else?" Belisent said. "I've known many a skilled spinner in my day but none so dangerous as him. Truth can pour from his mouth and still be false! You have my pity, dear, for what that is worth."

"And yet you serve him."

"Of course," Belisent said. "Don't be a fool. Now try some of this. It's from Dandilin."

She waved her hand and one of the servants placed a tray of cheese before Lara. She ignored it, but Bannertail fidgeted on her shoulder until she offered him a morsel or two.

"Do you bring that rat with you everywhere?" Belisent asked.

"No," Lara answered. "Now, what do you want?"

Belisent sipped from her glass and set it down.

"This is my eldest granddaughter," the countess said, jabbing her cane towards the first of the girls. "Melicent of Poictesme. She was to be wed to your brother, but of course that did not last. That little brat is her son, Bourdon. He will be lord of Tarsus one day if you can believe it. Assuming the Lord Protector does not put his head on a pike."

The youngest of the girls let out a sob.

"Oh, stop that," Belisent snapped. "*She* is not one of mine. Not yet at least, for I would add Genova to my grand collection. Though who we'll find to marry such a blubberer I do not know."

The girl did her best to stifle her tears.

"This other ingrate," Belisent went on, indicating the girl in burgundy, "Is cousin of yours by my Soredamor. Sansmerci, I call her. He who marries her will be the Count of Luxia. Is that not so?"

"Yes, grandmother," the girl said. She seemed to share her father's quiet gravity.

"Tarsus," Belisent said. "Poictesme, Luxia. I was born of a poor chevalier of Vyones, but I have conquered as much as any army could. And with far less pointless bloodshed."

She tapped her nail against her glass.

"Pointless," she said. "Stupid and cruel."

"And still," Lara said. "You serve him."

"Your pale brother's father killed my son," Belisent said. "Reynard slew him. Some would call that justice. Swift, even."

"Do you call it that?"

"I call it the past." Belisent drained her glass. "He was a sweet boy, though single-minded. He broke when he should have bent. I have not forgotten it. Nor will I. But it is done. No, it is the future that interests me now."

"What future would that be?"

"Yours, of course," Belisent said. "You are the future. And I must say, I find myself wondering where me and mine shall find our place in it."

"You seem as though you would fit anywhere you wish."

"Do I?" Belisent smiled. Lara was reminded of the sharks that swam off the coast of Verch.

"Like quicksilver," Lara answered. "Hot or cold, I imagine you'll find your place."

"Oh ho," Belisent said. "That's clever. But not so clever as to frighten him off it seems."

"How's that?"

"I was there the day you were promised to young Roland," Belisent said. "Had I known then what I know now, I might have made a different match. Alas! My Soredamor failed to snare him."

"I was charming," Soredamor spoke up. She had not touched her food.

"Too charming, my pet," Belisent crooned. "Too witty. Men like the Lord Protector may claim to want an equal, but they're lying. To themselves most of all. Ah, but I suppose I do not blame him. To be a match for a woman of our house is an exercise in wits. I imagine he found it exhausting."

"I feel exhausted myself," Soredamor grumbled.

"And I never tire." Belisent plucked a strawberry from her plate and studied it for spots. "Daughters, Majesty. I tell you, daughters are always trouble."

"My moder would have agreed with you," Lara said.

"The She-Wolf?" Belisent said, discarding the berry and choosing another. "Yes, I supped with her too once. Very serious. But that can be trouble of its own sort. Take my granddaughter, Sansmerci. Barons up and down the Isoile throw themselves at her feet and she- this thankless child-she treads on them like so much carpet."

"I do not love them, grandmother," the girl in burgundy protested.

"Love?" Belisent snorted. "Since when has *love* come into such things? Do you think I wed your grandfather for love, that red-faced lummox?"

Soredamor set down her wine glass. "Mother, please."

"The greatest thing he ever did was sit on his ass long enough to die in bed," Belisent said to Lara. "It seems to run in the family. This one will be an old maid by the time your children are fit to be wed."

"My children?" Lara said.

"Who else?" Belisent said, and then her face grew aghast. "Wulf, don't tell me you're barren? I've brought out the best cheese."

"I am not," Lara said. "At least, not that I am aware."

"Yes," Belisent said, relieved, "We have heard of your *friend.* The Lord Protector's guards talk too much. I do not judge, of course, there is no accounting for taste. But we both know that union is not like to bear fruit."

She gave the berry in her hand another look and finally took a bite.

"What *his* children will be like, though, I shudder to think."

"That is not what I shudder at," Lara said.

"Most of us do," Belisent said, "One way or another. It is not the match I would have chosen, of course. Heh! Were these the old days I might have been tempted to steal you away. The true heir? And Devoye has the men enough. But then who would I marry you to? Some headless brat?"

The Genovan girl whimpered again. The toddling heir to Tarsus began to sob as well.

"Oh, take them away," Belisent said, sighing. "The Queen-to-be has seen them, poor showing that they are."

The girls curtsied, the maid gathered up the weeping boy, and then the Lady Melicent helped to usher them from the chamber.

"Bourdon is the best that we can offer you," Belisent said. "And that is assuming you bear a daughter and not a son. We will see Sansmerci married of course, but she may die in childbed. There are no sureties when it comes to children."

"Or marriage," Lara said.

Belisent grunted and swallowed another berry. Soredamor took a sip from her glass. Both women eyed her, waiting.

"I do have a proposal," Lara said.

Even if it means the end of us.

"You have my attention," Belisent said, straightening in her chair.

"A private one," Lara said.

"Leave us," Belisent said, nodding.

The servants vacated the chamber with efficiency. Soredamor rose from her seat more slowly, but the Dowager Countess waved her towards the hall impatiently. The Countess of Luxia curtsied, and went, perhaps in search of her tardy husband.

The room was theirs alone. Unless-

Lara's eyes searched the walls. Reynard was with his captains, but that did not mean there weren't other ears listening. Had she known she might have brought Pierrot to play upon his lute.

"Perhaps you might sit closer, dear," Belisent said, clearing her throat. "My ears are still ringing with the cries of children."

Lara nodded and moved her seat. Bannertail she set down beside her plate. He gnawed happily.

"Now then," Belisent whispered, leaning close. Her breath smelt of fortified wine. "Speak."

Lara took a deep breath and made her bargain.

XII

The day came, gray and grisly. There had been rain during the night and the stones of the city looked dark and swollen to the eye. Water ran from tiled roof and battlement alike, pooling between the cobbles and turning the riverbank to a marshy fen.

Still, when the third bell of morning was struck, deep and sonorous, the great lords and ladies of Arcasia made their procession to the coronation dressed for better weather. Their silken skirts and woolen cloaks dragged through the muck of the broken streets, for they would not stomach the sight of servants amongst their ranks. Some of the younger ladies had brought parasols, and they used them now to shield themselves from the wet dripping from the gutters.

The Lord Protector had chosen the square before the Queen's Steps for the ceremony, and a platform had been constructed at the foot of the stair. Before it the nobles gathered, each to their place and according to their station. To its left stood Lothier and Osca, then Astolat, and finally the last surviving Baron of Engadlin, the ruddy-faced Pescheour of Listeneise, whose fiefdom was even now in contest with the rebels. Opposite stood the worthies of Tarsus, Luxia, and Genova, and with them Clarissant, Dowager Countess of Poictesme and eldest daughter of the Old Goat.

A crowd had been gathered to witness them, though there were far more soldiers than citizenry. Behind farmers and carpenters, butchers and fishmongers, the ranks of the Steel Heels stretched, their marshal Galehaut given a place of honor on the steps themselves.

The sky lightened. A chill breeze blew through the city, shivering the branches of the trees that grew beyond the square.

Then the fourth bell rang out, and the gates of the fortress of Carduel swung open. From it issued the Lord Protector, flanked by his Calvarian bodyguards and his chief captains. Lord Reynard had eschewed even a breastplate, and the Warden of the Muraille wore only his dull woodsmen's leathers, but the Baroness was girt for war. Her spiked mace, The Fairlimb, she carried on her hip, and her gauntlets were of polished steel.

Behind them came the hostages, escorted by the Baroness' sentries. They came to a point halfway down the Queen's Steps and halted, even the white sheepdog belonging to the heir of Astolat. The crowd murmured at the sight of them, for few had seen the *guests* of the Lord Protector with their heads still in place atop their necks.

Lord Reynard had nearly reached the platform when a winged shape took flight from one of the crumbling towers of the fortress. It swooped over the square, and then alighted on the platform in a storm of feathers.

"The Marquis of Carabas," Tisiphone sang out, "Baron of Maleperduys, and Lord Protector of Arcasia!"

The crowd knelt. The soldiers bowed their heads. The nobles found their knees.

He looked them over, and then took his place atop the platform.

"You may rise," Tisiphone intoned.

Boots scraped against cobblestones as the crowd found its feet. Reynard's herald stepped into the shadow of her father, her clawed fingers toying with the pendants hung round her neck as she drew her wings tight about her shoulders.

"Lords," Reynard said then, his voice carrying over the packed square. "Ladies, and all you true patriots of Arcasia, hear now my words! For near to twenty summers the throne of our fractious kingdom has stood unclaimed. And as Lord Protector I have served to defend the state from the rebels and pretenders that have sought to wrest it from us, dared even to stand between us and our rightful monarch!"

He paused, his good eye passing over the nobles arrayed before him.

No one dared to flinch.

"But no more," he said at last. "Now, at long last, I lay down my burden. I am Lord Protector no longer. For behold! I give to you your Queen."

There was a hush, and all eyes turned to the gates above, expectant. A long moment passed, so long that many began to wonder whether something had gone amiss, when a figure appeared at the head of the stairs.

The crowd stared, stunned speechless.

Lara wore a gown of ivory, her face veiled in a thin lattice that stretched to her toes. She did not know that it had been her mother's mourning gown, but the sight of her drove a chill into even the staunchest of hearts. Even in the gloom she shimmered as she made her way down the steps. Children quailed, and brave men shuddered.

Bad luck, some whispered, and *ill omen*, until they remembered the soldiers at their backs. But many of the Steel Heels were just as unsettled, for to them it seemed as though the Lady Genevieve herself had come, pale and bloodless, searching for the ones who had slain her children.

Then the high priest of Fenix and his retinue emerged from the gates, making their own hesitant way down after her, and the spell was somewhat broken. For those who knew 'Lord' Baldwin also knew that he would sooner drown himself in the Leucothea than walk in step with a phantom. And so they saw her again as she was, the defiant renegade so much blood had been spilled for, snubbing their lord and master with her choice of dress.

It hardened some against her, but to others she gained a measure of esteem. Who else would dare mock the Lord Reynard, and live to tell the tale?

"You look beautiful," Reynard said as she approached the platform. "My Queen."

"I thought it might please your humor," Lara said.

He nodded, his teeth flashing as he smiled. "You'll find I like to be surprised."

"Good," she said. "There are more surprises to come."

"I should hope so," he said, stepping aside as the high priest approached.

Baldwin bore the crown her mother had worn. Lara bent her head to accept it. The man reeked of cold sweat and there was more than a hint of Frisian brandy on his breath, but he managed to keep his hands steady as he placed it upon her brow.

Finally, Lara straightened to her full height and turned to face the square.

"Long live Larissa!" Reynard called out, finding his own knee. "Long live the Queen!"

"Long live the Queen!" the crowd repeated with a single voice. Then they were silent.

They were waiting for her to speak.

Lara's mouth went dry. She wet her lips as best she could.

"Lord Julien," she said, picking him out of the crowd. "Today you lead our armies to meet the rebels."

"Indeed, my Queen," he said, stepping from Faline's side. "This very hour."

"Then let us see you off," she said. "I will walk with you as far as the western gate, if it please you."

"It does My Queen," he said, bowing. "Indeed, you do me honor. But forgive me if I think it unseemly that you should walk all that way on this the day of your coronation, as we have done."

"A horse!" Galehaut called out. "A horse for the Queen!"

A groom led a horse through ranks of the Steel Heels. It was Maiden. She had been brushed and combed until her coat shone, and her blond mane had been pulled very neat.

Lara let Galehaut lead her down the steps of the platform. Maiden snuffled at her hand as another groom hurried forward with a mounting block.

She mounted, but she allowed the marshal of the Steel Heels to take Maiden's lead, and so was led herself through the square, the lords and ladies falling into step behind her as the Steel Heels closed ranks behind them. Count Julien walked directly beside her, before even Lord Reynard himself, his barons and chevalier following as honor guard, but he paid her little attention. She was little more than an ornament to him, a pretty feather in his cap as Danica might have said, and he had eyes only for the crowd gathered to witness his hour.

Lara did not spare him a second glance.

"You are gentle, Lord Galehaut," Lara said, admiring the ease with which he led.

"She is a fine horse, my Queen," he answered. "And needs gentleness."

She turned to regard him and swallowed a bitter pang of guilt.

"And do you go to meet the rebel as well?" she asked.

"I do, my Queen," Galehaut said. "Count Julien has given me command of the van."

"Then you have my pity," she said, quiet.

"And you mine," he answered. "My Queen."

Before long there were only Steel Heels to watch them pass. The mercenaries stared at her with hard eyes but raised a cheer for their captain. *Galehaut!* they shouted *Galehaut!* and beat the cobblestones with their pikes.

She held her tongue all the way to the western gate. Assembled upon the fields beyond were the ranks of Reynard's army, ready to march. Indeed, there were outriders and swift moving infantry bearing the banners of the Baroness already underway before the far margins of the rocky woodland west of the ruins. She guessed that Scyron would be amongst them, if he had not already been conveyed down the western road, from whence Roland's own host was indeed hurrying to meet them.

"Here I must beg leave of you," Galehaut said, handing over Maiden's reins. "Wulf's Fancy, my Queen."

"Wulf's Fancy," she replied, for was it not Summer's End?

Fresh horses were being brought up for Julien and his retinue. Lara deigned to nod to them as they bowed before her and then made for the serried ranks of Oscan foot. Count Pepin of Tarsus too made his obeisance, as did Tastevin of Genova, and the wolf-eyed Baron Jenner of Nym, who Count Coridon had chosen to command the Luxians in his absence.

Last to make a show of loyalty was the Baroness herself. She gave Lara the merest of nods before finding Reynard's eye upon her.

"Don't pout," Reynard said.

"The *rearguard*," Rukenaw said to him, her cheeks flushed. "My girls are wasted on baggage duty."

"And you will play along," he said, his gaze flicking towards Lara. "At least until the battle is joined."

"Oh?" the Baroness breathed. "And then?"

"Suffice it to say that should things go amiss for the Oscans, I doubt very much that Lord Julien will have any *objections* to you taking command."

"I see," she said, smirking. "And Galehaut?"

"He has his orders."

She beamed and brought her steed about.

"Farewell, Your Highness," the Baroness said, kissing the tips of her fingers. "I would wish you luck, but I imagine my lord will be gentle with you."

"I doubt that," Lara said.

"Yah!" the Baroness cried as she set her spurs. A score of riders bearing the emblem of her mailed fist flew after her and a score of shrikes took flight from the battlements above. The Steel Heels filed past at the quick step.

And then, save for the Graycloaks, they were alone.

"Do you like your present?" Reynard said, reaching out to stroke Maiden's neck.

The horse snorted, pawing at the soil underfoot, but accepted his touch.

"Present?" Lara said. "She was Arsinoe's horse. She is still."

"She has not my leave to ride her," Reynard said.

"And I do?"

"Of course," he said. "You are the Queen."

He beckoned to one of his bodyguards, and his own steed was brought from the gates. A coal-coated palfrey, speckled along the flanks.

He mounted smoothly, and then stared out over the plain, his gaze wandering towards the foothills north of the city.

"One last chance to run," he said to her. "I doubt they'd expect it. Not now."

"And give you the satisfaction of a chase?" she said.

"Just a thought," he sighed. "Come along then. We've a wedding to attend."

* * * * * *

They rode slow. The city felt empty, the wind sighing through cracked walls and leafless trees. A cheer met them as they drew within sight of the Queen's Steps, but it was a tempered thing, dull and fearful.

The sixth bell rung.

It was Summer's End, Wulf's Night as the common folk called it, and so there was no Crowning pole set up in the square, and there would be no Crowning queen. But a queen would be wed nonetheless, with a court to pay her homage. And, as it was Wulf's Night, the lanterns atop the towers of the citadel were already lit. In Frisia she had been told such things kept evil spirits at bay.

Here, she mused, *they might serve to keep them in.*

Tiecelin offered her his hand as she made to dismount.

She ignored it. A groom led Maiden away.

A feast for the common folk had been made ready in the square. For them Lord Reynard had supplied heaps of roast fowl, sizzling mutton on skewers, and golden pies that smelled of mincemeat and boiled apples. Chestnuts roasted in great pans over coal-fired braziers, and there were honeyed almonds to be had by the fistful.

For The Watcher's share the Steel Heels had laid out the carcass of a stag at the foot of the Queen Steps, still bloody from the morning's hunt. The shrikes had not sullied it, leaving it for the crows to feed upon.

Father had no doubt commanded it.

Lara stepped about the carcass, either unaware or unbothered by the way her gown trailed through the blood as she began the slow climb back to the citadel.

Reynard and the rest of the court followed, but at a distance.

He was not her husband yet.

Precieuse met them at the gates, and with her Baldwin stood, attended by a burly acolyte who looked as though he had been summoned fresh from the forge fires, so dark were his rough cheeks and hands with ash.

"Your Majesty," Precieuse said, and curtsied deeply.

The smith-priests bowed with far less grace.

"If you will?" Precieuse said, extending her hand.

Lara looked to the tower of the shrikes, searching for some sign perhaps. Then she took a deep breath and, turning away, she took the priestess by the hand.

"Come," Precieuse said.

She led her up the stairs to the sunken court, her face solemn as they drew near to the slender oak that had sprouted amongst the cold stones.

"Here," she said, releasing Lara's hand. "Where roots yet grow, will you be wed?"

"I will," Lara said.

They turned, and there Reynard stood, the high priest fidgeting by his side.

"Here," Baldwin said, his voice scarce above a whisper as he raised up his ornamental hammer. "Here, beneath her- Her-"

Reynard turned his eye on the man. The high priest's jaw quivered, but no sound escaped his lips.

"Do you have something to say, Master Baldwin?" Reynard asked, softly. "Or have you forgotten the words?"

"No, m'lord," the high priest said, a touch too quickly. "I know the words. Only, it is Wulf's Night. Could this, ah, happy day not wait until the morrow, my lord?"

"Baldwin used to shoe my horses," Reynard said, speaking to the crowd. "And before that he made blades for bandits in the hills of Maleperduys. Hardly a deep thinker, no? And yet it seems he's grown philosophical in his old age."

"No m'lord, but-"

"But now you think to question my judgement on this, the day of my wedding. Is that it?"

"No, m'lord," he whined, shrinking back. "No! Forgive me, please, I meant no disrespect-"

"I know, old man, I know," Reynard said, sounding a touch weary. "You are forgiven. But strange days call for strange measures, do they not?"

Baldwin nodded, *yes.*

"Good," Reynard said. "Now hold that hammer steady and say the bloody words."

"Here," Baldwin said, his right arm shaking only slightly, "Here, beneath her glory, will you be wed?"

"I will," Reynard said.

Baldwin lowered his hammer. Reynard approached the tree. Precieuse gave way.

He reached out to Lara with his true hand. She placed her hand in his.

Pierrot had been crouched within one of the archways, quietly tuning his lute. Even now he did not rise, but merely turned his head towards them, a silent question written across his face.

"We do," they said.

Reynard lifted her hand to his lips, kissed it, and they were wed.

Pierrot began to play, the strings of his instrument soft and sombre. Lara did not know the tune, nor did any then present, for it was a new composition. And in later years, when all who had stood before the oak had become equals in mortality, it came to be known as *Larissa's Lament*, a favorite of poets, recusants, and lovelorn fools.

From the court they wound their way upwards, servants and soldiers kneeling low as they climbed dark stairs and walked lonely corridors until they came at last to the throne room. The war table had been removed, and the chamber had been scoured of dust and cobweb, and yet it was still a dark place. Whatever glory of the Firebird there was in the heavens above was kept fast at bay by windows marked with the faces of long dead kings.

Only one thing truly shone in that place. It lay atop a cushion of velvet set before the thrones, a blood-red jewel the size of a man's heart. It was a strange thing to Lara's eyes, for it seemed to have a life of its own, pulsing softly, like a thing alive.

The gem of Zosia. The tales all said that the Demon King himself had worn it, set into his crown of iron, but that the spirit of the Faun Queen of old had blessed it, so that none could look on it unmoved. She had scoffed at such things when she was younger. These were fables spun by aunt Danica, or fictions from one of Pinsard's treasured books, fantasies to while away the hours.

She was older now. She had seen drakes and dragons. She had seen Vulp Vora. And now, when she looked on the gem a strange feeling crept over her. One that she had not expected.

She *wanted* it.

Not the jewel, exactly, she had never been driven by avarice, and up until that moment the reality of who she was had seemed a burden to her. But now as she stepped past the thing, the light within it softly changing as she made for the thrones beyond, she found herself thinking of how it might be to be a Queen in more than name. To wield *true* power. Reynard might rule through her for a time, but he was still mortal, and older than he liked to think.

Ten years? Twenty? He might yet die in battle. Either way, he would not live forever, and then to whom would they bow? Was she not the Queen of Arcasia, the heir to Aquilia himself?

Then she thought of Moder. Pinsard. Arsinoe. The heads of children above Traitor's Gate.

She took her place before the larger of the two thrones, took hold of her blood-stained skirt, and sat. And that was the span of her temptation.

No sooner had she taken her seat than Bannertail bounded across the throne room, having scampered down one of the banners hanging from the balcony above. He leapt from floor to arm rest, and then onto her shoulders, his long tail curling about the back of her neck.

She reached up to scratch under his chin. He chittered deep in his throat, and then lay silent, so still that one might have taken him for an expertly preserved stole.

Reynard moved to the throne beside her then, but he did not sit. Rather he waited for the nobles to take their places before the dais, the Northerners on the Queen's right, the Southerners on her left. Bradamante with two dozen of her Flycatchers filed in behind them to stand sentinel between the arches of the gallery.

Behind them came Tiecelin.

He crossed the chamber and mounted the first step of the dais. He had brought three of his shrikes with him. The one that had eaten Pinsard's eyes was perched atop his shoulder. The eerie one with the gift for mimicry was already perched atop a wooden mew, her wide eyes unblinking as she stared at the assembly.

Tisiphone lingered on the edge of the hall, half-hidden behind a curtain, her mouth a tight line.

Reynard quietly cleared his throat.

"Here is the gem of Zosia," Reynard said. "The heart of Arcasia, united once again through our Queen. Long may she reign!"

"Long may she reign!" the nobles echoed back.

"And here-"

Reynard looped the chain round his neck about the fingers of his good hand and held aloft the jagged piece of steel that lay at the end of it.

"Here I hold a shard of the sword, Thunderclap. And by it I claim the Princedom of Vireo, which I now make a gift to my bride, Larissa, our Queen."

Lara could see the doubtful looks written across the faces of some of the assembly, the men in particular, but no one dared to raise their voice.

Satisfied, Reynard took to his seat, and motioned for the others to approach.

One by one the great lords and ladies of Arcasia stepped before the throne and knelt, breathing rehearsed oaths before making gifts of their own. Cherax of Astolat shook and quivered as the Lady Elaine spoke of the pleasure barge that had been built for the Queen's comfort. Lord Pescheour had his valet display one of the bottles of his own private reserve, a vintage so old that it had been *laid down* (as he said) before the first Calvarian invasion. Young Luisant outdid the old baron, promising not only fifty tuns of the finest Oscan white, but a full third of the County's revenue from the fall harvest.

Then it was the Southerners turn. Count Terrien presented a full troupe of Tyrisian dancers to the court, as well as some two dozen servants from the Argyrian Isles to serve the royal house. From Count Coridon a great herd of horses bred in Ormond was promised, "For surely I have more horses than I can ride," the quiet man said from the comfort of his chair. Clarissant of Poictesme had a large cage carried in, within which bleated a winged chimera, an immense bird with the head of a stag.

Bannertail rose up on his claws and scowled, his tail whipping against the chairback.

"For your menagerie, my Queen," the Dowager Countess said, ignoring the outburst. "A chimera of my late husband's house."

"Set it free," Lara said as the thing batted at the bars with iridescent wings.

"My Queen?"

"Set it free," Lara repeated. "I will have no thing caged for my amusement."

"Of course," Clarissant said with an uncertain glance towards the cage. "As you wish."

"Take the bloody thing outside first," Reynard amended.

Clarissant curtsied, relieved, and waved her servants forward. They threw the cover back over the cage and began to trundle their way out, grunting with exertion.

Bannertail slipped onto Lara's other shoulder and resettled.

"Tiecelin," Reynard uttered.

The man stirred. "My lord."

"See it done properly," Reynard said.

"As you command."

Tiecelin spoke some quick words to the shrike on its mew. The little mimic repeated his *as you command* back to him, its head tilting sideways as it watched him go.

When the caged chimera had gone the Lady Belisent came forward. She bowed very stiffly, her hand gripping her cane.

"And what gift do you bring," Reynard asked. "Sweet lady?"

"I've already brought some thousand men with steel," she answered. "To serve at my Queen's command. Is that not gift enough, my Lord Consort?"

Reynard shifted in his chair. There was a smile on his face, but not in his eye.

"No," he said at last.

"I thought as much."

She rapped her cane.

Devoye stepped forward, as did a dozen of his chevalier. They had come in mail, and with blades on their hips.

"The late Queen had an honor guard," she said. "My son served it well. Kept his oath at any rate. But seeing as I have no more sons to spend, this lot will have to do. Will that suffice, my Queen?"

Lara felt Reynard's eye on her. She nodded.

"Good," Belisent said, rubbing at her own eyes. "I believe there are oaths to be sworn?"

"Speak now," Lara said, her voice carrying across the hall. "And truly. Do you swear by your life's blood to be faithful, and swear true allegiance to me, to uphold my laws, and bear arms on my behalf onto my death?"

"I do," they said.

"Then rise," she said.

"Rise," the mimic repeated from its mew. She had already mastered Lara's timbre.

The chevalier rose, bowed once more, and backed away with reverence.

Reynard turned his head to look at Lara now, a half-concealed smile on his lips.

"You knew that by heart," he said.

"And you think this is the first time I've had to say it?"

His lips pursed as he considered her words, the fingers of his false hand tapping ever so lightly against the armrest.

"As you say," he said, leaning close as he beckoned to the Lady Faline. "Then I suppose you might have committed this next bit to memory?"

Lara stared back at him. Bannertail hissed in his face.

He flashed his own teeth before leaning back into his chair.

The Lady of Lothier came forward then and recited the lineage of the kings and queens of Aquilia, from Altair's crossing of the Plain of Glass to the sad reign of Corus, deprived of both his crown and living breath by Basiliscus the Cruel. She did not speak of the Dukes of Arcas, nor the Counts of Luxia, nor any of the other lords and ladies of her lineage, save two: Nobel, the father Lara had never known, and Lionel, the brother she could only half-remember.

"And thus, onto his sister," Faline finished, "Larissa, Queen of Arcasia. Long may she reign."

"Long may she reign," the hall repeated.

Reynard rose then and motioned for Tisiphone to approach. The shrike-girl bowed her head obediently and approached, her clawed feet clacking against the stone.

He leaned close and whispered something in her ear. Lara saw her green eyes widen and felt her own cheeks growing flush.

He knows, her thoughts screamed at her. *He knows he knows he knows.*

He guesses, the more rational part of her urged. *He suspects. Keep quiet.*

She kept her peace.

So did Tisiphone, though she gnawed at her lip with pointed teeth.

"Hurry along then," Reynard said.

"As you wish, my lord," Tisiphone replied, her wings beginning to unfold.

The nobles flinched as she took flight, lighting on the balustrade above on her way to the tower that lay above Lara's own quarters.

Reynard's tower.

She was hardly gone when Reynard extended his left arm.

"Lyra," he said.

The mimic flew from its mew and landed atop his false forearm, her pin-sharp claws kneading the leather straps that held it in place.

"Follow," he said to her, soft yet firm. "Listen. Report."

The little mimic blinked her all too human eyes at him and then took flight, hurrying after her larger sibling.

Reynard turned to face Lara and *smiled*.

"Come," he said, extending his true hand. "My Queen."

She deigned to take it and rose. He led her down from the dais then, gentle but firm, and passed through the assembly with stately mien. From the throne room they passed into the arched passage beneath the viewing gallery and through the great doors that led to the feast hall.

The Graycloaks fell into step behind them, followed by the newly made honor guard of the Queen. Behind them the great lords and ladies of Arcasia trailed, the Northerners first, so that Lady Faline's sons, Luisant and Daguet led them, their heads held high.

They passed through a dark gallery and turned into a cavernous space lit by iron candelabras, a roaring stone hearth, and a trio of truly massive chandeliers, hanging by century-old rope. The walls were woodwork, stained dark and varnished so that the reflected fires seemed to dance within them, and the ceiling above all carved beams and painted rafters. The pair of tables which ran its length had been set for a royal feast. Crystal glittered and silver shone, and on either side of the chamber tables had been laden with decanted wine and tureens of steaming broth. Should the wine run dry, six tuns of the Felician lay on trestles, ready to be tapped.

But that was not what drew the eye.

Rather, it was the black mirror standing before the great windows at the far end of the chamber, through which Lara could still make out the faint outline of the tower of the shrikes. It stood where the top table might have been, upon a raised stone stage, and about its base a sort of pale mist clung, drifting amidst the supports keeping it upright.

At a distance from it an odd figure lurked, cloaked from head to toe in robe and leathers, a mask of sorts concealing the better part of its face. It was fiddling with something beside it, a low column with what looked like a helmet laid atop it.

Only this helmet was far too large for any man to wear. The odd holes in it would have rendered its wearer blind.

"Dramsind," she could not help but gasp.

"**Yes**," the helmet spoke, the word crackling like deep ice upon a lake, so loud that Lara could have sworn she could see it with her naked eyes.

But it was Dramsind's voice.

"He lives?" she asked, her fingers squeezing Reynard's hand almost involuntarily. Her joy, and her curiosity, had driven away her thoughts, if only for a moment.

"I'm not certain that he was truly *alive* to begin with," Reynard said, releasing her hand. "But yes. He lives."

She swept across the room, her bloodied skirts swishing until she stood before the column. She could hear the nobles streaming into the room behind her murmuring to each other, the word *mirror* slipping from many lips, but she did not care.

"Dramsind," she said, her voice low. "Is it really you?"

"**Yes**." There was no light behind the sockets of his 'eyes', not even a flicker.

"Are you . . . In pain?"

"**No**," he said.

She was aware then of the figure staring at her from behind the column. Or, at least, it seemed to be staring. She could not make out its eyes.

"How?" she asked, turning to find Reynard staring at her as well.

"Darrhon could answer that better than I," Reynard said, gesturing to the figure. "But I thought it might please you."

Lara saw the figure for what he was then, one of The Dragon's sorcerers. Reynard had stolen more than the mirror it seemed.

"But," she said, ignoring the sorcerer's stare. "He speaks? Our tongue I mean."

"Not much," Reynard said. "Only 'yes' and 'no.' But that will do for my purposes."

"What purposes?" she asked, her ire rising.

"Dramsind," Reynard said. "Show my guests what we spoke of this morning."

"**Yes**," Dramsind said.

Something hissed. Fresh gouts of white mist poured from the base of the mirror like steam from a kettle. A chill washed over Lara, like early morning in winter.

And in the black depths of the mirror, something began to take shape.

They looked like embers at first, glowing hot and cold as they drifted across the mirror's face. Then they grew larger, or closer rather. A dozen hulking ships, all ablaze, the blaze playing against a silvery sea.

She could not help but back away.

Gasps were rising from the crowd. Others stood transfixed, and then a great swell drove one of the fiery vessels against a dark shape. New flames blossomed, and as they ran along wood and plank one could clearly see the caravel it had struck, the little figures racing about its deck.

"The Frisians," she said.

"The enemy," Reynard corrected as another flaming cog crashed into a cluster of sloops, their sails catching almost at once. "You should know by now that I do not suffer my enemies to live."

The flames spread. They danced in the pool of his eye.

"But you see things that have already come to pass," he went on. "The survivors are already encamped with Roland and his rebels, less than a day's march to the west. Would you like to see their camp, my Queen? See how bold they are, how brave? How doomed?"

"No," she said.

"As you like," he said. "But tomorrow . . . Tomorrow, I will have other sights to show you."

He was close to her now. Close enough to kiss or kill. But she did not back away.

Behind her the mirror hissed.

"Continue, Dramsind," Reynard said over her shoulder. "Our guests may find what they see educational."

"**Yes**," Dramsind said.

Reynard stood aside and gestured to the high table. It stood before the great hearth, dwarfed by the flames that roared behind it.

She spared one last glance at Dramsind, and the images within the mirror and then walked the length of the hall, her head held high. The nobles remembered their manners as she passed and bowed. But their eyes were still on the ruin within the dark sheet of glass.

Lara did not blame them. She doubted any of them had seen *real* magic.

She found her seat. Reynard followed suit. The Graycloaks formed a loose circle about them, their hands resting on the hilts of their swords.

Her own 'guard' took position along the breadth of the hall, save for Baron Devoye. He waited for the Southerners to take their places, and then moved to stand behind the Lady Belisent, who had been given one of the places of honor closest to the high table. Opposite her sat Lady Faline and her sons.

Somewhere in the city bells began to ring.

Dusk. Wulf's Night had begun.

"Do you expect us to wear these," Lady Belisent said, frowning at something she had snatched from the table, "Lord Reynard?"

"Of course, my lady," Reynard said. "You would not want to risk The Watcher's displeasure, would you?"

Lara noticed the half-masks atop the tables then. They were fine things of silk and satin, set amongst the sea of silver cutlery. Each one suggested an animal. The Lady Faline had a silvery stag before her, her son Luisant a pale ghost owl. Lady Belisent had a golden goat with horns in her bony grip, scowling even harder. It seemed to scowl back.

"I suppose we should consider ourselves fortunate that it is not Midwinter," Belisent muttered as her granddaughter, Sansmerci, helped to slip on her mask, "Or we might be serving the servants."

Lara looked down at her own mask. It was quite plain, a black domino.

Reynard's was identical, only his was red.

Like blood, she thought as he slipped it on.

"Your father thought himself a lion," Reynard said. "Your mother a bird in a golden cage."

"And me?" Lara asked. There were beads of sweat already tickling at her neck from the heat of the hearth.

"A strange chimera," he said.

She slipped her mask on. Bannertail ran down her arm and onto the table, sniffing at the air with anticipation.

The feast began.

Servants and attendants outnumbered the royal guests. Dishes were served, grand platters savory and sweet, but Lara did not taste them. She ate sparingly, putting fork and knife to plate and then lifting some delicacy to her mouth. She scanned the hall as she chewed, studied the faces lit by candlelight. There were no smiles. No mirth. No one ate with relish.

On the far side of the hall the Frisian fleet blazed, brilliant and silent within the confines of the mirror. On the other, the hearth. It was the same one that the mad Queen Grisana had walked into, immolating herself at the close of her poisoned feast, the lifeless eyes of her guests watching as she burned, the hall catching with her.

The varnish had hidden the scorch marks, but they were still there.

The wine was poured, the strong Felician.

"Wulf's Fancy," Reynard said, raising his cup.

"Wulf's Fancy," the hall chorused, and drank deep.

Lara took a sip but seemed to misjudge the edge of her plate as she put down her crystal. It caught and then toppled over, shattering, its contents soaking into the tablecloth.

The hall grew quiet.

"Allow me, my Queen," Devoye said, and began to make for the high table, too fast for the Graycloaks comfort. Three of them put themselves between him and the Queen, loosening their blades from their sheathes.

Devoye stopped in his tracks.

"I meant only to refill the Queen's glass," Devoye rumbled, pointing to the carafe that stood close at hand.

"Your gallantry is admirable," Reynard said. "But unnecessary."

Reynard took his own glass and offered it to her.

"Here," he said. "A lover's cup."

She met his gaze and took it.

"My wits as sharp," she said.

She raised his glass and drank.

It took him a moment. Then he smiled.

"I'm not dead yet, my dear."

"Not yet," she said.

His smile deepened.

"Thank you, my lord," Lara said, turning to Devoye. A polite dismissal.

Devoye bowed and returned to his old mistress' side. The tension lifted. Guests went back to their meals, silver scraping against silver. Labete fought with Count Terrien's hounds for table scraps. Priest Baldwin fell from his chair, finally too drunk to stand. The Calvarian servants carried him out.

Lara motioned to one of the servants. Bannertail, full of sweetmeats, had fallen asleep atop a silver tray.

"Let him outside," she whispered. "The night air will do him good."

The servant nodded and carried both tray and chimera away.

The hearth roared. Count Terrien laughed at one of his own jests. A babe began to bawl- Little Bourdon, squirming as the Genovan girl tried to quiet him. Lara saw Faline wince at the sound, her hand gripping Daguet's. Sansmerci passed the weeping child to the Lucran girl, Melusine, who bounced him on her lap.

He quieted.

"Come!" Reynard called out suddenly, craning his neck towards the far end of the hall. "Where is the music? The dancing? This is Wulf's Night, is it not?"

There, near the foot of the mirror, Pierrot sat, cradling his lute. A woman stood with him, not another priest, but some singer from the city below, little more than a bawd. Lara had not caught her name, but she had been told that she knew her dreadfuls well enough.

As might be expected of any who sang for their supper in the shadows of Carduel.

Pierrot beat upon his lute and let its strings sing. The bawd nodded at the tune and swallowed the last of her cup to clear her throat.

"*The Watcher's Bride*," Reynard hummed to himself. "Your fool has excellent taste."

Lara did not answer.

Pierrot played, the bawd sang, and Precieuse slid from her own seat and began to sway to the music, her skirts twirling as she spun this way and that. Baldwin's second beat out a tempo on the table before him, his blackened fists like mallets.

The nobles turned their gaze from the priestess to the man watching from the high table, his eyebrows cocked as if to say, *well?*

One by one they began to rise. There were far more ladies than lords present, so they formed two lines between the tables, linked hands and began to move to the rehearsed steps of a courtly procession.

Lara watched them, hound and blackbird, stag and crab. A sea of animals.

Pierrot played. The Watcher had his bride and then the lady lost her diamonds. Zosia riddled with Graymask. The ocean swallowed Kerys.

Then he began to play the slow lay of Virago.

Reynard had been sitting, the fingers of his false hand flexing ever so slightly as he watched the nobles parade about the hall.

Now he straightened in his chair, his smile gone.

"Dance with me," he said.

"Is that a command?" Lara asked.

"A request."

She studied his face. There was nothing to see.

"Very well," she said, rising.

Reynard rose. She let him take her hand. Let him lead her around the high table to the center of the hall. The nobles parted for them, bowing, whispering.

Pierrot played on. The bawd faltered for a moment at the sight of them but then found her voice anew.

Lara curtsied. He bowed.

He took her hand in his, his false hand coming to rest against her waist.

She was glad of his gloves. She didn't think she could endure his naked touch.

They danced.

"How does it feel?" she asked. "To finally be king?"

"You think *that's* what I wanted?" he sneered.

"No," Lara admitted, "But I don't pretend to understand you."

"I think you do," he said, his false hand pulling her closer as they spun. "Or you wouldn't have the stomach to suffer through this."

"I suffer what I must."

His lips parted for a moment, words on the edge of his tongue. He closed them.

"What is it?"

"Nothing," he said.

"Secrets is it?" she teased. "On our wedding night?"

The barest flicker of a smile crossed his lips. It faded quickly.

"A crown won't make me king, Lara," he said. "Any more than rags would make you common."

He grew silent again. The lute wept. Lara stared into his eye and saw something behind it. It almost resembled regret.

"The song," she said. "It reminds you of her. My mother. Doesn't it?"

"Perhaps," he said. "Not you. You're many things, but no Virago."

"And you're no prince."

"No," he said. "But they'll sing songs of us I think."

She felt the fingers of his false hand quiver against her waist.

"I'd ask where you've hidden your dagger," he said. "But I don't want to seem improper."

"They're in my corset," she answered. "Precieuse helped to sew them in."

"One dagger not enough?" he asked.

"Not for you."

He slowed their pace, a two-step. Reynard's gaze wandered over the nobles dancing nearby. Lara followed it, saw what he saw: Young Luisant keeping some baron's girl from Monbranc at arm's length, a pair of Oscan ladies in matching satins, Sansmerci yawning as the brutish baron of Vyones gripped her hand like a butcher with a ham hock.

"Let's say that you manage it," he said. "What then? You can't believe your newfound allies will be enough to whisk you away. My guard will cut them down before they get within five steps of us."

"They're not here for *me*," she said.

"Oh?" he said. "Oh, of course. The *children*."

"The children," she repeated.

"And then your friends I suppose?" he sighed. "Your so-called brother. Your golden girl."

"Yes," she breathed.

"They may find that difficult," Reynard said, "When I've already ordered Tiecelin to have them executed."

Lara met his gaze. "I know."

Reynard was smiling again, his good eye gleaming.

"You bluff," he said.

"Do I?"

"Hm," he purred. "But then who will save you, my dear?"

"No one," she answered. "Myself."

"And how will you manage that?"

"Like this," she said, and ripped her hand from his.

He flew backwards, slipping away from her like an angry cat. He had expected a knife or a knee to his crotch. Instead, she made for the closest table, toppled Baron Pescheour clear over, slammed her hip into the wood and *reached*.

The Graycloaks had already drawn their swords, were already closing in, when she turned and hurled the carafe of Felician straight at the closest one's face.

He brought up his sword just in time to break its flight. Glass shattered. Wine soaked him from head to foot.

He looked more confused than hurt.

Then she thrust the candelabra at him.

The Felcian caught, tongues of flame racing over the man's tunic as he reeled backwards. He did not cry out, but Lara could see the panic in his eyes as the flames spread to the woolen cloak about his shoulders.

The man threw himself to the floor, rolling as the crowd began to shout. Another of the Graycloaks came at her, but she was ready for him too. She let go of the candelabra and threw herself right over the table, scattering plates and crystal as Count Cherax blinked at her, his mouth working to make sound.

"Get out!" Lara shouted at the Lady Elaine as she grabbed another full decanter and sloshed its contents against the curtains.

The Lady of Astolat did not wait for her to set it alight.

She took hold of Bastian and ran with Labete hot on their heels.

She was not alone. Nobles and servants alike saw the flames, and suddenly it was as if all the old stories, all the nightmares and dreadfuls that had kept them lying awake in the long hours of the night had come to life and they were in it.

They fled, some screaming, others choking as their eyes stung from the smoke. Belisent led the flight, her cane abandoned and quicker on her feet than her appearance might suggest. Luisant and Daguet nearly trampled their own mother as they shoved towards the doors. Sansmerci let out a frightened yelp as her brutish dancing party caught hold of her wrist and began to drag her away. The bawd from across the river tried to do the same to Pierrot, the fear of laying hands on one of The Watcher's servants driven from her head.

But when he would not budge, she gave up and joined the rout.

Devoye's chevalier were moving too, but not to help. Half of them took up the great mallets standing near the wooden tuns along the wall and began to smash them open. Felician began to pour like water from a breached hull, gushing across the floor.

The other half had drawn their swords, forming a circle of steel about the chamber's only exit. They let the nobles fly past, their eyes locked on the bodyguards tightening about the Lord Reynard.

Devoye was nowhere to be seen. A canny observer might have noticed him escorting Lord Coridon from the chamber when the royal couple began to dance. To visit the privy perhaps, or to retire early. Gone too were the Lady Melicent and her child, Bourdon. No one had complained when she carried the bawling babe from the chamber.

Not all were so fortunate. Count Terrien was wheezing in his seat, his face ashy as he clawed fruitlessly at his left arm. The big priest of Fenix had made the mistake of charging one of the Queen's chevalier, spittle flying from his mouth as he roared out a challenge. He managed to throw one of the chevalier aside before Southern steel cut him down.

The fire spread. The curtains went up like sheets of flame.

Lara tore at her bodice, freed the first of the knives sewn against the ribbing, and slashed open the stays that held up her cumbersome skirt, freeing her legs.

No one could have seen the weather-beaten boots beneath her silks.

They could now.

She moved along the table's edge, putting the flames at her back as another of the Graycloaks skidded over the table, his boot nearly taking her full in the chest as he flew forward.

Instead of dodging she took hold of him by the front of his tunic and slammed her forehead straight into his nose. Something crunched. The crown on her brow bit into her skin, drawing blood.

The man reeled backwards. She did not wait for him to recover but drove her knife through the underside of his jaw.

He fell, gurgling.

She tossed the crown aside, wiped the blood from her forehead with the back of her hand and caught Reynard's eye.

He had hardly moved. He hadn't even drawn his sword.

Instead, he brought his hands together, and clapped.

She spat on the floor and tore the other blade free.

"Pierrot!" she cried out, finding the man amidst the clouds of steam thickening about the mirror. He looked like one of Carduel's phantoms.

And he had a bundle of cloth in his arms. The guards had taken it for an instrument. He snapped the bundle loose, took hold of what lay within and flung it.

It flashed as it hurtled through the air. She caught it neatly. Loosed it from its scabbard.

Three-Merits.

And not a moment too soon. A shape came at her from the steam. The sorcerer, rasping. He had something like a knitting needle in his grip, a sack of some poison attached to it by a flexible stretch of pipe.

But he was no warrior.

She sidestepped his lunge and slammed the hilt of her sword into his face, the lens over his left eye cracking as he let out a metallic cry. He crumpled backwards, before skittering away like an insect, struggling for breath.

She looked about. Pierrot had vanished. The fires in the mirror were matched by the fires in the hall.

"Dramsind!" Lara shouted. "Will fire hurt you?!"

The trunkless head was silent. Perhaps it did not know.

"Will falling ten stories hurt you?!"

"No."

She ran up the dais and spun, putting all her strength behind her kick. The head came loose from its cords and went sailing through one of the stained windows behind it. Wind howled through the broken glass, cutting through the mist as it fanned the dancing flames beyond.

The mirror grew black.

Through the hole, Lara could hear steel ringing, voices raised in rage and terror. There was fighting within the walls below.

She put it out of her mind and turned to face Reynard.

One of the Graycloaks stood between them. Their captain, Ulfdregil.

"Drop your sword," the man said, drawing his own.

His voice was like slate grinding on slate.

"No," Lara replied.

She flipped the dagger in her hand and threw it.

He spun as she threw, cloak whirling, and then came charging towards her, his jaw set.

The *snap* of aged rope giving way was his only warning. He did his best to lunge, but the chandelier caught him full in the back as it fell, crushing the life from him with a tremendous *clang*.

Dozens of lit candles fell into the spilled wine. A river of fire ran up the length of the hall. Cinders were raining from the rafters, like lightning flies in the late summer.

"A pity," Reynard said, regarding the crushed wreck of Ulfdregil. "He was a good man. Loyal."

"He should have chosen a better master," Lara said.

The remaining Graycloaks began to advance on her, their eyes full of hate.

"*Stop,*" Reynard said, using their tongue.

They faltered, reluctant.

"*Leave her to me,*" he said.

He rattled off more: *Prisoners, tower, gates,* she knew that much Calvarian, but not much else.

Whatever the orders they obeyed, making for the hall. The pair of Tarsus men who dared to stand in their way died.

"Now then," Reynard said. "What shall we make of this wedding gift, Larissa?"

Lara leveled Three-Merits. A challenge.

"Ha." Reynard spared a cutting glance towards the chevalier. "Is this meant to frighten me? A half dozen fools, a fancy blade and a bit of fire?"

"No," Lara answered. "This is."

She nodded to the chevalier.

As one they retreated through the doors. Then they threw them shut. Something slid against the wood beyond. Something heavy.

"What are you doing?" Reynard asked.

"Killing myself," Lara answered.

The bemused smile on his face faltered ever so slightly, and she could see something there. Something she'd never seen before, something as sweet as if she had plunged a dagger through his remaining eye.

Surprise.

"You can't die," he said, simply. "You *can't.*"

"I can," she said. "And I will. And so will you. Isn't that what you wanted?"

"No," he said, skirting a pool of flame. He wasn't smiling anymore. "That's not how this game is played. I won't allow it."

"Try it," she said, flicking her blade. "Go on, *save* me. But I won't go willingly. Or do you think you're faster than the fire?"

His jaw worked. His good eye shone bright.

"What?" she asked. "Nothing clever to say for once?"

The ruby on his sword hilt flashed in the firelight as he drew.

"At last," he sighed.

XIII

She was watching from the parapet when the windows of the upper keep blew out, first one then another, opening like the eyes of some great demon. Black smoke tinged with licks of flame poured from them, and with them came the screams. Men, women, and children screaming, their cries carried on the wind.

"Volk," Arsinoe swore.

She had watched Lara from the tower, seen her crowned, seen her wed. She had seen too the army marching off to war beyond the crumbling walls of the city, a black mass of killers heaving beneath a gray sky. For a while she had watched the celebration in the square before the steps, her nostrils flaring as she caught the aroma of roasting shellbark. She would have killed both their guards for the sake of a single bite, had she a weapon.

And now the keep was on fire.

"Volk," she swore again, and began to move, pushing from the battlements and through the door to the interior of the tower.

As if that would help.

"What is it?" Pinsard's voice cut through the darkness. She could barely see him. He had let the fire dwindle down to its embers.

"Fire," she said hurriedly, looking for one herself. "She's set the keep on fire!"

"How do you-" he began to ask, and then, "Listen!"

Arsinoe could hear it too. Steel on steel. It sounded close.

In her rush she knocked something from the mantle. A dozen wicks scattered across the floor. Her fingers ached as she tried to snatch at them in the dark.

"*Volk!*"

She finally found a wick.

She thrust it into the hearth and lit one of the candles atop the mantle, then another. It was enough. Their new prison was larger than the last, but not much. Pinsard was standing in the archway, a pale silhouette, silent.

The fires outside outshone the ones within.

There was a cry in the stairwell beyond their chamber's only door, one she had heard a hundred times. Someone was dying. More sounds, steel echoing against stone. Outside the shrikes were shrieking.

What to do? She moved on instinct, flipping one of the hardbacked chairs provided *for their comfort* and aimed her heel at one of its legs. She kicked. The leg snapped free, and she caught it up. She doubted it would serve for a decent club, but something was better than nothing.

Pinsard had picked up the nearest thing at hand, his shaving blade.

Every night she had lain in bed, wondering when the door would swing open and Reynard's killers would come into the room, naked blades in their hands. But this was no knife in the dark, some subtle order being carried out. Who then? The rebels, or the enemy?

Then, a *click*. The door to the stairwell swung inwards and hit the wall.

Arsinoe slipped away from the candlelight. She caught a glimpse of Pinsard. The brave idiot had shifted into a fighting stance, a perfect target in the doorway.

If they have crossbows-

"Come on!" a man's voice barked from the stairwell. Arsinoe didn't recognize it. "Quickly!"

"Says who?" Arsinoe grunted, taking another step into the gloom.

"Your bloody rescue!" the voice snapped. Arsinoe could hear the fear behind his bluster. "Now move your hides before the shrikes eat us!"

She loosened her grip on the chair leg. They could have shot Pinsard. Still-

"Prove it!" she growled.

Someone in the stairwell cursed. *Hurry*, she could hear someone whisper.

"'Supposed to ask you," the man in the doorway spat. "Some nonsense about the stars. What they're worth. That make sense?"

"Good enough," Arsinoe said, "Husband?"

He nodded and reached out his hand.

She led him into the stairwell and found herself face to face with one of Reynard's minions, the kind she had been putting into the dirt for the past two years. This one was wearing the faux gold cloth and brassy mail of the Southerners. His beard probably covered the worst of his pockmarks.

There were five others with him, standing over the corpses of the Steel Heels who had been guarding the door. They looked eager to be elsewhere. One of them kept glancing up the stairwell, his bloodied sword shivering in his grip.

"Come on!" their spokesman said again, stepping aside so that he might take up the rear.

"A moment," Arsinoe said, pressing past him.

The man bit back a curse as she released Pinsard's hand and traded her chair leg for of one of the Steel Heels pikes. She would have taken his mail too, had she the time.

"Pinsard," she said. "Pike or sword?"

"Sword," he answered.

"Why do I even bother," she muttered, starting to undo one of the men's sword belts.

"Quit wasting time!" one of the other men snapped. "'es blind, ain't he?"

Arsinoe ignored him and the ache in her fingers. The belt slid free. She wrapped it about the scabbard and tossed both to Pinsard.

He caught them and slipped the belt smoothly about his waist. The Southerners shot each other looks.

"Done?" their spokesman asked.

Arsinoe nodded.

"Good," he said, and nodded to one of the others.

They began to make their way down the steps. Two of the Southerners in front, four behind. Arsinoe didn't ask where they were going. As long as it wasn't here, she didn't really care.

The sounds of battle beyond the tower were growing louder.

Her knees sang as they pounded down the steps. At least she could still feel them, she mused, and found herself wondering whether Pinsard would stumble, and if she would be able to catch his fall.

He didn't stumble.

They were well past the chambers of the Blue Prince, almost to the base of the tower she guessed, when the man leading them fell, his feet giving out from under him as he crashed down the steps on his back.

Arsinoe only caught a brief glimpse of the bolt protruding from his breast before she understood what had happened.

"Back!" the other Southerner said, raising his buckler as one of the Steel Heels came charging up the bend of the stairwell, sword outthrust. The two men met, steel and wood clashing, but there was hardly any room to maneuver. They were shoving at each other more than anything else.

She was trying to make use of her pike when another Steel Heel came up behind the first. There was another behind him, the one with the crossbow perhaps, and then another. She could hear them crowding the stairs.

"This way!" the Southerner in charge ordered, beginning to make his way back up the steps. "Over the walls!"

They followed, one of the Southerners joining the fray below without having to be told.

Some discipline. That's good. Now if only there were more of them . . .

They reached a landing, a door. One of the Southerners kicked it open, and they shoved through, passing into a dim chamber lined with weapon racks, the fires raging beyond the window slits their only light.

Someone howled in the stairwell behind them. And something else. A shrike, more than one, screaming like the Ruiner had come.

The next door flew open, and the night wind howled through it. Beyond a rampart stretched to the base of the citadel, its crenellations rimmed orange from the fires above. The sounds of battle poured from the courtyards beneath them, rising and falling like the wind itself.

No sooner had they stepped onto the walk when something whizzed right past Arsinoe's head. She ducked instinctively, yanking on Pinsard's hand. He grunted with annoyance but took the hint.

"Who's shooting at us?" she snarled as another missile shattered against the stonework of the tower behind them.

"Them," one of the men barked back. "Us. Both maybe. It's dark."

She shook her hair free from her face, wishing she had thought to tie it.

At least I'm not hungry.

"Stay low," the officer grunted, bending his head.

"No shit," she said.

They kept to the right as they picked their way forward, hustling past the bodies. Some were the lapdogs of the Baroness, but just as many wore the golden ram on their mail.

The bloody girls had put up a good fight.

She risked a look over the battlement. Beyond the stones, a sheer drop. The river looked like a ribbon of silver, or some thin curling wyrm. Her stomach dropped as she imagined the fall.

"What is it?" Pinsard breathed. She hadn't realized that she had slowed.

"Nothing," she replied, and kept her eyes on the man in front of her.

They were halfway across when a knot of figures emerged from the keep, the firelight against their mail picking them out in the night. Arsinoe tensed, the world growing quieter as her mind pushed out everything but the essential, but then she saw the ram's head etched into their captain's blackened breastplate, noticed the way their 'rescuers' straightened, temporarily more concerned with decorum than their own lives it seemed.

More new friends?

She kept her pike ready all the same.

The man strode forward, seemingly unbothered by the arrows flying over the rampart. He had another half dozen soldiers with him, tough-looking types with some gray in their beards. They at least had the sense to keep their shields up.

"Tower?" the big man rumbled as he came. The voice of authority.

"Steels Heels, m'lord," the spokesman said, ducking as something swooped overhead. "We're cut off!"

"No choice," The big man said and turned towards the fray below, silently calculating. "There's fire and steel behind us."

"Who're you supposed to be?" Arsinoe asked.

"Devoye," he said, sparing her a glance.

She recognized the name. One of Reynard's pet generals. A big man with a big reputation. And a turncoat seemingly. Arsinoe couldn't decide whether she admired that or not.

"You our saviors then?" Arsinoe said.

Devoye's lips thinned with distaste, just on the edge of speech, when something dark and winged flew out of the night. It collided claws first into one of the men trying to shield the Southern general from the missile fire. The man screamed as the shrike, a big one with dark feathers, dragged him over the edge of the rampart before letting go.

"Orders, m'lord?!" the spokesman managed.

"Carve us a path!" Devoye ordered, gesturing back towards the tower of the shrikes. "Bolk, see to our rear!"

The spokesman didn't argue, grunting *m'lord* as he turned about. One of Devoye's escort, Bolk presumably, took three of the others and threw shut the door to the keep.

"Move!" Devoye said, pushing past Arsinoe.

It was Pinsard who caught him by the arm.

"Lara," he said, his voice just loud enough to be heard over the din.

"No time," Devoye growled, tearing his arm free.

Arsinoe let go of Pinsard's hand. Then she sent the tip of her pike ringing against Devoye's gorget, just below the throat.

"M'lord!" one of the Southerners said, raising his sword to strike.

"Back off or he dies!" Arsinoe said and gave the general's gorget another gentle tap. Metal rang against metal. Devoye showed remarkable calm as he motioned for his guard to stand down.

They backed off, but only just. Another shrike came shrieking overhead. Pinsard had drawn his sword.

Devoye stared at her, his nostril flaring. *What?*

"You heard him," Arsinoe said, giving her pike a push. "What about Lara?"

Devoye licked his lips.

"Not part of the bargain," he said.

"What bargain?" Arsinoe said, though the pieces were already coming together.

"She dies," he said. "We join the rebels."

"Roland has to marry someone," she said, cynically.

He nodded.

"No deal," Arsinoe said.

"It is done," Devoye said, looking to the fires roaring above them. "Done!"

"Then we will undo it," Pinsard said.

"You want to die?" Devoye scoffed. "Fine, boy. You have your freedom, go and die! I doubt you've anyone left to shed many tears for you."

She was about to put the head of her pike through the man's face when the door to the keep flew open. *Exploded* might have been a better word for what it did. Hinges and iron bands came free as it split into three separate pieces. Smoke roiled from the breach.

Arsinoe releveled her spear.

A hulking figure emerged from the smoke, a giant Arsinoe thought at first, and then she saw the flycatcher in flight upon her tunic.

"Traitor!" Bradamante snarled, locking eyes with Devoye.

Half her hair had been singed off. There was blood running down her neck. Some of it might have been hers. The woman had the look of a *mormolykeia*, the so-called jackal men of Arsinoe's homeland: Feral and hungry for slaughter.

"Wulf," Devoye said, drawing his sword.

Bradamante charged.

One of the Southerners was stupid enough to get in her way. Arsinoe assumed that it was the weight of the woman's broadsword that killed him more than its edge. She cast another aside with her reverse swing, almost casually, as if he were some gnat buzzing in her face.

"She's mine!" Devoye said, shoving one of his own men aside to face the woman. "Clear the tower!"

Some sand, Arsinoe had to admit.

"You heard the general!" one of the Southerners said, turning about. "Move, the lot of you! At the quick-"

The word *step* barely escaped the man's lips. An arrow had sprouted from his neck. One with blood-red fletching.

It hadn't come from below. The angle was wrong.

Arsinoe flinched as another man was struck straight in the chest. The arrow had punched right through his mail. He stared at it in disbelief, and then keeled over, a second arrow joining the first.

She finally saw the bowman atop one of rooftops hugging the tower, almost perched near its edge, one of his legs thrown over the side of a crumbling balustrade as he loosed another arrow.

It was Tiecelin. The one who had watched his pet eat Pinsard's eyes. He didn't have the clearest line of sight from his position, but he still had the high ground.

How he had gotten up there Arsinoe didn't have time to wonder about.

"Archer!" Arsinoe shouted, mostly for Pinsard's benefit, and put one of the Southerners between her and the tower of the shrikes. "Up on the roof!"

Someone beside her collapsed in a crash of metal. Pinsard started to rush towards the tower, the tip of his sword screaming as he ran it across the battlements. An arrow hit the man in front of her. She grabbed onto him as he fell, using him as a shield.

She spared a glance backwards.

Devoye was trading blow after blow with Bradamante. The woman was forcing him to give ground with every strike. Then he misjudged one of Bradamante's swings. Her sword smashed into his left shoulder, his pauldron crumpling under the weight of the blow. He staggered backwards, trying to catch hold of the wall for support as he brought up his sword to deflect her next strike.

Bradamante's sword rose and fell.

There were more of the Baroness' bloody girls streaming onto the wall walk behind her. How many Arsinoe didn't have time to count.

Too many things were happening at once.

"Volk," she cursed, throwing the dead man in her grip aside. He was getting heavy anyhow and she might as well die on her feet.

Die well, husband.

She turned, pike ready, and began to sprint.

The world and the things in it came into sharp focus. To slow even. Details blurred to their most crucial parts. She didn't have a name for it, didn't call it anything, but to *burn* might have been choice. She imagined this would be how a piece of wood might feel as it blazed out in a fire.

If wood had feelings.

Something swooped overhead, wings outspread. She drove her pike right into its breast, felt the haft bend in her grip as she sent the shrike flying into the courtyard below. The noise it made as it fell was satisfying.

Bradamante saw her coming. The woman reared up, winding her sword the way some savage Irkallan might wield a piece of driftwood.

One misstep and she was dead.

Arsinoe dodged as the woman swung. The sword whistled past her head as she touched off the rampart, and then her spearhead was flying straight towards the woman's exposed face.

The woman surprised her by weaving backwards. She was quick despite her bulk.

Then she swung back.

Arsinoe ducked under the wide cut, doing her best to drive her pike into the woman's thigh. Chain took the brunt of it, but something must have sunk because the woman staggered a bit as she made her next cut.

It shattered Arsinoe's pike in half. The force of it nearly sent her over the edge of the battlements. The woman's little minions were already swarming forward, ready to put her down.

"Fine," Arsinoe snarled, pleased to find she still had the business end of the pike in her hands. "We'll do this the *hard* way."

* * * * * * *

The boy made an easy target. He was blind and the moonlight picked him out like a ghost. Some of Rukenaw's soldiers thought he was a ghost. You could see it in their eyes when they were in the yard, and Lyra heard their whispers.

A single shot through the breast would down him.

Later. He was not a threat.

The Telchine had seen him. The traitors too.

They were threats.

Tiecelin shot one of the traitors. He fell.

Griffe, perched on the balustrade above him, baited her wings.

"Not yet," he said, pulling another arrow from his quiver.

He drew. The Telchine was taking cover behind one of the traitors.

He loosed. The Telchine caught the traitor before he could fall.

Another of the traitors was leveling a crossbow at him.

He nocked, drew, loosed.

The arrow caught the traitor in the collar rather than through the throat. The wind was fouling his aim. He shot the man again for good measure.

Another of them had his shield up. He spent an arrow on the man's thigh and then shot him when he was down.

The boy was closer now. He was leaping over one of the dead women laying in his path.

He did not seem blind.

Tiecelin drew-

Denicher, Rohart's eldest, came barreling towards the ramparts, claws outstretched. The Telchine drove a pike into his breast. Threw him over the wall.

Tiecelin shifted his aim and loosed.

Too far. The arrow shattered against the stone behind the Telchine's feet. He could hear his breath quickening.

Not good for his aim.

He breathed. He nocked. He drew. He loosed.

The wind took the arrow. It ricocheted off the inside of the wall.

He pushed himself up from the edge of the roof. His kneecap popped. Needles ran up and down his foot.

He stepped over the tiles. The Telchine was fighting Bradamante. She had lost half her spear.

He held his breath and drew, aiming not for the Telchine but for where she would be.

The boy dragged himself onto the roof as he loosed, not two paces from where Tiecelin stood.

The arrow went wild.

Tiecelin gave ground. He drew, but the boy was already swinging at him. He was very fast. He did not seem blind.

A tile slipped under Tiecelin's feet. He lost his arrow as he caught himself.

"Griffe!"

She flew at the boy, screaming. He swung at her, but she was quick. She was beautiful. She flew at his face. He staggered backwards, shouting, swinging his stolen sword. She clawed at his eyes.

But he no longer had eyes. Griffe had eaten them already.

No matter.

Tiecelin found his feet. The boy backed toward the edge of the roof.

Tiecelin whistled, *kill*.

Griffe understood. She beat at the boy's face as she gained some height and then came swooping about in a wild arc, intending to drive him over.

Tisiphone's claws crushed her sister underfoot as she fell from above, the tiles cracking as she drove her body straight into the rooftop.

"No," Tiecelin said.

Griffe's feathers quivered. Tisiphone beat her wings.

"Father," she said, tiles shifting underfoot as she took a few steps towards him.

The boy was behind her.

"Step aside," he said, nocking. Drawing. Aiming.

"No," she said, wings outstretched.

Silver and gold glittered between her breasts.

"Step aside, daughter," he said. "I will not say it again."

"Then shoot me," she said. Another tile slipped free under her tread.

He breathed out. His bowstring pulled taut. His arrow quivered.

The wind caught her hair.

He faltered. She flew aside.

The boy was behind her.

He loosed. The boy swung. A proper Steel Heel blade.

The cut was meant to take his head.

It sheared into his left arm instead.

His own shot had gone wild. It had not struck his daughter.

Tiecelin dropped his bow and reached for his knife. The boy was too close.

The boy swung again, his blade meeting naught but air.

Tiecelin freed his knife and took a step backwards.

There was nothing behind him but air. Air and the river below.

He dropped his blade as he reached out, clawing at the sky, hoping to catch hold of something, anything.

There was nothing. His left arm swung loose, useless.

Then sharp claws dug into his sides. Held him on the precipice. His right foot found some purchase against the stone.

Tisiphone held him. Her wings beat furiously as she hovered there, staring into his eyes. Hers were so like emeralds.

He reached out, his fingers grasping at her waist.

"Come closer," he said.

She did not answer.

He was slipping from her grip. She beat her wings harder.

"Come closer," he said again. "And I will give you-"

His foot slid against stone. He tried to dig in his other heel.

"Pretties," he said, reaching for the filaments dangling from her neck. "All that you want."

He caught one of them. She winced as the chain dug into her flesh.

"Keep them, father," she said. "I don't need them anymore."

She let go of him.

The chain came loose.

Tiecelin flew.

* * * * * *

The wind beat against Pinsard's face, cold and true. He stepped away from the edge of the roof, testing each tile before putting his weight on them.

He did not wish to end the way the shrike tamer had.

Tiles clattered as something landed nearby. He brought up his blade.

"Stop," the husky voice said. "I am a friend."

He knew the voice. It belonged to the shrike girl.

He remembered her staring at him, back in the torture chamber. He thought she had come to gloat at first. Later he reckoned she wanted to eat him.

Maybe she still did.

"Friend," he repeated, letting her hear his skepticism.

Still, he lowered his sword arm ever so slightly.

"Are you hurt?" she asked.

"No," he said, before adding, "Are you?"

"No," she said, the word nearly swallowed by the wind.

Talons clacked against brittle clay. One of the tiles skidded off the roof.

She was close.

"Why?" he asked.

It was a simple question. She did not answer.

The clash of metal from below was tinny in his ears.

The fight was not over.

"Come," she said, almost as if she were reading his thoughts. "I will be your eyes."

"I do not need your help," he said.

"I offer it anyway," she said.

There was a rumbling boom from below. The roof shook.

"Alright," he said.

She went before him, tapping at the tiles with her claws. Easy for him to follow. The wind tugged at his jerkin. He wondered how high they were.

"Here," she said, "The edge. A short drop."

He sheathed his blade and slid over the edge, moving far slower than he had been going up. He hadn't even known where the edge of the roof was when he had leapt up to grab it, but he had been able to hear the shrike tamer's bow singing. It had not mattered then. With every step he had expected to be shot dead.

Now the fear of falling gripped him. He clung onto the lip of the roof, sweating in spite of the cold.

"Let go," the shrike girl said.

He let go.

He landed neater than he expected. She lit on the rampart from the flap of her wings.

"Lara," he said, "Where is she?"

"Inside," she said. "With *him*."

"Where?!"

Before she could answer there was a cry. No, *cries*. A dozen warbling throats and cackling voices screaming out one word like anguished spirits. Again and again, they shrieked it.

Father!

It was growing louder, both above them and beneath, a cry of sorrow that resolved into a hateful scream. His ears rang as it drowned out the wind, and with it the flapping of wings.

Something horrible was coming. Coming for them.

No, he realized. *Coming for her.*

"I must go," the shrike girl said.

"Wait," he said, reaching out. "At least let me-"

"I *must*."

"-thank you."

He did not know what else to say.

She brushed against him as she turned about. A moment of feathers and flesh against his arm. Her wings beat at the air.

"Farewell," she said.

Then she was gone. The voices came screaming after her, Pinsard ducking low as they poured over the side of the parapet and went shrieking into the storm.

He rose, began to move. He had tarried too long. Arsinoe needed him. Lara needed him.

And Reynard needed killing.

Anyone in his way, he would strike down as well. He did not trust the Southerners any more than he trusted the Steel Heels or the Bloody Girls. They had all been at Pikria. They had all helped guide the hand that had killed his *moder*.

But no one rushed to meet him. Their bodies were already strewn across the wall walk. He tripped over more than one of them before he began to use his blade as a guide.

At last he could hear Arsinoe. She was grunting, almost snarling, wet flesh squelching with every rough exhalation.

"Whoever it is," Pinsard said. "I think they are dead."

The squelching ceased.

"Punched me in the *ribs*," Arsinoe hissed through her teeth. "Feels like all of 'em are broke."

He offered her a hand.

"You're alive," she observed, taking his hand. He hefted her up and she sagged against him. The effort had clearly winded her.

"Surprised?" he asked.

"Always," she said, sucking in her breath as she threw something aside. It clattered over the stones. "Tiecelin?"

"Dead."

"Good."

She was letting go of his shoulder when the entire wall seemed to shake beneath them. It felt like an earthquake, great fingers beneath them rending at the foundations of the fortress.

"Kharetsin!" she said, catching hold of him. "What was-"

Her words were cut off by what sounded like a thunderclap. A flash of heat washed over his face. His ears rang. Arsinoe seemed to fall over, and it was not until she was laying on top of him and jagged pebbles were raining down from above that he realized that she dragged him into cover.

An all too familiar scent filled his nostrils. Black powder, bitter on the wind.

Another rumble, another explosion. This one sounded further away. Or was it the ringing in his ears?

"Come on!" Arsinoe was shouting then, dragging him upwards. "We have to move!"

He let her guide him, flinching at every new blast. The sounds of battle below had turned to cries of alarm, dozens of men shouting *fall back* and *move*.

Suddenly, he fought against her pull.

They were running the wrong way.

"What are you doing?!" she shouted at him. He could hear the terror in her voice.

"He has *Lara!*" he shouted back. "I have to face him!"

She balled her fist about his shirt and yanked.

"They're *dead*, Pinsard!" she cried, as much from the pain as anything else.

He tried to drag himself free, but she wouldn't let go.

"Do you hear me?!" she raged. "They're dead! They're dead!"

He stopped fighting. The wall shook. Pieces of Carduel rained down about them.

"She did it," Arsinoe said. He could not see her tears but he could hear them in her voice. "She killed him."

* * * * * *

The feast hall burned, the fiery sheets that had been tapestries dancing in the wind. So much wine had spilled from the tuns along the wall that it had formed a pool between the tables. Their boots sloshed in it. It made the footwork tricky. And yet the girl moved through it like it was nothing.

It gave her an edge.

He bore down on her. The tip of her sword danced towards his face, teasing.

"Getting tired already?" she sneered.

He slapped it aside and drove her back, Right-Hand gleaming as it met her steel. She waded backwards. Flames licked at her boots. There were flames in her eyes.

A good fight. A good death, even.

Could he ask for anything more?

He cut and thrust, kicking up wine as he tested her. It splashed onto the seatbacks and caught with the rest. She gave ground, refusing to meet him until the high table was at her back. Then, as some flaming timber groaned above them, she seemed to stumble, her guard lowering.

She let out a cry of dismay, *no*, or something like it.

He saw the ruse for what it was, and still it almost took him when her arm came whipping forward, wine meant for his face flying along the edge of her blade. He took it in the shoulder as he whirled away from the strike, felt her steel glance off his upper arm.

A cut. Not deep but it bled.

He parried her next strike without thinking and went into his riposte, a blow that would have skewered her if she had been standing still.

But she was already gone. She had disappeared into the smoke.

He leapt onto the nearest table, kicking plates and cutlery aside as he searched for her, Right-Hand easy in his grip.

"Come out," he said.

"Why?" she called out from the other side of the chamber. "Am I boring you?"

"Not at all," he said, turning. "I only thought that it might be time for us to retire."

"Dream on," she spat at him, but beneath her words he could hear her trying her best to stifle a cough.

The smoke was beginning to burn his throat as well. She was moving too, back towards the hearth.

He slipped from the table and slunk forward.

"Come now," he said. "It is our wedding night after all, and I grow tired of dancing. Have I not been . . . Patient?"

Her could hear her make a sound in the back of her throat, something between rage and disgust. Her foot scraped against solid stone.

There!

Their blades met before he could even see her. She was ready for him, and came at him in the Calvarian style, every slash a kill if it landed true. Deadly, but predictable.

Reynard grinned. It was easy to see Hirsent behind every strike.

He gave her some ground to work with, even waded backwards into the wine as she pushed him. She quickened her strikes, mixing their economy with a hint of Frisian panache. No wonder she had killed so many of his men.

It was art.

If only it could go on forever.

He leaned across one of her cuts and thrust. Not too fast, just enough to put her on her backfoot again. She parried, riposted, sidestepped. He put more pressure behind his cuts, Right-Hand flying at her face with every strike.

She parried them all. But her blade, her arm rather, was beginning to shake.

"A shame," he huffed, and drove his blade straight at her brow.

She was still quick enough to parry but as their blades met, he *pushed*, his left hand lashing out to grab the edge of her blade and wrench it from her grip as he pivoted.

Her blade slipped from her grip easily. She had let go.

Then she drove her left fist into his jaw.

He was lucky. She had probably been aiming for his neck, and with enough force to crush his windpipe.

Hirsent again.

He cast her sword into the wine as he staggered backwards, slashing at the air to keep her at bay. It was hardly necessary. She dove after her blade and then went scrabbling through the overturned chairs.

Running. Or-

Then he heard the rope snap. He flew backwards.

The chandelier slammed down in front of him, more candles spilling into the Felician. He took another step, out of the wine, and caught her gaze through the fire.

"Almost," he said to her and began to wade through the flames.

The fire beat at his face. His cloak began to smoke. But he would not burn.

He could see by her face that she wasn't surprised.

She leveled her blade and waited to meet him.

This time he did not hold back.

Right-Hand sung. Three-Merits quivered. The fires rose and fell.

She began to cough. His own lungs cried out for air. Behind him a window exploded from the heat. Or was it the mirror?

He did not care.

He swung. She recoiled, her back slamming against the wall as she tried to twist away. He reached for her, his false fingers closing about her forearm, but they were not made to grip cloth. She slipped from them and made to fly under his arm.

He curled his false fist. The hidden blade slid free.

She cried out as he slashed at her, tried to backpedal, only to find that there was nothing but stone at her back.

He leveled Right-Hand at the center of her chest.

"Do you yield?" he asked.

To his surprise, to his delight, she looked down at the blade with distain.

"You want your wedding night?" she asked.

"Of course," he said, pressing his blade closer. Blood beaded beneath its tip.

"Then follow me!"

She slammed her free hand into the stonework, and the masonry behind her slid inwards.

She half-fell into the darkness beyond, and then he could hear her feet echoing as she ran up hidden steps.

He smiled. Of course she knew.

He followed her into the dark.

He did not need light to see. He knew these passages inside and out. This one lead upwards, to the royal chambers. No escape that way.

Good.

The stairway ended. A corridor twisted this way and that, clinging to the edges of the royal apartments like vines. He could not hear her. Perhaps she had already chosen a door.

He tried the first one he came across, the one that let into the parlor. It gave an inch before catching against something trapped in the hinges. A spike no doubt, jammed into place with a mallet. Hardly surprising.

She had told Sigyn she would do it.

The next one was stuck too. So was the next. He quickened his step. The smoke was getting thicker. He could not help but cough. Still, he grinned, and passed the next entryway at a run.

He knew where she was leading him.

The way to her bedchamber flew open. It wasn't even sealed. The false door he had ordered the laborers to install in place of the one that was already there had not fooled her.

The chamber seemed empty. The doors were shut. The wind whistling through the windows had blown out the candles.

The windows were open.

"Nowhere to run now," he said. "Or have you learned to fly?"

The secret door swung shut behind him. The locks *clicked*.

He spun about, ready to parry, but there was no one there.

"That's a good trick," he said.

"Isn't it?" she whispered.

Still here. Good.

But where?

He padded forward, blade first, his gaze shifting from one end of the chamber to the other. The thought of her slashing at his hamstrings occurred to him, so he kept some distance from the postered bed.

The floor creaked beneath his tread. Smoke hissed through the looser boards. It wouldn't hold forever. Outside he could hear the Steel Heels he had held in reserve trying to hold the gate against the men the Old Goat had thought to hide from him. That and the screaming of the shrikes.

"Hot or cold?" he asked.

One of the tapestries behind him rustled. He slashed at it, centuries old fiber tearing as it collapsed into a shapeless heap.

Just the wind.

And, beneath that, he could hear her snicker.

Across the chamber, behind one of the shutters, a dark shape loomed, half nestled between vanity and folding screen.

He shifted towards it, changing his grip.

"Warmer," she said, her voice scarce above a whisper.

He took another step. The shape remained still.

"Warmer," she repeated.

Much closer now.

Slowly, deliberately, he turned his back on the shape in the corner.

A floorboard creaked. Metal scraped against sheath, the quick draw.

He spun and brought Right-Hand straight down in a savage cut.

The dressing mannequin standing in the corner toppled under his blow. Its head went rolling into the cold hearth.

Her blade glanced against his false hand, and then whipped against his left shoulder blade. As he turned, she stabbed at him again. This time the mail failed him. Steel bit through the links.

He slashed without thought. She didn't even feel the cut, kept fighting. Their blades met again and again, until he pushed hers away and kicked her back against the bed.

She coughed. Spat blood. Her eyes widened as she realized it was her own.

She raised her free hand instinctively but did not touch her face.

Reynard had split it open, from cheek to chin.

"Something to remember me by," he said.

She spat more blood and came at him afresh. She fought with abandon now. Desperation. Sloppy.

"Just like your father," he said as he cast aside her strikes, ignoring the pain in his side as he weaved. "He let his pride blind him too-"

She sent her blade glissading over his. He flinched away from its tip and sent her staggering with his riposte. She was slowing. The blood loss was making her woozy.

That and the smoke rising from below.

"No *patience*," he snarled, driving forward, smashing at her blade with every breath. "No *thought*. All of them."

Her arm began to waver. She staggered back against a table. It toppled, spilling fruit and silver, but she kept her feet. Moved to put the wall at her back.

He did not let up, but lunged forward, the false blade whistling as he drove it straight into the wardrobe. She only just managed to dodge.

"They could have lived," he grunted, extracting the blade from the splintered wood. "Your mother, Hirsent . . . Isengrim."

She was staring at him, her blade raised but shaking in her hand. Her chest heaved. She was trying to catch her breath.

"But no," he breathed. "They wouldn't *listen*. They couldn't *wait*. Just. Like. You!"

Their swords met. She lost her grip. Three-Merits went clattering across the floorboards. She collapsed backwards, too exhausted to stand.

She looked up at him. He could see it in her eyes. She had lost and she knew it.

They both had.

He took a breath, coughed.

"It's over," he said. "Come."

He lowered his sword and extended his hand.

Somewhere, deep beneath the cold stones of Carduel, something stirred. A shudder ran through the walls. Plaster cracked and ancient mortar spilled from the arches above.

She cracked a smile, her teeth slick with blood.

"What was that?" he asked, though he already knew the answer.

"I beat you," she said.

The walls beyond the window lit up as some great fire beneath them blossomed into life. The room shook. He barely kept his feet.

"Blackpowder," he whispered, looking at her with new admiration. "How much?"

"All of it," she said.

A fresh explosion rocked the fortress. The floor groaned and split. Flames rushed up from below to swallow the royal bed. He leapt as the vanity fell into the fire raging beneath them.

He found himself balancing on what remained of the floor. There wasn't much left. Support beams and a handful of boards, already aflame. Smoke choked him. Heat upon heat washed over him. Gouts of fire climbed the walls.

He blinked back his tears and saw her, clinging to the edge of one of the windows directly across from him. Her hair was whipping in the wind, and her face bloody but her eyes still were bright.

"Is this how you imagined it?" she asked.

"Something like," he answered, managing not to choke. "But it's not so bad. At least I'm not alone."

She stifled a laugh.

"What's so funny?"

"You," she said. "You still don't see it, do you?"

"See what?"

"The windows," she laughed, stepping onto the ledge. "They weren't built to open!"

She leapt into the night. He watched her fall, her body twisting as she threw out her arms . . . And caught the rope stretched between the keep and the tower of the shrikes.

Her own weight snapped it free. Or perhaps she had cut it. Either way, she sailed into the gloom, the lanterns blowing out as they fell. Like falling stars, almost.

Beside the windows he could see the stacks of glass, propped against the wall. She had neatly chipped them free. It must have taken her weeks.

"Ah," he mused. "Clever."

Then Carduel erupted.

EPILOGUE

"Don't smell so bad from 'ere," Blackeye muttered, rubbing at his nose all the same.

"What don't?" Cloak snipped.

"Fires, ya twist," Blackeye said. "What else?"

Cloak sniffed at the air and spat, but his old associate was right. Down here in the Styes, the fumes that poured from the old fortress weren't more than a whiff. They'd been burning for a month or more now, and no sign of stopping. Some folk said it would burn 'til the stars went out.

Fools, Cloak knew. Even the biggest fires go out eventually.

"Still *stinks*," Cloak said.

"Yeah, yeah," Blackeye grumbled. "Now, hush up. We're close."

Everything felt close in the Styes. Alleys too narrow, rooftops practically kissing overhead, wood all gone to rot. Usurper's lot had turned a blind eye to it.

And now it was King Roland's turn.

Cloak had come from the Tumble, worst slum in Nemea. The Styes were far worse. Haunted too they said, but what wasn't in Carduel? Only folk who kept their doss here were desperate. Or they were the sort that didn't like attention. Rats, say, with prices on their heads. But rats still had to eat, had to poke their squidgy noses out of their holes now and then. Rat gets hungry enough, it might even risk the market off Victory. Lots of stalls there now for a cheap and easy tuck. And why not? Most folk might not even see a rat for a rat.

But for those that did? Well. That was opportunity.

This one had arms like a swordsman, and a scar that weren't no cat scratch. Following her had been easy, Blackeye said.

Almost like she wanted to be found.

At the end of the alley, a dingy court: Old brickwork and crumbling plaster, stairwells plunging into pitch black cellars, rags and baskets.

Blackeye put up his palm. Cloak went still.

He could see it too. Candles behind curtains.

"Wait 'til she puts 'em out," Blackeye whispered, already looking for a likely place to lean.

Cloak crept backwards and found a spot himself. He watched his breath mist in the air as he kept his eyes fixed on the curtains. After a while his eyes got heavy.

"Cold," he said, shoving his hands beneath his pits.

"Quick work this," Blackeye reminded him. "Quiet."

Cloak shivered. "Shadows is always quiet."

They waited. The Watcher lurked between the clouds. A cat slunk across the court, bone thin.

Finally, a shape moved past one of the windows. Then the candles went out. First one, then another.

"There," Blackeye sighed. "See?"

He drew his knife. It fair near gleamed in the moonlight.

Cloak flexed his fingers to get some blood flowing. "You sure she's alone?"

Blackeye paused to consider.

"Didn't see but her, did we?" he said at last. "Bloody doxy, though. Wulf, could be another."

Cloak hesitated. Time was, Fairlimb's lot would cut you up just for looking at them sideways. Fancy or no, they weren't no doxies. Kingfishers were supposed to be her hardest.

Time was. Lord Protector was ash now, and the Fairlimb? Well, she was running north like her ass were on fire, weren't she? Her girls were just that again, *girls*.

No one left to protect them.

"More coin," Cloak said, drawing his own blade.

"Even split," Blackeye agreed.

They crept forward, hugging the walls as they kept to the edges of the court. No sound but the soft tread of their boots.

The door loomed close. It was half-open. Practically an invitation.

Blackeye nodded. Cloak took the opposite side of the door, blade raised to strike as he put his hand to wood and pushed.

The door swung open. Inside it was dark.

Blackeye peered inside.

"Nuthin'," he whispered, and made ready to slip through the gap.

Behind them, back in the alley, something *snapped*.

Cloak turned, squinting into the gloom.

There was nothing to see.

"Cat," Blackeye growled between his teeth. "Leave it."

Cloak nodded and was already turning back towards the opening when Blackeye made a sound halfway between a gasp and a wheeze. Then he fell over.

There was a bolt in his breast.

Cloak ran. Not the way they had come. The alleys all looked the same, so he chose the nearest one. His footfalls echoed against the stones.

The alley narrowed, turned. Ended.

He'd picked a blind alley.

Behind him, he could hear boots scraping ever so slightly against stone. He whirled about, fingers tight about the hilt of his blade.

There was no one there. No one he could see.

The footsteps came to a halt.

"Who's there?" Cloak rasped, his heart pounding in his ears.

Boots scraped against stone. From out of the darkness, a figure emerged.

"No one," it said. "Only a shadow."

Steel flashed in the moonlight.

* * * * * *

The dead men were tied to the foot of the Queen's Steps, their backs set against the thick limestone newels like a pair of beggars. The placards in their laps were made of half-rotten wood, but the paint was fresh. The script, neat.

Bounty Hunter, they read.

Arsinoe studied the men's faces. She did not know them. They weren't Steel-Heels, or Genovans, or even sea-reavers from the look of them. Just two dead men whose hard faces had gone slack before growing stiff.

Their eyes had been closed at least.

"Orders, Captain?" one of the watchmen ventured.

It took her a moment to realize the man was talking to her. The closest she had been to playing officer before had been when she had been fighting for the Karks. She hadn't liked it then either.

"Orders?" she repeated the man's words, her gaze wandering over the nearby rooftops. Blackbirds roosted there. Nothing unusual.

"Crowd's starting to gawk," the watchman said with a nod towards the growing knot of onlookers. "You want we should cut 'em down?"

"What's the point?" Arsinoe snorted. "They're already dead. It's the living I'm worried about."

"Can't just leave 'em," the watchman said. "Looks bad."

Arsinoe looked at the man, a sergeant by the extra embellishments on his coat. Like many of the new men of the so-called watch, he was a Lornishman. Probably worked a net before Roland put a sword in his hand. His beard didn't make him look any less young.

"You want 'em down?" Arsinoe asked. "Run for the temple, boy, and see if you can rustle up some priests. Making bodies disappear is supposed to be their trade."

"What about the crowd?"

Arsinoe ground her teeth together.

"You two." She pointed at the nearest watchmen. "Keep an eye on the gawkers. Discourage the curious ones. The rest of you, get back on patrol. *Now.* There's a murderer on the loose, remember?"

Maybe it was her tone of voice, maybe it was the fact that she outranked them, or maybe they simply wanted to be anywhere else but here, but the watchmen began to move. One of them started to bark at the crowd. *Get back, nothing to see,* and all that rot.

She went back to searching the rooftops, dimly aware that the sergeant with the wispy beard was still staring at her. He was shuffling his feet, no doubt getting up the courage to ask her what it was she was looking for.

"You still here?" she asked without turning to look at him.

He mumbled something that sounded like an apology, made an approximation of a salute, and made himself scarce.

She hated being in charge.

She left the square and walked the battlements overlooking the river. The sky had turned pink. Soon it would be sunup. She sighed. This was going to be a long day and her knees were already aching.

But she had told them to fetch her if there were bodies again on the Queen's Steps.

The first time she hadn't batted an eye. There had been a lot of scores to settle after Wulf's Night, and there were no Steel Heels left to keep the peace. The placards were a colorful addition, but a belt of spiced rum had chased away any of her doubts.

The second time, well, that could be a copycat. That the corpses in question had been executioners under the old regime, well that was irony, wasn't it?

But three times? Experience had taught her that there were no such things as coincidence. Someone was sending a message.

She thought she knew who.

Something on a nearby roof caught her eye. A bird's nest, built right up against a chimney. There were no eggs inside. Or, rather, there were, but something had been at them. There was nothing left but cracked shells.

She shifted her gaze to the edge of the roof.

A fox-squirrel sat there, gnawing on what remained of a sparrow.

Arsinoe leaned against the battlements.

"You can come out," she said. "I know you're there."

Lara emerged from the ruins of the nearby tower. Beneath her hood, she looked half feral. But most of that was the scar. It ran jagged from cheek to chin. She must have stitched it closed herself.

The scar is what most people would see from now on.

Not a queen who was supposed to be dead.

"You finally showed," Lara said.

"I had to know," Arsinoe said. "Know it wasn't *him*."

"Satisfied?" Lara asked.

"Almost," Arsinoe said.

Lara smiled ever so slightly. Arsinoe knew that even that must hurt. They walked.

"They made me a captain of the royal guard, you know."

"I know," Lara said. "I saw you take your oath."

"Figured you might," Arsinoe said. "I suppose I wouldn't miss my own funeral either. *Volk*, what a day that was."

It had been held in a square beyond the Traitor's Gate, the morning after Roland had ridden into the city at the head of his army. With

- 264 -

no body to burn, they had made do by building a pyre as big as a house and setting it alight. Afterwards the prisoners had been brought before the King to beg clemency. And to the surprise of many he had granted it.

Chief amongst these was Galehaut, marshal of the Steel Heels. The boy prince and his army had met them near some place called Hest, and both the marshal and his men had fought until they were surrounded by a sea of foes. Arsinoe had expected his head to be set above the gate that day, and she was far from alone. The man had been Reynard's right-hand for many a year, second only to The Baroness, and had proven a loyal servant to the end. But as he knelt before the King in chains, the ladies Faline and Sansmerci came forward to speak of his gallantry, his forbearance, and (more quietly) of the need for experienced generals to help defend the realm from its many enemies. And so Galehaut was not only pardoned, but rewarded, and was named Marquis of Carabas so long as he swore unwavering loyalty to the crown. This he did, and what were left of his Steel Heels were given free leave to follow him or, failing that, to divest themselves of arms and remove themselves to Mandross.

Most chose to keep their blades.

More pardons followed. The barons of Astolat and Osca who had not fallen in battle at Hest were forgiven their folly, as were the young lords of the tower who now found themselves Counts. They had been hostage to Reynard's cruel whims, after all, and were deemed blameless. As for Count Julien, no pardon was necessary. He had died in the fighting, shot through the jaw with an arrow even before the Southerners had a chance to turn their coats, the Luxian foot slamming into the flanks of the Steel Heels just as Roland's troops met them head on.

There was no clemency for The Baroness however. Nor was there judgement. She had escaped capture, having retreated into the foothills with captains and troops in tow. The reports all told that they were heading north, an army turned brigand, as if there was a difference. Arsinoe didn't envy her. The bounty on her head was nowhere near as large as Lara's had been . . . But it was large enough.

That done, the great lords and ladies of Arcasia, those who were left, made a new show of loyalty to their new King and master, bowing and scraping, and swearing oaths, and practically kissing his boots. And, of course, it was announced that, come spring, he and the Lady Sansmerci would be wed properly, reforging the ties between the houses of Arcas and

Luxia, re-knitting the realm, and so on, and so forth. Arsinoe had yawned through most of it. She had hoped Scyron could keep her company, but they had put him with the Frisians and she could not catch his eye.

And so, it took her by great surprise when she was called forward. Why not, she had figured. The offer they made her was generous.

"And?" Lara said.

"It's not so bad," Arsinoe said. "Pay is good, I get better cuts of meat from the kitchen, and it's mostly just standing around, looking like a bad day. Not as much time to myself as I'd like of course. But it beats being lonely."

"And all you have to do is stop the Queen from being killed."

"It's a tough calling," Arsinoe said.

Lara smiled again and sighed, softly.

"What's she like? I only met her once."

"Pretty," Arsinoe said, considering. "Vapid. She has the wits of a myrmik. Course, that could all be a show."

"Roland fancy her?" Lara asked.

"Hard to tell with him, isn't it?" Arsinoe said. "But he's building her a big castle 'cross the river. Already laying out the lines. Better than nothing."

"Old Goat must be happy," Lara said.

Now it was Arsinoe's turn to smile.

"At least someone is."

They came to a halt. Above them the fortress loomed, weeping clouds of soot. Somewhere on the crag below the blackbirds picked at the bones of Tiecelin.

"Who were they?" Arsinoe asked.

"Murderers," Lara said.

"That what you do now? Hunt murderers?"

Lara did not answer. She put her hands on the parapet, closed her eyes, and took a deep breath.

"It smells sweet," Lara said.

"The smoke?" Arsinoe scoffed.

"Vengeance," Lara said. She opened her eyes.

Arsinoe chuckled. "Careful," she said. "That's a taste turns bitter quickly."

"Shame," Lara said, quietly.

Arsinoe joined her. Watched the river run its course.

"You should have drowned him," Arsinoe said. "Let him drift in Domdaniel for a century or two."

"He would have swum out," Lara said. "Still, the rest must be happy."

"The rest?" Arsinoe asked.

"The ghosts," Lara said. "They've suffered long enough."

"Haven't we all?"

Arsinoe put her hand on Lara's. She wished she could feel it.

"Speaking of which," Arsinoe said. "There's someone else wants to see you."

"I know," Lara said. "Where is he?"

"Up there," Arsinoe said, turning her head towards the keep. From here it looked like a thing adrift, cleaving from a sea of smoke.

"I did not see him at the funeral," Lara said.

"No," Arsinoe said, swallowing her next words. *He refused to come.*

"How is he?" Lara asked, wearily.

"You," Arsinoe said, "Should see for yourself."

They did not have to take the Queen's Steps to reach the lower courts of the citadel. The black powder had blown a hole in the side of the crag so large that it had exposed the upmost dungeons, so that one could climb exposed stairs and rubble all the way to the foot of the tower of the shrikes, which stood amidst a sea of upturned masonry.

Lara spared it a fleeting glance before pressing on. Arsinoe kept her own eyes on the way ahead. She could hear Bannertail scrabbling after them, soft against the rocks.

The sunken court was no longer sunken, half of the arcade having fallen into the depths beneath, but the little oak was still there, clinging to life amidst the wreck of Carduel. Pinsard was there, bent over an overturned block of limestone. His brow was furrowed, and his pale fingers were questing at some shape in the dirt.

Dramsind's head hung from his hip, a makeshift harness helping to keep his gaze level. Beyond them, a human scarecrow lurked, half propped against a fallen bit of statuary.

"I thought you might be here," Lara said.

The scarecrow caught her gaze and smiled knowingly, his impish eyes squinting with delight.

Pinsard did not look up. His hands brushed at something in the dirt.

The ruins of a dead man's face. He had been crushed by the rock.

"Is it him?" Pinsard asked.

"No," Dramsind answered. You had to strain to hear him now, his words like to someone speaking under a soft yet insistent wind.

Pinsard seemed to stare at the corpse beneath him. Then he beat his hand against the soil and rose.

"Pinsard," Lara said.

"Lara," he said.

"What are you doing?" she asked.

"What does it look like I am doing?"

Lara did not answer.

Pinsard turned towards the court fool and said, "Show us another."

The scarecrow yawned but did as he was bid.

Pinsard followed the fool into the shadows of an alcove. They watched him struggle to overturn some jagged slab that had cracked a beam in half. His hands searched beneath it. He settled on something, lifted it up, his fingers running over its hilt.

It was a sword. But not his father's.

He cast it aside.

"Pointless," Pinsard said, rising. "He is not here. But you knew that."

The fool did not nod at this. Nor did he shake his head. He merely smiled. Or was it a grimace? It was hard to tell the difference.

"We are wasting time," Pinsard said. "Come."

He made for the ruined stair that wound its way to the gatehouse. The fool followed on his heels, like an obedient dog.

Lara stood in their path.

"He's dead, Pinsard," she said.

He seemed to stare at her, his face as cold as the desert by night.

"Then where is his body?" he asked.

"Gone."

"Yours is too," Pinsard said. "Are you dead?"

"No," Lara said, shifting. "But, that night, Pinsard, the fire, no one could have survived-"

"You made us a promise," Pinsard said. "Remember?"

Her mouth grew hard. "I kept it."

"No," Pinsard said. "No, all *you* have done is rob us of our vengeance."

"You don't mean that," Lara said.

"Don't I?"

He brushed past her. Arsinoe did not get in his way.

"Pinsard," Lara said, her voice tight.

"What?" he said, turning.

"You said *don't*."

Something unspoken passed between them, and for a moment they reminded Arsinoe of their old selves, like children, lost in the wild.

"Don't go," Lara said. "There's a place for you here."

There wasn't. Arsinoe knew that. So did Lara. He was too inconvenient.

Reynard was dead, Lara was dead, and Roland was King.

There was no room left for the truth.

Bannertail slipped from the shadows and weaved his way through Pinsard's legs. The boy bent to scratch the fox-squirrel behind the ears.

"I love you, little sweoster," Pinsard said, straightening. "And I forgive you. But, let me go. Please. I *beg* of you."

She nodded. They embraced.

"Husband," Arsinoe said.

Pinsard turned. His cheeks were wet.

"You take care of him," she said, glancing at the empty helm riding on his hip.

"I will."

"And you," she said, bending to one knee. *"Fepasa. Bolapo."*

"Yes," Dramsind said, like stone grating on sand.

"Farewell," Pinsard said.

Arsinoe nodded. Words were too hard.

Pinsard walked down the stairs. The fool hesitated for a moment, turned. Then he bent. A bow.

"Who are you bowing to?" Lara asked.

He raised his head and shrugged.

They went. She did not need to ask where.

Arsinoe walked to the oak and took one of its branches in her hand. The leaves had turned golden red. As red as the setting sun. She plucked one.

"They all think he's mad," Arsinoe said.

"Do you?" Lara asked.

"I gave Maiden to him," she said, turning the leaf in her fingers. "So, maybe he's only half-mad."

She let the leaf fall.

"Getting late," she said. "Will there be more bodies, you think? Lara?"

She was already gone.

It was alright. She would see her again.

There were years left.

And if I ever get tired, there's a box to dig out of a river. Live like a Queen in Irkalla.

The firebird was up. Across the river the forest was a wildfire of color. Red leaves and golden fields.

It can wait.

* * * * * * *

The wood was hard to light. It was still wet from last night's snow and his fingers shook. He could barely feel the flint strike in his hand, but he kept trying at it. Pierrot could have done it easier, but he was still out foraging.

That or he had found a warm barn to sleep in.

Pinsard was tired of waiting. He struck flint to steel until his thumbs ached.

At last, heat. The sparks had taken. He bent over them and blew, gentle, the way *moder* had taught. When he could hear the wood begin to hiss, he held his fingers close.

A little more. Just enough for warmth.

He chose one of the branches from his bundle and snapped it in half before feeding it to the flames. The fire crackled. He could feel something wet on his face. Snow again.

He pulled his cloak tighter about his chest.

A bird landed in the boughs above him. Small, with quiet wings. An owl perhaps. He wondered if it was watching him, its head tilting to regard him as he huddled by his fire.

Behind him, Maiden stamped her hooves. Then she went still.

Pinsard reached out and touched his hand to Dramsind's brow.

Still there, yes, but silent. And yet-

Tsh tsh tsh.

Something close. In the brush. Dead leaves shushing . . . And beneath them, nettles. Nettles crunching underfoot.

It wasn't Pierrot.

Pinsard rose, loosening his sword from its sheath with a flick of his thumb.

The woods grew quiet.

"Who's there?"

The fire snapped. The night bird's claws dug into bark.

"Just a wanderer," a man called back. "Cold. Like you."

His voice was grizzled. Probably fond of smoke.

"Alone?" Pinsard asked.

The man shifted his feet.

"I've a little one with me," he said. "My girl."

"I don't hear her."

"Fia," the man said. "Come out so the man can see you."

Footsteps, light as a feather, rustled against the brush. Maiden whickered. The night bird took flight.

"There," the man said. "Only us. No need for steel."

Pinsard ungripped his hilt.

"Come," he said. "Sit down."

The two of them stepped closer to the fire. He could hear the worry in their steps. But the warmth soon overcame their shyness. The man settled down and no doubt set the girl in his lap. She must be very small.

"Are you hungry?" Pinsard asked.

The man chuckled darkly. "Yes, master. Very."

Pinsard reached for his pack, his fingers brushing against his mess kit as he dug deep. Finally, he found a bit of waxed cheese and hardtack.

"Here," he said, offering it over the flames.

The man was silent for a moment. Then he took what was offered.

"Say thank you," the man said.

"Thank you," the girl repeated. Her voice was frail as a morning frost.

They ate in silence. The snow fell in large flakes. Pinsard added a pair of branches to the fire. Afterwards the man hummed a tune.

The girl's breath grew easy.

The fire hissed.

"Blind?" the man asked at last.

Pinsard nodded.

"But no beggar."

"No," Pinsard said.

"Where are you headed?"

"North," Pinsard said. "Maleperduys."

The man shifted. The girl let out a sigh in her sleep.

"Long road," the man said.

"I don't need any help."

"Wasn't offering," the man said.

His voice had taken on a harder edge.

"You're one of them," the man said. "Aren't you?"

Pinsard felt his cheeks grow flush.

"No," he said, trying to bite back his anger. "I am no Graycloak."

"Yet you go north."

"I do."

The man let out a shivering breath. "What for?"

"I am looking for someone."

"A man?"

Pinsard nodded.

"And when you find him?"

Pinsard was silent.

"I see," the man said.

The wind blew through the trees. One of the branches fell into the ashes.

"Lots of folks these days, with vengeance on their minds," the man said. "Can't blame them. Him who was hurt a lot of folk. Even if it weren't him held the blade."

The man shifted forward. Embers scraped against embers. The fire blazed hotter. Pinsard could imagine the sparks rising against the snowfall.

"That what you're after?" the man asked. "Revenge?"
Pinsard took a breath. Then he nodded.
"Well," the man said. "You seem a good man."
The fire snapped and crackled.
"I hope you find him."

Acknowledgements

The journey to Carduel was not without its challenges. To all who helped me keep my feet, my thanks: As ever, my dedicated editor, Marguerite Hickernell, sharp-eyed proofreader Brian Morey, and the patient support of Kirsten Foster, who helps me walk dungeons both dark and deep.

www.ingramcontent.com/pod-product-compliance
Lightning Source LLC
Chambersburg PA
CBHW060342030726
47497CB00003B/566